A Note Yet Unsung

Center Point
Large Print

**This Large Print Book carries the
Seal of Approval of N.A.V.H.**

A BELMONT MANSION NOVEL • 3

A Note Yet Unsung

Tamera Alexander

CENTER POINT LARGE PRINT
THORNDIKE, MAINE

The text of this Large Print edition is unabridged. In other aspects, this book may vary from the original edition. Printed in the United States of America on permanent paper. Set in 16-point Times New Roman type.

ISBN: 978-1-68324-305-2

Library of Congress Cataloging-in-Publication Data

Names: Alexander, Tamera, author.
Title: A note yet unsung : a Belmont mansion novel / Tamera Alexander.
Description: Center Point Large Print edition. | Thorndike, Maine : Center Point Large Print, 2017.
Identifiers: LCCN 2016055201 | ISBN 9781683243052
   (hardcover : alk. paper)
Subjects: LCSH: Large type books. | GSAFD: Love stories. | Christian fiction.
Classification: LCC PS3601.L3563 N68 2017b | DDC 813/.6—dc23
LC record available at https://lccn.loc.gov/2016055201

To Jack,
my little writing buddy.
It was so hard to finish this one without you.
We miss you still. . . .

"For the LORD sees clearly
what a man does,
examining every path he takes."

Proverbs 5:21 (NLT)

Preface

Music is an important part of our lives and comes in many forms. Most definitely, the term *one size fits all* does *not* apply when discussing the vast number of styles in this time-treasured art form.

As can be said pretty much across the board when comparing the mores of current society to those of times past, what was taboo then—be it for better, or worse—has now become the norm. In nearly every country in the world today, women are welcome to participate in orchestras, and their talent is lauded.

But such was not always the case.

In the nineteenth century, women were not allowed to play in orchestras or symphonies. They were considered too genteel and delicate natured for the rigors of practice and dedication required to master an instrument. (O ye of little faith . . .)

As I researched, I came across a popular opinion of the time that not only supported the preclusion of women playing in orchestras, but that also set forth that a woman playing a violin in public would be scandalous. Far too sensuous and suggestive. No proper woman would ever consider doing such a thing!

And from that . . . the idea for *A Note Yet Unsung*, a Belmont Mansion novel, was born.

Most of the novel you're about to read is fictional, though there are certainly elements of real history and people woven throughout. For instance, there really is a Belmont Mansion in Nashville, built in 1853, that still stands today. And Mrs. Adelicia Acklen, a character in the novel, is the dynamic, born-before-her-time woman who lived there.

Adelicia had three defining loves in her life—art, nature, and music. So as I began writing the Belmont novels (of which you're holding the third and final installment), their singular themes rose rather quickly in my thoughts: art (*A Lasting Impression*), nature (*A Beauty So Rare*), and finally, music (*A Note Yet Unsung*).

At times, as I wrote, it felt almost as if these stories and characters had been waiting for me to begin writing, and I'm so grateful they did. It's been a pleasure and an honor to take these journeys with them.

In addition to Adelicia, many of the other characters in the novel were inspired by real people who lived during that era—people who worked at Belmont and who visited there. But the characters' personalities and actions as depicted in this story are purely of my own imagination.

A bonus to this book! On my website (www.TameraAlexander.com) I've included links to all the music "performed" in this book. So if you want to listen as you read, please visit the book page for *A Note Yet Unsung* on my website and click the playlist tab.

I invite you to join me as we open the door to history once again and step into another time and place. I hope you'll hear the not-too-distant strains of Beethoven, Mozart, and other grand masters of music just as I did while I penned Tate and Rebekah's story.

Thanks for joining me on yet another journey,
Tamera

1

NASHVILLE, TENNESSEE
JANUARY 12, 1871

Rebekah Carrington stood shivering across the street from her childhood home, satchel heavy in hand, cloak dusted with snow. She counted the strides it would take to reach the front door. How could such a brief distance feel so insurmountable, so much greater a course to navigate than the ocean she'd just traversed? She wished she could blink and be back in Vienna.

After ten years, Austria felt more like home than the city in which she'd been born and lived the first half of her life. But the letter delivered nearly four weeks ago, only days before Christmas, had changed every—

The front door to the house opened.

Rebekah pressed into the shadow of a nearby evergreen, its pungent pine needles sharp and prickly with cold. She lowered her head to peer through the icy branches—breath fogging, hanging ghostlike in the air—and her stomach turned with something more than hunger.

It was *him*.

How many times since leaving Nashville had she pictured the man?

Yet looking at him now, a decade later, through

a woman's perspective, he seemed so different than when she'd peered up at him as a girl of thirteen. Though thicker through the middle with age, he was still tall, standing nearly six feet, and still possessed a commanding presence.

But he wasn't quite the towering figure her memory had conjured.

For years, recollections of the encounters—and that one night, in particular—had haunted her. With time and distance, she'd moved beyond it. She was no longer that young, naive girl, and she wasn't afraid of him anymore.

So why was her heart all but beating out of her chest? She straightened her spine, pulling her courage up along with it.

Her stepfather climbed into a carriage, one far grander than what she remembered him and her mother owning years earlier. Perhaps a purchase he'd made with money he'd gained in a recent *inheritance*. That possibility only deepened her resentment toward him, and made her question, yet again, the untimeliness of her grandmother's recent passing.

Not a word from Grandmother Carrington about feeling unwell, much less being ill, and then the shocking news of her "sudden and tragic death." It didn't make sense, and the ache of loss reached deep.

Rebekah eyed the carriage, and the silhouette of the man inside.

Barton Ledbetter was *not* an honorable man, she

knew that well enough. But surely he wasn't so devoid of morals that he would have dared to—

"Who you hidin' from?"

Rebekah jumped and spun, her thoughts veering off track.

A young boy peered up from beneath the bill of a ragged red cap, his belligerent expression repeating the question.

She frowned. "I'm not *hiding* from anyone."

The tilt of his head told her he thought differently.

"I was merely . . . considering my plans." Hedging the truth, she found the tug at her conscience easily allayed by the fact that her actions were decidedly none of this boy's business.

A half-empty sack of newspapers hung from a slim shoulder. And as though he sensed an opportunity, he whipped one out, rolled it up in a flash, and offered it to her as though presenting the crown jewels of the Habsburg family.

"Nickel for a paper, miss. Make it *two*"—a smirk tipped one side of his mouth—"and I'll keep quiet 'bout what I seen."

Rebekah eyed him. "And what exactly *is* it you think you've seen?"

"I caught you spyin'. On that family what lives right there." He pointed to the house.

She looked back at the carriage. It was about to pass her! Her stepfather looked up, seemingly straight at her. And she froze. He and her mother weren't expecting her until tomorrow. She'd arrived a day early due to fair weather while crossing the Atlantic, but—

She pressed into the spiky secrecy of the piñon pine, realizing she wasn't ready to face him after all. She needed time to plan her next steps—steps that would take her away from him. And sadly, from her mother too. Unless . . . she could persuade her mother to leave with her.

The carriage continued, and only after it turned the corner did Rebekah breathe easier.

"Well, lady? What's it gonna be?"

She turned back to find the boy still there, watching her, triumph in his expression. Recognizing an opportunist when she saw one, she leveled a stare. "You don't even know who resides there, young man."

"Yes, I do!" His tone and set of jaw were almost convincing. "That man there." He pointed in the direction the carriage had gone. "Him and his wife. That's their place. I see 'em comin' and goin' all the time."

Judging from his meager height and frame, Rebekah didn't think the boy more than seven or eight years old. He was on the lean side, as though regular meals were a scarcity, and his threadbare coat was tattered at the collar and absent its buttons. But he had a shrewdness about him she recognized. Similar to that of boys his age who'd grown up on the streets of Vienna. It was a savvy she both admired and pitied.

No child should be without a home, a safe place

from the world. And yet having a home didn't necessarily guarantee a child's safekeeping, she knew.

An idea came to her, and she set down her satchel. She hadn't been raised on the streets, but neither was she an innocent. She reached into her reticule, deciding that—either way this went—the decision about her homecoming would be made for her, and she would accept it.

"I'll purchase *one* newspaper for myself." She met his scowl with a firm stare. "Along with another. And I'll give you an extra nickel if you'll agree to do something for me."

His eyes narrowed. "What's it you're wantin' me to do?"

"Deliver the second newspaper to that house across the street. Knock on the door, and when the housekeeper answers"—which Rebekah felt certain she would—"ask her to deliver the paper to Mrs. Ledbetter. *If* Mrs. Ledbetter is at home."

A grin split his face. "Told you, you was spyin'!"

She stared. "Do you want to earn an extra nickel or not?"

He adjusted his cap. "What if she ain't home? You gonna try 'n cheat me outta my money?"

"Not at all. You'll still get three nickels either way. Do we have ourselves a deal?"

He held her gaze, then nodded once, slowly, as though considering another, unspoken, alternative. "I'll do it, just like you said."

Rebekah took the newspaper from him and pressed three coins into his grimy palm. His brown eyes lit, and she gripped the hem of his coat sleeve, having seen how swiftly these boys could run. "I warn you, young man, I'm fast on my feet. Keep your word or risk being chased down the street by a girl."

He snickered. "You ain't no girl. You a lady. And ladies, they never run."

She narrowed her eyes. "This one does."

His expression sobered as he turned, but Rebekah was certain she glimpsed a trace of amusement—and admiration—in his eyes.

From her niche behind the tree, she watched him pause at the edge of the street, waiting for conveyances to pass. She pulled her cloak collar closer around her neck as the flutter of nerves resumed in her stomach, same as happened every time she imagined seeing her mother again after all these years.

Her grandmother had managed to visit Austria every two years, staying a handful of months when she did. But her mother? Not once did she visit, despite Grandmother Carrington's offer to pay. Which had hurt more than Rebekah had ever revealed in her correspondence. Growing up, she'd always been closer to her father, responding to his warm, patient manner. The memory of her mother's attention in those earlier years, while consistent and plentiful, was tainted with the memory of her cooler demeanor and a propensity toward the critical. As though nothing Rebekah had done was quite good enough.

Still, Rebekah couldn't remember exactly when her relationship with her mother had gone so awry. Sometime after her father died. But, no, that wasn't it, though that loss certainly had changed their lives.

It was after her mother married Barton Ledbetter. That was when she'd become more solemn, distant. And . . . far more censuring.

They'd exchanged letters through the years, of course. Letters that had grown less frequent as time passed. Yet Rebekah still loved her and knew the affection was reciprocated, in her mother's unique way. But the thought of seeing her again after all these years was an unnerving prospect.

She rubbed the taut muscles at the base of her neck, weary from travel and uncertainty. After having been back in the city scarcely two hours, she knew that Nashville—and her family home—would never feel like home again.

In a flash, the boy darted across the street, skillfully dodging a lumber delivery wagon and outwardly oblivious to the heated curses the driver called down on him. The boy headed in the direction of the house—then stopped cold.

Every muscle in Rebekah's body tensed.

She gathered her skirt, debating whether she'd truly give chase over two nickels, despite her threat, but the boy glanced back in her direction and grinned—*grinned,* the little urchin—before continuing on to the front door.

Rebekah let out her breath and felt a speck of humor, even though she wanted to throttle his scrawny little neck.

She followed his progress and then found her gaze moving over the house, which had not aged well in her absence. Though her family had never been landed gentry, her father had inherited several parcels of land surrounding their home, which had allowed them to raise animals and keep a substantial garden. A nicety when so close to the city.

But after her mother remarried, Barton sold most of that property. Though where all the money had gone, she didn't know. Now a mixture of clapboard houses squatted one after another along the street that had once been a country-like thoroughfare where low-limbed oaks, decades old, had lent such joy and adventure to childhood summers.

Rebekah pictured the rooms of the house as they were when she'd last lived there, and still found it difficult to believe Grandmother Carrington was gone. *Oh, Nana . . .*

Grief was a strange thing. You could try to avoid it, keep it at arm's length, even maneuver around it for a time, but grief was patient and cunning. And always returned. With a vengeance.

She sucked in a soft breath, her vision blurring.

The letter from her mother had been succinct,

void of any detail other than "your grandmother passed unexpectedly, yet peacefully, in her bed," and had spelled out in no uncertain terms that it was time for Rebekah to return home. Then her mother had effectively cut off her funds.

Rebekah wiped her cheek. Dealing with the sudden loss of her grandmother—and benefactor, though of so much more than money alone—was difficult enough. But being forced to return to Nashville, and with the unequivocal expectation of her residing in that house again—with *him*—was unfathomable.

She couldn't do it. She *wouldn't*.

Yet she didn't have her paternal grandmother to side with her anymore. To insist on the importance of an education abroad. As if that had been the impetus behind her leaving for Vienna years earlier than originally planned by her father, God rest him. Her grandmother had believed her about the events of that horrible night. But her mother? *"Certainly you're confused, Rebekah. There's no way he would even think of ever doing anything like that. You're his daughter now. He's simply trying to be a loving father. Something for which you should be grateful . . . instead of misconstruing."*

At her grandmother's urging, Rebekah hadn't confronted him about it. They'd all acted as though it had never happened. At times she wondered if that had been the wisest choice . . . or merely the easiest.

The boy rapped on the front door, three sharp knocks, and when the door finally opened, Rebekah's heart squeezed tight.

Delphia.

The woman was still as round and robust as Rebekah remembered, almost as wide as she was tall. Even at a distance, the cook's apron appeared perfectly starched and gleaming white, same as every day of Rebekah's youth.

Like pearls gliding on a string, her thoughts slipped to Demetrius, and she wondered if Delphia's older brother was there or on an errand, or perhaps in the garden out back that he loved so much. In nearly every letter her grandmother had written, she'd included kind regards from Demetrius, oftentimes along with something witty he'd said.

Of all the people she'd thought about since receiving her mother's letter, she'd thought most of him. Demetrius was the one bright spot about returning. And she could hardly wait to show him what she'd finally mastered, thanks to his patient kindness and all he'd taught her.

She reached into her cloak pocket and pulled out the wood carving she'd carried with her for nearly fifteen years now. The carving was of the dog she'd had as a child. The likeness to the cute little pug—Button—was amazing, as was everything Demetrius carved. He'd told her he simply saw things in pieces of wood and then carved until he'd set them free.

Rebekah watched as Delphia stared down at the boy, hands on her hips, and it occurred to her that she hadn't bothered asking the lad his name before sending him on this errand. Delphia took the newspaper from him—the boy talking as she did, though Rebekah couldn't make out what he was saying—and Delphia slowly shook her head.

So then . . . Rebekah sighed. Her mother *wasn't* home.

Part of her felt disappointment, while the greater part felt relief. So the decision was made. She'd just bought herself another day to work up the courage for her official *homecoming,* and to try to find another place to live, though the two dollars and twenty-four cents in her reticule wouldn't stretch far.

Grandmother Carrington had told her during her last visit to Vienna almost two years ago that, in the event of her passing, she'd laid aside some money for her. Rebekah didn't know how much, but she was grateful. Even a small amount would help until she found a way to support herself.

Delphia spoke to the boy again—this time glancing beyond him to the street—and Rebekah held her breath, waiting for him to turn and give her away.

But he merely shrugged his slim shoulders and tipped his red cap in a way that drew a smile from the older woman. Something not easily done.

The little urchin was a schemer *and* a charmer.

When the front door closed, the boy retraced his

steps to the street. He looked briefly in Rebekah's direction and gave his cap a quick tug, his smile claiming victory. Then he took off at a good clip down the street.

Rebekah watched him go, feeling a peculiar sense of loss when he turned the corner and disappeared from sight. Which was silly. She didn't even know the boy.

Yet she felt beholden to him in a way.

The growling in her stomach redirected her thoughts and dictated her first course of action, so she headed toward the heart of town in search of a place to eat.

But the Nashville she'd tucked into memory years earlier was no more. Everywhere she looked, she saw remnants of the heartache her grandmother had written to her about during those awful years of conflict. What few buildings she did recall seemed to have aged several decades in the past one, their brick façades riddled with bullet holes, the dirt-filmed windows cracked and broken or missing altogether. Such a stark contrast to the opulent wealth and beauty of Vienna.

But what she found most surprising was the number of Federal soldiers walking past or standing grouped at street corners. She had no idea so many were still assigned to the city. Surely their continued presence wasn't helping to mend any fences.

Finally, nearly half an hour later, she discovered a small diner and claimed an open table by the front window, grateful to be out of the cold. Having had only a package of crackers since yesterday afternoon, she splurged on a breakfast of hot cakes, scrambled eggs, and bacon.

By the time her meal arrived, she'd scanned the list of advertised job openings in the *Nashville Banner*, which left her more discouraged than before. She perused the first column again as she ate.

The majority of openings were for factory positions, all of which sought experienced seamstresses. She could sew—if her life depended on it and patrons didn't care if their garments fit properly. But an experienced seamstress? No one would ever accuse her of being that. And the pay—ranging from thirty to seventy-five cents per week, depending on experience—was scarcely enough to buy food, not to mention a place to live and the barest of necessities.

The porter who had stowed her luggage at the train station warned her that life in Nashville would be far different than when she'd left. He hadn't been exaggerating.

December 2, 1860. The day she'd departed Nashville for Europe, and only a handful of months before war had broken out. And one year, to the day, following her dear father's unexpected passing.

The server returned and wordlessly refilled both Rebekah's water glass and empty cup. The coffee was strong and bitter, and the steam rose, mesmerizing, as she sipped and searched the remaining listings with greater care.

WANTED: EXPERIENCED CHEF FOR NEW HOTEL VENTURE.

She perused the lengthy requirements for the position, secretly impressed with anyone who could meet such stringent expectations. She sighed. She couldn't sew, she couldn't cook.

Why was it that what she knew how to do well seemed so useless? If she were a man, that wouldn't be the case.

As though poking fun at that very thought, a cartoon in a side column caught her attention, and she frowned. The sketch was an obviously satirical depiction of an all-female orchestra. Because the woman in the foreground, the most pronounced, was holding her trombone *backward*. Same for all the other female musicians with their instruments.

Rebekah read the caption beneath the cartoon and her eyes narrowed. *Ladies in Concert.* She huffed. The illustration had been drawn by a man, of course. Of all the—

Just below the cartoon was an article about the New York Philharmonic, a concisely written piece—only a few sentences long—that had originally appeared in the *Washington Daily Chronicle*, according to the first sentence. It announced that the symphony there had recently admitted their first female, a monumental feat of which Rebekah was already aware. But that was all the article said. No musician's name, no mention of what instrument the woman played. Nothing. And the article itself was *dwarfed* by the cartoon. Rebekah shook her head.

Yet she was grateful to the journalist for including even that much. She looked for the reporter's name and finally found it in almost minuscule print following the last sentence. SUBMITTED BY MISS ELIZABETH GARRETT WESTBROOK.

Feeling a sense of womanly solidarity with Miss Westbrook of the *Washington Daily Chronicle*, Rebekah returned her attention to the list of job openings.

SERVERS WANTED: YOUNG, ATTRACTIVE FEMALES ONLY. No description followed that listing, only a postal address. And it didn't take her imagination long to fill in the blanks as to what requirements that job might entail.

Just as she'd noticed the boys living on the streets of Vienna, she'd seen women, even young girls, standing on street corners after dark and loitering in alleys—and she'd glimpsed the same near the docks after disembarking in New York following the voyage. No matter the culture or continent, the baseness of human nature didn't ever seem to change. Which was particularly disheartening, under the circumstances.

She moved to the next column and felt a stab of melancholy at reading the last listing. A governess position. Now that, she was qualified for. She was good at it too, as the Heilig family would attest, if they could. She'd served their family for over two years. Though being a governess was hardly her heart's aspiration.

Especially considering—her eyes widened as she read—she'd be caring for six children. *Six!* She let out a breath. But the remuneration was almost a dollar per week, as well as room and board, and with less than three dollars to her name, she couldn't be choosy.

Not to mention the alternative staring her in the face if she didn't secure a job immediately was ample motivation. So a governess she would be, again, if she could manage to get hired.

She drained the last of her coffee, left enough money on her place setting to cover the meal and a little more, and stood. The young server, about her age, she guessed, was clearing dirty dishes from nearby tables, her apron soiled with stains. Her movements were efficient and experienced, but the stoop in her slender shoulders and the dullness of routine in her expression told a deeper, more touching story.

And suddenly, being employed to teach a family's children didn't seem so poor a prospect.

Rebekah gathered her reticule, newspaper, and satchel and crossed to the door, then remembered and returned for her cloak. Slipping her arms in, she acknowledged the truth hanging at the fringe of her thoughts. She should've stayed in Vienna. She should have searched harder for another way to remain there. She wrapped the woolen garment tightly around herself and shoved the buttons through the buttonholes, her frustration mounting.

But there was no way. She'd searched, she'd tried, however briefly, in the time she'd had. That was why she was standing here now.

She was almost to the door when a gentleman seated nearby opened his newspaper and gave it a good shake, then folded it back on itself. The noise was overloud in the silence, and Rebekah glanced his way. Then paused.

A bolded caption caught her attention.

She read it, then read it again, already telling herself she was foolish to feel hopeful. But the hope inside her paid no mind. With purpose, she returned to her table, withdrew the small glass bottle from her satchel, and poured the remaining water from her glass into it and capped the lid tight.

Once outside, she searched her copy of the newspaper until she found the article. She quickly scanned the newsprint, a cold breeze stinging her cheeks and making it difficult to hold the paper aloft to read.

Her lips moved silently as she devoured the text.

She pulled her father's pocket watch from her cloak and checked the time. Already half past twelve. She winced. She'd never make it. But she had to try.

After all, it wasn't as though she had anything left to lose.

• • •

Winded, she stepped into the dimly lit hallway and closed the roughhewn oak door behind her, grateful to be out of the wind and cold. Her legs ached from the freezing trek across town, and her confidence lagged. If only she'd seen the article in the *Nashville Banner* earlier, perhaps her chances of leaving here with a *yes* might've held more promise.

As it was, the advertised time for auditions had ended over an hour ago, and she could well imagine what conclusions a man such as Mr. Nathaniel T. Whitcomb would draw about a person who was tardy.

Nathaniel T. Whitcomb. Even the man's name bled blue.

According to the newspaper, Mr. Whitcomb hailed from the highest level of society. No surprise there, considering his education at the prestigious Peabody Conservatory of Music in Baltimore, then later at the Oberlin Conservatory of Music. Whitcomb's lengthy list of honors was impressive, and was made only more so considering his age.

Only thirty-two. Nine years her senior.

Quite a feat, she had to admit, even if begrudgingly. Yet if past experience proved true—and she felt sure it would—the man was guaranteed to possess an ego to match. That always seemed to be the way with male musicians.

Conductors, in particular.

But far more important than the man's view on

punctuality was his opinion about women in the orchestra. If only he was as forward thinking as the article had led her to believe. It indicated the Nashville Philharmonic was still in its infancy, and the newness of the organization could play in her favor. And surely it would help her case that the philharmonic societies of New York and Philadelphia had each recently admitted a female into their ranks.

Still . . .

The South had always been slower to accept change, especially when said change issued from the North. Years had passed since the war, but it was clear scars along those lines continued to fester.

"May I *help* you?" a woman announced, her tone sharp.

Startled, Rebekah turned to see a woman seated behind a desk to her right. The older woman's dour expression proved a good match to the mustiness of the building.

Palms clammy despite the chill, Rebekah approached, not having anticipated this particular hurdle—and silently berating herself for not. She was comfortable with symphony conductors, thanks to her experience in Vienna, but their gate-keepers . . .

They were a dreaded lot. And this one looked particularly formidable.

Best she phrase her request carefully, or she'd find herself back out on the street before she could blink. Her arm aching, she shifted her satchel from one hand to the other. "Yes, ma'am. I'm certain you *can* help me. Thank you." Rebekah offered a smile that went unreciprocated. "I'm here to inquire about—"

"The new position," the woman said, her gaze appraising. "Allow me to guess. . . . You *adore* the symphony, and it's always been your heart's deepest desire to somehow be part of it."

The woman's none-too-subtle sarcasm assured Rebekah she wasn't to be trifled with, but it was her slow-coming smile that made Rebekah feel as though the outside cold had somehow worked its way into the room.

Whatever her reason, the woman had apparently taken a disliking to her. Either that, or she simply didn't like the idea of her applying for the "new position." But were they even speaking about the *same* position? Instincts told Rebekah they weren't, but she followed the woman's lead.

"Thank you again for your offered assistance"— Rebekah glanced at the nameplate on the desk— "Mrs. Murphey. I'm so grateful for your help. And you're correct. I've long appreciated the symphony and would love to be involved with it. In fact, I—"

"Precisely *how* did you learn about it? That's what I'd like to know."

Rebekah hesitated. "Learn about . . ."

"The position for the conductor's assistant," the woman said slowly, as though addressing a daft child.

Rebekah forced a pleasant countenance. She'd learned at a young age that lying was wrong, but there was also such a thing as being too forthcoming. She'd learned that the hard way.

"Actually, Mrs. Murphey, I was speaking with someone this morning about Nashville, and we were discussing how much has changed in recent years. Then I read the article in the newspaper and learned about the new conductor and decided—"

"That you'd try and beat the others to the head of the line." Mrs. Murphey gave a flat laugh. "Well, you're too late, Miss . . ."

"Carrington, ma'am." Rebekah forewent the curtsy she knew wouldn't be appreciated. "Rebekah Carrington."

The woman looked her up and down, her gaze hesitating a little too long on Rebekah's jacket and skirt peeking from beneath the cloak. Rebekah brushed a hand over her attire. Being in mourning, she'd chosen her dark gray *panné* velvet jacket with matching pleated basque skirt and bustle. It wasn't her most elegant ensemble, but it suited her circumstances. And besides, the fashions in Nashville—at least what she'd glimpsed thus far—were considerably less elegant than Europe, and Vienna, specifically.

"Well, Miss Carrington . . . It befalls me to inform you that scores of young women have already inquired about the position. Women from Nashville's finest families, not to mention daughters of our most generous patrons of the philharmonic. So with that understanding, may I suggest you turn your attention toward other more *promising* employment opportunities. Good day to you."

Mrs. Murphey returned her focus to the papers atop her desk. But Rebekah didn't move.

Whether it was the woman's abrupt manner or the paralyzing truth about her own dire circumstances, she knew she couldn't leave without exhausting every last ounce of opportunity. And she didn't care one wit about the assistant's position. She'd come here with something far greater in her sights. Something that would turn the dear Mrs. Murphey's already graying hair to a shock of white. An entertaining prospect at the moment.

"Pardon me, Mrs. Murphey."

The woman's head slowly came up.

"I appreciate your counsel, but I still request that you ask the conductor if he has the time to speak with me. A few moments is all I require."

Mrs. Murphey stood slowly. "Perhaps I did not make myself clear enough, Miss Carrington. There's no reason for you to expect that—"

"You made yourself perfectly clear, ma'am. But I'm determined to speak with Mr. Whitcomb. So I can do that today. *Now*. Or . . ." Rebekah raised her chin. "I can come back first thing in the morning. And every morning after that."

The woman's lips thinned. "He's a very busy man, with a most demanding schedule."

Rebekah set down her case. "Which is why I don't wish to waste his time. Or yours."

Her sour expression only grew more so. "Very well. Remain here until I return."

Mrs. Murphey strode down the long corridor, her heels a sharp staccato in the silence.

Rebekah let out a breath, relieved . . . but also not. She stood for a moment, letting the silence settle around her as the musty smell of the opera house tugged at a cherished memory.

The image of her father dressed in his Sunday best, and she in hers, drifted toward her. She remembered that evening so well, although they'd entered through the ornate front doors of the building on that occasion. She'd never forget that night. Her first symphony. A traveling ensemble from New York, her father had explained. The experience had been magical, and changed everything for her. Her father had known it too.

What she wondered, and guessed she would never know for certain, was whether or not it had been his intention for the experience to change everything. Most certainly, it hadn't been her mother's.

Rebekah unbuttoned her cloak but left it on, still chilled, and let her gaze drift.

Peeling plaster walls and warped wooden floors belied the once rich opulence of the building. Yet somehow, the rear corridor of the opera house still managed a regal air, as though the timeless beauty of Mozart, Beethoven, and Schubert had seeped into the brick and mortar until it haunted the corridors and side halls with a presence she could all but feel and was certain she would hear in the stillness if she listened closely enough.

A shame the structure was scheduled to be torn down.

The article she'd read earlier recounted the city's plans to have the old opera house demolished soon, then followed with a description of the *new* Nashville Opera House, as it was being touted, scheduled for completion that summer. The details gave every indication of the building being spectacular. But apparently, numerous mishaps had delayed the project's completion.

The most startling being when an upper balcony collapsed during construction. Several workers had been seriously injured, but thankfully, none killed. From the tone of the newspaper column, a bout of scandal had followed involving the city's then mayor and his son, the architect first assigned to the project. Both father and son had lost their positions and, subsequently, a new architect—from Vienna, of all places—had been appointed to oversee the project.

And any structure in Nashville involving an architect from Vienna was one she intended to see.

As a young girl, she hadn't thought anything about Nashville having an opera house—modest though the building was when compared to those in Europe—but it was quite an impressive claim for so modest-sized a city. Nashville wasn't New York or

Philadelphia, after all. But the delights of theater, opera, and symphony were still appreciated. Especially following such a dark time of war.

The journalist had alluded to an "unnamed Nashville benefactor's extravagant generosity" in the construction of the new opera house, which explained how the project was being funded amidst such a depressed economy.

She glanced down the hallway, saw no sign of the gatekeeper, and so took a seat to wait in a chair along the wall. She pulled out her copy of the newspaper and perused the article again, eager for anything that might help her in her meeting with this *Nathaniel T. Whitcomb.*

The reporter emphasized the conductor's penchant for original scores and his leanings toward newer techniques, which she found encouraging. But that it took this much effort simply to get an audience with the man didn't bode well for her chances. She only hoped—

The reprisal of staccato heels drew her attention. But it was the utter consternation darkening the older woman's face that dared her to hope.

Rebekah started to rise.

"Stay seated," Mrs. Murphey commanded, her tone brittle. "The maestro is with someone at present, so you'll have to wait."

Hope reared its encouraging head. But . . . the *maestro?*

Rebekah searched the woman's expression. Surely, even with all the acclaim he'd received so early in his career, the man had yet to merit the distinguished title. Still, Mrs. Murphey's expression held not a hint of misgiving.

Fifteen minutes passed, then thirty.

Rebekah waited under the woman's watchful eye.

But when Mrs. Murphey stepped away from her desk, Rebekah furtively reached into her satchel, opened the bottle of water, and slipped a reed inside. Best to be ready, just in case. Her cherished oboe within wasn't her first instrument, nor her favorite, but it felt like an old friend, and—in light of public opinion regarding women playing the violin—the oboe was a far safer choice for this audition.

She rubbed her hands on her cloak, her nerves getting the best of her. Why was she so anxious? She'd auditioned for a symphony a thousand times—in her dreams.

But could she do it when it really counted?

Nearly two decades of playing or studying music—ten of those in Vienna—should have inured her to the panic in her stomach, especially considering her experience assisting one of Austria's most famous conductors. But assisting a conductor with score preparation and copying musical scores in his home—following dinner and after completing her duties as the governess to his children—was a far cry from being directed by one.

His dear wife, Sophie, once confided to her that Herr Heilig considered her quite talented—for a woman. But he also considered women to be *"far too delicate natured for the rigors of an orchestra."* So Rebekah had watched—and learned—as much as she could, waiting for the day when she could prove to him that she was, indeed, strong enough.

But that day had never come.

"Miss Carrington?"

Rebekah looked up.

Mrs. Murphey nodded down the corridor. "The maestro is available now. Let's not keep him waiting."

The sound of footsteps registered, and Rebekah peered down the hallway to see an older gentleman, hat in hand. He paused and glanced her way, his expression severe. Then, with a hasty gait, he departed in the opposite direction. She gathered that his meeting with the maestro hadn't gone as desired.

She only hoped she fared better.

2

Rebekah thought again of what she was about to do, and a knife of uncertainty cut through her. But this opportunity wouldn't likely come again. At least not for her. She expelled the stale air in her lungs in exchange for fresh and removed her cloak, then draped it over the chair and reached for her leather satchel.

"You *did* bring references with you, I trust, Miss Carrington?"

Rebekah hesitated, then swiftly smoothed her features. "I've brought everything that's required, I assure you."

She hurried down the hallway to avoid further questions, and felt Mrs. Murphey's disapproval boring into her. But it was an uncanny sense of being otherwise observed that drew her gaze to her right.

The eerily similar gazes of esteemed conductors, five in all, stared at her with resolute examination—Mozart, Handel, Beethoven, Bach, and Haydn—their portraits hanging in perfect symmetry, one after another. Each man wore an expression of triumph, as though having been deeply satisfied with his own accomplishments. And with good reason. Yet though their pasty complexions and slightly sagging jowls, captured with such detail by the artists, lent testimony to lives dedicated to perfecting their craft, a day or two in the sun would've done them all considerable good.

She slowed her steps, her gaze settling briefly on Haydn, a favorite Austrian son and the composer honored on the special evening her father had brought her to the opera house. Symphony No. 94 had been performed. One of her favorites. She'd tried to tell her mother about the experience and recalled her mother's response. *"An indulgence that will come to no good end—mark my words."*

Perhaps her mother would yet be proven right.

But her father—familiar longing tugged at her emotions—had been the kindest, gentlest man she'd ever known, passing away far too soon and leaving a hole in her life and in her mother's. Which her mother had filled too hastily and without knowing the true character of the man she'd married only five months after Papa died.

An empty space at the end of the row of portraits drew her attention, and she moved closer to read the engraved bronze plaque, similar in size and placement to those beneath the other portraits: NASHVILLE PHILHARMONIC, NATHANIEL TATE WHITCOMB.

Already they had commissioned a portrait of the man to hang beside the greatest composers in history? She shook her head. A dangerous undertaking to feed the ego of a symphony conductor, which that would most certainly do.

Gathering her nerve, she approached the doorway on the left, the one the man had exited earlier, only to find another hallway, shorter, beyond it. She stepped around the corner, eager to exit the scope of Mrs. Murphey's condescending gaze.

She smoothed the front of her bustled skirt as she mentally rehearsed her audition piece. Mozart's Oboe Concerto in C Major. She could play it flawlessly, and had, many times—alone in her room or when demonstrating proper technique to a young student.

But never when so much was at stake.

The partially open office door stood a mere four yards away, but her legs suddenly felt like lead.

It wasn't the audition she feared so much. She knew she could play. What she didn't know, and couldn't predict, was the new conductor's decision. If he said no, where would she go? What would she do? Be a governess? *Again.*

The weight of that possibility, and what it meant for her future, hung like an anvil about her neck.

But anything was better than returning home.

Beneath the weight of the moment, she paused, feeling self-conscious for not having done this in too long a time. *If you're listening, Lord, if you're really as patient and generous-hearted as my father always said, then let this Mr. Whitcomb prove more open-minded than his peers.* More like the conductor she'd read about in New York last year, or perhaps like Herr Dessoff, a *true* maestro from the Vienna Philharmonic. *Help me to play with confidence. And please . . . please let him say yes.*

Lifting her head, she fixed her gaze on the door, covered the distance, and raised her hand to knock—

"So you're telling me your performance Saturday meets your definition of 'playing with full emotion'?"

Rebekah stilled. The voice coming from the other side of the door was decidedly male—and decidedly displeased.

"Because if that's the case," the man continued, "I fear you're one of the most emotionally *trammeled* musicians I've ever encountered."

"But, sir, I—"

"I trust you're familiar with the definition of *mezzo forte*?"

Sarcasm thickened the rhetorical question, and the very air seemed to crackle with it.

"Of course, I am, sir. But—"

"*Moderately loud* is the meaning of the term. And yet you play as though the bars in question were marked *pianissimo*. I could scarcely hear you. *You* are the concertmaster! I expect you to display the leadership and ability a musician of your experience should possess. And to play as though you actually have an ounce of passion for the music, instead of merely *regurgitating* the notes on the page."

"But, Maestro, I'm quite certain that I, along with the other violinists—"

"Did you or did you not hear what Edward Pennington, the director of the symphony board, said to us just now? Our performances must be *sharper, better, more evocative*." An exasperated sigh. "Confirm with the section leaders that everyone received the new rehearsal schedule. Monday's practice will now be at seven o'clock in the morning, and no excuses from *anyone* about the schedule conflicting with jobs. Each man made a commitment when I accepted him into this orchestra, and I expect each to live up to his word. That will be all."

Dismissal punctuated the man's already sharp tone, and alarmed at the possibility of being discovered standing out here listening, Rebekah scurried to put distance between her and the office—

When the door opened wide.

A man strode from the room, face flushed, features dark with anger. But seeing her, he stopped.

Rebekah knew instantly that he wasn't Nathaniel Tate Whitcomb. Because this man was no stranger. She knew his face. Or more rightly, a younger version of it.

His eyes narrowed, as though he, too, were sifting back through time to more youthful years.

"Rebekah?" He said the name almost like a curse, surprise thinning his voice. "Rebekah Carrington." He spoke with certainty this time, and even greater displeasure.

But it was the look in his eyes—the animosity Rebekah remembered only too well—that caused the slender thread of hope she'd had for this audition to snap clean in two.

"Darrow Fulton," she said softly, the name resurfacing despite years of attempting to forget it. Her childhood nemesis, at least in a musical sense. The same age as she, he'd taken violin lessons from Mr. Colton just as she had, his hour coming always right before hers. And somehow Darrow still managed to be there to torment her as she was walking home.

How many taunts had he thrown her way? How

many bows had he broken? Her skill had never exceeded his, as Mr. Colton had always reminded her. The violin master had made it clear that he thought teaching girls was a waste, but her father's generous payment for lessons had somehow served as adequate persuasion. But the fact that she'd been close to Darrow Fulton's equal—at least at one time—had more than rankled her childhood nemesis. It seemed he had hated her for it.

The scrape of a chair in the office beyond broke the tense silence between them, and Darrow briefly glanced back in that direction. A flicker of embarrassment crossed his features before his expression went hard again.

"Finally back from Europe, I see. After all these years." A smile formed, though not a friendly one. "Dear ol' grandmother kicks the bucket and the money runs out." He made a *tsk*ing noise. "Pity."

The emotion that had threatened earlier wrapped around her throat like a three-strand cord and pulled taut. But she kept her composure, choosing to focus instead on the abuse he'd inflicted in her youth. Only now she had the strength of womanhood—and perspective—to fight back.

"I'll tell you what's *pitiful,* Mr. Fulton." Her voice held steady despite the hammering in her chest. "That after all these years, it appears you haven't changed. Not one bit. Now *that* is what I find most pitiful."

The creak of a door sounded.

"Mrs. Murphey, I instructed you to—"

Rebekah looked past Darrow and found herself staring at Nathaniel T. Whitcomb. Only, he looked nothing like she'd expected, or like any other symphony conductor she'd ever seen. This man wasn't the least bit pasty or weak. And nothing about him sagged either.

With a firm-set jaw, lean, muscular build, and piercing blue eyes, he seemed better suited for cross-examining a witness or ripping trees up by their roots than penning a sonata or conducting Beethoven's Fifth. Except for the beard. The beard, a cross between neatly trimmed and days-old stubble, gave him an air of casual distinction that firmly placed him in the category of musician.

Commanding was the first thought that came to her mind—*exceptionally handsome* was the second—and the combination threw her off-balance.

Darrow Fulton brushed past her, giving her a look that said their conversation wasn't over, and Rebekah swiftly found herself standing alone with the man who unknowingly held the bits and pieces of a dying dream in the palms of his hands.

Not another daughter of a rich patron . . .

Tate growled inwardly. How many of these vexatious creatures did they expect him to tolerate?

When Mrs. Murphey had told him that a young woman was here to interview for the assistant's position, he'd cut her off midsentence, tempted to refuse the meeting altogether. Time was scarce. And he was certain he'd already interviewed every young woman in the state of Tennessee.

But he needed the funds the wealthy patrons supplied and knew what he had to do to mollify them—meet their daughters. Though granted, this particular daughter was particularly lovely and had an air of maturity the others thus far had lacked. His gaze lingered briefly on her high-collared shirtwaist and jacket.

She wasn't flaunting her womanly *charms* as the others had either. At least not yet. Sometimes the longer these meetings went, the more *warm-natured* the young women became.

"I'll grant you five minutes, Miss . . ." He couldn't remember her name, if Mrs. Murphey had even told him.

"Carrington, sir," she supplied a little too eagerly. "Rebekah Carrington."

The last name didn't strike a chord with him, but he was still becoming familiar with this circle of society, and the list of Nashville Philharmonic benefactors. The list was surprisingly lengthy, ranging from one-time givers to those more committed, though the list needed to be lengthier still, considering the construction costs of the new opera house and the plans for growth the board had proposed.

Which meant the inaugural symphony in June— scarcely six months away—had to be an over-whelming success in every way. Winning the public's support was paramount, as were lucrative ticket sales and, of course, excellent musical content.

The musicians under his direction were fair at best. But what could he expect when he'd been handed an odd collection of music teachers, college professors, and amateurs to form Nashville's first philharmonic? Despite numerous practices over the past few weeks, they needed to be *so* much better than they were. Same for the symphony he was writing.

Or rather . . . attempting to write.

The philharmonic board had agreed to give him time to compose. But their directive was clear—they wanted a symphonic masterpiece in exchange. No pressure there.

He could feel the lifeblood of the music deep within him, but the notes refused to find their way onto the page. At times, mainly in the wee hours of the night when the world was still and the muse stubbornly silent, he wondered if he could do it. Then wondered if, in the process, he might be going a little mad.

For the umpteenth time that day, the dreaded *tick-tick-tick* of the infernal clock inside him rose to a deafening thrum.

"After you, ma'am." He gestured the young woman inside his office, eager to be done and on his way to the train station. He glanced at the clock on the mantel, then at the box from the apothecary in the corner, thinking of another place a world away.

He could *not* miss the last train today.

"Thank you, Mr. Whitcomb, for agreeing to see me." The young woman flashed a nervous smile as she claimed the wingback chair opposite his. "Mrs. Murphey conveyed that you're quite busy, so I appreciate your sparing the time for me."

He nodded and smiled, a useful gesture he was swiftly perfecting.

"The way you describe what it's like to conduct an orchestra, sir, the methods you use . . ." Her eyes widened. "I read this morning's article in the *Nashville Banner* and found it most enlightening. Especially the section the reporter included about how you—"

"Miss Carrington . . ." He held up a hand. "I'm honored you read the article. But . . . I'm aware of its contents. And you have only four minutes remaining. So perhaps it would be best to get directly to the subject at hand."

Her smile dimmed, and the eager sparkle in her eyes dissolved to desperation. "Of course." She clutched the brown leather satchel in her lap. "From what I've gathered, sir, you're a forward-thinking man. A true visionary in terms of the symphony and conducting. The strides you've made are so admirable and . . ."

Tate watched her as she spoke, gradually feeling more and more disappointed, yet unable to pinpoint why. Then it came to him. He'd somehow hoped for so much more from this woman. She was attractive—exceptionally so—with reddish-blond hair that set off keen hazel eyes. And her attire was quite elegant, even by Nashville's wealthiest standards.

But it was the intelligence in her expression, the way she held her head erect, and the direct manner in which she met his gaze—straight on, not in the least demure or simpering, as though she considered herself his equal—that had led him to hope for more. But as it was . . .

She apparently needed some help. And though it was out of character for him, he decided to lend her a hand.

"So having said all that, Mr. Whitcomb, I—"

"Are you well studied in the area of music, Miss Carrington?"

Her mouth, momentarily clamped shut, slipped open. "Yes, sir. I am. But what I'm trying to tell you is—"

"And can you transcribe a concerto?"

"Of course, but what I'm here to—"

"And a good cup of coffee. Stout, not bitter. Is that also in your repertoire?"

She searched his gaze. "Have you been listening to what I've been saying, Mr. Whitcomb?"

He heard a spark of displeasure in her voice, and genuinely smiled. Intelligent *and* spirited. He wished now that the decision of whom to hire as his assistant was really up to him. The board insisted it was, but everyone knew the truth, which made the charade of meeting their daughters even more infuriating. The position would ultimately go to the highest bidder, and he had a good idea of whose daughter would be awarded the position.

The very thought filled him with dread.

"Of course, I've been listening, Miss Carrington. I was merely outlining some of the duties required of my assistant. However . . ." He regretted this more than she would, he was certain. "I'm afraid the position has already been filled. But," he added quickly, "if you'll leave your address with Mrs. Murphey, we'll be certain to contact you should the situation change." Which was doubtful, but a fellow could hope.

He started to rise.

"Mr. Whitcomb." She lifted her hand. "I need to say something to you, sir."

More than slightly impressed with her assertiveness, Tate settled back in his chair, his interest sufficiently piqued.

"I didn't come here today, sir, to interview for the position of your assistant. However *important* and esteemed a position I'm certain that is."

He didn't think he imagined the trace of sarcasm in her tone, yet he couldn't account for it either. Had he offended this woman in some way? Apparently so, but . . . *how?* Eager to find out, he gestured. "Continue."

"I'm here . . ." She paused to open her satchel, then withdrew a case. "To audition for you. For the open seat of oboe. *If* you will allow me, Mr. Whitcomb."

There weren't many ways to surprise him anymore. But this woman had managed to find

49

one. *"You* want to audition for the open oboe chair?" As soon as he said it, he heard the disbelief in his voice and could well gauge what reaction that would draw from her.

Her brow knit tight, and determination swiftly replaced the desperation in her expression. "That's correct. I'm a fine oboe player and would appreciate the opportunity to audition for you. I know the formal auditions are officially over, but I only found out about them this morning."

She opened the case and began assembling the instrument, which looked slightly shorter than the usual oboe. The fingering system looked different as well.

"Miss Carrington, I—"

"Don't decide anything until you've heard me play. *Please,"* she added softly.

"Miss Carrington," he said again, growing less impressed with her assertiveness as the seconds ticked by. All she'd said at the outset was merely flattery to prime the pump. He realized that now. But what she was asking was completely out of the question.

He'd be run out of town on a rail if he allowed a woman in the orchestra. And if the continued success of his own career didn't hold enough importance to discourage him from such a foolhardy consideration, the circumstances in his personal life certainly did.

Regardless of his opposition to the idea of females being admitted to symphonies in general, for a host of reasons—not the least of which was what it would do to the already tenuous concentration of the current members under his direction—admitting a woman, no matter how talented, would be the equivalent of throwing away everything he'd worked so hard for—including the symphony he was writing for the upcoming inaugural concert.

Seeing the intensity in her expression, he continued. "The Nashville Philharmonic is comprised solely of males, of which I'm quite certain you're aware."

"Yes, sir, I am." She continued to adjust the upper and lower joints of the instrument. "But things don't always have to stay the way they are. Isn't that what you said? In the article?"

Now the woman was quoting his own words back to him?

She withdrew a reed from a bottle of water and placed it on her tongue, holding it between her lips as she finished tightening the connections on the oboe. Tate had seen this simple gesture performed countless times by musicians, but watching her do it was different, and garnered his attention in a way the simple routine hadn't before. Which made him infinitely grateful she wasn't watching him as he was watching her.

She held the upper joint, inserted the reed, and licked her lips, pressing them together intermittently as she did. "I'll be playing Mozart's Oboe Concerto in C Major."

"Miss Carrington." Tate shifted in his chair, still mesmerized by her mouth. "I would prefer it if you wouldn't—"

She began playing, and he fell silent. Not because the music she played was so exquisite—though it *was* beautiful—but because he could see her fingers trembling as she played, yet the music itself reflected none of that fear.

She played pianissimo at first but with a deepness and clarity not only of note, but of soul. Her skill was hardly flawless, but he could *feel* her passion for the heart of the piece and wished Mr. Fulton was here to witness it too.

This was what he'd been trying to describe to the man, but had failed, judging by Fulton's confused expression. Darrow Fulton's skill with the violin was exemplary. He was the finest musician among the fifty men who comprised Nashville's newly formed philharmonic. Darrow simply didn't love the instrument as a man with his level of talent ought. And the remainder of the musicians were ragtag compared to this. To *her*.

Drawn deeper into the music, Tate could all but hear the orchestra's accompaniment playing behind her, and Miss Carrington kept in perfect tempo. Her timing was excellent, and her vibrato . . . pure pleasure. She managed the descending arpeggio with practiced ease, and he closed his eyes and allowed himself to be carried along on the fluidity of the score.

This particular concerto was a personal favorite,

and he anticipated each shift—*allegro aperto*, *adagio ma non troppo*, and finally *allegretto*—and wasn't disappointed once. Disappointment came only when she finished.

And even then, the silence seemed to hover on the edge of the last lingering note, as though sharing his momentary regret.

Not wanting to open his eyes yet, he did so anyway, and discovered hers still closed, the instrument resting in her lap.

"Miss Carrington . . ." He spoke softly, aware of the rapid rise and fall of her chest and recognizing the blissful aftermath of having experienced the power of music flowing through her. Just as this music had flowed through Mozart a hundred years ago, and through myriad other musicians who'd performed the piece in the years between. Though he'd wager few had performed it with this woman's skill and passion.

Still . . .

All he could think about was . . . *What a gift.* Followed by a second thought that stung even before it was fully formed . . . *What a shame.*

Finally, she opened her eyes, their hazel color having taken on a deeper hue, and he read a singular question in her gaze—one he wished he didn't have to answer.

"Well done." His voice sounded overloud in the silence between them. "That was . . . exquisite. Thank you."

She smiled, and he was surprised at how much

he would have given in that moment to be deserving of such warmth and gratitude from her.

"But," he continued, the weight in his chest bearing down hard, "what you're asking, as I said before, is not possible. I'm sorry."

She blinked, and the beauty of the moment faded. "But . . . you just said—"

"I know what I said, Miss Carrington. And I meant it. Every word. But the fact remains, you are a woman. And women—"

"Aren't allowed to play in orchestras."

He let the silence answer for him.

"Are you aware, Mr. Whitcomb, that the philharmonic societies of New York—"

"—and Philadelphia have each admitted women into their memberships. Yes, I am aware."

"And yet?" she responded, incredulity edging an even tone.

"And yet we are in Nashville, Tennessee. Not in New York or Philadelphia. And the fact remains that the majority of people in this city, and certainly those who have pledged to financially support the symphony, as well as those we hope to draw to the box office, are not of that same mind. At least not for the present. But who knows what the future will bring, Miss Carrington."

"It won't bring anything new, Mr. Whitcomb, if those of us in the *present* don't work toward change. Toward bettering our society and *all* of those who comprise it."

Tate studied her, admiring her zeal—and

courage—while also wondering how on earth he'd ever gotten himself into this situation. He blamed the reporter and that blasted article. Nothing good ever came from speaking with a journalist.

He rose from his chair, hoping she would follow his lead. She did, slowly, and with a sadness that caused his chest to ache.

The clock on the mantel chimed the half hour, and he glanced over.

Half past four?

The last train left in one hour, and he had to be on it.

"Miss Carrington, I offer you my sincerest apology, ma'am, but I must ask you to excuse me. I have a pressing appointment that I cannot reschedule. So again, accept my thanks for the pleasure of hearing you play, and know that I, most sincerely, wish you all the best."

The words felt patronizing coming off his tongue, and—judging by her injured expression—she took them as such.

"I appreciate your time, Mr. Whitcomb. And I certainly don't wish to detain you further." She quickly disassembled the instrument and slipped it back into the satchel. "Good day."

Tate accompanied her as far as the hallway, though she didn't acknowledge him, nor did he blame her.

He retrieved his packed suitcase and portfolio from his office, grabbed the box filled with bottles of laudanum, and raced to the train station.

3

Rebekah hurriedly retraced her steps down the rear corridor of the opera house, disappointment clawing the back of her throat. *"Accept my thanks for the pleasure of hearing you play, and know that I, most sincerely, wish you all the best."* Could the man have been more condescending?

Gaze fixed on the exit ahead, she was grateful beyond words that Mrs. Murphey was nowhere in sight. Now, if she could only make it outside before the knot in her throat broke loose and—

"Bite your tongue, Matilda Murphey! I wouldn't wish being employed by that woman on my worst enemy, much less—"

From an open side door, Mrs. Murphey stepped into the hallway, and Rebekah stopped abruptly to avoid colliding with her.

Their gazes locked, and Rebekah found that even without words the woman could still wound.

"Ah, Miss Carrington . . ." Mrs. Murphey's eyes narrowed, and her expression dripped with unmistakable *I told you so.* "I take it your interview didn't go as hoped?"

Rebekah glanced at the door at the end of the corridor. So close, and yet still so far. "No, ma'am . . . It did not."

Another woman stepped from behind Mrs. Murphey, about the same age, it appeared.

Rebekah sensed her focused attention and braced herself to meet it as she shifted to face her. But she found only kindness there.

"Oh, my dear, are you all right?" The sweetness in the woman's voice was nearly Rebekah's undoing.

"She's fine, Agnes," Mrs. Murphey supplied. "I tried to warn her about interviewing for the assistant's position but she would have none of it. She insisted on wasting the maestro's time."

"Well . . ." Agnes gave Rebekah's arm a brief squeeze. "Who can blame a lovely young woman for wanting to improve herself with new experiences? Not to mention vying for a chance to work with such a fine man." Her cheeks puckered as she smiled and winked. "But never you mind, dear, I'm sure you'll find another position soon enough."

Eyes burning, Rebekah managed a nod. "Thank you, ma'am."

"The name's Mrs. Bixby, dear. And you're so welcome."

"Well . . ." Rebekah dipped her head. "If you'll both excuse me, I best be on my way."

She was halfway to freedom when someone called her name. The patronizing tone assured her it was Mrs. Murphey. The woman must have taken lessons in intonation from *the maestro*. Remembering what he'd said—*"Well done. That was exquisite"*—only deepened the ache in her throat. Why say such things when he didn't truly mean them?

Clenching her jaw to stem the tears, she turned back to find Mrs. Murphey smiling. Rebekah's guard instinctively rose.

"I've only recently—in the past hour, in fact—been made privy to a position that's currently open. I thought you might be interested. Considering your lack of success here."

"Matilda, *no*." Mrs. Bixby shook her head. "I don't think—"

"That Miss Carrington is qualified?"

Agnes Bixby frowned. "That wasn't what I was going to say at all. It's only that—"

Mrs. Murphey shushed her with a wave of her hand. "Do you have experience being a governess, Miss Carrington?"

Rebekah looked between the two women, reading concern in one expression and irrefutable challenge in the other. Clearly, Mrs. Murphey had an agenda, and Rebekah was certain the woman didn't have her best interests at heart. Far from it. But she needed employment and was willing to sacrifice her pride in order to gain it. Because employment was the only way to escape living at home.

With *him*.

"Yes, ma'am." She lifted her chin. "I have experience, and references."

"Well, then . . ." The sparkle in Mrs. Murphey's gaze turned almost catlike. "This is, indeed, your lucky day. Insomuch as you're not averse to hard work, of course, and to truly applying yourself."

Imagining again the shock of white hair on the woman's head, Rebekah added a face full of wrinkles to match. And maybe a wart or two. "I'm not afraid of hard work, Mrs. Murphey, and I *am* in need of employment. So if you're privy to a position with a family, I'd be obliged if you'd share the information with me." She only hoped it wasn't the family with six children she'd read about in the *Nashville Banner.*

"Oh, I'll do better than that, Miss Carrington. I'll write it down for you." With a jaunt in her step, Mrs. Murphey crossed to the desk and put pen to paper.

"I still think"—Mrs. Bixby came alongside them—"it would be best if Miss Carrington were to—"

"It's best to let her decide for herself, Agnes. If there's one thing I've learned very quickly about Miss Carrington, it's that she prefers to make up her *own* mind. Isn't that correct . . . Miss Carrington?"

Mrs. Murphey handed her the slip of paper. On it was a name and an address, neither of which were familiar to her.

Rebekah slipped the piece of paper into her pocket. "Thank you, Mrs. Murphey." The words came more easily than she'd imagined. "And to you as well, Mrs. Bixby. Your kindness is much appreciated," she added softly, gaining a bit of satisfaction when seeing Mrs. Murphey's frown.

Eager to leave, she retrieved her cloak and

hurried outside. She paused on the street long enough to slip into her cloak and wrap the woolen garment around herself. A cold wind bit her cheeks, making her eyes water, helped along by the memory of what Mr. Whitcomb had said. . . .

"I meant it. Every word. But the fact remains, you are a woman."

Was it possible that a portion of his compliments had been sincere? That he'd considered her skillful—only . . . not skillful enough? Or was it solely her gender that had informed his decision?

Whichever it was, she guessed it didn't matter. Because in the end, whatever the reason, she hadn't earned her place in the orchestra. And yet . . .

It did matter. It mattered a great deal.

She made her way down the street, frustration and chill quickening her pace. The thoroughfares were less crowded than earlier, the skies a touch grayer, and her outlook far less hopeful. How would she ever be able to overcome an obstacle she couldn't change?

The question wasn't a new one for her.

God had made her a woman. He'd planted the love of music in her heart from the very beginning, her father had always said. He'd recounted for her the many times he'd caught her sitting at her open bedroom window, late at night, listening to the music coming from the slave cabins just over the hill. God had gifted her with the desire and ability to play, an ability she'd worked for years to perfect.

So why would the Creator have placed that love inside her if not for a purpose? And why put people in her life to help her toward that goal— *dear Demetrius*—if performing wasn't part of God's plan for her life?

Thinking of Demetrius made her think of home, and home reminded her of decisions—and confrontations—that awaited. While she couldn't delay returning home forever, she could at least postpone it one more night. She checked her pocket watch. It was too late in the day now to call on the family about the governess position. But tomorrow was Friday, so she would seek an interview bright and early in the morning. Best find a place to stay for the night.

First, however, she needed to return to the train station to make arrangements for the trunks she'd left in the porter's care. He'd made it clear she couldn't leave them there overnight, but a man in his position would be able to recommend a reputable hotel or boarding room. She'd have him deliver the trunks there.

She headed back in that direction, her satchel heavy in her grip, her mind churning.

Nathaniel T. Whitcomb.

Perturbed when her thoughts returned yet again to the man, a third suitable descriptor for him came to her, besides *commanding* and *exceptionally handsome.*

The man was *supercilious,* most definitely thinking quite highly of himself. The way he'd stared at her, as though he couldn't believe she would deem herself worthy to audition for him.

The maestro, indeed.

Then again, the one time she'd chanced to briefly open her eyes while she played, she'd discovered his own eyes closed, and his expression leaning toward what was almost certainly appreciation. Even pleasure. At least at the time. Until the flippant manner in which he'd chosen to end her audition. And her dreams.

"I must ask you to excuse me. I have a pressing appointment that I cannot reschedule." She laughed beneath her breath. A pressing appointment. At the very least, he could have been honest and simply asked her to leave.

She rounded the corner, and the question that had reared its ugly head earlier returned with renewed vigor.

What if she had been given this ability, this desire to play, for some purpose other than playing in an orchestra? What if scaling a descending arpeggio on her oboe—her fingers expert on the keys, the music flowing from deep within her through the instrument, born of her very life's breath—was simply intended for her own pleasure? Or when she cradled the violin, holding the instrument firmly but gently, as one might hold a fragile bird—with enough conviction so it wouldn't skedaddle away, yet gentle so as not to crush it—what if that was for her delight alone?

Yet how did she balance that with the fact that

when she played—the violin, especially—she felt more alive, purposeful, closer to God, and at home within herself than at any other time in her life?

The shrill blast of a train whistle jerked her back to the present, and she paused for a second, waiting for her thoughts to catch up. She was only three or four blocks from the station at most.

Wishing again that the afternoon wasn't so far gone and she could call upon the family about the governess position, she pulled the slip of paper from her pocket and read Mrs. Murphey's tight, even script.

Mrs. Adelicia Cheatham. Belmont Estate.

Rebekah stared at the name, searching the distant past for any shred of remembrance. She did the same with the estate, which seemed vaguely familiar to her. But . . .

Nothing firm.

Her grandmother, God rest her, had been faithful in her letter writing through the years. Remembering her handwriting—shakier as she'd gotten older—tightened Rebekah's heart with grief. Yet she'd also been faithful not to share overmuch about Nashville and the families in their acquaintance. Which proved just as well. Because whenever Nana had shared, the majority of the news had included countless deaths of fathers and sons in the war, followed by the losses of family homes and property.

Another blast sounded, and a telltale plume of smoke and cinders rose above the buildings in the near distance. Rebekah hurried on, mindful of the icy streets and eager to retrieve her luggage from the hold and secure lodging for the night.

Winded, Tate reached the station platform just as the final train whistle blasted and sent a billow of smoke lofting into the late-afternoon sky. The gray clouds were beginning to make good on their threat, and a fine mist fell like icy lace over the plank wood beneath his boots. He paused to allow an elderly couple to precede him on the walkway.

The detour he'd taken by his house had cost precious time, but after promising Opal he'd bring this—he patted his coat pocket—with him on his next trip, he couldn't very well show up without it. Her smile would be worth it.

A porter knelt to pull up the step, then saw him and paused, and said something to him. But the man spoke so softly, Tate couldn't understand him.

"Beg your pardon?" Tate offered, having seen the man before.

"I said . . . You almost missed it, Maestro Whitcomb."

"That, I did." Tate glanced at the name sewn on the front pocket of the man's jacket, knowing he should be familiar with the employee's name by now. "I appreciate you holding her for me, Mr. Barrett."

The man beamed. "My pleasure, sir. Headed to Knoxville again? Important symphony work, I imagine."

Tate briefly looked away. "The symphony keeps me busy."

Barrett nodded. "Nice article in the paper this morning, sir. I'm saving up to surprise the missus by taking her to one of your concerts. She's always wanted to go." His expression turned sheepish. "I've never been too keen on that kind of music myself, but . . ." He stood a little straighter. "No reason I can't give myself a little extra culture for one night."

Tate laughed. "There's a concert three weeks from tonight. An evening with Ries and Bach."

"They local fellows?"

Tate smiled, deciding not to elaborate. "Visit the box office before the show. There'll be two complimentary tickets waiting for you."

The man's expression faltered. "No kiddin', sir?"

Tate clapped him on the shoulder. "No kiddin', Mr. Barrett. Only thing is . . . now I'll be nervous knowing you're there."

Tate climbed aboard, the porter's laughter following him inside. He kept his gaze averted from the other passengers and chose a seat toward the back, away from others. Not that any of them would recognize him. Anyone who might would more likely be traveling toward the back, in the first-class passenger cars—far from the bothersome soot and cinders.

Hence, why he'd chosen this one.

The air in the passenger car was frigid, and also ripe with humanity. So after stowing his bag in the overhead rack, he cracked open his window a little and settled in for the trip. Nearly four hours, but the distance and time traveling never bothered him. He'd always slept well on a train. And after the week he'd had, sleep sounded marvelous.

He leaned back, crossing his arms and brushing an envelope protruding from his coat pocket—the note Mrs. Murphey had shoved into his hand as he left the opera house. Sighing, he rubbed his eyes.

Guessing who the missive was from, he debated whether to open it now or leave it for later. But considering the donation the sender had recently pledged, he lifted the flap.

The fine deckle-edged stationery confirmed his suspicions, and as his gaze moved over the page and down to the elegant signature in closing, he heard the woman's genteel, yet somehow strikingly authoritative voice . . .

Dear Maestro Whitcomb,

It is with extraordinary pleasure that I congratulate you once again on your impressive accomplishment in being named the Nashville Philharmonic's first official conductor. We are most honored to have you in our midst, and I consider it a privilege to partner with you in laying a firm foundation for our symphony. Your exemplary leadership coupled with lavish support from the most loyal patrons will be the brick and mortar of our success. But, of course, you understand that full well.

Tate had to smile. Mrs. Adelicia Cheatham was certainly diplomatic—he gave her that. Better she simply say, "I'm giving the symphony exorbitant amounts of money and, in exchange, expect the new conductor to be at my beck and call."
Curbing a slight scowl, he continued on.

Thank you for agreeing to be an honored guest at my upcoming dinner party, and also for your gracious offer to arrange a string quartet for the evening of this Saturday, only two days hence.

Gracious offer? He still had no idea how she'd managed to rope him into doing it. In fact, thinking back on it, he couldn't remember saying yes. She'd simply acted as though it were a given.
If the woman wasn't so rich, he would've been tempted to check his wallet when she'd left his office that day.

Is there any more ethereal music than that of the violin and cello? If such a sound exists, it has yet to fall upon these ears. Please remember to include Mozart's Spring Quartet, for it is among my favorites.
You, of course, will be an honored guest, and I will consider it my personal duty to

introduce you to everyone in attendance. While several of the guests have already agreed to partner with the symphony, many have not. We will combine our efforts to make converts of them yet!

The event begins promptly at eight o'clock, so please arrive with your musicians no later than one hour prior, as my husband, Dr. William Cheatham, and I wish for the timeless strains of the masters to greet our guests as they step into the entrance hall. Is there anything more welcoming on a cold winter's eve than the warmth of candlelight in a window and Beethoven beckoning you in?

Personally, he could think of a few things. Yet there *was* a certain Mozart concerto—and musician—that came to mind as being exceptionally pleasing. Thoughts of Miss Carrington challenged his concentration as he scanned the last paragraph of the letter.

In addition to Mozart's Spring Quartet, Mrs. Cheatham requested several other pieces to be performed, but he gave her preferences little heed. The woman could command a performance, but not what instrumental pieces to perform.

He had to maintain *some* control.

He folded the letter and returned the envelope to his pocket as another woman took precedence in his thoughts. He welcomed the change, even if the similarities Miss Carrington shared with the author of the letter were a tad alarming. Both determined and decisive, the two women knew what they wanted and weren't afraid to pursue it.

But Miss Carrington's pursuits were so far outside the boundaries of acceptable, not even the independent-minded Adelicia Cheatham would approve.

Miss Carrington had entered his office with an agenda, yet left with it decidedly unfulfilled. Which had given him no pleasure. Where had she learned to play like that? With such precise yet fluid grace? At none of the conservatories he'd attended, that was certain. Women weren't admitted, and rightly so. They would be a distraction. Just as she most certainly would be in his orchestra. She was . . .

Exquisite was the word that came to mind. And it suited both her talent and her physical attributes. She was—

"But I requested that you keep the luggage *here,* sir! I only gave you that address in the event that I—"

"I'm sorry, miss. But it wasn't me. I did like you said and set the luggage aside. Another porter must've seen it and had it delivered a while ago. Again, my apologies."

The conversation drifting in through the window caught Tate's attention, but it was the exasperated sigh that brought his head around.

It was *her*.

He leaned forward to peer through the rivulet-streaked window, the icy mist having turned to rain.

"I can arrange for a carriage, ma'am," the porter continued, tone earnest. "Stand over there beneath the awning, and I'll—"

"No." Miss Carrington shook her head. "I don't need a carriage, sir. What I *need* is for my trunks to *not* have been delivered to my—" Her lips firmed. She closed her eyes, and Tate felt more than saw a shudder pass through her.

The train lurched forward, and he fought the urge to get off and go to her. Try to help, if he could. Not that she would welcome his assistance. Not the way things had been left between them. And since someone else was waiting for him at the other end of the tracks, someone who *would* welcome him . . .

He turned in his seat to watch her as the train pulled away. She bowed her head, her shoulders gently trembling.

4

Soaked from the rain and trembling with cold, Rebekah raised her hand to knock on the front door—

The door jerked open.

She steeled herself for the wounded—no, *furious*—expression on her mother's face. But

70

found herself instead staring into depths of deep brown love and warm concern instead.

"Land sakes, child!" Delphia grabbed her by the arm and drew her across the threshold into a hug that would've crushed a slighter woman. "It's about time, Miss Rebekah! We been waitin' on you."

"I'm s-sorry for being late. And"—Rebekah's chin shook—"for b-being so wet."

"A little water ain't killed me yet, child." Delphia's breath was warm against her cheek. "Oh, it's good to have you home, Miss Rebekah."

Unable to remember the last time she'd been hugged this way, Rebekah relished the warmth and the woman's familiar scent—like warm sugar cookies and love. A savory scent intermingled with the sweet, and in a blink, Rebekah was carried back to earlier years.

"But, Lawd . . ." Delphia held her at arm's length. "I got one thing wrong for sure."

Rebekah searched her expression.

"You ain't no child no more. Is you, ma'am? Just look at them curves."

Rebekah smiled. "But *you* look exactly the same, Delphia. You look wonderful."

The woman's grin shone bright when she laughed. "If by wonderful you mean fat and full o' sass, then that I am." She squeezed Rebekah's hands. "Gracious, you chilled to the bone. You shoulda sent the porter to fetch the carriage." Delphia shook her head. "But you here now, and that's what matters. Now, let's get that door shut 'fore the freezin' moves in and gives us all the fever."

Rebekah stood in the entrance hall, regretting the water marks she was leaving and feeling even more like a stranger in this house than she'd feared.

Crystal and bronze oil lamps flickered on mahogany side tables that had been shined to a high polish. The tables had belonged to her paternal grandparents, crafted from a tree her grandfather had felled when he and her grandmother first married. Rebekah remembered playing beneath the tables as a child, and the countless times her father must have clearly spotted her during their games of hide-and-seek, yet never let on.

Odd, the childhood moments one remembered.

Odder still that, though she knew better, she half expected her grandmother to walk around the corner at any moment, arms outstretched to greet her, smile at the ready. Still so hard to believe she was gone.

The clock on the mantel faithfully marked time's irrepressible march, while matching the cadence of a phrase repeating in her mind. *I should have stayed in Vienna. I should have stayed in Vienna. I should have stayed in Vienna.*

And for the thousandth time, she attempted to silence the voice.

She was here, *home,* with her mother likely only a room away, and all she could think about was leaving again. The distant relationship between them wasn't right. She'd always known theirs was a different sort of kinship, and she hoped to change that now that she was grown. But how to begin such a long and uncharted journey? Especially when she wasn't sure whether her mother shared that desire.

"Give me that cloak, Miss Rebekah, and let's start gettin' you warmed up. I'll tell Rosie to get a fire goin' in your bedroom too."

Rebekah surrendered the sodden garment and waited, shivering, for Delphia to return. When she did, Rebekah's earlier suspicion about her grandmother's death rose again to the surface.

"How did she die?" she asked quietly, hoping to get more details.

"I found her in her bed upstairs. It was still early, sun just peekin' up. Your grandmama always did like a cup of hot tea first thing. Said it helped her wake up with the day." Delphia sighed. "Only, she didn't wake up that mornin'."

"Had she been sick? Or not feeling well?"

Delphia stilled and looked at her, then hurriedly hung the cloak on the coat rack. "Not that I recall, ma'am. But . . . you know how it is. All our days are numbered by the Lawd. It was just her time, I guess."

Not fully convinced, Rebekah nodded.

A moment passed, and Delphia's arm came around her waist. "But look at you now, Miss Rebekah . . . All growed up and lookin' so much like her."

Rebekah's heart lightened. "Really? You think so?"

"Sure do. You got her smile and that way of lookin' at a person that makes 'em feel listened to, like they matter. You both always had that way about you." Her brown eyes glistened. "Not to mention you's all filled out and ladylike. Not too skinny, not too plump. And them fancy clothes! *Mmm-hmm* . . ." Delphia shook her head. "Like you come straight from some kind of palace or somethin'."

"No palace. I promise. Although Sally and I *did* live a few streets away from one." She smiled. "The house we rented was small. Only three rooms, but it was nice."

"Oh, that Sally . . ." Delphia's expression softened. "I still ain't believin' what your letter to your grandmama said." Delphia laughed. "Sally done gone and found herself a man! A foreign one too!"

"More like Sebastian found her and wouldn't take no for an answer. He has a family home they'll be moving into soon."

"Awfully kind of you to let her stay, Miss Rebekah."

"*Sally* was the kind one. Leaving here like she did all those years ago. Leaving everyone behind." Not that the woman had had any choice in the matter. Sally, twice her age, had been a slave in her grandmother's household. But after Nana left Austria—having stayed several weeks to see them settled and Rebekah's education under way—Sally had served not only as handmaiden and guardian, but eventually as confidante and dear friend as well.

It was a relationship her mother would never have approved of. But Nana had, and that's all that mattered.

"Is . . . she here?" The question was out before Rebekah could call it back.

The briefest shadow eclipsed Delphia's kindness. "Missus Ledbetter, she restin' for a bit. But you better know she's all afire and kindlin' to see you again." As swiftly as Delphia's laughter bubbled up, it settled. "But them trunks arrivin' afore you did . . . well . . ."

Delphia shot her a look that Rebekah had all but forgotten, yet instinctively understood. She would pay a price for choosing not to come straight home. Yet she wasn't about to admit where she'd been that afternoon and what she'd been doing. Not even to Delphia.

"She a proud woman, your mama. But she good too. Just don't take too well to change. And surprises . . . well . . . they get her a mite flustered."

"That's putting it mildly." Seeing Delphia's frown, Rebekah lowered her head. "I'm sorry, Delphia. I . . ." She clenched her jaw, peering up. "I had some errands I needed to take care of in town. I never intended for the trunks to be delivered early."

Delphia brushed a wet curl from Rebekah's temple, much as she'd often done when Rebekah was a child. "We all have us our own ways of dealin' with things." Wisdom deepened her gaze. "That's one thing that ain't changed through the years. And likely never will."

Rebekah nodded, sensing an answer to her earlier thought about altering the relationship with her mother. Only, it wasn't the answer she'd hoped for.

Delphia escorted her to her old bedroom, where a fire crackled in the hearth. With Delphia's assistance, she changed into a fresh jacket and skirt—dark brown with deep blue piping. Not nearly as elegant as her now-wet traveling ensemble, nor as nice as her mother would be expecting, but nothing could be done about that.

Rebekah fished through one of her trunks until she found her hairbrush and combs.

"You need me to send someone up to help with your hair, ma'am?"

"No, thank you, Delphia. I'll manage. But before you leave . . . Is Demetrius here? How is he? I'm so eager to see him again."

Delphia paused beside the chifforobe. "Demetrius, he . . ." She smoothed a hand over the damp skirt, opening her mouth to speak, then her lips briefly firmed. "He ain't here right now. But I know he'd like nothin' more than to see you too." Her smile held reminiscence, and a flicker of something that tugged at Rebekah's heart.

"Now I best get back downstairs to the kitchen. Get y'alls dinner fixed up."

As Delphia closed the door behind her, Rebekah settled at the dresser and did her best to set her still-damp hair to rights. So much for making a good impression upon returning home.

The special haven of a bedroom she remembered from childhood was gone, stripped bare of every last memento, as though someone had tried to erase the memories—and her—from the home. In its place was a lovely bedroom with which she felt absolutely no connection, which made the once-cherished space seem even more lonely.

Her styling efforts finally exhausted, she left the bedroom and paused on the second-floor landing, grateful to find it empty. She crossed to her grandmother's bedroom. The door was closed, and she hesitated, wanting to open it, yet not wanting to all the same.

The knob turned easily in her grasp, and the first thing her gaze touched was the old cherrywood rocker by the window—absent the colorful crocheted quilt that always occupied the seat or was draped across the back. Her focus went next to the bed, where the hand-stitched coverlet Nana had pieced together and sewn from several of Grandfather Carrington's shirts always rested. Only, it wasn't there either. In its place lay a simple white coverlet. Pristine. And sterile.

In fact, the entire room was sterile. Absent of any of her grandmother's things. It was as if Nana had never lived there. A rush of grief—and anger—swept through her. Why would her mother have gone through her grandmother's things without her? She should have known that—

"Rebekah."

She froze at the voice behind her. And despite all the mental and emotional rehearsing she'd put herself through in preparation for this moment, she still felt taken aback.

Feeling his gaze, she turned—and quickly realized that distance had distorted her estimation earlier that morning. Barton Ledbetter was still an imposing man, with eyes darker than she remembered and more assessing. Sharp prickles needled up her spine as memories of that night rushed back.

Watching the slow curve of his smile, she broke out in a cold sweat and her stomach knotted tight. She consciously unclenched her fists at her sides, not wanting to give him the satisfaction of seeing her discomfort.

"Barton . . ." Voice tight, she still refused to call him *Father,* as he'd asked when he and her mother first married. Only one man would ever hold that distinction in her heart. So they'd settled on a first-name basis instead. "I didn't hear you there." His intention, no doubt. She glanced beyond him to the open door of the fourth bedroom across the hall.

As though reading the question in her mind, he gestured, his smile turning oddly sheepish. "Some evenings when I arrive home later than planned, I

78

find your mother already abed. So I stay in there out of concern for her rest."

"Of course." Rebekah nodded, not believing him for a minute. Several reasons came to mind as to why a man would be out so late at night. None of them respectable.

He moved toward her, and she tensed, the memory of his hot breath on her neck and the stench of liquor and sweat all too vivid.

He stopped a few feet away, his gaze appraising. "Let me be the first to welcome you home, Rebekah. It's been far too long, my dear, and the house far too quiet without you. This is a very happy occasion for your mother and me. One we've long awaited, I assure you."

She wasn't fooled by his greeting or the oily sincerity of his tone. In fact, his falsity aligned perfectly with the kind of man she knew him to be. And with what he'd done to her—or would have done. If not for Demetrius.

Demetrius . . . Thinking of him gave her renewed boldness.

"From my perspective, Barton, my homecoming is hardly a joyful one, considering the circumstances. Though I *am* looking forward to seeing Mother again. Speaking of . . ." She glanced toward what had been her parents' bedroom, eager to be rid of his company. "Do you know where she is?"

He didn't answer her immediately. "I believe I heard her leave the room a few moments ago. She's likely waiting for you downstairs. In the parlor."

Rebekah turned toward the staircase.

"I must add," he continued, "looking back on things now, I do believe your grandmother, God rest her, was right when she suggested you go abroad for your education when you did."

Rebekah paused at the head of the stairs. She didn't look back but knew he'd moved closer, because she could smell his sickeningly sweet shaving soap. Cherry laurel. How she'd grown to hate that scent.

"You know I didn't agree with your grandmother—at first. And was adamantly against the decision, to be truthful. It hurt to see your mother so wounded. To have her only child taken so far away . . . But in light of the war and the horrific events that soon followed your departure, I believe it *was* best for you to be removed from this city. The years in Europe were far kinder than those you would have experienced here. And I can't help but believe, especially upon seeing you now— such a striking and . . . beautiful young woman— that it was, indeed, for the best."

Unable to believe what he was saying, she slowly turned back—and found he'd all but closed the distance between them.

She'd expected him to behave as if nothing had happened, as he'd done before she'd left. But for him to *intentionally* bring up the subject of why she'd gone away and then lay the wisdom of the decision on the war . . .

It gave new meaning to the word *gall*.

She stared up at him and, in the space of a blink, she saw him through the eyes of her younger self, and realized how she'd been so taken in by him at first. He was *smooth,* as her grandmother had once described him. Some might have called him handsome too. And he possessed a charisma that he used to cultivate trust on the one hand, while skillfully manipulating with the other.

"If there's anything I can do, Rebekah, to make this adjustment easier for you, dear, please don't hesitate to make that known. You need time to heal, I realize. The news of your grandmother's passing must've come as a great shock to you, as it did for us. It was so sudden. So unexpected." He shook his head. "But the doctor assured us Ellen died peacefully in her sleep. Which is of great comfort. And not a bad way to depart this world, compared to some."

His false piety and pretension she could stomach. She was accustomed to that. But hearing her grandmother's name from his lips ignited her anger. "Why have all of Grandmother Carrington's belongings been moved from her room? And what's been done with them?"

"Your dear mother found it too difficult to deal with at the time, so I took care of it all for her."

"You *took care* of it?"

His focus never left her face. "Yes. Understanding that your grandmother was always such a . . . gracious and benevolent woman, I made sure

81

her clothing and belongings went to those in need. I'm sure you'd agree that that was what she would have wanted."

The news arrowed through her. "You got rid of *everything?* Her clothing? Her quilts? Her jewelry?"

"Don't think of it as having gotten rid of it, Rebekah. Think of it as . . . blessing those less fortunate. Much as she did for you by sending you abroad."

Her eyes threatened to water as she thought of all those pieces, those precious, tangible memories of her grandmother . . . gone. But she steeled herself, not wanting him to see how much it hurt her. "I don't know what kind of charade you think you're playing, Barton, but know this . . . You don't fool me. Not anymore. I know what kind of person you are. I know what you're capable of."

His expression turned pain-stricken. "My dearest, sweet Rebekah . . . I've obviously done something to offend you, child. But I'm at a loss as to what that could be."

Her face went hot. "How dare you stand there and pretend that—"

"Miss Rebekah? You comin' down, ma'am? Your mama, she waitin' for you. Wantin' to see her baby girl."

Hearing Delphia, Rebekah took a deep breath and steadied her voice. "Thank you, Delphia. I'll be down momentarily." Waiting for the telling retreat of the woman's footsteps, Rebekah faced him again, every inch of her body tense and ready to strike. "I'll say this once to you, Barton, and once only. *Stay away from me.*"

She turned and took a step, only to find the floor wasn't there.

Realizing her miscalculation, she grabbed for the bannister—and missed. She fell forward, and saw the stairs rushing up to meet her. She braced herself for the impact—when an iron grip encircled her upper arm.

Barton pulled her back against him. "There, there, child. I've got you."

Regaining her footing, Rebekah jerked away. "Let go of me!"

He gave her quick release. Trembling, she glared up at him, furious with herself. And with him.

"Careful, my dear." His smile came slowly, even affectionately. "Best watch your step."

How did he do it? Not a trace of deceit in his eyes. No guilt or remorse either. Though she doubted he was capable of the latter.

Heart pounding, she descended the stairs, the sickening scent of cherry laurel clinging to her clothes.

The entrance hall lay ahead, the front door just beyond, and she wished more than anything that she could throw it open and keep on walking. But her love for a mother she scarcely knew anymore—and the love of a father that still beat steady and strong inside her—dictated otherwise.

She stepped into the central parlor to see her

mother sitting posture perfect in the wingback chair by the fireplace, in a pose strikingly similar to one Rebekah remembered from their final moments together before she'd left for Europe. And for some reason, the observation warmed her heart.

"Mother . . ."

Her mother turned, and her eyes lit. "Dearest Rebekah . . ." She held out her hands, and Rebekah went to her and knelt before her chair. Her mother squeezed her hands tightly.

Her mother had never been one for displays of affection, so Rebekah counted this as near exuberance, and an indicator of better things to come.

"I'm so grateful you *finally* decided to come home. You've been dearly missed."

"I've missed you too." Rebekah's heart swelled. "It's good to see you again."

The last ten years had left some not-so-gentle reminders of their passing in her mother's appearance. Her blond hair, slightly darker than Rebekah's, shimmered in the candlelight as it always had. But through the soft curls at her temples, time had woven coarse strands of silver. And at the corners of her eyes and mouth, nature had left definitive quotes, as though determined to accentuate a lifetime bent toward the more negative, including fear and worry.

"Although . . ." Her mother gently pulled her hands away, her smile waning. "I must admit . . .

if you'd come home sooner, as I requested—many times—you could have seen your grandmother again. Which would have given her such great joy, as it would have given me. But as it is . . ." She sighed, her eyes glistening even as they narrowed slightly. "We must all learn to accept the choices we make and live with the consequences, however painful, must we not?"

The warmth in Rebekah's heart cooled by a degree, and disappointment knotted at the back of her throat. "Yes," she finally managed. "As difficult as those choices—and consequences— may be at times." She hesitated to broach the next subject, but decided it best to get it out of the way. "I went into Grandmother's room just now, and saw that all of her things are gone. I wish you could've waited for me to—"

"Your stepfather very kindly volunteered to take care of that difficult task. And you should be grateful to him, just as I am." Her mother's already perfect posture stiffened even more. "You have no idea how I suffer at times, Rebekah. The aches in my head, in my back, the unsettledness in my stomach. I simply couldn't face that dreadful undertaking. It needed to be done, and you weren't here, so Barton saw to it. I should think you would show your gratitude instead of complaining."

A defense on the tip of her tongue, Rebekah bit it back, knowing it would only do more harm. "Do you know if he kept anything?" she asked gently. "One of her quilts? Her journal?"

Her mother frowned as though only now considering these more personal items. She pressed a hand to her temple. "I can't remember for certain. There may be a box somewhere . . . from your grandmother. Perhaps it's in the closet in your bedroom."

"Dinner's served, Missus Ledbetter." A young woman stood in the doorway, offered a brief curtsy, and disappeared back down the hallway.

Grateful for the reason to hope, Rebekah stood, only to find her hope short-lived when Barton entered the room.

"May I have the honor of escorting you two lovely ladies to dinner?"

With smile restored, her mother stood and accepted Barton's invitation, slipping her hand into the crook of his arm, gazing up at him. Rebekah walked ahead as though she hadn't heard.

Dinner was an awkward blend of stilted conversation and strings of overlong silences, but eating Delphia's cooking once again was nothing short of heartwarming.

While Austria's *Wiener schnitzel*, goulash, flaky apple strudel, and their scrumptious Viennese culinary specialty, the *Sacher torte*, had more than satisfied, Rebekah had never forgotten Delphia's skill in the kitchen.

She spooned her last bite of Delphia's warm sweet potato pie topped with candied pecans and fresh whipped cream into her mouth—no small feat after consuming fried chicken, field peas with potatoes, and pan-fried buttered corn—and she savored the sweetness and the memories it brought.

How many nights had she crept downstairs after bedtime to find Delphia and Demetrius in the kitchen eating cold sweet potato pie? Right from the pan. She couldn't wait to see him.

"It's part of maturing, sweetheart."

Rebekah looked up from her plate to find her mother eying her from the foot of the table, apparently continuing the chosen topic of dinner conversation—*her* life.

"Part of coming to terms with what's most important." Her mother arched a brow. "Which I hope you've managed to do despite being away from those who love you most. It's so important to maintain one's standards. People are always watching."

"Oh, I'm certain she has, Sarah." Barton gestured, and a servant standing off to the side refilled his glass with bourbon. For the third time. "I'm convinced our lovely Rebekah has matured in that way. As well as in every other."

He lifted his glass in a silent and solitary cheer.

Rebekah confined her gaze to the table, counting the minutes until she could politely excuse herself. Convinced the moment had come, she feigned a yawn, which encouraged a real one. "If you'll both excuse me, I'm very tired from the journey and would like to retire to my room."

Her mother sat a little straighter. "I was hoping you might wish to take tea with me in the study.

We have much to discuss regarding your home-coming. There are plans to be made. Barton and I have conversed at length, and—"

"Plans?" Rebekah looked between them.

"Yes." Barton set down his glass. "Plans about what you'll be doing now that you're home."

Rebekah gave a short laugh. "Pardon me, Barton. But I don't see how my plans are any of your concern."

"Rebekah Ellen!" Her mother's face flushed crimson. "You will not speak to my husband in that disrespectful manner. Is that understood?"

Clenching her jaw, Rebekah forced a nod.

"Now . . ." Her mother tucked her folded napkin by her plate. "Much has changed in our circle of society, and you need guidance as to how to reenter that world. Never fear, there *are* still eligible gentlemen who are open to considering a woman who is . . . a little further along in years. But don't let that concern you," her mother added quickly. "I've already begun sowing seeds that I'm certain will bear fruit."

"Mother, I don't mean to seem ungrateful but—"

"Your mother has been preparing tirelessly for your return, Rebekah. And I know you're not eager to disappoint her."

Feeling the walls closing in around her, Rebekah found herself swiftly growing to loathe Barton Ledbetter even more than she already did. Yet she checked her temper, knowing better than to cross him in front of her mother.

"And yet, Sarah . . ." Barton leaned forward in his chair. "Considering all that Rebekah has been through in recent days, and all you've been doing—so unselfishly, I might add—I do believe it would be best if we save these discussions for tomorrow. Don't you agree, my love? After all, we're finishing dinner later than usual, and you do need your rest."

Feeling slightly ill and knowing it had nothing to do with the food, Rebekah watched her mother as Barton's suggestion gradually found a foothold.

"Of course, you're right, Barton. As always. It's best we wait. Rebekah, we'll see to this tomorrow instead."

Barton rose and moved to escort her mother from the room. Her mother had always been a dutiful wife—Rebekah remembered that from childhood. But when had she ceased having her own opinions whatsoever?

Whatever the answer, at least the discussion about the "plans for her life" had been postponed, and *her* plan was to make sure it stayed that way. But there was one more thing she needed to know. And though now likely wasn't the best time to broach her next question, she doubted a right time existed.

"Mother, before you go . . ."

Her mother paused, her hand tucked into the crook of Barton's arm.

"Grandmother Carrington . . . she said she'd laid aside some money for me. On the event of her passing." Rebekah smiled to soften the abruptness of the topic. "Do you know who I need to contact in that regard?"

Her mother's expression clouded, and then she peered up at Barton, who looked at Rebekah and sighed, with a little too much feeling.

"Rebekah, I fear your grandmother spoke out of turn. Though I wasn't going to share this with you, and wanted to spare you any embarrassment . . . upon your grandmother's death, I was forced to cover her outstanding debts. Which I did happily, considering what a fine woman she was, and how special a part of this family."

His smile, meant to appear condoling, she knew, felt like a punch to the gut. Rebekah pressed a hand to her midsection, glad she was still seated. "Her debts?" Her voice came out small. "Grandmother Carrington didn't have any debts."

"You've been gone a long time, Rebekah." Barton's deep voice gained an edge. "And it's been a difficult few years. But don't worry. I'll take care of you—just as I take care of your dear mother." He patted her mother's hand and shifted to look Rebekah in the eye. "Perhaps tomorrow, Rebekah, you and I can find a few moments to speak at length about this."

Rebekah bowed her head and didn't look up as they left the room, her hands trembling in her lap. He'd taken it. The money. He'd taken it all. But what could she do? She had nothing in writing from her grandmother. Nothing to substantiate her claim. And even if she did, where was the money now? Nowhere she could get to it.

She pressed against the pounding in her temples. It would seem the bulk of her hope now lay with Mrs. Adelicia Cheatham at the Belmont estate. Because it certainly didn't lie with Nathaniel T. Whitcomb.

She had no doubt such a man had never had to work for anything in his life, that it had all been given to him on a polished silver platter. And though it wasn't a charitable thought, she hoped that one day he would drink from the same cup of disappointment he'd served her earlier that day.

And that she'd just been made to drink of again.

Determined to put him out of her mind, she found Delphia and two other women—neither of them familiar to her—in the kitchen. Gone was the houseful of staff from before the war. At dinner she'd learned it was only Delphia now, along with two day servants. And Demetrius, of course, though her mother and Barton had not spoken of him.

She visited with Delphia, Rosie, and Nissa as they worked. The playful banter between the women helped to lift her spirits.

Once the dishes were washed and the kitchen straightened, the day servants left for the night. No sooner had the kitchen door closed than Delphia pulled a covered dish from the cupboard—and grinned.

"The last of the pie!" Rebekah said in an

exaggerated whisper. "You and Demetrius always saved me a slice."

"*He* always saved you a slice. I woulda eaten it soon as look at you."

Rebekah laughed, knowing that wasn't true. "I've missed you, Delphia."

"And Lawd knows I've missed you, Miss Rebekah. It weren't the same here without you. Weren't the same at all."

"So where is he?" Rebekah accepted the sliver of pie on a linen napkin, unable to believe she still had room for it. But she did.

"Where is *who?*"

Rebekah turned to see her mother standing in the doorway and nearly choked on the bite of pie.

Delphia rose from her chair and brushed the crumbs from her apron. "Somethin' I can help you with, Missus Ledbetter?"

"I thought you said you were tired, Rebekah."

Rebekah swallowed. "I was. I mean . . ." She cleared her throat. "I *am*. I came in here to say good night to Delphia, and . . . we started talking."

Her mother's gaze trailed to the pie plate, then back to her. "*Who* is it you're looking for, Rebekah?"

Rebekah placed her napkin on the table. "Why don't we talk about this tomorrow?"

"Where is *who?*" her mother repeated.

"You know who," Rebekah answered.

Her mother looked pointedly at Delphia, who confined her gaze to the floor.

"Mother, please. Let's not play these games. I just want to visit with him. To see how he is. Tell him about Europe and about how I finally—"

"Demetrius is dead, Rebekah. He died shortly after you left."

As though suddenly seeing her mother from down a long tunnel, Rebekah stared, her world tilting. She shook her head, trying to bring it aright. "Th-that's not true. That's not possible."

"I told your grandmother when it happened that we should tell you, but she insisted"—her mother's lips formed a thin line—"that it would be too much for you to bear. Then as time went on . . ."

Her mother's sentence trailed off into silence, and Rebekah looked over at Delphia, knowing she'd find reassurance and the truth. But the tears pooling in Delphia's dark eyes told her just the opposite.

And Rebekah felt her knees give way.

Delphia's strong arms came around her, supporting her, as Rebekah collapsed into a chair. And through the pounding of shock and disbelief, one thought broke through.

"You knew," Rebekah whispered, peering up at her.

"Of course she knew."

Rebekah heard her mother's voice from somewhere in the room, and—even though she knew better—it struck her as peculiar that her mother wasn't the one helping her, holding her in that moment.

Delphia was.

Why was it that those who had suffered most always seemed to be the ones who comforted best? *"Sufferin's a cruel teacher, Miss Bekah,"* Demetrius had said to her on more than one occasion, using his nickname for her that still warmed her heart. *"But she teaches you good, sufferin' does. A wise learner'll come to 'preciate her over time. But usually only after they's on the other side of the pain."*

"Rebekah, there was no point in telling you." Her mother's voice bled through the memory. "Besides, you always thought too highly of that man and his opinion. Need I remind you, he was only a—"

"Don't!" Rebekah half screamed, half cried. "Don't speak about him. Don't even say his name, Mother."

"Rebekah Ellen Carrington! How *dare* you address me in such a—"

Rebekah stood, fury coursing through her so fierce it left her quaking. "Please leave the room *now*, Mother. Right this minute. Don't speak another word, or . . ." Her chest ached with betrayal and hurt. "Or I'll leave this house and I'll never come back. *Ever.* Do you understand me?"

Face pale, eyes wide, her mother stared,

unblinking, and Rebekah could see in her pained, shocked expression how much she'd wounded her. Which hadn't been her intention. But what her mother had done, hiding the truth from her all these years . . . And what she'd been about to say about the man who had saved her from humiliation and heartache . . .

Her mother did as Rebekah demanded, letting the door swing closed behind her, and Rebekah sank into the chair again.

A heavy sob clawed its way up her chest. "You should have . . . told me, Delphia." She had trouble catching her breath.

Delphia brushed the hair back from Rebekah's face, her look full of love and remorse. "How's I s'posed to do that, ma'am? Just go against your mama's say so? Your grandmama's too?" She shook her head and hugged Rebekah tight. "Even if I *did* know how to write my thoughts onto paper, ain't no way I coulda done that, Miss Rebekah. Not with them sayin' I can't."

Knowing she was right, Rebekah bowed her head. Nana had known too, yet hadn't seen fit to tell her. But why . . . Why would they have hidden such a thing? She should've had a chance to grieve his passing. Then again . . .

She could almost hear her grandmother's voice. *"You had just started your life there in Austria. There's nothing you could have done. And he would have wanted you to be happy in your fresh start. Not looking back with regret and grief."*

The image of Demetrius breaking through the barn door and pulling Barton off of her that night was burned into her memory. He'd thrown Barton into a stall as though the man weighed nothing at all. Then he quickly helped her back to the house, her shaking like a leaf, the bodice of her dress ripped open, her hair a disheveled mess. Grandmother met her sneaking up the stairs, and when Rebekah told her what happened, she'd moved Rebekah's bed into her room that very night, claiming she needed assistance during the early morning hours.

Not a month later, they'd departed for Austria.

Rebekah took a deep breath. "I'm sorry," she finally whispered, wiping her cheeks. "I know you're right." Then, slowly, the fog inside her began to clear. Once dispelled, it left a chilling question. Had Demetrius's actions, how he'd protected her, cost him his life? Was Barton responsible in some way?

Rebekah was certain that Delphia didn't know anything about what had happened in the barn—because Demetrius swore he wouldn't tell a soul, and his word was as binding as an oath.

Trembling, Rebekah peered up. "What happened to him, Delphia? How did he . . ." She couldn't finish the sentence.

Delphia settled into the chair beside her. And it seemed like a long time passed before she spoke. "Demetrius, he . . ." She glanced at Rebekah but couldn't seem to hold her gaze. "He just didn't come home one night. I didn't know 'til next mornin' come near six o'clock. Sun was up and the wood bin for the kitchen stove was still empty. Not like my big brother to be tardy like that. So I sent Sissy down to see 'bout him. Next thing I know, Big Ike from over at Belle Meade come knockin' on the back door. Tells me he and some other men found my brother in a field on their way to town 'fore daybreak. Demetrius, he was beat real bad." Her brow knit tight. She closed her eyes, tears squeezing from the corners. "And bleedin' somethin' fierce. Never knew so much blood could be in a man and him still drawin' breath. I tended him, but . . ."

Tears wove their way down Delphia's cheek, and she looked away.

Rebekah wiped her own tears, not certain she wanted to know the answer to her next question. "Did you find out who did it?"

Delphia lifted her watery gaze. "There been so many killin's, ma'am—back then, 'specially. And it ain't like somebody gonna do somethin' 'bout it even if you *do* know. That's just the way of things."

Feeling as if she might be sick, Rebekah hurried over to an empty pail by the back door . . . and made it just in time. Her stomach convulsed as images filled her mind. "I should have"—she gasped for air, her chest and back muscles spasming—"been here. I should have . . . known."

Delphia came alongside and held her hair back as Rebekah's stomach emptied a second time.

Rebekah wiped her mouth on the handkerchief Delphia held out.

"I'm so sorry, Delphia. You loved him so much. And he . . . loved you."

"That I did, child. And . . . I still do."

Moments passed, as did the nausea, and Rebekah eased back to the chair at the table. Her throat vile and raw, she sipped from the cup of water Delphia offered.

"This ain't been much of a homecomin', has it, child?"

Seeing the woman's feeble smile, Rebekah returned it.

"Truth be told, Miss Rebekah, up 'til Miss Ellen's passin', I'd been thinkin' you might never come back. And I wasn't blamin' you one bit. It's a hard world we livin' in here."

Rebekah swallowed back fresh tears. "I'm grateful for the time I spent in Austria. But . . . I think it's a hard world everywhere."

Delphia's eyes held her gaze, some undefinable emotion in their depths. "Amen to that, child. Amen to that."

Later, in her bedroom, her emotions numb and her body wearier than she could remember, Rebekah changed into the nightgown she found hanging in the chifforobe. Delphia, or perhaps another of the servants, had unpacked her clothing. Although, if her plans went the way she hoped, she would only be packing them up again.

She checked in the closet for the box her mother mentioned might be there. But . . . nothing. A couple of wooden crates containing clothes from Rebekah's childhood but nothing from her grandmother.

A soft thump sounded from the hallway beyond the bedroom, and she quickly crossed to the closed door, her bare feet noiseless on the carpet. No lock on the door.

She blew out a breath.

She hadn't seen Barton since dinner. Delphia had told her he went out almost every evening. *Important business meetings* was the explanation Delphia had heard him give her mother. Rebekah could tell from Delphia's tone that she didn't believe his explanation either.

She'd never been certain about Barton's exact profession. He claimed to be in "acquisitions and trade," whatever that meant. She only knew that his occupation took him away at odd hours and that he oftentimes traveled, according to her mother's letters through the years.

Rebekah pressed her ear to the door, and listened.

Only night sounds—the occasional sigh of the house as it settled, the squeak of a carriage passing by out front, a dog barking some distance away.

Still . . .

She grabbed the handle of one of her trunks—the one containing her books, judging by the weight of it—and dragged it across the floor, then pushed it up against the door.

Her stomach still unsettled, the effort left her queasy, but she repeated the action with a second trunk, this one empty, and managed to situate it atop the other, then stood back. She needed one more thing.

She scanned the room and her gaze settled on the appropriate item. She retrieved the empty silver vase from the mantel and placed it near the edge of the trunk. If anyone tried to open the door and force their way in, she would know it.

Bone weary, she pulled back the covers, removed the bed warmer, and returned it to the hearth. She turned down the lamp on the bedside table and climbed onto the overstuffed down mattress, toasty warm where the bed warmer had been, but otherwise icy cold. The fluffy down rose up around her, and she curled her body into the warmth.

Shadows danced on the walls, the wind outside swaying the tree limbs at will. As she lay there, emotions she'd struggled to keep at bay suddenly gained the upper hand in the dark.

She hugged the second pillow to her chest and buried sobs into its softness. She hadn't seen Demetrius in over ten years, but the comfort of knowing he'd been there—or, *here*—and remembering all he'd taught her, had given her strength.

Only, he *hadn't* been here.

Shouldn't she have sensed something when he

died? A distancing of some sort? An inexplicable sadness, perhaps. But she'd sensed nothing.

She used the corner of the bedsheet to wipe her face, then sat up in the dark, accepting that sleep was a distant wish. She wondered if her mother, in the bedroom down the hall, was able to sleep. But knowing the medication Delphia said she oftentimes took, Rebekah figured she was.

Her eyes adjusted to the dark, she slipped from bed and over to the partially unpacked trunk in front of the window, and withdrew the leather case from inside. The worn latches lifted without complaint, and as moonlight filtering through the window fell onto the violin and bow, she felt as if she were seeing an old friend again.

She lifted the violin from its velvet bed and tucked it against her collarbone. The very act brought comfort, as did holding the bow.

The chin rest formed perfectly to her contours, and she slowly drew the bow across the A string in a smooth up-bow stroke. She adjusted the coordinating peg and repeated the movement, listening, eyes closed, before doing the same with the remaining strings.

She stood in the silence, darkness huddling close, and heard—from a great distance away, across time and memory—the sweet strains of a song drifting toward her.

She moved to the window seat and sat cross-legged, as she had as a girl, and stared out to where the rows of slave cabins once clustered near the back of the property. The cabins were gone now, a row of clapboard houses having taken their place. Delphia was the only servant in residence and occupied a room off the kitchen.

But in the silvery light of winter, Rebekah could still see, in her mind's eye, the outline of the rustic dwellings. No bonfire burned in the distance, no voices lifted in song. All was dark and quiet.

Yet the melody of the song filled her heart and mind, and she drew the bow across the strings and gradually joined in, the lyrics of the song carving deeper meaning into her heart in light of the present. *"Come, thou fount of every blessing, tune my heart to sing thy grace . . ."*

She closed her eyes and was there again— listening to Demetrius play and sing—and she gave herself to the memory and the music, trilling effortlessly over ascending and descending arpeggios that once tripped her up and frustrated her to no end.

But now they poured from bow and strings with a beauty she knew didn't originate from herself alone.

The music was a culmination of so many who had contributed to her life—Papa; Maestro Heilig; her somewhat reluctant violin tutor, Mr. Colton; even Darrow Fulton, who had fanned her already-competitive spirit to flame, unknowingly pushing her to accomplish what she might not have on her own. But the one person who had contributed most to her love for this instrument, to her affinity for the beauty a violin could create . . .

Demetrius.

As she played, she heard his patient counsel in each and every note. *"You gots to keep your chin tucked against it, Miss Bekah. Right here. That's it. Cradle it real gentle, like it's the sweetest thing you ever did hold."*

And his voice, a rich baritone, like deep water coursing over smooth rock. She'd always wished she could sing more like he had, and like the Negro women did, with such convincing clarity and truth. Such strength and richness. Not like her own softer voice. Some things could be taught or trained, but other things were gifts from the Giver.

That's what their voices had been to her, their songs—a gift.

As the music swelled in her memory, so did the sweet strains of the song she played, the lyrics as familiar to her now as the notes. *"O to grace how great a debtor, daily I'm constrained to be! Let thy goodness, like a fetter, bind my wandering heart to thee. Prone to wander, Lord, I feel it. Prone to leave the God I—"*

A loud thud sounded from across the room, and she went stock-still, then looked toward the door. The vase was gone. It was on the floor. And the trunks . . .

They appeared to be moving.

6

In a blink, Rebekah crossed the room and found the door inching open, the trunks proving to be a poor deterrent. "Who is it?" she asked timidly.

"Open the door, Rebekah. I want to talk to you about—"

Grimacing at the stench of liquor and stale cigar smoke, she shoved the door hard, and it slammed back into place. But no sooner did the latch click than the knob turned again. And this time, the opposing force grew in insistence.

Summoning strength, she put her back to the stacked trunks and braced her full weight against them, digging her heels into the carpet.

But still, the trunks moved.

"Miss Rebekah?"

Suddenly the momentum on the other side of the door halted, and the door closed with a thud. Muffled footsteps retreated down the hallway.

Her shoulder and back muscles burning, Rebekah refused to trust the supposed retreat and kept pushing, the smell of him, the very thought of his intentions, his hands on her, causing a bitterness to sting the back of her throat.

"Miss Rebekah?" came the voice a second time. *Delphia.*

The staircase creaked beneath the woman's steps, and Rebekah went limp with relief. She slid to the floor and rested her head in her hands, her heart still pounding.

"Miss Rebekah . . ." A soft knock sounded. "I's just comin' to see if you's feelin' all right, ma'am. You bein' sick earlier and all."

The concern in Delphia's voice was like a balm, and Rebekah slowly found her footing. She started to push the trunks aside to open the door, then caught herself. What if Barton *was* somehow responsible for what happened to Demetrius? Would the man consider taking action against Delphia for interfering? He certainly seemed brazen enough. Not to mention persistent. Rebekah quickly decided she couldn't take that chance.

"Yes, Delphia." She spoke through the closed door. "I'm fine. I'm feeling much better now, thank you."

"I can get you some tea, miss. Or some warm broth, if you think that'd be some help."

"No, thank you. But . . . I appreciate the offer all the same. Thank you, Delphia. Truly."

"Ain't no trouble. I drank me some coffee earlier and just ain't got the tiredness yet. I'll keep an ear out for you. Come and fetch me should you need anything."

Hearing Delphia's retreat, Rebekah felt her own relief ebb. She moved closer to see the clock on the mantel. Half past one. A weariness came over her that seemed years in the making, yet she couldn't give in to it. Not until she was out of this house and far away from him.

Only then did she realize how cold she was. She grabbed a blanket from the bed, wrapped it around herself, and then settled again on the floor, her back against the trunks.

Moments passed, and her chin slowly dipped forward. She snapped her head back into place and widened her eyes in the darkness, determined to stay awake.

She looked across the room at her violin on the bed where she'd hurriedly laid it, the contours of the instrument beautiful even in the shadows, and she tried to summon a remnant of the peace and warmth she'd felt only moments earlier.

But it was gone.

Hours later, Rebekah knocked on the bedroom door off the kitchen. The sun would soon be up and she'd determined to be gone by then. She'd tried to stay awake, but sleep had finally over-taken her. Her neck sore from sleeping propped up against the trunks, just like her backside, she wouldn't begin to breathe easier until she was *out* of this house.

She knocked a second time. No response.

The knob turned easily in her hand, and as she opened the door, the oil lamp she carried cast a golden arc over the dark room.

The form in the bed stirred. "Who's there?" came a rough voice.

"It's me, Delphia. Rebekah."

The woman yawned deeply as she sat up.

"Lawd, ma'am. It still be dark. What you doin' up 'fore the sun?"

Rebekah knelt by her bed. The fire in the small hearth had cooled through the night, and the wooden floor was cold beneath her knees. "I'm leaving," she whispered, choosing her words carefully. "I don't need to stay here, Delphia. I *can't* stay here. I've been living by my own leave for far too long to come back and try to make a home beneath this roof."

Delphia squinted and rubbed her eyes, studying her for a moment. Rebekah sensed disapproval in the pause and hoped she wouldn't offer argument.

"Do your mama know yet?"

Rebekah shook her head. "I left her a note, slipped it beneath her door. She won't be happy with my decision, I realize, but it's for the best. For everyone."

Delphia pushed back the covers. "Let me get you some breakfast 'fore you—"

"No, I'm leaving now. But I do have a favor to ask. My trunks are packed. I'm only taking my satchel and a small travel case with me. As soon as you can, would you see that my trunks are delivered to this address?"

She laid the slip of paper on the bedside table, hoping the right person would be there to accept the trunks when they were delivered.

"Yes, ma'am. I get 'em moved down here 'fore the house even wakes. Then out the door first thing this mornin'."

"Thank you, Delphia. I appreciate your help. You've always been"—her throat tightened—"so special to me. Same as your brother."

"Oh, child . . ." Delphia took hold of Rebekah's hand, hers feeling as rough and firm as a man's. "You's just like your grandmother. A good woman. And strong. Stronger than you look."

With a weak smile, Rebekah prayed that was true. Because she needed every scrap of strength she could muster.

She rose, then paused. "My mother . . . Is she . . ." How to ask the question. Yet she had to. She couldn't leave her mother here without being certain. "Is she all right? With him, I mean? Is she safe?"

Delphia stared appraisingly. "I ain't never seen the man lift a hand to her. Or his voice, neither. Mr. Ledbetter, he come and go as he wishes, and I don't think much truth sticks to him. But I don't think he ever hurts her. Nor will he, long as I'm here."

Rebekah let out a breath and gave her hand a squeeze. "Thank you, Delphia." She was nearly to the door when she heard her name. She looked back.

"You even know where you're goin', child?"

"No. Not exactly. But anywhere is preferable to here."

Careful of the deep, frozen ruts in the road, Rebekah navigated her way between the two massive columns of chiseled limestone marking the entrance to the Belmont estate, not pausing to admire the display of wealth. Despite the two pairs of stockings she wore, her feet and legs were like ice, and her gloved hands ached with cold.

She was accustomed to walking, so the two-mile distance from town wasn't the issue. It was the bitter cold seeping into her bones every step of the journey that left her feeling as though her limbs were about to snap clean in two. Even so, she had to admit the scenery was beautiful. The oak and poplar trees, their limbs winter barren, were laced in ice and glistened in the morning sun like cut crystal beneath a candelabra.

"Please . . ." Her breath puffed white. "Please let the governess position still be available."

No doubt such an elite family would have received numerous applications for the job, all of them from well-qualified candidates. So somehow she needed to impress this *Mrs. Adelicia Cheatham.* Because she needed a job. And a place to live.

She was surprised to see a stag standing stone-still in the shadow of a stalwart pine, its antlered head lifted heavenward in a majestic pose. Only on closer inspection did she realize the beast was made of cast iron. And other animals—dogs, lions, and several deer, all cast from iron like their fearless leader—made appearances as she covered ground.

A soft brush of ice touched her cheek. Followed by another. And another. She paused long enough to look up. Then sighed. It was *snowing?*

She quickened her pace toward the bend in the road ahead, mindful of her step across the frozen ruts and eager to reach the house before her hair was a complete mess. She rounded the corner and spotted the mansion—still a good distance away, sitting atop a gently rising hill like a queen on her throne.

She blew an already damp curl from her temple and clenched her teeth in order to keep her chin from trembling. So much for making a good first impression.

She quickened her pace.

The estate's residence appeared regal in its pristine winter setting, tall white columns framing the entrance to the reddish-brown home. *Exquisite* described it well, although it didn't begin to compare to Schönbrunn Palace, the summer residence of the Habsburg monarchy, only blocks from their house in Vienna. She and Sally had strolled past that palace countless times, discussing the history of the royal family and imagining what wondrous splendors presided behind the palace walls.

What a life she and Sally had shared in Vienna together. Lonely at times, yes. But also exciting, and a privilege, she realized. Like another world away.

And one forever gone. For her, at least.

The road gradually widened, and Rebekah followed its curve as it edged the boundary of what would most certainly be lavish gardens come spring. It appeared they were designed in a circular pattern, the largest circle closest to the mansion, while its smaller counterparts descended downhill, diminishing in size.

She passed a large, all-glass conservatory and spotted greenery of plants and trees within, but couldn't make out any detail due to the fog masking the windows.

Marble statuary dotted the expansive grounds. And numerous gazebos, their painted cast iron soft white against the pale of winter, stood silent in the cold, reserving their welcome for warmer days.

Finally, every part of her aching from the bitter cold and her teeth clattering, she climbed the front steps and crossed the limestone patio, watching for slick spots. She managed the last of the stairs up to the ornate front door and set down her bags, grateful for the shelter of an upper porch that extended over the entrance.

She brushed the snow from her cloak and, without benefit of a mirror, did the best she could with her hair and the rest of her appearance. She whispered a quick prayer—trying to ignore the feeling when it fell flat—and firmly knocked on the door.

A long moment passed.

She knocked a second time, and as the door finally opened, a heavenly brush of warmth and the scent of cinnamon and spice issued from within before the cold pushed back and won.

A woman dressed like a head housekeeper greeted her with a curious and even censorious expression. Her dark spectacles rested midway down her sharp nose—the precise angle necessary to peer ominously down at one's prey and render a despicable little rodent weighed, measured—and doomed.

The woman looked past her, first to the left, then right, before her gaze settled decidedly on Rebekah's satchel and travel case, then slid back to Rebekah's eyes. "Good day. State your business, please."

Rebekah swallowed. An image of Mrs. Murphey chuckling softly from behind her desk in the opera house eroded her fledgling confidence, as did the more sobering images of women and young girls loitering on street corners.

"I . . . I'm here to interview."

"And do you have an appointment?"

The tone in which the woman asked the question answered it as well.

"I thought not." Her smile was the very definition of condescension. "Mrs. Cheatham entertains candidates by appointment only. So may I suggest you make one, as required, and come back another day."

As she started to close the door, Rebekah felt a surge of desperation—and impertinence.

"Pardon me, but I'm here at the personal behest of Mrs. Murphey at the opera house."

The woman stilled, and Rebekah took that as her cue.

"Following my meeting with *Maestro* Whitcomb

yesterday, Mrs. Murphey encouraged me to contact Mrs. Cheatham posthaste." The embellishment—and reference about Nathaniel Whitcomb—felt somewhat false, with reason. Yet when Rebekah saw the tiniest muscle at the corner of the woman's eye flinch, she knew she'd found a chink in her armor. "However, if this isn't a good time, as you indicated, perhaps I should come back . . . after meeting with other families who are interviewing as well."

She gave a curtsy and turned, the reckless bubble of hope swiftly sinking inside her. Counting the limestone steps leading down to the patio—and trying not to panic over what to do next—she braced herself for the long, frigid walk back to town.

"Mrs. Cheatham is indisposed at the moment. So you may wait inside while I converse with her on the matter."

Rebekah turned back, her hope cautiously buoyant again. The woman's stern expression communicated displeasure, and Rebekah knew she was treading on very thin ice. But better thin ice than freezing water.

She climbed the stairs and stepped inside the entrance hall, already anticipating the warmth of the home and trying not to appear like the beggar she felt.

Sure enough, a fire blazed in the foyer hearth, and by sheer will alone she stayed exactly where she was instead of running over to it and kneeling to soak in its warmth. Her teeth resumed their clattering, and she realized then that her initial encounter with this woman must have temporarily scared away the chill.

But it returned with fierceness, and her cheeks burned like fire.

"Place your cases there, in the corner. And give me your cloak."

She did as the housekeeper bid, taking in her surroundings. Mrs. Cheatham was apparently fond of statuary. A handsome piece crafted of white marble took center stage in the middle of the foyer—a woman kneeling as she gathered grain, looking upward, her gaze beseeching, all while apparently oblivious to her robe having slipped from her slender shoulder to reveal a rather shapely right breast.

Rebekah was tempted to smile. Quite a bold statement for an entrance hall in America. Yet the statue's elegant face, her poised bearing, were simply stunning.

She did not consider herself an art aficionado, but living in Vienna had afforded her privileged exposure to centuries of European art and architecture that she never would have gained otherwise.

"My name is Mrs. Routh. I'm the head housekeeper at Belmont. And you are?"

Rebekah curtsied a second time. "Miss Rebekah Carrington, recently returned from an extended time of study and travel in Europe. Specifically,

Vienna, Austria." Phrasing it that way sounded so much better than "banished to Europe so as not to be ruined by a licentious stepfather."

"*Sie sprechen also fließend Deutsch?*" the woman asked.

Jolted by the unexpected transition, Rebekah worked to catch up. She nodded. "*Ja, Frau Routh. Ich spreche Deutsch.*"

"*Et parlez-vous français aussi, Mademoiselle Carrington?*"

Rebekah had to smile, admiring the woman's lingual versatility while also realizing she'd underestimated her. A mistake she wouldn't make again. "*Oui, je parle français, Madame Routh.*"

Without appearing the least bit impressed, Mrs. Routh gestured. "Follow me to the tête-à-tête room."

Rebekah shadowed her path, slowing briefly when she noticed another piece of statuary in the foyer, one resting on a draped table directly beneath a large portrait of a woman and child, presumably Mrs. Cheatham and her daughter. The sculpture was as beautiful as that of the young woman gathering grain, but it touched her in a way the first hadn't.

The sculpture depicted two sleeping children, their images flawlessly captured in smooth white marble, their ringlets and chubby hands rendered in exquisite detail by the sculptor. An inscription carved on the front, along the bottom, caught her eye. . . .

Laura and Corinne.

She peered down into the precious faces of the children and wondered whom the names belonged to. Whatever the answer to that question, she somehow knew this statue represented more than sleeping children. More likely a love that continued beyond the grave. A love with which she was well familiar.

"Tea will arrive presently, Miss Carrington. Enjoy the refreshment until I return."

Hearing the implicit command in her statement, Rebekah nodded. "I'll wait here, Mrs. Routh."

The door closed with a definitive *thud,* and Rebekah swiftly crossed to the fire burning in the hearth, removed her gloves, and laid them aside. She extended her hands toward the flames and flexed her fingers. Finally, they were beginning to thaw.

Once her front side was warmed, she turned and backed as close to the hearth as she dared, the radiant heat gradually penetrating the layers of fabric to drive off the chill. *Oh, heavenly . . .*

A knock on the door, and a servant entered carrying a silver tea service. A woman—petite, her dark hair tied back in a kerchief—wordlessly set the tray on a side table, poured a cup, and handed it to Rebekah.

"Thank you," Rebekah whispered.

The servant—older, but not *old*—had friendly eyes and a matching smile. A memorable combination.

"You're welcome, ma'am. You need anything

else, just ring." She gestured toward a brass bell on a side table, then dipped her head and closed the door noiselessly behind her. All very efficient. Precisely how Rebekah imagined Mrs. Routh ran this entire household.

Sipping her tea—hints of cinnamon, clove, nutmeg, and orange in the brew—Rebekah relished its warmth and let her gaze wander.

While she found the tête-à-tête room cozy, even charming, she also decided it was a bit dizzying. Beautiful though they were, portraits inhabited nearly every inch of wall space and gave the room an overcrowded feel. Adding to that, every horizontal surface was covered with either crystal vases, miniature sculptures, gilded books, or decorative bowls, which only—

Her quickly forming opinion lost all momentum when she saw the portrait on the wall directly behind her. Her breath locked tight in her lungs, and she had to remind herself to breathe.

Guido Reni Sketching Beatrice Cenci.

She knew the painting well, and the one to the right of it of Beatrice alone. She'd seen the portrait in Europe years earlier and—once learning the story behind the young sixteenth-century woman—had felt a sickening kinship with the girl. She also held admiration for her, because of what she'd finally done. Though Rebekah would be loath to admit it for fear of what someone might think.

Paintings of young Beatrice were popular in

Europe, and apparently had become so in America too. These two copies were especially good. Interesting that Mrs. Cheatham had them hanging in her home. Something Rebekah would never be able to bring herself to do. It would be a constant reminder of that night, and what Barton would've done to her, if not for Demetrius.

Seeking a needed distraction, another object caught her eye—the family Bible—and she stepped closer to where it lay on a table before the hearth.

Acklen was the name on the cover. Not Cheatham.

So was Acklen Mrs. Cheatham's maiden name? Or perhaps she'd been married previously. Rebekah gently lifted the cover of the thick leather volume and peered within. Her gaze fell on the name *Joseph Alexander Smith Acklen,* and beside his name the years *1816–1863.*

Feeling as if she were trespassing, she started to close the cover, but the names *Laura* and *Corinne* rose in her memory, and she wondered whether they were listed anywhere in the—

Footsteps sounded outside the door, and Rebekah quickly stepped back from the Bible to the spot where Mrs. Routh had left her.

Mrs. Routh opened the door. "Mrs. Cheatham has agreed to spare you a few moments. Come with me, please."

Both thrilled and terrified, Rebekah returned her teacup to the tray and matched Mrs. Routh stride for stride, careful not to fall behind.

They cut a path back through the entrance hall

and into a larger and far grander salon. Their heels clicked on the black-and-white, tile-painted wooden floor, and Rebekah glanced behind to gain a better view of a cantilevered staircase behind them. The staircase divided halfway up and spiraled to the left and right before continuing to the second-floor landing.

So elegant.

Mrs. Routh paused by a set of glass-paneled double doors, and Rebekah did likewise. The head housekeeper rapped softly on the glass pane, then turned the knob and indicated for Rebekah to precede her.

Scraping together confidence, Rebekah stepped into the room.

The moment she saw Mrs. Adelicia Cheatham, she knew with certainty that when Mrs. Murphey had given her this woman's name and address, she hadn't done so with her best interest at heart. On the contrary.

Mrs. Murphey meant to destroy her.

7

The woman's smile appeared so serene, so welcoming, yet it dripped with unmistakable censure. It had been a mistake to come here—Rebekah knew that now. But how to remedy it? She felt like a fly caught in a web, and had only herself to blame.

Mrs. Routh stepped forward. "May I present Mrs. Adelicia Cheatham. Mrs. Cheatham, *this* is Miss Rebekah Carrington."

The way the head housekeeper said her name caused Rebekah to shrink inside, as though the woman was secretly referring to a conversation Rebekah wasn't privy to. And Rebekah was fairly certain she hadn't imagined the woman's emphasis on the word *this* either.

Rebekah curtsied as though being presented to a member of the House of Habsburg. "It's an honor to make your acquaintance, Mrs. Cheatham."

Again that lovely, dangerous smile. "Thank you, Miss Carrington. Please, be seated."

She claimed a spot on the edge of the settee opposite the woman, making note of the exits in the room—the door at her back, then one on the left, though where the latter led she didn't know.

Exquisite ivory lace embellished Mrs. Cheatham's dress, and Rebekah ran a hand over her own gray skirt and jacket, feeling underdressed and outranked.

"Would you care for tea, Miss Carrington?" She gestured to the adjacent serving cart. "It's my cook's special winter blend of spices."

"I already enjoyed tea in your front parlor. And it was delicious. Thank you."

She gave a slight tilt of her head. "How reassuring to know that guests arriving at Belmont continue to be treated with courtesy and consideration."

Rebekah hesitated, thinking she heard a certain tone in Mrs. Cheatham's voice. Then a sparkle lit the woman's eyes, and Rebekah began to feel more at ease. "Yes, ma'am. Rest assured, you have no reason to question in that regard. And if I may add at this time—"

With a delicate nod, Mrs. Cheatham granted permission.

"—I truly appreciate the opportunity to interview with you. I'm most grateful and want you to know that, if I'm chosen, I'll always give my very best."

"*Indeed.* How wonderful to know." Mrs. Cheatham held her gaze for longer than necessary, then took another sip of tea before placing the delicate china cup and saucer on the table to her left. "Before we start, Miss Carrington . . . I would be most grateful if you would enlighten me on one matter."

Slightly taken aback, Rebekah nodded warily. "Of course, Mrs. Cheatham. If I'm able to do so."

The woman's pleasant countenance suddenly lost a shade of its bloom. "Precisely why would one who claims to be so grateful for this opportunity arrive unannounced on my doorstep, without extending the least courtesy or consideration in regard to her visit prior to her arrival? No letter declaring her interest in the position or even her desire to be considered for such. I find this oversight a most curious oddity, Miss Carrington. One upon which I sincerely hope you're capable of shedding light."

Wondering where all the air in the room had

gone, Rebekah heard a tiny gasp, then realized it had come from her. She swallowed. "Mrs. Cheatham, please allow me to explain. I—"

The woman lifted a single forefinger. Not even a hand. But Rebekah knew without question that to continue speaking would be a severe misstep. One she would regret.

"The reason, Miss Carrington, that I granted you audience rested solely on the merit of your acquaintance with Maestro Whitcomb."

"Acquaintance . . ." Rebekah's voice rose almost an octave. "With Maestro Whitcomb?"

Mrs. Cheatham eyed her. "You *are* here this morning, are you not, at the recommendation of Nashville's newly formed philharmonic? Of which Maestro Whitcomb is conductor. Hence, I presume you enjoy an acquaintance with him, and that he will vouch for your character and experience once I contact him. Which I most assuredly will do as soon as you leave."

Bewildered, Rebekah glanced at the door to her left, tempted to bolt. But racing from this interview and out of the mansion wasn't an option, and it would scarcely improve her lot. But what would happen when Mrs. Cheatham discovered there was no *acquaintanceship?* That the man knew little to nothing of her.

Feeling the heat of Mrs. Cheatham's steady appraisal, Rebekah felt the sweat beading beneath her chemise. Most certainly, this woman wielded considerable influence over the prominent families in this city. Which meant that after this failed interview, the chances of gaining a position for governess anywhere else in this city would be precisely what her chances were for this one. . . .

Nil.

"Well, Miss Carrington? I'm waiting to be enlightened."

Rebekah's gaze fell to the woman's diminutive hands resting demurely in her lap, while her own were white-knuckled and aching.

"Mrs. Cheatham, I've made a grave mistake in coming here to interview for the position of governess. I see that now." She also saw the streak of warning flash across her hostess's expression. "I sincerely regret having wasted your time, ma'am, and ask that you, please, allow me to take my leave."

"Position of *governess?*" Mrs. Cheatham's eyes narrowed. "I filled that position yesterday, Miss Carrington."

Rebekah's lips moved but no words came at first. "So . . . what am I . . ." She caught herself. "For what position was I interviewing just now?"

"Music tutor. To my ten-year-old daughter, Pauline."

"Music tutor," Rebekah repeated softly, finding the irony nothing short of rich. Tempted to tug on that thread, one look at Mrs. Cheatham's stern expression made her think better of it. Besides, she needed a governess position, which usually provided room and board, not merely an agreement to give a child lessons once or twice a week.

Her empty stomach chose that moment to rumble, and she quickly cleared her throat and pressed a hand to her midsection, hoping to mask the noise.

"Again, Mrs. Cheatham, my apologies for having wasted your time." She rose to leave.

"Did you or did you not inform Mrs. Routh that the Nashville Philharmonic recommended that you contact me?"

Not wanting to, Rebekah eased back onto the settee. "No, ma'am. And . . . also, yes."

"And why mention that—if, indeed, the stated referral is bona fide—if you were interested in the *governess* position?"

"I assure you there was a referral. From Mrs. Murphey at the opera house."

She frowned. "And just who is this *Mrs. Murphey?*"

"A woman who, I am quite certain"—Rebekah curbed a humorless laugh—"will gain enormous pleasure upon learning I came to see you."

Sensing Mrs. Cheatham's mounting frustration, she hurried to explain. "Following my meeting yesterday with Maestro Whitcomb, Mrs. Murphey, who is employed at the opera house, wrote down your name and address, and encouraged me to contact you about the governess position. Looking back on it now, I realize I should have been more suspect. And you are right. I should have taken the time to write an introductory letter. But my personal situation is such that I need *immediate* employment, Mrs. Cheatham. And I simply didn't realize at the time with whom, or where, I would be interviewing this morning."

"One's place in society should hardly determine whether a person is, or is not, accorded common courtesies, Miss Carrington."

Rebekah bowed her head. "No. You're right, of course. It shouldn't."

"Clearly, you believe this woman did not have your best interest at heart. Why would that be?"

"I honestly can't say, other than I believe she took an initial disliking to me. Mrs. Murphey can be very . . . *protective* of Maestro Whitcomb."

Her brow furrowed. "Protective in what sense?"

"Of his time."

"And she felt you were encroaching upon that? By your meeting with him?"

Rebekah knew when someone was digging for the truth, and this woman was up to her elbows in dirt. "Yes, ma'am."

The clock ticking on the mantel sliced off the seconds, and Rebekah felt them piling up between them. Compared to this, trudging back into town through the snow didn't sound half bad.

"So . . . to summarize our last few moments, Miss Carrington. You came here to interview for the position of governess, which you learned about following a meeting with Maestro Whitcomb yesterday. Yet you have backed off your prior claim of an acquaintance with the man, even though you used his name to gain entrance into my home and to an audience with me." She leveled a stare. "Which leaves me to wonder . . . why? And what it is you're not telling me."

"I give you my word, Mrs. Cheatham, I'm not hiding anything. I simply came here to interview for a position. Although"—she took a deep breath, and exhaled—"when Mrs. Routh was about to turn me away earlier, I *did* mention Mr. Whitcomb's name, thinking it might hold sway with her, and with you. And for that, I sincerely apologize. Yesterday was the first time I ever met the conductor. Our interaction was brief and . . . most uneventful, I assure you."

A single dark eyebrow lifted in silent, unmistakable question, but Rebekah wasn't about to share why she'd been meeting with Mr. Whitcomb.

She could well imagine how Adelicia Cheatham would react if the woman knew she'd dared to challenge Nashville's new conductor about a woman's place in an orchestra. A married woman like Mrs. Cheatham, insulated by such wealth, could never begin to understand what it meant to fight for every foothold in a world dominated by men.

"Mrs. Routh told me you've been living in Europe. Am I correct in understanding, Miss Carrington, that Nashville was originally your home?"

Rebekah nodded. "That's right. I've spent the past ten years in Vienna pursuing my education and . . . being a governess." She forced a tiny smile.

126

Mrs. Cheatham responded with an even tinier one. "An education in Vienna. That's quite an opportunity. Especially for one so young at the time."

"My father recognized my love for music early on. And also . . . my talent, he said. It was his wish that I study music more in depth once I was older. But since none of the American universities or music conservatories admit women into their ranks, he looked abroad. To Vienna."

"And very wisely so," Mrs. Cheatham said. "I cannot imagine a better place in which to study music."

"My father died before I was of age to study abroad on my own, and my late grandmother"—speaking of Nana, remembering the sacrifices she made, stirred Rebekah's emotions—"decided it would be best if I left earlier than planned. Shortly before the war started, as it turned out. And it was the right decision."

"Without a doubt." Mrs. Cheatham regarded her. "Do you still have family here?"

"Yes, ma'am. My mother and . . . her husband. My . . . stepfather." She could still see the door inching open as he'd tried to force his way into her room earlier that morning. And the stench . . .

"I see. And do these people have names?"

Rebekah blinked. "Yes, ma'am, of course. Mr. Barton Ledbetter and, my mother, Mrs. Sarah Carrington Ledbetter. But I wouldn't expect you to know them, Mrs. Cheatham."

"I know a great many people, Miss Carrington, from many varied walks of life. I find it unwise to make presumptions about others. Wouldn't you agree?"

Feeling the sting of yet another rebuke, Rebekah nodded, her pride rubbed raw. "Yes, ma'am."

"You were not familiar with my name, were you?"

Rebekah heard no pride in the question. Only curiosity. "No, ma'am. I was not. I'm sorry."

Mrs. Cheatham huffed a most unladylike breath. "One does not say one is sorry when they have committed no wrong. How many times must I correct you young women on that fact? Offering an apology for an offense and admitting you were mistaken on or not aware of a subject are two quite different responses to two quite different circumstances."

Rebekah stared, wondering where that outburst had come from, and who the other young woman was who had likely suffered a similar scolding. "I . . . appreciate your correction, Mrs. Cheatham."

If this woman's intention was to put her in her place, she'd accomplished her goal—several times over.

The clock chimed three times—a quarter of ten—and Rebekah's thoughts turned to the family with six children and whether they still needed a governess—and if she could get to them before Mrs. Cheatham did. To that end . . .

She stood. "Thank you, Mrs. Cheatham. You've

been most gracious with your time this morning. But I refuse to take any more of it. Will you excuse me, please?"

Mrs. Cheatham looked up at her, her expression inscrutable. "Yes, Miss Carrington, you may go."

Rebekah turned.

"*After* you answer one more question."

Her back to the woman, Rebekah winced before smoothing her expression and turning.

"I take it you play an instrument, Miss Carrington."

Having experienced one too many rebukes in the past hour, Rebekah kept her answer brief. "I do."

Mrs. Cheatham's eyes brimmed with curiosity. "And what instrument would that be?"

"The piano, of course, and the oboe. And the violin."

On admission of the latter, the woman's expression actually warmed. "Indeed? And are you well trained?"

Rebekah lifted her chin. "Exceedingly."

A slow, almost catlike smile curved Mrs. Cheatham's mouth. "And do you still refuse to tell me the nature of your acquaintance with Maestro Whitcomb?"

Mrs. Cheatham held her gaze, and Rebekah didn't dare look away. To do so would make her look weak. And though she was beaten and bruised and couldn't wait to be out of this house, she didn't want Mrs. Cheatham's last impression of her to be one of weakness.

Hand on the doorknob, Rebekah knew full well what Adelicia Cheatham was really asking. "You want to know the topic of my meeting with Maestro Whitcomb."

A telling sparkle lit the woman's eyes.

"I went to see Maestro Whitcomb yesterday"—Rebekah let her own smile come slowly—"to audition for the Nashville Philharmonic."

8

I beg your pardon?" Mrs. Cheatham's eyes went wide.

"I auditioned. For an oboe seat. I was not, however, selected."

"*You* . . . were allowed to audition for the Nashville Philharmonic?"

Enjoying the look of shock on the woman's face more than she should have, Rebekah held up a hand. "To be completely forthcoming . . . Mr. Whitcomb didn't so much *allow* me to audition, as he didn't immediately demand that I leave his office when I began playing. That came soon enough."

And she'd never forget his response. *"But the fact remains, you are a woman."* Remembering how he'd looked at her when he'd said it—as though she were something to be pitied, like some poor, wet kitten left out in the rain—only rallied her frustration.

Mrs. Cheatham rose from the settee, the skirt of her dress a sea of ivory lace as she crossed the room. "I don't suppose you have your violin with you?"

Not expecting, or quite following, this turn in the conversation, Rebekah glanced in the direction of the front hall. "No, ma'am. But I *do* have my oboe."

She shook her head. "I want my daughter Pauline to learn to play the violin. She's been taking lessons for some time now, but she's not progressing as I believe she should. Her teacher is, in fact, a member of the orchestra. But I get the sense he's not as dedicated to her instruction as I would have him be."

Rebekah could well imagine that. After all, Mrs. Cheatham's daughter was a *girl.* "How long has Pauline been playing?"

"Two years. She started at the age of eight."

"I started at the age of four."

Mrs. Cheatham's jaw tensed. "So you're saying I was late in beginning her lessons."

"No, ma'am. I'm simply saying that your daughter has a lot of work ahead of her compared to other girls her age who've been studying longer. Your enthusiasm for her to learn, while a gift in itself, is incidental to *her* enthusiasm. She must want to learn for herself, or it will never happen."

"A good teacher can help instill that love, can he—or *she*—not?"

Rebekah eyed her, wondering if she was

correctly interpreting her meaning, and what that would mean if she was. "Certainly, they can. But that love will be challenged every step of the way. I enjoy playing the oboe. It gives me great pleasure. But when I play the violin . . ." She briefly closed her eyes. "It takes the pleasure of playing to an altogether different level. Even so, there are moments when the instrument can still be as much foe as it is friend."

Mrs. Cheatham laughed softly. "Not unlike husbands, from time to time."

Unprepared for such candor, Rebekah felt her mouth slip open, which only seemed to encourage the pertness in Mrs. Cheatham's demeanor.

"If I were to provide you with a violin, Miss Carrington, would you be able to play it?"

Rebekah stared. "Well, of course. But I—"

Mrs. Cheatham reached for a silver bell on a nearby table, rang it, and within the space of a minute, Mrs. Routh opened the door.

"How may I be of service, Mrs. Cheatham?"

"Bring me the red leather case from my trunk room, please."

Mrs. Routh hesitated, looking between them, her expression one of confusion.

"The red leather case, Mrs. Routh," Mrs. Cheatham repeated more pointedly.

"Yes, ma'am." The head housekeeper nodded. "I'll get it right away, ma'am."

Mrs. Routh returned soon after and carefully laid a violin case on the settee beside Mrs. Cheatham.

"Very good, Mrs. Routh. Thank you."

The head housekeeper closed the door as she left.

Mrs. Cheatham smoothed her hand over the case. "Did you ever have opportunity to visit Italy while in Europe, Miss Carrington?"

Rebekah nodded. "I did. Once. I went to Florence."

"Ah . . . The cathedral of Santa Maria del Fiore, the Palazzo Vecchio. Florence is divine, is it not?"

"Yes, ma'am, it is." Rebekah's gaze flitted to the case, guessing what was inside, and her curiosity was more than a little piqued.

As if reading her thoughts, Mrs. Cheatham opened the latches. "Above all other instruments, the violin and cello are my most favored. Sadly, I do not play either. Though I do play the piano well, which is comforting to the soul. But there are places in the heart where only the violin can reach. Would you not agree?"

Rebekah nodded, watching as she slowly lifted the lid. As she'd assumed, a violin nested inside, along with a bow.

"I acquired this in recent months, having admired it from afar for some time." Mrs. Cheatham ran a finger down the slender neck of the instrument, then lifted the violin from its cushioned vault and held it out to her.

Rebekah took it, uncertain of the woman's expectations.

"She's a thing of beauty, isn't she?"

"Yes, she is." Rebekah inspected the violin. Elegantly proportioned and fine in detail, the instrument was gorgeous. And old, by her guess. But well maintained. The original varnish, she felt certain, not shiny but matted, was in pristine condition.

"I'd like you to play for me, Miss Carrington." Rebekah eyed her.

"Would it help, or hurt, if I told you this is to be your *formal* interview?"

"My formal interview?" Rebekah realized she'd guessed correctly.

"I want my daughter, Pauline, to not only learn how to play—I want her to fall in love with this instrument. So far, that has not happened. And I believe time is running out. So . . ." Mrs. Cheatham waved a delicate hand. "Please, play."

Rebekah smiled. "Mrs. Cheatham, I'm honored that you would consider interviewing me as a tutor for your daughter. Truly. But . . . I need to seek a governess position. One that includes room and board. Because I need a place to live."

"But you said your stepfather and mother live here in town. Could you not live with them and . . ."

Rebekah wasn't certain why, but Mrs. Cheatham let the sentence fade. Perhaps the truth of her situation at home showed in her face. She hoped not. But whatever the cause, she was grateful the woman let the subject die.

For a second time, Mrs. Cheatham gestured toward the violin. "Play, Miss Carrington."

Hearing the insistence in her voice, Rebekah took hold of the violin by the neck, accepted the bow from Mrs. Cheatham, and proceeded to tune each of the four strings.

She cradled the instrument against her collarbone, suddenly a little nervous, aware of Mrs. Cheatham watching her every move. She started to ask her if she had a request. Then she thought of Demetrius and simply began to play.

The violin's resonance was breathtaking. She would've sworn the instrument was guiding her along, that it had played this song before and knew it better than she did. Even playing pianissimo, the sound was brilliant, like the purest light beaming down from heaven. The instrument had incredible power, and she played for a moment, then two, for the sheer joy of it, and because of the look of pleasure on Adelicia Cheatham's face.

Finally, Rebekah let out a sigh. "This is a *splendid* instrument, Mrs. Cheatham."

"Yes, it is." Mrs. Cheatham's mouth tipped as though she were contemplating revealing a secret. "And well it should be, Miss Carrington. It's the Molitor Stradivarius."

Rebekah blinked. Then looked down at the violin cradled so casually in her lap. "*This* is the—"

"It's named after one of Napoleon Bonaparte's—"

"Generals. Yes, I know!" Rebekah's pulse quickened.

"Antonio Stradivari crafted it in 1697. The seller told me that the general owned it for many years. It's rumored to have been in Napoleon's possession as well. And I must say, it does my heart good to see someone who realizes its worth as much as I do."

Rebekah inspected the violin more closely, drinking in its beauty anew from the top of its curled scroll to the tuning pegs, down to the bridge, then the tailpiece. She'd read about this violin in her studies in Vienna. Masterful. And almost two centuries old.

A little light-headed, she looked up. "May I play it again? Please?"

Mrs. Cheatham laughed, then granted permission with the slightest nod.

A little awestruck but mostly humbled, Rebekah cradled the violin against her collarbone again, reverently this time, and fought back emotion as she started to play.

The music wrapped itself around her, and she gave herself to it. To the softness of the verses she knew so well, and to the swell of the chorus that seemed to be made up of many violins instead of just one. She felt a connection to all the musicians who'd ever held this piece of history and wished she knew who they were.

She held the final note longer than usual, not wanting the song or the moment to end. But it did end, and when she opened her eyes and met Adelicia Cheatham's watery gaze, she couldn't help but believe she'd just been given a new beginning.

● ● ●

Adelicia Cheatham was going to be the death of him.

Tate grabbed the extra folder of music for the string ensemble from his desk drawer and shoved it into his satchel. He wasn't playing this evening, but he knew musicians. Especially the amateurs.

But he'd wanted a challenge in establishing an orchestra. And he'd gotten it.

He checked his pocket watch. An hour, that's all the time he had to get to the Belmont estate and see the musicians set up before guests started arriving.

Usually, an hour would be ample. But with the lingering snow on the roads and the temperature hovering below freezing, it would take longer.

And Mrs. Cheatham would be livid.

His day had started coming apart almost before it began. First, when he nearly missed the train due to heavy rains, and then a downed tree had blocked the railway just outside of Chicory Hollow. Then to top it all, the train from Knoxville broke down halfway back to Nashville. The two hours spent stuck on the tracks was time he'd needed to prepare for Mrs. Cheatham's party tonight. Why he'd ever agreed to coordinate this ensemble, he didn't know.

And yet, he had.

The woman's financial generosity to the symphony comprised well over half of their annual donations, and the symphony board had made it beyond clear that part of his job was keeping their major donors happy.

So this was him working to keep Mrs. Cheatham *ecstatic*.

He spotted an envelope on his desk chair, his name scrawled across the front, and he circled his desk to read it. His mood quickly went from bad to worse. He wadded up the stationery and threw it across the office. If Adelicia Cheatham didn't do him in, Edward Pennington and the man's overzealous symphony board certainly would.

Tate strode from the opera house and climbed into the waiting carriage, the icy wind whipping his coat. He rapped twice on the door, and the conveyance lurched forward.

The usual bumpy ride was made even more so by ruts that the cold and ice had clawed into the roads. The windows on the carriage doors were partially fogged, and he leaned back into the seat, weary from the quick two-day trip but grateful for the opportunity to go.

He questioned again the wisdom of promising Opal he'd return within a month's time. But she had a special way of bending his heart to her will, something not easily done.

Every time he made the trip, he was reminded of how far away from the world here in Nashville a person could travel in only a few hours' time. He leaned forward and rested his head in his hands. The slight ache that had begun behind his eyes earlier in the day was steadily building.

His thoughts raced a thousand different directions at once, but they swiftly narrowed to the one weighing most heavily on him. The prognosis for his—

The carriage suddenly careened to the left, and Tate pitched to the side with it. His head and shoulder slammed against the wall, and the pounding in his temples exploded. His eyes watered from the pain. Ears ringing, he looked out the window in time to see a freight wagon passing within inches of them.

The carriage came to a jerky halt, and Tate heard the driver yell some choice words to the pair of mares harnessed up ahead.

"Sorry, Maestro Whitcomb," the driver called down. "The gals, they're a bit skittish with the snow and ice. I'll have us out of here in a jiffy."

Out of here? Feeling slightly off-balance, Tate opened the door and peered down—and realized why. The left rear wheel was wedged a foot deep into a rut.

"Maestro!" The driver appeared at the door. "If you don't mind waiting off to the side here, sir, I've enlisted a couple of men to help me get her unstuck. Don't you worry, though, I'll still get you to Belmont on time!"

Tate climbed out into the brisk wind. Adelicia Cheatham was going to eat him alive. Rubbing the soreness from his shoulder, he moved close to a gas streetlamp. Foot traffic was surprisingly heavy for this time of evening, especially considering most of the shop windows were already dark, shades pulled. He tugged his coat collar up around his neck, grateful again for Mrs. Pender, his widowed housekeeper, who'd made sure his clothing for the evening was freshly pressed and ready when he'd dashed home earlier to change. What would he do without her?

Seeing the driver and his two enlistees struggling with the carriage, Tate finally decided they needed a fourth man if he wanted to make it to Belmont before dawn. So much for freshly pressed. He waited for a wagon to pass, then started across the street when someone bumped him from behind.

"Sorry, sir!"

Tate turned to see a boy peering up and immediately checked his coat pockets, then remembered his wallet was in his satchel in the carriage. He'd had his first run-in with one of these little pilferers years ago, on the streets of New York. He'd learned quickly.

"Got one last paper here, sir. A special edition. Let you have it for a dime."

"Papers cost a nickel, young man."

The boy grinned. "Guess I could let you have it for that."

"No, thank you. Not interested."

The boy's grin faded by several dramatic degrees. "I understand, sir." He bowed his head, a tattered red cap briefly hiding his face. "I was just trying to get some extra . . . so my sister could eat tonight."

Tate eyed him. "What's your sister's name?"

"Lula."

"How old is Lula?"

The boy blinked. "Four."

"How old are you?"

"Seven," he said, jutting out a cocky chin.

"Where's your sister now?"

"At home."

"Where's home?"

"Few streets over."

"What's the address?"

The boy swiftly glanced away, then back again. "Two-ten Flour Mill."

Tate stared. He didn't usually give these little pickpockets the time of day, much less engage them in conversation. The boy appeared to be slight of build by nature, but judging by his threadbare clothes, life had only helped that along. And yet the boy hadn't learned how to lie. At least, not well enough. Maybe that was it. . . .

Tate rubbed the back of his neck, the ache in his head still pounding. Maybe he saw something still worth saving in the lad.

"When did you last eat, son?" Tate asked him.

A layer of bravado fell from the boy's expression. But it wasn't softness waiting beneath.

"Don't need your charity, mister. Just wanted to sell my last paper."

Tate smiled. Yes, something definitely still worth saving here. He reached into his pocket, glancing toward the street to discover that the men nearly had the carriage righted.

"Tell you what . . ." He pulled the change from his pocket. "I'll take the paper, and I'll give you an extra nickel . . . for *Lula*. But I want you to promise me that you'll—"

In a flash, the boy snatched the coins from Tate's hand and ran. Or tried to. Tate overtook him easily and grabbed him by the collar of his coat. The boy fought and squirmed, pummeling his chest with clenched fists—still full of coins, no doubt. But the boy was no match for him.

"Hold still!" Tate commanded, gripping him by the shoulders. "I'm not going to hurt you." He leaned down.

The boy lunged for him, teeth bared, but Tate kept him at arm's length.

"Listen here, you little culprit! There aren't many people in this world who will care enough to help you. Best not make enemies of those who would. Do you understand me?"

The boy gentled, then lowered his head. "Yes, sir," he said softly. "I understand."

Tate took a breath. "Now—"

"Maestro Whitcomb! Your carriage is ready, sir!"

Tate glanced behind him. "Thank you, I'll be right—"

Pain exploded on his shin, and the boy wriggled from his grip and took off down the street. Holding his leg, Tate stared after him, wishing he could give chase. But losing a few coins didn't begin to compare to the price he would pay for being late to

Adelicia Cheatham's party. Hopefully, the kid would buy himself a couple of meals. And maybe one for *Lula*.

He limped back to the carriage, his head pounding anew. The driver opened the door for him, and he climbed in.

"Get me to Belmont within thirty minutes and there'll be a generous tip in it for you."

As the carriage lurched forward, Tate spotted a sign in a mercantile window across the street, the words illuminated by a gas streetlamp. *Flour Mill. Two dollars and ten cents.*

He smiled to himself as he rubbed his shin.

9

Just shy of half an hour later, the carriage rounded the circular drive leading to the steps of Belmont Mansion. An elderly Negro man dressed in a dark suit, shaved head gleaming in the lantern light, hurried to open the door.

"Welcome to Belmont, sir. The name's Eli. If there's anything I can do for you this evening, please let me know." The man spoke with distinction, his Southern accent thick, yet every syllable perfect.

Tate gave him a quick nod, handed a double tip to the driver, and strode toward the mansion, which was lit up like an evergreen at Christmas. Light warmed every window, and the lanterns dangling from decorated poles and strung from tree to leafless tree caused the snow blanketing the grounds to sparkle like diamonds.

Mrs. Cheatham's desired effect, he felt certain.

He'd been to the mansion only once before, but once was enough to realize how wealthy this woman was. She'd remarried in recent years, he understood, after the deaths of her first two husbands. And from what he'd been told, she'd entered marriages two and three already a very wealthy woman. And had only grown more so through the years.

Tate lifted his fist to knock on the door, but the Negro man—Eli—got there a split hair of a second before him and opened the door wide. Tate nodded his thanks as he entered the house, still uncomfortable with such close attention from servants, even after all these years. A man could transplant himself from one world to another, but his roots had memories that reached deep inside, and over time those memories tended to find their way back to native soil, to home.

And standing here in the opulence of this mansion as the newly ordained conductor of the Nashville Philharmonic, his own roots were tugging hard, reminding him of who he really was—and who he wasn't.

"Maestro!"

Tate looked up to see Mrs. Cheatham floating toward him in a haze of expensive lace, silk, and diamonds—diamonds in her tiara, on her hands, at her waist. Everywhere he looked, the woman glittered.

"Maestro Whitcomb, you're here! Thank goodness. I feared something had gone awry and you weren't coming." Her tone was cordial, but her eyes held a shade of displeasure.

"My apologies, Mrs. Cheatham. I've faced numerous delays today, but all is well now."

She glanced past him. "Did the fourth musician not travel with you?"

"Fourth musician?"

"Yes, only three have arrived thus far. You promised me there would be four. By definition, a string quartet must have four players. Must it not, Maestro?"

The ache in his temples spanned to the back of his head. "Of course it does, Mrs. Cheatham, and I'm certain the other musician will be here any moment."

"I certainly hope so. Because I made special mention in the invitations about the music tonight. If that part of the evening falls flat, I fear it will negatively influence my guests' desire to be more deeply involved with the symphony. And that is something neither of us wants to happen. Especially at this crucial outset."

"I could not agree more, Mrs. Cheatham. Now if you'll point me toward the minstrel gallery, I'll see who is missing."

She led him through the entrance hall to the grand salon, and to the cantilevered staircase ascending to the second floor. The familiar sound of stringed instruments being tuned drifted downward.

"Maestro, you remember my husband, Dr. Cheatham."

Tate turned to see the man walking toward them. "Yes, of course. Good to see you again, Dr. Cheatham." He offered his hand, feeling the seconds tick past.

The older man's grip was firm. "You as well, Maestro Whitcomb. I must say, my wife has spoken of little else but your ensemble this evening. Your musicians, as well as your own presence here tonight, is an honor for us. One we're eager to put on display."

"The honor is all mine, Dr. Cheatham. Thank you, sir. And thank you, Mrs. Cheatham." Tate bowed slightly at the waist. "We'll begin playing well before your first guest's arrival. You have my word."

Wanting to take the stairs in twos, he instead took them as would a cultured maestro—mainly because his shin still ached. When he reached the second-floor landing, he saw his cellist, his violist, and one violinist—then the empty chair. He didn't even try to hide his frustration. "Darrow Fulton. Where is he?"

The three men looked at one another. And finally, Wallace, the cellist, spoke up. "Good evening, Maestro. We don't know, sir. We've been here for almost an hour and haven't seen him."

Tate checked the time. Scarcely fifteen minutes before guests were scheduled to begin arriving. He raked a hand through his hair, his frustration fueled by exhaustion and the constant ache in his head.

He gestured to Adams and the violin the man held. "I don't suppose you have an extra one of those in your back pocket, do you?"

Adams gave a timid smile that quickly faded. "No, Maestro, I don't."

Tate blew out a breath. Just as well. Of all the instruments in the orchestra, the violin was the most beautiful—and exasperating—to him. He'd never come close to mastering it, though he'd tried for years.

His skill had excelled early on with the piano, which, as it turned out, was integral with his chosen path. Give him a violin, and he could manage to find his way through a sonata, though not without foibles. Which he would prefer not to display in front of members of his orchestra, be they amateurs or not.

Best find Mrs. Cheatham and get this over with.

He pictured telling her the news, and then he imagined Edward Pennington, the symphony board's director, arriving tonight only to find everything was *not* as it should be—which Pennington had so forcefully stressed needed to be the case in the note he'd left on the desk chair earlier.

Tate didn't know for sure, but he suspected Pennington had voted for the other candidate for the conductor position. Yet somehow, when all the cards were dealt, Tate ended up with the winning hand.

But, as conductor, he still served at the will of the new symphony board. And it wasn't unheard of for a conductor to come and go before his portrait was even hung in the gallery—and he hadn't even scheduled the first sitting for his yet.

He aimed a look. "Gentlemen, the three of you begin playing in eight minutes."

Adams frowned. "But, sir, the opening piece calls for two violins. How will we—"

"Eight minutes!" Tate glared, then took the stairs back down again in search of Mrs. Cheatham.

Amidst the bustle of servants scurrying here and there with trays of food, chairs, and silver platters laden with champagne glasses, he spotted a young woman carrying a tray who seemed slightly less preoccupied. "Excuse me, miss." He gestured in an effort to get her attention. "It's imperative I find Mrs. Cheatham immedi—"

The woman turned, and Tate's request died on this tongue. "It's . . . *you*." No sooner had he said it, than her eyes—that lovely shade of hazel—darkened, and his memory quickly rose in defense. "Miss Carrington."

Not looking the least impressed, she stared up at him, the lack of exuberance in her expression telling him she had no trouble placing who he was. "That's right, Mr. Whitcomb. And if you're looking for Mrs. Cheatham, she's in the central parlor." She gestured to the room at his back.

"You . . . work here?" Tate appraised her manner of dress. She wasn't wearing the standard black frock and starched white apron like the other servants, yet she *was* carrying a tray.

"I do. But I'm quite busy at the moment. So perhaps it would be best if you came directly to the subject at hand." Her smile, though pretty, was anything but genuine.

Remembering having said much the same thing to her when she was in his office days ago, Tate felt something akin to a gut punch, and a good one. But despite the jab, he was mindful of the time, so he forced a pleasant countenance and followed her suggestion. "The second violinist hasn't shown for the ensemble tonight, and I need to discuss this with Mrs. Cheatham."

Miss Carrington's eyes flashed with an emotion he couldn't define, and that departed just as swiftly. "Music is of utmost importance to Mrs. Cheatham, especially for her gatherings. This won't be . . ."

A young woman pushing a cart stacked with china passed close by, and Tate missed the last of Miss Carrington's comment.

"This won't be *what,* Miss Carrington?"

"I said, this won't be pleasing news for Mrs. Cheatham."

"Nor do *I* consider it such. Now, do you know where I might find her?"

"Absolutely." She nodded, shifting her gaze over his shoulder. "She's right behind—"

"Maestro Whitcomb . . ."

Tate turned to find himself squarely in the hostess's sights.

"Pray tell, my dear sir, why do I not hear the ethereal strains of Beethoven's String Quartet No. 6 in B-flat Major, as I requested, filling every corner of my home?"

Tate tried for a smile. "My deepest apologies, Mrs. Cheatham. But we are, indeed, absent a violinist this evening." He caught the slightest narrowing of her eyes. "However, considering the talent of the musicians present, I'm certain that we can—"

"You play the violin, do you not, Maestro?" Mrs. Cheatham pierced him with a look. "I believe I read that fact in the papers you submitted for review to the committee of select symphony patrons."

Feeling chastised and not liking it, especially in front of Miss Carrington, Tate wondered where the symphony's lead benefactress was headed with her questioning. And call it pride, but—considering immediate company—he didn't wish to admit his deficiency with the instrument. And under the circumstances, saw no need.

"Yes, in fact, I do play the violin, Mrs. Cheatham. However, the fact remains, we don't have a second violin, which makes it a—"

"Miss Carrington, would you please procure my violin for the maestro?"

"With pleasure, Mrs. Cheatham."

Tate looked from the younger woman, now hurrying toward a side corridor, back to the older. "You own a violin, Mrs. Cheatham?"

"My guests will begin arriving at any moment, Maestro Whitcomb. Please assure me there will be music from a string *quartet* to greet them, as you promised."

He ran a finger around the inside of his collar, feeling a little warm. "Yes, Mrs. Cheatham. There will be. However, I consider it my duty to inform you that I—"

"You mustn't play the entire evening, of course. You must join us for dinner and conversation following." She placed a hand on his arm ever so briefly. "I knew you wouldn't disappoint me, Maestro. Now if you'll excuse me, final details await my attention."

Left to stand alone in the center of the grand salon, Tate felt as if he'd been resolutely put in his place. Because he had been. Yet the woman had done it with such politeness and—

"Here you are, Mr. Whitcomb." Miss Carrington appeared at his side, red leather case in hand, and with—if he wasn't mistaken—an even deeper sense of satisfaction in her expression. "I didn't realize you played the violin, sir."

Sensing challenge, he took the case from her, his pride sufficiently prodded. "Thank you, Miss Carrington. And yes, I do. But it's not that uncommon. Most professional musicians play more than one instrument."

"Indeed?" She smiled. "Well, I look forward to hearing it. Which"—she glanced beyond him toward the front entrance hall—"I hope will be any second now, since the first guests are arriving."

Tate turned to see the front door standing open and guests disembarking from a carriage. He was up the spiral staircase in record time, the ache in his head drumming with each step. When he reached the top, he stepped forward only to have the second-floor gallery begin to spin.

The earlier ringing in his ears returned with a fierceness and grew so loud he gripped the bannister. The world and its sounds swirled around him—distorted, mangled—as though being siphoned through a tiny tube inside his head.

His heart pounded in his chest.

He squeezed his eyes tight for several seconds, then opened them to see the three musicians staring at him, their expressions confused. One of them spoke, or at least . . . moved his lips. But no words came.

Then in a flash, as if the siphoning had been reversed, all sound came rushing back, wave after punishing wave, and Tate pressed a hand to his left ear, the volume almost overwhelming.

"Maestro? Are you all right, sir?"

Tate heard the voice as if from far away, yet knew it came from only feet in front of him. His breath coming hard, he heard the laughter and merriment of guests and motioned for the three musicians to begin playing.

"Beethoven's Serenade . . . in D Major, opus 8!" he managed, needing to buy himself some time.

Adams frowned. "But I thought we were to open with No. 6 in—"

"Change of plans!" Tate seethed.

The three men stared at him, then at the violin case in his hand, then back again, their expressions slack with uncertainty.

"You *do* have the music," Tate asked hurriedly.

The men nodded.

"Then *play!*" he commanded.

They shuffled through the sheet music on their stands, faces flushed, then simultaneously raised their bows. Adams, the violinist, cued the others with a nod and they began.

Hearing the chatter of conversation rising from below, Tate regained his breath—and balance—and laid the violin case on a side table. He took a moment, breathing deeply. He must have hit his head harder back in that carriage than he'd thought.

And these headaches . . .

He was working too long of hours, and too many. Too little sleep. But it couldn't be helped. He could sleep later, once his career was solidly on track and once the symphony he was writing was finished.

Feeling some better, he opened up the violin case—then paused. How was it Adelicia Cheatham owned such a fine instrument? He ran a hand along the curves of the violin, then his gaze snagged on an inscription along the inside lip of the case. He angled the case toward the candlelight to better see the writing—then took a full step back, nearly colliding with the tip of Wallace's bow.

Tate stared. It couldn't be. But it was. *Antonio Stradivari.*

He laughed, but no sound came. He couldn't play this. It had to be nearly two hundred years old. And why did Mrs. Cheatham have it? The woman had money enough, for certain. But *why* would she buy so exquisite and rare an instrument? *Because she could,* came the swift and silent reply.

The woman did hold great affection for the violin—she'd made that clear, even in the short time he'd known her.

He touched the slender neck of the stringed beauty, reverence for the instrument and its creator causing his fingers to tremble. He squeezed his hands, then alternately flexed and relaxed them to work out the jitters.

He glanced behind him at the three musicians, knowing he had five minutes at most until they completed the Serenade. He retrieved the violin from the case, along with the bow, and stepped into a nearby bedroom illuminated by a single oil lamp on a side table.

The bedchamber belonged to one of the children, judging by the drawing easel and dolls taking up residence on the bed. He closed the door, needing to tune the instrument.

It had been months since he'd picked up a violin, which was testament in itself as to how he'd played the last time—not well. Oh, how he envied musicians who could pick up this instrument and make it sing. With the exception of Mozart's Spring Quartet, a personal request by Mrs. Cheatham, the pieces he'd chosen for this evening weren't overly difficult—for an experienced violist, cellist, or violinist.

For him, it would be near torture. Why hadn't he simply told the woman he couldn't play well enough?

Because he hadn't wanted to give Miss Carrington the satisfaction of seeing him tragically humbled after he'd been forced to put her through a similar experience days earlier.

And she *had* forced him on it.

While, granted, certain few of the female gender were gifted at playing an instrument—as she was on the oboe—the fact remained that the symphony was a stressful, even brutal, environment. Competition was fierce and allowed no room for emotions characteristically displayed by the weaker sex. A woman wouldn't last a day in that environment. Nor would any sane woman wish it upon herself, if she knew the truth.

So, in fact, what Miss Carrington probably considered as a great slight from him, was really his effort to protect her, though he doubted she'd ever be convinced to see it that way.

With all the confidence of a schoolboy at his

first dance, he tucked the instrument against his collarbone, and felt the age-old stories about these violins—stories that had been passed down through the years—flooding his mind. Some musicians actually believed the instruments absorbed part of the talent of every musician who'd ever played them, and that's why their sound was so rich and full of tone.

Other musicians went a step further—a grand leap, in his opinion—and claimed that each Stradivarius absorbed a bit of the soul of each player and was, in essence, haunted. He'd heard outlandish stories of people claiming to have heard the strains of a Stradivarius only to enter the room and find the violin locked away in its case.

Almost wishing that nonsense was true at the moment, and that the violin would just up and start playing, all by itself, Tate knew better. He'd internalized middle C since early youth, and he tuned the A string, using an upward stroke. Surprisingly, it was close to being in tune. Same for strings D, G, and E.

He pulled the bow across the strings, listening, until a perfect fifth interval separated them all. If only playing the instrument would prove so easy.

Needing something familiar, he chose a Mozart piece—Twelve variations of "Ah! Vous dirai-je, Maman"—as familiar to him as the keys of a piano upon which he'd played this song countless times as a boy. The words of the familiar English lullaby accompanied each note internally as he played.

Twinkle, twinkle little star, how I wonder what you are . . .

The resonance of the Stradivarius breathed new life into the simple tune and gave beauty to chords tentatively, even poorly, played. He grimaced, wishing there was a way out of this.

Not only was he risking humiliation in front of Mrs. Cheatham and her guests—Miss Carrington included in that number—but three members of his symphony would witness his mediocre performance. He didn't know which rankled him more.

But hearing the final strains of Beethoven's Serenade drifting through from the other side of the door, he knew he was out of time.

10

After butchering his way through Beethoven's String Quartet No. 6 in B-flat Major—or at least that's how it felt—Tate knew he'd chosen his career as a conductor wisely. Four instrumental pieces later, he also knew he was nowhere near worthy enough to play this magnificent instrument.

As he did his best to keep up with the other musicians, the only complaint he had was that, at times, the other men played too softly. Why was it no one seemed to understand the proper application of pianissimo?

By the time he played the final note of the

second violinist's part in Mozart's Spring Quartet, his concentration was spent and the pads of his fingers ached from the lack of developed toughness, especially when he played vibrato. He'd never been more relieved to finish a piece of music in his life, and also to discover the pounding in his head had eased.

He lowered his bow, and in the sudden quiet, the lilt of conversation rose from the first-floor parlors and grand salon, followed, a moment later, by the tinkling of a bell—the signal for the presentation of dinner, and for him to join the guests. The other three musicians would continue playing through dinner and dessert.

As the men readied their next set of music, Tate realized that, though he'd appreciated their individual talent before tonight, his respect for that talent had deepened considerably over the past hour. He was certain, however, that their respect for *him* had lessened considerably. Not that he could blame them. He'd especially struggled with the arpeggios and tempos. How he wished he could play the violin better than he did.

With more than a little relief, he returned the priceless Stradivarius to the sanctuary of its case, the bow along with it, and made sure the latches were securely fastened.

He momentarily weighed the option of telling the musicians about it, then quickly decided it best he not. After all, it wasn't his to share.

He headed toward the bedroom he'd used earlier,

then thought better of it and sought another bed-room. Finding what he was certain to be Mrs. Cheatham's, he stepped inside, placed the violin on her dresser, and closed the door behind him.

Footsteps sounded on the stairs, and servants appeared with refreshment for the musicians, which Tate took as his opportunity to head downstairs.

"Maestro Whitcomb?"

At the top of the stairs, Tate turned to see Wallace, the cellist, looking at him with an odd expression. Same as that of the other two.

"Maestro," Wallace continued, his expression showing hesitance. "It was an honor to play with you tonight, sir."

Taken aback, Tate saw the other two men nod in agreement, which touched him more than he dared let on. "Thank you, gentlemen. But the honor was mine, I assure you."

Once downstairs, he was surprised to estimate nearly sixty people in attendance for the "intimate dinner party." Then again, he was learning that Adelicia Cheatham never did anything on a small scale. The social events she hosted at Belmont were legendary—parties consisting of upwards of fifteen hundred to two thousand guests, he had been told.

So, in those terms, he guessed this gathering *was* intimate.

"Come, Maestro!" Mrs. Cheatham appeared at his side, still sparkling. "Allow me to introduce you to my guests."

"Your violin is quite something, Mrs. Cheatham," Tate whispered as she led him toward the crowd, which earned him a mischievous smile. "I stored it in what I believe is your bedroom. On your dresser, ma'am. But I'll retrieve it if—"

"It will be fine, I'm certain. Now come, Maestro Whitcomb. We have much work to do," she whispered.

Mrs. Cheatham maneuvered her way through the crowd of elegantly clad men and women, speaking and commenting to each couple with the same ease in which he cued the various sections of an orchestra in a concerto. Her timing was impeccable. She never missed a beat. Or an opportunity to encourage hearty support of the new symphony.

Conversation over dinner and dessert proved every bit as exhausting as he'd anticipated. And while he managed the social aspects of his job with outward aplomb, inwardly he craved the solitude of home. Namely, the small study with his books and piano.

Still . . .

He found his gaze scanning the faces, searching. But he saw no sign of her. She worked here. He knew that much from her own admission. Though, precisely what Miss Carrington did at Belmont, he didn't know. She'd been carrying a tray, but as to its contents, he couldn't say.

Yet he did remember, in perfect detail, the softness of her profile, the curve of her cheeks when she smiled, and the provocative sway of her hips as she walked away.

"Tell us, Maestro Whitcomb . . . Do you have an opinion on this controversial subject?"

Tate blinked, and discovered the older woman seated across from him wearing a somewhat challenging expression, along with the rest of the guests around them. Having not heard a word she'd said before addressing him personally, Tate eased into a smile, not about to admit such.

"Of course I do." He laughed softly, feeling a number of eyes shift in his direction. "Although . . . after this slice of Mrs. Cheatham's apple cake slathered in warm buttered rum sauce, I'm not altogether certain I can remember it."

Laughter erupted, along with scattered applause and a few shouts of "Hear! Hear!"—then conversation gradually resumed among the guests.

Tate caught the faintest nod of approval from Adelicia Cheatham from her place at the foot of the table, and it pleased him to see her apparently pleased as well.

But his curiosity was roused as to what *controversial* matter he'd avoided addressing.

The next hour crept by even more slowly than the one previous, and when it finally came time to leave, Tate had to work to hide his true feelings when Mrs. Cheatham requested he join her and her husband in bidding the guests good evening. "One last chance to make sure they remember the symphony," she whispered.

He almost wished he could run upstairs and play with the other musicians again. And play the three men did, to the enormous pleasure of the guests, who still seemed not the least eager to leave.

Tate recognized the Beethoven piece as being the ensemble's finale, and he hoped Mrs. Cheatham wouldn't mind her guests walking to their carriages in the hush of night, unaccompanied by one of the masters.

As conveyances slowly made their way up the long circular drive, couples clustered in the entrance hall and on the porch outside. Tate spotted Dr. Cheatham speaking to Adams, Wallace, and Peters before handing each musician an envelope. Good. The men deserved it. They'd played well.

Seeing his own carriage approaching, Tate decided it wasn't outside the boundaries of etiquette to take his leave as well. He approached his hosts and bowed at the waist. "Dr. and Mrs. Cheatham, may I say what an honor it's been to—"

Conversation fell silent around him as the exuberant strains of Mozart's "Rondo alla turca" suddenly filled and enlivened the night air, and he felt the hairs prickle on the back of his neck. Each note was perfection, the challenging tempo a paragon, and every guest entranced.

No one moved. No one said a word. He, himself, barely breathed.

Never had he heard Mozart's Turkish Rondo played so intuitively, so brilliantly on the violin.

He looked around for Adams but saw only

Wallace and Peters. So Adams had decided to finish the evening with a solo. Tate had no idea the man had that level of talent in him. Adelicia Cheatham would be over the moon. Speaking of their hostess . . .

Tate sought out Mrs. Cheatham and found her standing, eyes closed, as though she were drinking in the timeless beauty of the music and the giftedness of the one playing. Then—

Tate blinked. It couldn't be. But . . . it was.

Adams stood not ten feet from him, off to the right, his own violin case in hand. Tate slowly turned back toward the grand salon and the cantilevered staircase, and all he could picture was the Stradivarius where he'd left it—

Locked away in its red leather case.

The second the solo ended, thunderous applause filled the house, and Tate made for the stairs, slowed by the number of hands reaching out to shake his.

"Well done, Maestro!" one man said, clapping him on the back.

"Saved the best for last, did you?" another joined in.

"Ending the evening with Mozart. Splendid choice, Maestro. Splendid!"

Tate managed what he hoped was a gracious smile, all the while working to get to the staircase. He took the stairs by twos this time, not caring who saw. But when he reached the second-story landing, it was empty—save for the Stradivarius nestled cozily inside its open case on a side table.

He looked up and down the landing, then took the liberty of peering inside the darkened family bedrooms.

No one. All was quiet—as a ghost.

He returned to the violin and stared down at it, recalling the stories he'd been told. He picked up the violin and the bow . . .

And smiled.

Unless ghosts had begun leaving behind the warmth of their grip, someone made very much of flesh and blood had been standing here seconds earlier, playing this violin. And whoever it was . . .

He had to find him—and implore him to become part of the Nashville Philharmonic.

Pulse racing, Rebekah pressed farther into the shadows in the corner behind the wardrobe, still able to see Mr. Whitcomb's silhouette in the hallway.

When she'd first heard the sound of footsteps racing up the stairs, she'd darted toward the closest bedroom, only to remember it was Dr. and Mrs. Cheatham's. So she'd turned and bee-lined into one of the children's rooms instead. Exhilaration fired through her veins, but she ignored her body's demand for more air and took quick, silent breaths, certain she would be discovered at any moment.

But oh . . .

Playing that violin had felt superb. No, beyond

superb. It had been *sublime*. And the guests' response that followed, their applause . . .

Her eyes watered with emotion. *Overwhelming* didn't begin to describe it.

The eruption of applause had felt like a sudden downpour after decades of drought, and she drank in the affirmation even now, partly ashamed that it meant so much, yet so grateful to have it.

She'd always wondered what it would be like to play for an audience. Not in a recital setting, but a *real* audience who knew and appreciated music. She'd overheard musicians say that playing before an audience had an almost addictive quality. That once you performed and felt that connection, you wanted to perform again and again.

And now that she'd tasted it, she understood.

The retreat of Mr. Whitcomb's footsteps down the stairs helped to loosen the tangle of nerves in her chest, and she finally took a deep breath and leaned her head back against the wall.

She stayed put, already knowing how the carpeted floors in this bedroom creaked, telling more tales than a magpie. Plus, she'd read one too many dime-store novels in which the heroine emerged too quickly from her hiding place only to find the villain lying in wait. And regardless of how handsome Nathaniel Tate Whitman looked tonight, he was most certainly a villain.

For her, at least.

Moments passed.

Finally, deciding it was safe, she emerged from

hiding and crossed the bedroom to peer out a front-facing window. Two stories below, carriages lined the circular drive, their flickering headlamps illuminating the darkness, much like their cousin lanterns suspended from the trees.

Then she spotted him, climbing into a carriage a ways down the drive.

She felt a slow smile, watching Mr. Whitcomb and imagining again what must have been running through the man's mind as he'd raced upstairs only to find the Stradivarius alone, tucked in its case, *sans* musician.

What would he think if he knew she was the one who'd played? A *woman!*

She'd listened to the string ensemble as the final Beethoven selection had drawn to a close, yet still the attendees lingered, laughing and visiting, waiting on their carriages. It was then she'd seen Mrs. Cheatham look pointedly in the direction of the staircase, and she knew what the woman was thinking. Because she'd heard her say as much. *"I desire for music to greet my guests as they arrive at my home and as they depart from it."*

Then not a moment later, she'd caught Mrs. Cheatham's slight frown as the musicians descended the stairs, cases in hand, and the idea occurred to her. Yet as much as the thought of Mr. Whitcomb falling out of Adelicia Cheatham's good graces appealed to her, she knew the success of this evening meant a great deal to her employer.

Plus, she could only imagine how grateful Mrs.

Cheatham would be if the guests departed to the memorable strains of Mozart instead of the dull clomp of horses' hooves.

She'd waited for the final guests to make their way into the entrance hall, then she slipped upstairs. It took her a moment to find the Stradivarius, while weighing the risk of what she was about to do. But the possibility of someone discovering her was next to nil. No guest would *dare* venture upstairs to the second floor where the family bedrooms were located, just as Dr. and Mrs. Cheatham would never abandon their guests. And with the couple's children tucked away with their governess in another part of the home, the only person she'd had to worry about seeking her out was—

The maestro. And sought her out he had. He'd almost found her too.

Rebekah watched the line of carriages slowly circle the illuminated drive, Mr. Whitcomb's among them.

She'd gained glimpses of him throughout the evening—from behind a fern in the corridor leading to her bedroom. Mrs. Cheatham had never said she couldn't show her face this evening, but it had been understood. And Rebekah wasn't the least offended. She was merely Mrs. Cheatham's daughter's music tutor, after all. A person in employ. Not a guest in this home, and certainly not a guest on tonight's list.

But—her smile deepened—she was a person in employ who had negotiated room and board with a family that was certainly one of Nashville's wealthiest.

Courting a satisfied feeling, she made her way downstairs, pausing briefly on the staircase to make sure no guests lingered. Then she hurried across the grand salon toward the corridor to her bedroom. A silver tray still laden with petit fours sat invitingly on a side table, and she sneaked a couple as she passed.

Moist white cake with buttercream frosting. *Divine.*

Already she'd discovered that Cordina, Belmont's head cook, worked culinary magic with herbed pork roast and potatoes. And the breakfast of eggs and hot cakes with sausage that morning had been delicious as well. But one thing Rebekah didn't understand . . .

Why were her meals being served to her in her room? She wasn't about to complain, but she wouldn't have minded going down to the kitchen either, like the other servants and employees.

Brushing past the corner fern, she thought again of Nathaniel Whitcomb and how he'd moved among the guests that evening with such skillful ease—chatting, smiling, offering what must have been the most witty repartee, judging by the laughter his remarks drew. And how the women had behaved. . . .

She huffed. *Shameless* was the word that came to mind.

Females, young and old, stared after the man as

though he were Adonis in the flesh. Mr. Whitcomb was handsome, admittedly, and made quite the dashing figure in his black waistcoat and tails, but there was something about him she found distinctly off-putting.

Perhaps it was his entitled upbringing, or prestigious education in the country's most distinguished schools, or maybe the outlandish volume of awards and praise he'd garnered at so young an age. Or perhaps . . .

It was the cavalier manner in which he'd laid waste to her dreams in one devastating blow. How she'd relished handing him the Stradivarius earlier, eager to put him in his place.

But to her dismay, he played the instrument disappointingly well—for a conductor. Conductors were infamous for boasting they could play numerous instruments *well,* when their actual talent more than stretched the definition of the word.

Rebekah shoved open the door to her bedroom, a fraction of her earlier satisfaction evaporating as she did. The man had no idea what it was like to have doors slammed in your face for reasons that couldn't be changed.

A servant laying the fire in the hearth suddenly jumped to her feet. "I'm sorry, ma'am. The usual girl who does this is ailin', and I'm runnin' a bit behind. But I'll be done soon enough."

"Oh, it's no worry." Rebekah recognized her as the woman who'd delivered tea to her yesterday, the one with the friendly eyes and matching smile.

Only, she wasn't smiling today. Rebekah wished to set her at ease. "My name is Rebekah Carrington. I'm Pauline's new music tutor. And you are?"

The woman fingered her stained apron, her gaze darting to the door and back. "My name be . . . Esther, Miss Carrington."

"Well, it's nice to make your acquaintance, Esther. And thank you for the fire."

Esther dipped her head and knelt again on the drop cloth, intent on her task.

Rebekah watched her, the woman's behavior so different from yesterday.

Through the years, and with some prompting, Sally had shared with her about life as a servant—and about what life had been like as a slave. And even though Sally had insisted that Rebekah's grandfather and father had been kind and decent owners, it was the first time Rebekah could ever remember being ashamed of her family. She hated what the war had done and what it had cost in lives, but she was so grateful that the late President Lincoln had declared freedom to those enslaved. Especially after she'd grown to love Sally as she had.

"Have you been at Belmont long, Esther?" she asked, perching on the edge of the bed.

Esther's movements quickened. "Awhile, I guess, ma'am."

"I only arrived yesterday. But . . . of course you know that. Do you have family here in—"

"All done, Miss Carrington." Esther gathered the

drop cloth, grabbed the bucket, and hurried to the door. "Sorry again for disturbin' you, ma'am."

"I promise you, Esther, it wasn't a . . ."

The woman closed the door softly, and Rebekah stared after her, the crackle of the fire accentuating her sudden exit. Unable to account for the change in the woman's demeanor since yesterday, Rebekah rose. Apparently being a guest at Belmont was different than living here. Mrs. Routh, or even Mrs. Cheatham, might have a rule against house servants and employees of the family fraternizing. Herr Heilig did, after all.

The fire swiftly devoured the kindling, and Rebekah added another log to the flames, already having learned that the chill in the room was stubborn to leave. She shed her skirt and shirtwaist, chemise and undergarments, and hurriedly slipped into her gown.

Mrs. Cheatham had seen that her trunks were delivered from the opera house last night. When she'd left home before dawn yesterday morning, that had been the only place Rebekah could think of to send them. She'd hoped against hope that the kind Mrs. Bixby—and *not* Mrs. Murphey—would be the one there to accept them. And Mrs. Bixby had been, bless her.

Because if it had been Mrs. Murphey, Rebekah was certain the trunks would've been sent straight back to her mother's house. Or to the nearest rubbish pile.

Only one of the trunks remained at the opera

house—left behind due to its weight and the limited space in the wagon, Mrs. Bixby penned in her note. It was the trunk containing her books and folders of music, including the bound collections of musical scores she'd painstakingly copied through the years, along with orchestrations Maestro Heilig had generously allowed her to transcribe for her own personal library.

She turned back the bedcovers, grateful again to have found a place to live. Mrs. Cheatham was a shrewd negotiator, and room and board was all the remuneration Rebekah would receive for giving Pauline violin lessons. Which meant she needed to find another way to earn money, either through securing a second job or teaching more students. But for now, at least, she was safe—and far away from Barton Ledbetter.

A knock on the door drew her around.

"Yes?" It was probably Cordina with the tea cakes the woman had promised to set aside for her. Rebekah grabbed her robe and cinched it at the waist as she opened the door. "Cordina, you're the most—"

"Good evening, Miss Carrington."

Rebekah blinked. "Mrs. Cheatham."

Her employer smiled, looking radiant amidst a bejeweled glow, diamonds at her neckline and waist, and on her tiara, all glittering white and gold in the oil lamp she held. "I'm sorry to bother you at so late an hour, but this cannot wait till morning. May I come in, please?"

Rebekah felt her face grow warm. She'd expected Mrs. Cheatham to be pleased at her performance, but for the woman to come to her room . . . "Yes, certainly. Please, come in." She stepped back and opened the door wider for Mrs. Cheatham to enter, then closed it in an effort to keep the heat in the room.

Mrs. Cheatham glanced about, and Rebekah trailed her gaze. She'd taken for granted that no one would object to her repositioning some of the bedroom furniture. Now she questioned that call.

Mrs. Cheatham motioned. "You prefer the dresser against that wall instead of nearer the window?"

Hearing a sliver of displeasure in her voice, Rebekah hastened to explain. "I spend several hours a day practicing, and I enjoy looking outside when I play. It helps to break the monotony. But if you'd prefer, I'll happily move it—"

"No, no. It's your room, Miss Carrington. You may arrange the furniture as you see fit."

"Thank you, Mrs. Cheatham."

The woman moved toward the bank of windows, the lamp's illumination dancing off the darkened panes. Rebekah watched her, sensing something amiss but at a loss as to what it might be.

"Your performance tonight was exquisite, Miss Carrington. My guests were quite enthralled." She glanced back. "Though, no doubt, you're already aware of that, judging by their applause."

Rebekah warmed at the compliment. "I'm glad they were pleased. I remember you stating your preference for music when hosting dinner guests. And when I realized the ensemble had concluded, then saw the musicians coming downstairs—"

A single dark eyebrow rose in a perfect arch, and Rebekah realized what she'd foolishly admitted.

Her smile took effort this time. "I saw the musicians because . . . I was standing just inside the hallway." She gestured toward the closed door. "I simply wanted to watch the guests as they left. Everyone looked so lovely."

Mrs. Cheatham stared. "Continue," she said softly.

"After the musicians came downstairs"— Rebekah decided not to mention having seen her employer frown—"I thought how pleased you would be if your guests departed to Mozart instead of the squeaky wheels of the carriages. So . . . I sneaked upstairs. But no one saw me," she said quickly. "I made certain of that."

Mrs. Cheatham smiled and returned her gaze to the darkness beyond the window. "Mozart's 'Rondo alla turca.' A most ambitious choice. And one masterfully executed."

Rebekah let out a breath, the tension inside her easing. "Thank you, ma'am. I'm so glad you're pleased."

"*Pleased* isn't exactly the word I would use in this instance, Miss Carrington." Mrs. Cheatham turned back, her smile fading. "Don't misunderstand me. Your skill is exemplary. You play with a passion that runs deep, yet with a tenderness that touches the furthest corners of one's heart. Which makes what you did tonight . . . especially perilous for me."

Rebekah frowned. "Perilous? I . . . I don't understand."

"Your behavior tonight has exposed me to risk, Miss Carrington. Risk I neither sanctioned nor welcome. You see, after you finished playing, after the silence returned only to be filled with thunderous applause, after everyone fawned over how we *'saved the best talent for last,'* my guests demanded to know the identity of the master violinist. Including Maestro Whitcomb. So you see, Miss Carrington, if your attempt was to please me, you fell *woefully* short of your mark."

Rebekah stared, her joy quickly souring, replaced with a dread that tasted like ash on her tongue. She swallowed. If she lost this job—

Suddenly, all she could see was Barton Ledbetter. All she could feel was the man's hands on her and how he—

"Mrs. Cheatham, I assure you, I believed with my whole heart that you would be pleased. It never occurred to me that what I did might reflect poorly on you. If I'd thought for one moment that—"

"But that's the problem, my dear. You didn't think. You made the decision in an instant. With emotion as your guide, instead of logic." With a sigh, Mrs. Cheatham placed the lamp on a side table. "While I do believe you wanted to please me, I believe the overwhelming motivation behind your actions this evening was to prove a point to Maestro Whitcomb. The man said no to your audition, and that hurt you. Deeply. So you wanted to show him up, so to speak. Prove you could play, even perform, as well as any man."

Mrs. Cheatham leveled her gaze, her blue eyes unwavering in their appraisal. "Would you care to contradict me on that point?"

Rebekah broke out in a cold sweat and felt herself growing smaller inside, even as a shrill voice cried out from deep down that Mrs. Cheatham was wrong, that her reasons for playing had been completely innocent, even altruistic, and that Nathaniel Whitcomb had absolutely nothing to do with her decision to—

But truth tightened Rebekah's chest and only grew stronger as it surfaced, suffocating the smaller, less honest voice, until every other reason for why she'd done what she did fell stone-cold silent—

Except for the truth.

"You're right," Rebekah whispered, shame—and fear—adding a quiver to her voice. "I cannot contradict you. What Mr. Whitcomb did and said hurt me, and most definitely entered into my decision. But please believe me, Mrs. Cheatham. In that moment, as I was preparing to play for your guests, my most conscious thought *was* of how pleased you would be. And also of"—she blinked back tears, her voice tightening—"how wonderful it would be . . . to be heard."

For the longest moment, Mrs. Cheatham held her

gaze. And the longer she did, the more Rebekah's throat ached. Finally, Mrs. Cheatham blinked and her countenance seemed to soften.

"I believe you, Miss Carrington."

Rebekah took a quick breath, a single tear slipping down before she hurriedly wiped it away.

"I can see the earnestness in your eyes even now. But what I stated earlier is also true. I know what it's like to be a woman in a world dictated by men. I know what it's like to possess certain abilities customarily attributed to a man—abilities to conduct business, for instance, or argue points of law—and then to be set at naught, to be ignored or ridiculed, simply because you are a woman who possesses those attributes."

The silence lengthened, and Rebekah realized she was shaking. Whether from the cold or the aftermath of nearly losing her job, she couldn't be sure. *If* she hadn't lost the job yet.

"Not that long ago"—Mrs. Cheatham's voice took on a softer quality—"a dear niece of mine— you'll meet her soon, I'm sure—told me that the world is changing, and with those changes are coming new opportunities for women. While Eleanor proved that statement true for herself, it came at a high cost. For her, *and* for me. In the end, it was a price I was willing to pay because . . . she is my niece. And family does not abandon family."

Clearly hearing what she was saying, Rebekah nodded. Exceptions were made for family. Of which, she was not.

"So while changes *are* coming for women, and many of those changes I welcome, you must remember, Miss Carrington, that you are an employee in my home. And while so employed, you will conduct yourself with the utmost propriety and decorum. Because your actions are a direct reflection upon me. And as much as I admire your talent, allowing a female musician to perform—even anonymously—at one of my parties is unacceptable and would be found offensive by many.

"Earlier this evening, in fact, at dinner, one of my guests, Mrs. Schaefer, questioned the maestro about his opinion regarding females participating in orchestras." Mrs. Cheatham frowned. "Mrs. Schaefer fancies herself a suffragette and is quite a vocal supporter of Susan Brownell Anthony. And while I am in full favor of women being given the vote, I do not condone some of the methods the suffragette gatherings undertake to further their goal. The end does not always justify the means, Miss Carrington."

She retrieved the lamp. "This is my home, and you're teaching my daughter. Hence . . . my ways, my rules. Do we have a clear understanding?"

Feeling worn and bruised, Rebekah nodded. "Yes, ma'am, we do. Thank you . . . for allowing me to stay on."

"You're welcome, Miss Carrington. Now I'll bid you good night." She strode toward the door.

Rebekah hurried to open it for her. "May I ask you one last question, Mrs. Cheatham?"

The woman paused, the cold air from the hallway sweeping in like an unwelcome intruder.

"How did Maestro Whitcomb respond? To the woman's question this evening."

Mrs. Cheatham gave a soft laugh. "Maestro Whitcomb deflected it, actually. With humor and skill. He committed his opinion to neither side, therefore offending none of my guests. I view it as a deliberate kindness to me on his part. Even though you and I both know where he stands on the issue."

Rebekah nodded, also knowing that Mr. Whitcomb was likely looking out for himself too. If he offended potential donors, that meant no money for the symphony. Or its new conductor. So perhaps the act was less a kindness done for Mrs. Cheatham than it was for himself. Though that was scarcely an opinion she could voice.

Mrs. Cheatham turned to go, then paused. "Every person employed here at Belmont is carefully scrutinized, Miss Carrington. The information you provided about your mother and your stepfather has been confirmed, as was the information about your recent return to the United States. It's also been confirmed that you've had no dealings with the local officials here in Nashville, nor in Vienna."

Rebekah felt her eyes widen.

"I share this with you because, although I don't know what it is, my intuition tells me that you're running from something. Or more likely hiding."

Concern deepened the woman's expression. "I have entrusted the care of my daughter's musical education to you, and in doing so, I am allowing you to have a relationship with one of the most precious people in my life. I need to be assured that the young woman now living in my home, spending four hours a day with my daughter, is of unquestionable character and has Pauline's best interests at heart."

Tender steel threaded the woman's tone, and again, Rebekah felt her throat tighten with emotion. "I pledge to you, Mrs. Cheatham, I do have your daughter's best interests at heart. I'll teach her well, and I won't do anything to bring reproach upon you or your household. I give you my word."

Mrs. Cheatham nodded, then looked beyond Rebekah to the bedroom. "Another young woman, not so unlike yourself, once occupied this room while employed as my personal assistant. As it turned out, she was *not* what she appeared to be upon first impression."

Rebekah winced. "I take it . . . that young woman is no longer in your employ."

Adelicia Cheatham's smile came slowly, if not almost with pleasure. "She most decidedly is *not*. One might say that life took Claire in a . . . very different direction. Rest well, Miss Carrington."

11

Would it help if I massaged your shoulders, Maestro?"

Tate paused, pen in hand, and looked up, irritated by the continued interruptions while also not believing what he'd just heard. "I beg your pardon?"

Smiling coyly, Miss Caroline Endicott skirted around to his side of the desk. "You seem . . . rather tense, Maestro. And Papa said that as your new assistant, I need to do everything I can to make you comfortable and to"—she squinted as though the act of thinking demanded her entire focus—"foster an environment in which you are able to create and fulfill your duties to the symphony."

Tate sighed and laid aside his pen. *Miss Endicott, your presence in this office over the past two days has made it the very antithesis of a creative environment,* is what he wanted to say to the young woman. But since her father was on the symphony board and had recently made a substantial donation—hence, securing for his daughter the coveted position of "personal assistant to the conductor"—he managed a smile.

She was trying her best, he knew. Problem was, her best was sorely trying his patience, and the frustrating orchestra rehearsal from earlier that morning wasn't helping either.

The odd collection of amateurs, college professors, and music teachers—most of whom thought they knew more than he did—made conducting nearly impossible. He felt more like a ringmaster in a circus than someone trained at Oberlin and Peabody.

The orchestra wasn't *horrible*. At times, they came close to sounding good. But they still had so far to go. Because good wasn't good enough. Which reminded him . . .

He must ask Mrs. Cheatham again if she had discovered who serenaded them on the violin at her house that evening. The woman had claimed having no responsibility for the event and had honestly seemed as surprised as he'd been. But enlisting the talent of such a violinist would make an enormous contribution to the orchestra. To have such a soloist to perform. A conductor's dream.

Sensing Miss Endicott's growing impatience, Tate did his best to mask his own. "Miss Endicott, as I attempted to explain to you on Monday, I need to concentrate. And concentration requires a quiet, uninterrupted setting. So if you would—"

Before he knew it, she'd slipped behind his chair and began kneading his shoulder and neck muscles.

A knock sounded on the partially open door.

"Excuse me, Maestro Whit—" Mrs. Bixby's eyes widened as she entered the office. "Oh, I'm sorry for interrupting. I—"

"*Please* come in, Mrs. Bixby." Tate stood and

effectively removed himself from Miss Endicott's grip. But in the process, he knocked a stack of sheet music to the floor. The pages scattered in disarray. Frustration mounting, he wondered if he would have to go back home in order to get anything done.

"You're not interrupting, Mrs. Bixby. My door is always open to you."

The older woman approached timidly, envelope in hand. "A letter just arrived from Mr. Pennington, Maestro. I knew you'd want to see it straightaway."

She handed it to him. He read it—and literally felt the pressure building inside of him. The director of the symphony board requested a meeting. And this, after receiving the latest report from the architect responsible for building the new opera house. That never boded well. And would bode even worse if Mrs. Bixby mentioned to anyone what she'd just witnessed. Not that he thought she would.

Tate tossed the letter on his desk. "Mr. Pennington will be stopping by today, Mrs. Bixby. Show him in when he arrives."

"Yes, sir. Of course, sir."

"And leave the door open as you go," Tate added, noting the sideways glance Mrs. Bixby gave the younger woman as she departed.

Hearing the shuffle of paper, he turned to see Miss Endicott picking up the strewn pages of sheet music.

A quizzical expression lit her face, and she paused and held up a page of the orchestral score he'd been writing—or attempting to write. "Can you really read all of these notes at the same time? And then make them come together?"

Tate looked at her, certain he could hear the strain of tiny little wheels inside her brain. But since she was his assistant, and he *did* need help . . .

"Every instrument has its part, Miss Endicott. And it's the conductor's responsibility to bring them all together and make them one. It's about timing, and rhythm, knowing the sum of the parts so well that their integration—what's being played and what's yet to be played—almost becomes like breathing. When walking down a familiar street, for instance, a person doesn't have to consciously think about drawing each breath while also maintaining his balance as he places one foot in front of the other while he also converses with a friend. He simply . . . walks and talks. It's much the same for a conductor."

She gazed up at him. "You're *such* a gifted man, Maestro."

Seeing her doe-eyed look, Tate knew she hadn't heard a word he'd said. But he had an idea that might prove her presence helpful after all, while also keeping her hands otherwise occupied. "You said you play the piano, did you not?"

She blinked. "Yes, sir . . . I do."

"Very well." He held out his hand, and she relinquished the sheet music. He crossed to the grand piano. It was an older instrument, but he'd recently had it tuned and it more than served for practicing. "I want you to sit here and play this opening for me. The first twelve bars. Play it, then wait until I ask you to play it again. Do you understand?"

She looked down at the piano keys, then back up at him, and nodded.

More hopeful in theory than in reality, Tate returned to his desk and picked up his pen.

He'd been working on this symphony for over a year and had only two of the four movements completed. The third was partially written, but badly, in his estimation. It lacked the soul of the music he could hear deep inside him—if he could only draw it out. He had four months, at most, to finish it. Then a month for rehearsals before the opening concert at the new opera house. Hardly a schedule for success.

With a whispered, desperate prayer, he focused. "All right, Miss Endicott . . . play."

She did. Only, the tune she played sounded nothing like what he'd written. Or at least he hoped it didn't.

"Stop, Miss Endicott." He retraced his steps and checked the sheet music. "What were you playing? Because you certainly weren't playing this."

She gazed up at him. "I . . . I play the piano, but"—she blinked—"I don't read music all that well. But once I hear something," she said quickly, "or hear it a few times, I can play it perfectly! Or close to perfect." Her expression brightened, and she scooted over on the bench. "So why don't you play it a few times, then once I learn it, *I'll* play it for *you!*"

Tate stared, the response that came to mind not suitable to say aloud, much less to a lady. He took a deep breath. Her "working" for him five days a week was out of the question. He was having trouble enough composing on his own. The music of his childhood kept intruding and all but drowning out the treasured influences of Beethoven, Bach, Pachelbel, and Mozart that he'd tried so hard to coalesce within him. "Miss Endicott, I will not—"

A knock sounded on the door again, and he turned, bracing himself for the meeting with Edward Pennington. But it was Mrs. Bixby again.

Only this time, her expression was frantic.

"Please forgive me, Maestro Whitcomb. Mrs. Adelicia Cheatham sent a wagon for the last remaining trunk, but the trunk's too heavy for the driver to lift on his own." Her words spilled out one atop the other. "Now the driver says he's leaving and that Mrs. Cheatham *will not* be pleased if he doesn't bring it with him. I don't know what to do. I couldn't find anyone else. Would *you* please come and help him lift the trunk into the wagon, sir?"

Tate's breath left him, part laugh, part sigh, though he felt not a shred of humor. "*What* trunk are you referring to, Mrs. Bixby? And why did Mrs. Cheatham leave it here?"

The older woman wrung her hands. "It doesn't belong to Mrs. Cheatham, sir. It belongs to her governess, the young woman who was here last week. Oh, sir, please come quickly. I don't wish to anger a woman like Mrs. Cheatham."

"Her governess? Do you mean . . ." But Tate didn't finish the sentence, fearing Mrs. Bixby might implode on the spot, and already having a good idea to whom she was referring. He strode to the door, then remembered and glanced back. "That will be all for today, Miss Endicott. Thank you."

The young woman rose, nursing an injured look. "But I'm supposed to spend the entire day here. Helping you!"

Undeterred, Tate took a backward step. "Which is quite generous. But I won't require your assistance on Tuesday or Wednesday afternoons. Or on Thursdays and Fridays at all," he added quickly, knowing he would likely hear from her father on the issue. "So I'll see you again on Monday morning. Good day, Miss Endicott!"

Not waiting for the argument her pouty lower lip promised was forthcoming, Tate caught up to Mrs. Bixby, who was already halfway down the hall. "You said the trunk belongs to—"

"Miss Carrington, a young woman whom Mrs. Murphey directed to the advertised governess position at the Belmont estate. Miss Carrington sent her trunks with a note asking that I hold them for her. Which, despite Mrs. Murphey's resistance,

I was happy to do. Then the next thing I know, Mrs. Cheatham herself sends word requesting that the trunks be sent to Belmont. So the young woman must have been awarded the position!"

So *that's* why Miss Carrington was at Belmont. She was the children's governess. Tate could well imagine her in that role. Yet he could still hear her playing the oboe as she had that day in his office. Such control and emotion. Every note precise.

"The wagon's right outside that door." Mrs. Bixby gestured.

Tate strode ahead and opened the back entryway to see a wagon, driver on the bench, reins in hand.

"Hold up!" Tate called, a cold wind rushing in. "I'll help you with the trunk."

The driver looked back, and his already perturbed expression became more so. "I got to pick up another shipment 'cross town for Mrs. Cheatham. She said she had to have whatever that is *today,* and that place closes soon."

Tate met his glare. "It won't take us long to load this. And like I said, I'll help."

The driver gave the lever at his side a hard shove and set the brake.

"The trunk is just inside here," Mrs. Bixby instructed.

Waiting as the driver climbed down from his perch, Tate glanced beside him. "Mrs. Bixby," he whispered, "what you witnessed back in the office . . . I promise you, it was completely—"

"Innocent, Maestro. Rest assured, I know that

full well. I'm getting up in age, and most folks think I don't notice such things, but I do. I have a strong sense about people, and in the first moments of meeting Miss Endicott, I became fully convinced she was a *coquette*."

Tate blinked, surprised—and impressed. "Mrs. Bixby!"

"I know I look sweet, Maestro. And I guess I am, compared to Mrs. Murphey." She winked. "But she and I are apples that fell from the same orchard. Granted, mine fell a year or two later than hers, and from a more appealing branch."

Wanting to hug the woman, Tate settled for a wink instead.

Once inside, the driver took one end of the trunk and Tate took the other. They lifted, and Tate quickly realized why the man had threatened to leave it behind. What did Miss Carrington have packed in there? Anvils?

When they reached the wagon, they hefted the trunk to the back bed—when Tate felt a sharp pain in his ears. The world fell silent. All sound vanished. Then, almost as quickly, came flooding back again. His head spinning, Tate lost his grip on the trunk, and the corner hit the edge of the wagon. The trunk tipped and the top came open.

Momentum took over and books and papers flew everywhere. The luggage landed in an upside-down heap on the ground.

Mrs. Bixby gasped. "Oh, my gracious!"

The driver cursed. "It weren't my fault! And I

ain't got time to wait 'til this is cleaned up. I'll be back for it tomorrow."

"Oh no!" Mrs. Bixby reached for him. "You must take it today!"

Tate's equilibrium quickly returned, and he blinked to clear his head. This episode wasn't nearly as bad as the one at the Cheathams' house the other night. Still . . . Somehow, he had to get more rest.

He glanced at the mess at his feet, then bent to pick up a file still intact, bound with a leather cord. Papers peeked from the edges, and when he realized what was within, he felt the hint of a smile. "Not to worry, Mrs. Bixby. I'll deliver this to Belmont myself."

"As long as your other duties would in no way interfere with Pauline's lessons—four hours a day, five days a week, as we agreed—then I have no issue with your seeking additional employment." Mrs. Cheatham briefly glanced down at the files on her desk. "But I do care deeply about *what* other employment you seek. And please assure me you're *not* planning on opening a cafe, or restaurant, or some other such rogue undertaking."

Rebekah looked across the desk. "I can assure you, opening a cafe is nowhere in my future. I hardly know how to cook."

"Music to my ears." Mrs. Cheatham gave a little half smile, then eyed Rebekah across steepled hands. "So tell me . . . How is Pauline progressing? What is your opinion on her level of skill with the violin at this juncture?"

Rebekah smiled at her intensity. "We've only had four lessons thus far, so I hesitate to predict what her propensity will be. That will be revealed with time and observation. But I do find your daughter most enthusiastic about the prospect of playing the instrument." Rebekah hesitated to share her next thought, however true it was.

"Come, Miss Carrington. We shall have no secrets between us regarding my daughter. Say whatever is on your mind. I value straightforwardness in people, and most certainly in my employees."

Rebekah hated the fact that she was so easily read. She needed to work on that. "Pauline is a very spirited young girl, Mrs. Cheatham. And I believe part of her desire in learning to play the violin lies in the fact that, for a female, playing the violin is considered rather . . ."

"Gratuitous?"

Rebekah couldn't help but laugh. "*Bold* is what I was going to say, ma'am. But I suppose, in most people's minds, your description fits far better."

Mrs. Cheatham smiled, and it was a lovely thing to behold, so different from the first time Rebekah met her. The woman had to be in her fifties, yet she was radiant, still endowed with a measure of beauty customarily reserved for more youthful women. A sense of wisdom and grace surrounded her as well, one that only came with age—and that certainly didn't come to all.

For some reason, thinking about Mrs. Cheatham in this way made her think of her own mother. She'd mailed a letter to home, informing her mother that she was still in town and had secured employment. Rebekah had also promised to visit in the near future. But she hadn't revealed to her mother where she was staying. Because she wouldn't put it past either her or Barton Ledbetter to show up unannounced at Belmont and demand she return home.

Something that would *not* be happening.

"As I shared with you yesterday, Miss Carrington, it is imperative Pauline be ready for the girls' spring recital in May. That is the primary reason you are here. You mentioned challenging her with more complicated music. Have you done that yet?"

Rebekah shook her head. "But as soon as my music trunk arrives, I will. And I'll be sure to let you know the outcome."

"The trunk should arrive today. I sent a driver for it." Mrs. Cheatham rose and crossed the small library to the hearth. She stretched her hands toward the fire, and the crackle of wood succumbing to flame filled the silence.

"What was *your* motivating factor in learning to play the violin, Miss Carrington? I doubt anyone was standing in the wings encouraging you to play that instrument."

"Actually, there was someone." The words were out before Rebekah fully considered them, and they tore at the still-recent wound. How could she share with Adelicia Cheatham about Demetrius, about what he'd meant to her? She couldn't. A woman like Mrs. Cheatham would never understand.

Rebekah only hoped, as she had so many times in recent days, that Demetrius had known how much his life, his generosity, had changed the course of hers. Feeling Mrs. Cheatham's continued attention, she hurried to expound.

"It was my father," she answered, still truthful. "When I was a young girl, he let me accompany him to hear the occasional visiting symphony. It was magical," she said softly. "Not only that he considered it important enough to take me with him, but the way I felt walking along with my arm tucked into the crook of his. For as long as I can remember, he'd told me that God had planted the love of music in my heart."

Warmth filled Mrs. Cheatham's expression. "There's nothing like a father's love for his daughter, and hers for him."

Rebekah sensed a deeper undercurrent in Mrs. Cheatham's comment, one she understood well. "My mother, however, wasn't in favor of my father taking me there, nor of my learning to play. She felt it was . . . *gratuitous*"—she gave a knowing smile—"a foolish indulgence for a daughter, one that would never come to any good."

Mrs. Cheatham turned toward the window, the panes icy with frost. "Almost as powerful as a father's love . . . is the knife of a mother's disappointment. Thankfully, to some extent, and with time, the former helps to overshadow the latter."

Rebekah stared, unable to see her employer's face and equally unable to imagine a mother not being proud of such a daughter as Adelicia Cheatham. Strange as it was though, it heartened her to know that Mrs. Cheatham had apparently shared her experience in regard to parental favor— and the lack thereof.

But it pained her more than she could say to think of carrying the weight of her mother's disappointment for years to come. Not to mention how her mother must feel toward her now, since her daughter had left home during the wee hours that morning. Rebekah had promised Delphia she would be in touch soon, and she intended to keep that vow.

"Pardon me, Missus Cheatham. You ready for your tea service, ma'am?"

Rebekah turned to see Cordina in the doorway and hoped the woman had made tea cakes again. They were addictive little delicacies, and it had been a while since lunch.

"Yes, Cordina. Thank you." Mrs. Cheatham returned to her seat.

Cordina poured the tea and handed the first cup to Mrs. Cheatham, then paused. "You gettin' one of them head pains again, ma'am? The neuralgia?"

Mrs. Cheatham gently rubbed her temple. "How

is it that you know it's coming on almost before I do?"

Cordina shook her head. "They's comin' more often these days, it seems. Want me to send for the doctor?"

"No, I'll be fine. It will pass."

Rebekah leaned forward. "My mother suffers from head pain on occasion. She takes a powder from the doctor. I could go into town for you, if you'd like, and get some."

"Oh, Missus Cheatham's doctor give her some already." Cordina handed Rebekah a cup of tea. "I'll go fetch a powder for you, Missus Cheatham. Be right back."

Rebekah noticed Mrs. Cheatham didn't argue. She also noticed . . . no tea cakes.

They sipped their tea in silence, Rebekah feeling as though, over the past few moments, she'd been given a glimpse into an Adelicia Cheatham not seen by many. And she felt . . . honored.

"Tutoring other children." Mrs. Cheatham placed her teacup and saucer on the desk, the pain evident in her eyes. "I'm *certain* there are parents who would pay for your services in tutoring their children on the oboe. I'm willing to pen some notes to determine interest, if you'd like."

"Thank you, Mrs. Cheatham. I'd be most grateful for that." Although tutoring other children wouldn't fulfill her heart's desire, she was certainly equipped for it. However . . . "There's one problem. I don't have transportation. I don't mind walking in the least. I enjoy it, actually. But the time spent walking to and from town will greatly decrease my time available to teach."

"You're welcome to make use of a carriage while you're here, Miss Carrington. Or if you ride . . ." Mrs. Cheatham paused, question in her expression.

Rebekah nodded. "I do."

"Then you may take a horse. There are plenty of both."

"Again, I'm so grateful. But I wouldn't feel right about doing that without paying, Mrs. Cheatham."

"Well, yes, of course. That's understood. But not to worry, I'll figure out an arrangement that's equitable to us both."

Rebekah smiled and nodded, hoping her surprise didn't register too vividly on her face. But judging by the momentary gleam in Mrs. Cheatham's eyes, she knew it had.

"I got your medicine for you, ma'am." Cordina bustled back into the room, unfolded the medicinal paper, and sprinkled the white powder into Mrs. Cheatham's tea. "You got a guest too, Missus Cheatham. Mr. Whitcomb just arrived. Says he brought a trunk with him that belongs to Miss Carrington here."

Rebekah turned and looked behind her at the closed door that led directly into the entrance hall, then at the second door that led from the library through the family dining room and into the grand salon. The second was most definitely her first choice.

"How opportune!" Mrs. Cheatham drank the last of her tea. "We were speaking about that trunk only moments ago. Please show him in, Cordina."

Rebekah stood. "I'll leave so you can meet with him alone, Mrs. Cheatham. I'm sure you and Mr. Whitcomb have much to discuss."

"I desire that you stay, Miss Carrington." Mrs. Cheatham gave her a pointed look. "At the very least, I'm certain you'll want to thank the maestro for personally delivering your trunk. And even if appreciation is not foremost in your thoughts, I believe in facing one's challenges square on. It makes us stronger. Be those challenges situations . . . or people."

Rebekah swallowed and sat down again, believing she'd faced enough challenges recently. Yet she could hardly refuse. Hearing footsteps behind her, she felt her guard rising. And she couldn't decide which irked her more—having to show gratitude to Nathaniel Whitcomb after he'd been so *un*gracious to her . . .

Or actually having to call the man *maestro* to his face.

P lease join us, Maestro Whitcomb." Adelicia Cheatham gestured.

Tate claimed the chair to the right of Miss Carrington, not missing the passing look the young woman gave him, which held equal parts dislike and resentment. It was unfortunate, how their acquaintance began. Especially considering what he'd come to ask her.

All the way here, he'd tried to think of a way he could get back into her good graces. But there was only one thing Miss Carrington wanted from him. And it was something he could not grant her.

"Miss Carrington and I were enjoying a pot of tea, Maestro. Would you care for a cup?"

"Yes, Mrs. Cheatham, I would. Thank you for your hospitality."

Mrs. Cheatham poured. "Do you take milk and sugar?"

"Neither, thank you." He looked to his left again. "How are you today, Miss Carrington?"

"I'm well, thank you . . . *Maestro* Whitcomb. And you?"

Tate couldn't help but smile. She'd practically had to force the title out, like shoving a button through a slit sewn too small. "I'm still a little chilly at the moment. But I'm well also. Thank you for asking."

She turned her attention back to her cup of tea and, despite the warmth from the hearth, Tate felt a chill—coming from about two feet away. Considering the young woman's aloofness, convincing her to accept his offer seemed next to impossible.

"So tell me, Maestro"—Mrs. Cheatham leaned back in the desk chair—"what brings you to

Belmont? Other than to deliver Miss Carrington's trunk, a task which falls decidedly outside the scope of your responsibilities."

"You know as well as I do, Mrs. Cheatham, that the boundaries of a conductor's responsibilities alter according to the needs of the symphony's most generous donors."

He raised his teacup in silent salute and drank, looking up in time to catch what appeared to be a silent exchange between the women.

Miss Carrington shifted in her chair. "Thank you, sir, for bringing my trunk all the way out here. That was . . . very kind of you."

Tate marveled at how genuine the young woman's behavior could appear when she deemed it necessary—if not for her eyes. Her eyes revealed all. "You're most welcome, Miss Carrington. It's my pleasure. May I also extend my congratulations to you on your new position here as governess. I failed to do that the other night, as I wasn't yet aware."

Miss Carrington paused midsip and, for an instant, looked like she might choke. She cleared her throat. "Actually, sir, I'm . . . not the governess. That position was already filled by the time I applied. I'm tutoring Pauline, Mrs. Cheatham's daughter . . . in music."

She cut a quick glance at Mrs. Cheatham, whose serene countenance revealed nothing. Yet he heard a definite note of caution in Miss Carrington's voice.

Then it hit him—was Miss Carrington worried about him mentioning something about her audition with the symphony to Mrs. Cheatham? He'd never reveal such a thing, for both their sakes. If word ever got out that he'd even allowed a woman to audition—which he hadn't, not technically. She'd simply begun to play—he'd be out of a job and on his way back east before he knew what happened to him.

"Tutoring, in music." He nodded, looking from her to Mrs. Cheatham, then back again, and he quickly realized he couldn't say anything about her playing the oboe because the only reason he knew about that was the audition. Treacherous waters, these. So best he tread carefully. "Well, congratulations again, Miss Carrington. I think it's important that every child have an opportunity to learn about music. Because children grow up. And, hopefully, they'll attend the symphony one day, and then, for my sake, at least"—he laughed softly—"they'll eventually come to support it."

"Hear, hear! Maestro." Mrs. Cheatham lifted her teacup in his direction. "Well said."

He glanced at Miss Carrington, but after the briefest of smiles, she averted her eyes and, therefore, kept her thoughts to herself.

But at least one hurdle he'd anticipated was out of the way. She was a music tutor in this household, not a governess, which meant a great deal more of her time should be open to use at her discretion. And he knew just how she could use it.

"So tell me . . ." Mrs. Cheatham quickly filled the silence while pouring him another cup of tea. "How is your symphony progressing? I trust you're finding the time to compose amidst all else?"

His grip tightened around the delicate china cup. "I am. It's taking more time than I first imagined. But . . . the piece is coming along well."

"Splendid! That's wonderful news." Mrs. Cheatham smiled approvingly. "I'm eager to hear it."

He tried to mirror her enthusiasm but fell short. Because *well* was a relative term considering his progress to date. Yet what else could he say to the woman? Her expectations were high, as were those of the symphony board. As were his own. After all, he wasn't writing this symphony solely for the opening concert at the new hall.

At the heart of his endeavor was his desire to honor the man who'd first started him down this road. The man who had believed in him long before he'd ever believed in himself.

But regardless which motivation drove him at any given time—and they both did—time was running out.

"I presume"—query tinged Mrs. Cheatham's tone, pulling Tate's focus back—"that Mr. Pennington was in touch with you earlier today?"

"Actually, no." He set the teacup on a side table. "He sent word that he wanted to meet, and I waited until finally leaving to come here. But he never came by."

"Well, I'm certain he'll be in touch soon enough."

Something in Mrs. Cheatham's expression didn't ring quite true, and Tate felt an alarm go off inside him. "Do you happen to know what he wants to discuss with me?"

Mrs. Cheatham's hesitance immediately answered the question.

"In fact, I do know, Maestro, as Mr. Pennington and I visited yesterday afternoon. But since he's the board director, he should probably be the one to tell you the good news."

Tate felt his spine go stiff. Edward Pennington's note hadn't had an air of "good news" about it. And he was familiar enough with Mrs. Cheatham's persuasive powers to know that the woman could wrap a dead skunk in silk and lace and pass it off as a mink.

"In his note," Tate began, sensing Miss Carrington's attention, "Mr. Pennington indicated he'd received the latest report from the architect. So I assume this has something to do with the new opera house."

Adelicia Cheatham delicately firmed her lips. "That's correct, Maestro. And . . ." She sighed. "Oh, I suppose I *could* go ahead and tell you since you're here. Then you and Mr. Pennington can work out the details as you both see fit." She withdrew a file from the bottom of a stack of folders on her desk but didn't open it. "Mr. Geoffrey, the architect, and husband to my niece,

Eleanor," she added with obvious pride, "informed us yesterday that the project is moving along quite smoothly. So much so that he estimates the hall to be completed an entire month earlier than expected."

Tate's heart rate kicked up about five notches. Surely she didn't mean—

"So I'm happy to report that we have the opportunity to host the opening concert earlier than planned."

"*May* instead of June? That is completely unacceptable." Tate rose from his chair, suddenly feeling caged and needing to move. "With all respect, Mrs. Cheatham, it's impossible for my orchestra to be ready in that time frame. I don't think anyone grasps the measure of work there is in . . ." He took a breath, telling himself to calm down. But the idea that someone could make a decision that so greatly affected his area of responsibility, without even contacting him . . . "You should have heard the orchestra at rehearsal this morning. To say there's room for improvement is being overly kind. The woodwinds kept coming in a bar late, and those that didn't were flat. The horns couldn't keep tempo, which threw off the clarinets, and the violin section is a disaster. The first violin played sharp thirteen times. *Thirteen!* And he's my concertmaster!"

He blew out a breath, hearing the anger in his voice, a realization helped along by noting the intense disfavor in Mrs. Cheatham's expression and the utter disbelief in Miss Carrington's.

Mrs. Cheatham leveled her gaze. "Are you quite finished, Maestro?"

Again, Tate sighed. "I am. And please forgive me, Mrs. Cheatham, for speaking so freely. The past few weeks"—*and years,* he thought to himself—"have exacted a cost."

"One which, I trust, can be recovered from."

Hearing the not-so-subtle challenge in her tone, he nodded. "Yes, Mrs. Cheatham, most certainly it can be. And will be . . . with time and focus. And by my completing this symphony."

"I appreciate that assurance and would ask, Maestro, that you take this next bit of counsel under advisement as you would from a friend." Her smile reached her eyes. "Perhaps a way to increase your time would be to cease taking so many out-of-town trips, guest conducting on the weekends, as you've been doing. Yes, it increases awareness of the new opera house and what we're doing here, but it appears that your time would be far better spent on first priorities."

The comment stung more than he would've expected, and for reasons that Adelicia Cheatham couldn't begin to fathom. Which was the only thing that kept his anger from resurfacing. "I appreciate that counsel, Mrs. Cheatham, and will certainly . . . take it under advisement."

Not so much embarrassed as he was frustrated, he sneaked a look at Miss Carrington, and their eyes met. He would have given much to read her mind at the moment. Because not a trace of dislike or resentment lingered about her now. A keen watchfulness framed her lovely face, replacing the disbelief from moments earlier.

Tate suddenly remembered the mystery still needing to be solved. "By chance, Mrs. Cheatham, have you discovered the name of the violinist who performed the final Mozart piece at your party? Perhaps you checked your guest list and, through the process of elimination, derived the name of the gentleman. I can assure you that adding such talent to the orchestra would be a phenomenal boon to us all."

Mrs. Cheatham's gaze never wavered from his. "I fear I have no gentleman's name to give you, Maestro. As I told you that night, I was as surprised by the performance as you were. And because you found no one when you went upstairs, I am of the opinion that the individual prefers to remain anonymous." Her quick smile seemed to act as a bookend to the subject. "Now . . . as I said earlier, Maestro Whitcomb, Mr. Pennington and I met yesterday, and he informed me that the assistant position you requested has been fulfilled."

Tate gave a humorless laugh. "Indeed, it has been. And if this *assistant* continues to help me the way she has this week, not only will I never finish this symphony, I seriously think only one of us will be alive come June. And I know it will be her. Because she will have talked me to death."

Mrs. Cheatham's laughter was abrupt but swiftly

contained. "Remind me, if you would, who was awarded the position."

Tate cast a look at Miss Carrington, not wishing to speak out of turn.

"It's all right, Maestro. Rebekah Carrington is completely trustworthy. Otherwise, she wouldn't be in my employ."

Rebekah. So *that* was her Christian name. Thinking back, he *did* recollect she'd told him her name that day in the office. He simply hadn't been paying close enough attention. "It's Harold Endicott's daughter."

An emotion flashed across Mrs. Cheatham's face that looked akin to mirth. "I see. . . ."

"You find this amusing, Mrs. Cheatham?"

"In truth, yes, a little." Her eyes sparkled. "And yet, also . . . no." Her expression sobered. "I understand the importance of having an assistant, Maestro Whitcomb. And the even greater blessing of having that person become like an extension of yourself. So . . . we must find that person for you."

It took everything within him not to look over at Rebekah Carrington in that moment. But, oh, he wanted to. Because already knowing what he knew about her, combined with what he'd seen in that trunk—the collection of bound notebook after notebook filled with music, entire symphonies she'd transcribed in perfect penmanship and notation, her initials, REC, revealing the authorship, as if the trunk's ownership hadn't already—

he was certain he'd found the perfect assistant.

Never mind the fact the woman could scarcely look at him, much less stand to be in the same room with him for more than five minutes.

She'd copied Haydn, Beethoven, Mozart, and Chopin in painstaking detail. For the experience, he supposed, learning their patterns, their methods, same as he'd done. And apparently she held a special appreciation for a certain Maestro Heilig's work. Because she'd also copied numerous sonatas, cantatas, and concertos composed by him.

But he had no idea how to broach the subject with her without simply asking outright, which wouldn't end well—that was guaranteed.

Movement outside the window caught his eye, and he turned to see what it was. As he did, he caught the pointed look Mrs. Cheatham leveled in Miss Carrington's direction. Then, thanks—or perhaps, not—to the mirror over the mantel, he saw equally strong objection darkening Rebekah's expression.

If that didn't confirm the young woman's true feelings on the matter, the firm shake of her head did.

Not wanting to let on that he'd seen, Tate looked out the window to find twilight settling over the estate. On the distant horizon, a flock of geese flew in formation against the dusky purple sky, their distinctive honking barely distinguishable. He wondered where they were headed, and if the destination would be as they had imagined once they arrived.

He shook his head inwardly at the frivolous thought, grateful no one else could hear it.

"Maestro Whitcomb?"

Hearing his name, Tate turned to find Mrs. Cheatham staring at him, rather intensely. "I'm sorry, ma'am. Did you say something?"

"Indeed, I did. Though you apparently weren't listening." Mrs. Cheatham turned purposefully in her chair and gave him a look similar to the one she'd given Rebekah. Only this time, it had a conspiratorial quality to it. "I asked you, Maestro, precisely what qualities you're looking for in an assistant."

He stared for a beat, and it occurred to him that, the way Mrs. Cheatham was turned, Rebekah likely hadn't seen that look. Then it registered with him what Mrs. Cheatham was attempting to do. And why she was doing it. She had a great deal invested in the new opera house—and in him. She was one of his biggest supporters.

So, in essence, she was protecting her investment. And he had no choice but to take all the help he could get.

He reclaimed his seat and sighed as though giving the question extensive thought. "Ideally, Mrs. Cheatham, my assistant needs to be someone who is accomplished at playing an instrument. The piano, for instance. Or the flute. Or even . . . the oboe." He glanced at Rebekah but didn't dare linger. "And he—or *she*—would need to read music well, and be able to transcribe. They must also express themselves with great economy. I find incessant talking a vexation to the spirit."

He guessed Rebekah hadn't uttered more than fifty words since he'd walked into the room. Which, when compared to Caroline Endicott, made her seem almost mute.

"And finally," he continued, "my assistant needs to appreciate the difficulty of composing while also possessing the ability to tell me when something doesn't sound right, or when they believe it could be better. I value honesty in a person, and their ability to collaborate. I seek someone who will speak their mind, who will feel comfortable sharing their own ideas. Yet who, in the end, will accept my final decision without question or rancor."

Silence, heavy and thick, filled every inch of the library.

After a long moment, Rebekah Carrington turned to him. "You don't expect much, do you, Maestro Whitcomb?"

Not surprising, he found a hint of sarcasm in her eyes that matched the subtle color of her tone.

"I do expect a lot, Miss Carrington. But I don't expect anything from others that I do not demand of myself." Knowing the masquerade was all but over, he owned up to the moment. "I admit, I came here today with the express purpose of asking you to be my assistant."

She frowned. "Me? Why would you think of me?"

"Because . . ." He actually felt his face heat. "When the driver and I were lifting your trunk onto the wagon, it slipped. And fell open."

She sat forward, her expression turning panicked. "Are my—"

He held up a hand. "Everything is intact. It's not as you packed it, of course. And you'll find some of the pages a little worse for wear. But nothing was lost, I assure you." He glanced at Mrs. Cheatham and sensed her silently urging him on. "Picking up the notebooks, I couldn't help but notice what was within. It was . . . exquisite. You're a gifted woman, Miss Carrington." Not to mention, she'd been an avid concertgoer—in Europe! The woman had apparently lived in Vienna, judging by the number of symphony playbills she'd kept as mementoes.

Vienna, Austria. The home of Wolfgang Amadeus Mozart himself. Who better than this woman to be his assistant?

Miss Carrington's eyes narrowed slightly, and he wondered if she was thinking back to that day in his office when he'd said no to something she'd obviously desired a great deal.

"I appreciate your offer, Maestro Whitcomb. But I already have a job."

Mrs. Cheatham rose. "If you'll both excuse me, I need to check with Mrs. Routh about dinner. Maestro, would you care to join us?"

Surprised that Adelicia Cheatham would give up so quickly, he felt his opportunity slipping away. "No, thank you, ma'am. The symphony calls and my small study awaits. But I appreciate your kind invitation."

"Perhaps next time, then." She inclined her head. "Thank you again, Maestro, for your dedication to your craft and to our philharmonic, fledgling though it may be. This endeavor is near and dear to my own heart, as you well know. I want nothing less than a spectacular evening to dedicate the new opera house . . . for everyone involved. Whether it be May . . . or June. This new auditorium is not only important to Nashville, it's important to this part of the country, and to its people. Because, as Miss Carrington and I were discussing just the other day, the world is changing so quickly. And we must take advantage of every opportunity that's afforded us. Would you not agree, Miss Carrington?"

Rebekah's grip noticeably tightened on the arm of her chair. She briefly bowed her head, then lifted it and nodded. "Yes . . . I would."

Mrs. Cheatham laid a gentle hand to her shoulder, then left the door ajar when she departed. Tate stared after her, not quite knowing how she'd managed it. But if he wasn't mistaken, Miss Rebekah Carrington was now his assistant. And yet . . .

Though the silence from moments earlier had been somewhat uncomfortable, it was nothing compared to the pressure building in the room now. He'd wanted to leave here with Miss Carrington's agreement to serve as his assistant, but he felt as if she'd been given no choice in the matter. Because she hadn't.

Miss Carrington rose, and he did likewise, feeling the tension roll off her in waves.

"Miss Carrington, if I could—"

"Allow me to see you out, *Maestro* Whitcomb."

She strode from the library into the entrance hall and retrieved his coat from the rack in the corner. She held it out and he quickly took it, fully believing she would've dropped it on the spot if he hadn't.

She reached to open the door, but knowing he couldn't leave with the situation between them like this, he held it closed.

"Please hear me out, Miss Carrington. That's all I ask."

Footsteps sounded from the grand salon, and they both glanced in that direction. When no one appeared, Miss Carrington turned to him.

"You do not want to work with me, Mr. Whitcomb. Such a collaboration will not produce the desired end, I assure you. And then we'll both find ourselves in trouble with Mrs. Cheatham."

"Miss Carrington, if I don't reach my desired end, my trouble will be far greater than with Mrs. Cheatham alone. And you're wrong . . . I do want to work with you." He lowered his voice. "Don't forget . . . I've heard you play. I've seen your transcribing skills. And I know that you'll give your opinion of my work without the slightest window dressing. Of that, I have no question."

He smiled in an attempt to ease the tension between them, but the stubborn set of her chin went unchanged.

"I'll pay you, of course. That's understood. And we'll work around your schedule for tutoring Mrs. Cheatham's daughter."

She reached for the doorknob. "This isn't fair," she said softly, so softly he almost didn't hear.

"No, I suppose it's not. But as someone very close to me has long said . . . life isn't always just. But God, who sees everything, *is*. And He will bring good from it."

She looked up at him, her eyes so full of disappointment, he was almost tempted to release her from the obligation. But his own needs wouldn't let him.

"Good night, Miss Carrington."

"Good night . . . *Mr.* Whitcomb."

Not begrudging her that final jab, he took his leave and climbed into the carriage waiting at the foot of the steps.

On the way home, he replayed the encounter over and over in his mind. And no matter how he looked at it, he could only see it one way. The way Rebekah Carrington saw it. He was the skunk in this scenario, and he doubted there was anything anyone could do—Mrs. Cheatham included—

to change him into a *mink* in Rebekah's eyes.

Once home and sequestered in his study, he sat at the piano and played, the fire crackling in the hearth behind him. First Mozart, then Bach, then Beethoven. He willed the music—and the inherent talent and life within it—to wash over him. To fill him until it permeated every ounce of his creativity. He didn't wish to drive out the music he'd learned to play as a boy, the music that flowed through him as surely as his ancestors' blood. He only needed to silence it, for a while. Long enough for the masterpiece he knew he was capable of writing to be given birth.

Because in the end, what was most important was the music. And despite his inability to grant Rebekah Carrington her dream, he was convinced she possessed the fire and the passion he needed in order to achieve his.

Only now, he had one month less in which to do it.

13

Tate heard footsteps in the corridor outside his office and rose from his desk. But when Mrs. Murphey walked by, continuing down the hallway, he sat back down, perturbed. He raked a hand through his hair.

Last Wednesday, when Rebekah Carrington acquiesced to becoming his assistant, he'd assumed she would start the next day. So he'd expected to see her on Thursday. Then Friday.

After she failed to show up either day, he'd sent word to her over the weekend, asking when he could expect to see her in his office. He'd been surprised by her swift response, though not by its brevity.

He'd opened the envelope addressed to him in perfectly formed script and pulled out a single sheet of stationery.

> *Dear Mr. Whitcomb,*
> *Monday.*
> > *Sincerely,*
> > *Miss Carrington*

He smiled to himself again, recounting her candor. But now it was Monday and almost one o'clock. Another day was winding away, and he had no idea when she would arrive.

Thankfully, Miss Endicott had taken her leave around noon—and had nearly taken his sanity with her. But under threat of Miss Endicott's father withdrawing his funding, the young woman would be "assisting" him on Monday and Tuesday mornings, much to his chagrin. And lack of productivity.

He returned his focus to the notes he'd made during the latest rehearsal, yet another source of frustration. He'd lost count of how many times he'd had to yell, "Anticipate!" to the wind section.

They'd come in late after nearly every rest. And the violins and violas . . .

He'd dismissed the rest of the orchestra and had kept the entire string section behind. Following rehearsal, he'd spoken with Darrow Fulton, his concertmaster, about the various issues in the sections. He found the man's excuses as flat as his playing.

Fulton had used the weather—*the weather,* Tate huffed—as his excuse for missing Mrs. Cheatham's party. Tate had told him in no uncertain terms that if he missed an event again, he'd be looking for another orchestra with which to play. In which case, Tate would be looking for a new concertmaster. Not an easy hire, nor transition, to make. Especially among his current pool of musicians, if one could call them all that.

So hopefully, the man's erratic pattern of behavior would improve.

Hearing the distant sound of a French horn playing—Mozart's French Horn Concerto No. 4, if he wasn't mistaken—Tate closed his eyes and followed along. He knew the piece well and pictured the musical notations in his mind. The concerto was beautiful, haunting in parts, and reminded him of the mountains back east. He could almost see the wispy, smoke-like clouds hovering over the forested peaks, shrouding them in mist.

The music ended, the misty mountains faded, and Tate opened his eyes.

His gaze fell to the calendar atop his desk, and he thought again of his promise to Opal that he would visit before another month had passed. Which meant he needed to head out of town again soon. *Guest conducting,* as Mrs. Cheatham had phrased it.

Her opinion on the matter was clear. But . . . the truth was, she didn't have all the facts on the matter. Nor did he desire her—or anyone else—to have them. It wasn't in his nature to hide things, so these occasional trips were becoming more difficult to—

Footsteps sounded again from down the hallway, but he didn't rise. It could well be Mrs. Murphey or Mrs. Bixby again, or one of the musicians coming to practice in one of the back rooms. But when the footsteps halted abruptly just outside, he knew.

He stood, watching, waiting for her to walk around the corner. He tugged on the sleeves of his coat, wondering why he was suddenly nervous. *She* was the one arriving—late—for her first day of work. Not him.

Yet even as he shrugged off the anticipation, he was struck by the urgency of his circumstance, and by how much he needed this collaboration to be a success.

And by how much he needed her.

Rebekah took a deep breath, only steps away from his office. All the way here in the carriage she'd been fine. Still angry over being forced into this situation, yes. But nervous? No.

So why now?

She exhaled, knowing she could do this job. Practically speaking, she already had. She'd been Maestro Heilig's assistant. Informally, of course. She hadn't been paid for the work, and she'd worked in his office in their home, not in the symphony hall. And she'd never actually helped him compose either, she'd only copied pieces for him and discussed the music with him.

Although, even then, their *discussions* were mostly her listening to him—learning, drinking in his knowledge and experience. So . . .

Her stomach did a flip. *Was* she qualified?

What if her prediction to Nathaniel Whitcomb about what would happen if this didn't work actually came true? What if they failed? And Mrs. Cheatham turned on them both? She braced a hand against the wall for support.

". . . adding such talent to the orchestra would be a phenomenal boon to us all."

Recalling what the man had said about the *anonymous* violinist who had played that evening helped calm her nerves, while provoking her ire at the same time. But to know that a man such as Nathaniel Tate Whitcomb considered her talent worthy . . . well, that meant something.

Unless he turned out to be like the majority of musicians she'd known in Vienna. Men who made secretive weekend visits to opium dens or spent late night hours imbibing special potions they swore increased their creativity and ability to play. Laudanum and morphine were most popular, she'd learned.

She'd never understood the attraction to concoctions or medications for enhancing one's playing ability or inspiring the muse. Consistent practice and communing with nature were her remedies. Without any of the aftereffects.

She pulled back her shoulders, determined. She could do this. She *would* do—

"Miss Carrington."

She nearly jumped and looked up to find him standing there. "Mr. Whitcomb!"

"Good morning, ma'am. I thought I heard footsteps."

"Yes. I . . . I was on my way to your office."

His dark hair was a bit disheveled and his blue eyes seemed especially intense. It took her little imagination to picture him atop the conductor's dais, baton slicing the air, his well-muscled shoulders filling the contours of his black coat and tails as he held his musicians' combined attention in the palm of his hand.

"Well . . ." He gestured for her to precede him. "Right this way."

She'd been in his office before. But as she walked in, it all felt new to her.

She remembered a grand piano but couldn't have said definitively where it was placed in the spacious room. And though she'd read in the

Nashville Banner about his awards and prestigious accomplishments, she didn't recall seeing the framed evidence plastered all over the walls.

She'd long held that someone who felt the need to proclaim their accomplishments so boldly must be trying to accommodate for some shortcoming.

Or perhaps it was her own jealousy, rooted in the wish that she could have the same opportunities to do all that person had done, while wondering if she would have succeeded as well. Not wishing to examine that thought any further, she tucked it away.

"May I take your cloak, Miss Carrington?"

"Yes. Thank you." She handed it to him, and noticed stacks and stacks of sheet music on a table in the corner.

He gave a one-shouldered shrug. "I'm a little behind on my filing."

Rebekah nodded, assuming that would be one of her duties. Then it occurred to her . . . "Was filing not part of Miss Endicott's responsibilities?"

His mouth tipped in a half smile. "I believe the act of filing assumes that the filer knows the alphabet. So . . . the answer to your question is no."

Knowing he was joking, she laughed, then instantly regretted it. Not only because she felt as if it gave him the upper hand—and the upper hand was something she did not want Nathaniel Whitcomb to have with her—but also because it felt a little mean. She schooled her features.

"Actually, I should tell you that Miss Endicott is still assisting me two mornings a week. As long as you understand that *assisting* can have a very broad definition. Now, please"—he gestured toward the two chairs in front of his desk—"have a seat. I thought we'd begin by discussing your experience and musical skills. There's nothing more frustrating than two people working together with different expectations."

Rebekah could think of a few things. Like working for someone for whom you didn't want to work. But for the sake of unity—what little there would be—she kept that to herself.

He leaned back in his chair, the creak of worn leather marking the gesture. "You play the piano, I assume."

"I do."

"And would you say you play well?"

Feeling as though she were being interviewed, and resenting it, Rebekah crossed the room to the piano and took her place on the bench.

Her fingers were yet a little stiff from the cold, so she rubbed them together until they warmed. Tempted to play Mozart's "Rondo alla turca," as she had the other night on the Stradivarius, she refrained. But she smiled to herself, imagining what his reaction would be if she did.

She began playing, her fingers flying across the keys.

The piece she'd chosen wasn't extremely well known, and she doubted Mr. Whitcomb would be familiar with it. But it was one of the most challenging she'd encountered. Before his untimely death, Robert Schumann, the composer, had been a colleague of Maestro Heilig's in Vienna. Hence, she'd become familiar with his work. Or with his masterpieces, as they were lauded in Europe.

She only intended to play the opening bars of the opus, but she hadn't played a piano in weeks, and this instrument was exquisite, so the experience was pure pleasure. Mrs. Cheatham had a piano in her central parlor, but Rebekah didn't dare play it without permission, and she hadn't yet scrounged up the courage to ask.

Not wishing to push her point too far home with her newest employer, she cut the opus short, then turned on the bench to face him.

He held her gaze for a moment, then nodded once. "I'll take that as a yes. However"—he picked up a page of sheet music from his desk and brought it to her—"can you play a piece without having heard it before, and without previous preparation or study?"

She took the music, placed it on the music rack of the piano, gave it a brief scan—and played.

The delivery wasn't nearly as crisp and polished as a moment earlier, but she got through the page with only a handful of minor mistakes. "I'm a bit out of practice with reading and playing on sight."

He nodded. "Yes, I noticed your tempo wasn't quite on the mark on the fourth and seventh measures."

She looked up at him, and caught the gleam in his eyes.

"Well done, Miss Carrington."

Against her will, and even as she told herself not to, a place within her responded to his praise.

"I assume you can sing as well?"

She eyed him. "Is that a requirement?"

"The symphony I'm writing doesn't include a vocal part. I'm merely trying to gain an accurate assessment of your abilities."

Not overly fond of being *assessed,* and especially not by him, she rose from the bench, wishing to be closer to eye level with him. "I can sing. But I'm certainly no Jenny Lind. If that's a talent you wish for your assistant to possess, Mr. Whitcomb, then I'll happily step aside and—"

"That won't be necessary." The glint of a stubborn streak shone in his expression. "You're more than qualified for the position. But one alteration *is* needed. We'll be working closely together on a near daily basis, so I suggest we dispense with the formalities. My given name is Nathaniel, but I'd appreciate you calling me Tate. Likewise, may I call you Rebekah?"

"Tate? Why Tate instead of Nathaniel? Or Nathan."

He shrugged. "I've always preferred Tate. Less formal, I guess. And now . . . Rebekah"—he took a seat on the piano bench and gestured for her to join him—"why don't we get to work?"

Sensing a definite challenge in his tone, she

looked at the bench, then back at him, and claimed the narrow space beside him.

"I'd like to begin," he continued, "by requesting you play the opening movement of this symphony. If you can manage Robert Schumann's Toccata in C Major, opus 7, one of the most demanding pieces ever written for the piano, I believe you'll manage this quite well."

Giving her a look that said to think twice before trying to stump him again, he reached for a folder of music on the table behind them, and his thigh brushed hers. Warmth traveled the length of her body, like a rush of warm air on a frosty eve, and it swirled inside her, round and round, until finally settling in a tantalizing coil deep inside her.

The effect was dizzying, and it took concentration just to breathe.

He placed the music on the rack before them, attention focused, seemingly unaffected. "This is only the piano arrangement, of course, but it should give you a good idea of the theme of this symphony. And I welcome your candid opinion afterward."

Rebekah struggled to focus on the music instead of him seated so close beside her, and though she didn't see a name or initials on the first page— or even a title, for that matter—she instinctively knew that this was his work.

She glanced over at him. "I've been here fifteen minutes, and you already want me to play the opening to your symphony and then give you my opinion?"

He matched her stare. "Precisely."

She looked at the music, then nodded and sat up straighter. "All right. But you'll have to move over. I need more room."

Wordlessly, he did as she asked, which gave her immense satisfaction. And for the first time since having been forced into this arrangement, the potential of the opportunity began to take root. She would be assisting a conductor in composing a symphony. A *symphony!* One that would be played publicly.

Granted, the conductor was Nathaniel *Tate* Whitcomb.

She began playing and was pleasantly surprised. The balance of tension in the chords was quite good, and she quickly fell into the rhythm of the—

"Stop, stop . . . You're playing it too fast, Rebekah."

She stilled, hands poised on the keys.

He tapped the sheet music. "Take note of the correct timing. It's a fast tempo, with spirit, yes. But it's not like you're on a runaway train."

She took a deep breath, not caring for the sudden change in his tone—or his insinuation. "It says *allegro con brio*, and I'm playing it at the tempo in which it was written. It's in two-four time. See it here?" She tapped the meter and rhythm notation on the page, much as he'd done, in the hope it would aggravate him as much as his comment was aggravating her. Then she smiled up at him. "Perhaps you meant to compose the symphony in four-four time instead?"

The blue of his eyes hardened, and he turned his attention back to the piano. "Play it again."

Swallowing another retort, she did as he asked, starting over at the beginning. As she played the same measures again, her understanding of the theme began to deepen, and she found herself anticipating the direction the music was—

"Stop, stop, stop!" He sighed. "You must play it with *feeling*. Not as though you're simply reading and regurgitating the notes."

With the chords still resonating from the grand piano, Rebekah clenched her jaw, grappling for calm that was scarcely there. "I *am* playing with feeling. However, the emotion of any piece is always open to interpretation to some degree. So perhaps if you'd—"

"Let's give it another try. Shall we? And mind the notations in the music."

She bristled. The condescension in his tone—not to mention the manner in which he'd interrupted her—was more like that of a teacher with a first-year student than a fellow colleague desiring a candid opinion.

However, considering who had arranged—or *demanded*—she be here . . .

For the third time, she started over from the beginning.

"Better," he said as she played. Yet to her, it was the very same tempo she'd played before.

She doubted he was even aware of it, but he was directing her with his right hand. Able to see him from her peripheral view, she tried to read at least a measure ahead in the music, while trying to follow his pace, while also trying to *feel* the music.

And the music was quite beautiful, even if a tad awkward or . . . *off* at times. Already, she thought of a minor alteration he could make that would greatly enhance the—

"Stop, stop, *stop!*" He gave an exasperated sigh. "You failed to fully realize the desired dynamic shift from bars thirty-two to thirty-eight. What you need to do, Rebekah, is—"

"And what *you* need to do, *Tate,* is let me play!" She turned to face him. "You need to listen to the music you've created. Not the music inside you, but the music that's on the page. Because the music on the page is what the orchestra members will have. That's all! They won't have the music that you're hearing in your head. So if what you're hearing doesn't match what you thought you wrote, then *perhaps* you need to look again at what's on the page!"

She heard the strident quality in her voice, but the offended arrogance darkening his expression didn't help her attitude. "Look at the construction of your theme. Granted, I'll play the notes more skillfully once I have more than *two seconds* to look at the music before you demand I play! But if the desired dynamic shift still isn't happening, perhaps *you* need to look at what precedes that shift. Because what comes before is as important as what comes after. And sometimes what you think is on the page is really still inside of you. So, while I know this may come as a shock to you, it could be the composer's oversight in this instance—and not the musician's!"

The sound of someone pointedly clearing their throat stopped Rebekah cold. She looked up to see Mrs. Murphey standing in the open doorway, tray in hand, disapproval and anger lining her face.

And Mrs. Bixby stood close behind her . . . smiling.

14

Your afternoon tea, Maestro Whitcomb!" With a loud *clank,* Mrs. Murphey plunked the tea service down on a nearby table and aimed a murderous scowl at Rebekah.

Working to control his own temper, Tate stood to intervene, sensing the situation about to go from bad to worse. He had to deal with Rebekah Carrington—and would, once they were alone again.

But for now, he had another woman to restrain.

Mrs. Murphey took a step toward Rebekah as if about to address her—or throttle her—and he held up a hand. "Thank you, Mrs. Murphey, for the refreshment. I believe we can serve ourselves this afternoon."

On a day-to-day basis, Mrs. Murphey was a force to be reckoned with. But when properly riled, her talons came out. Never with him, of course. Only with those who dared treat the conductor with less respect than she deemed worthy. She was the gatekeeper, after all, and she performed her duties well. And anyone with eyes could see that she considered Rebekah an intruder to be eliminated.

Only then did he notice Mrs. Bixby's bright countenance. He gave the woman a furtive glance, wondering at the cause. But her smile only deepened as she took her leave with a very rankled Mrs. Murphey.

Tate pushed the office door almost closed behind them, blurring the line of acceptable office decorum. But he preferred that no one else overhear the conversation to come.

He turned to face Rebekah. "Well, that was unfortunate."

She stared for a beat. "I completely agree."

Despite the cool air in the room, he was overly warm and removed his coat. He tossed it over the back of a chair, then loosened his tie. "If we're to work together, Rebekah, we must be able to speak to one another plainly, without tiptoeing around issues. But we're going to have to do it respectfully. Do you agree?"

She nodded, her features softening in what appeared to be contrition. "I do."

"Good." He forced a smile. "I'm glad that's clear between us. Because I'm more than willing to overlook your outburst just now. But in the future—"

"*My* outburst?" She stood, the piano bench scraping the floor as she did. "You're the one who scarcely let me finish playing a measure before you interrupted, *'Stop, stop, stop!'*" She spoke the words in a deeper register as though trying to mimic him, but it only came out sounding like some self-aggrandizing, pride-bloated buffoon. "And if you didn't want my candid opinion, Tate, then why did you ask for it?"

"I do want your opinion. But . . ." How to phrase this in a way she would accept? That wouldn't send her traipsing out the door? He looked beyond her to the wall of awards and accomplishments, and wondered if those meant nothing to her. "Since I was a young boy, I've studied music. I've dedicated the greater part of my life to learning from the masters—Bach, Haydn, Mozart Beethoven, Schubert. I've pored over their work until I feel as if I now know it as well as they did. Likewise, I've apprenticed with the most gifted conductors of our day. I've tirelessly pursued every available venue to hone my talent, to get me to the place where I am now." Tiny lines began to gather in her brow, and he hurried to finish before she aimed another assault. "So as I said, I *do* want you to share your opinion. All I ask when you do . . . is that you remember with whom you're sharing it."

She blinked, stared for the longest time, and then slowly nodded. To his surprise—and pleasure—her expression lit with understanding.

"I believe I see what you're saying, Tate. You're telling me that *you're* the conductor and I'm not."

He let out a breath. "Those aren't the exact words I would have chosen, but, yes . . . I'm the man charged with writing the symphony, and the man who has been trained to do such."

Her smile formed slowly, but still, he took it as a good sign.

"And furthermore," she continued, "you're saying that, in order for this to work between us"—she motioned—"I must follow your lead."

Tate started to nod, then hesitated, wondering if he'd detected defensiveness in her tone. Yet she was still smiling. "Again, I believe we're now on the same page, so to speak, Rebekah. And I appreciate your understanding and acceptance of the situation." He gestured toward the piano bench. "Shall we get back to work?"

He sat, but she made no move to join him.

"Tate." She looked squarely at him, as though he were a child of three instead of a grown man. "You . . . *cannot* . . . conduct me." She gave a short, caustic laugh that acted like a hot poker to his pride. "Primarily, because I'm not in your orchestra. But more importantly, because two people cannot *truly* collaborate on something if one of them holds both the reins. That's especially true in music. Each must hold a rein, and then work together to set the pace. How do you expect me to form my own opinions if I'm supposed to follow your lead? It makes no sense!"

"It actually makes perfect sense. Because I am the—"

"Conductor. Oh yes, I believe we're all well aware of that, *Maestro* Whitcomb." She took a step toward him, her expression resolute. "For the first time, I understand what my father meant when he warned, 'Be careful of anyone who has to tell you who they are more than once.'"

Tate stared, anger warring with thinning patience. Never had anyone spoken to him like this. Much less, a female. And to think, he'd once considered this woman nearly mute. And yet . . .

Something burned within him, separate and apart from his anger. At its sharpest point was a scalding pinprick, and it literally stole the words from his tongue. His chest tightened, and all he could think about was how hard he'd worked to get to where he was and how much those accomplishments deserved to be respected. How much *she* should respect him for all that he'd—

A knock sounded on the door. "Excuse me, Maestro Whitcomb?"

Tate's gaze locked with Rebekah's, and he caught the subtle rise of her eyebrow, ostensibly at the mention of his title.

"Come in," he said, voice hoarse.

Mrs. Bixby entered, wearing a smile that swiftly faded as she glanced from him to Rebekah, then back again. "Two quick issues, Maestro. First, Harold Endicott sent word that he'd like to speak with you about his daughter's schedule. He feels that with Miss Endicott serving as your personal assistant sponsored by the symphony, she should work with you more than only on Monday and Tuesday mornings."

Mrs. Bixby slid him a surreptitious look he understood only too well. But it was the slightly raised eyebrow from Rebekah that goaded his temper.

"Secondly, Maestro, and more importantly, the carriage is here to convey you to Mr. Cooper's residence."

He frowned.

"Mr. Washington Cooper, the artist commissioned by the symphony board for your portrait." Mrs. Bixby signaled behind her. "For the hallway, Maestro. It's the first of four sittings, sir."

Tate grimaced. He'd completely forgotten— and what a time to be reminded. "Tell the driver I'll be right there, Mrs. Bixby. *Please,*" he added as the door closed, sensing judgment from Rebekah's corner of the room—then seeing it confirmed in her eyes. "I'm afraid we need to cut our time short today."

She turned to retrieve her cloak and reticule, and muttered something beneath her breath.

"If you have something to say to me, Rebekah, then say it loud enough to hear."

She gave him an odd look. "I said, '*Yes,* I gathered that.'"

He found himself looking at her mouth, at the fullness of her lips, imagining their softness, which only frustrated him further.

She crossed to the door and paused, an almost hopeful look on her face. "I'll completely understand, Tate, if, in light of today—and the fact that I'm not your *only* personal assistant—you've decided it best that we not—"

"I'll see you tomorrow afternoon as planned. And don't be late. We have much work to do."

Reality hardened the hope in her eyes, and she exited, wordless, leaving the door wide open.

He gathered his work for the evening, stuffed it into his satchel, and left not two minutes behind her.

He hurried past the portraits of the composers, the afternoon light falling across their faces, and he noticed similarities in their expressions he'd not noticed before. Each of them sat erect, head held high, unmistakable pride lighting each of their gazes. The same attribute seemed to puff each chest out full, vest buttons straining as though fearful of failing to meet their obligation. Likewise, each man's chin was similarly lifted as if he himself had found ample reason to look down upon the rest of the world.

Tate gave himself a mental shake, realizing the

thoughts in his head sounded suspiciously like those of Rebekah Carrington instead of his own. He continued down the hallway and outside, determined to leave her behind for the day.

He climbed into the carriage, a frigid wind whipping at his coat. Each of those composers had the right to be proud of his accomplishments. Yes, they were demanding and had leaned toward being harsh in their criticism—as he knew he could be on occasion—but excellence wasn't born of coddling. Excellence was forged through fiery discipline. And regarding the conductors' similar postures in the portraits, that could easily have been the result of the artists' instruction during the sittings, rather than the conductors' individual personalities.

As the wind rocked the carriage, the wooden wheels seemed to find every pothole in the road, and Tate could still feel that hot pinprick inside him, like a match shoved dagger-deep and burning hot.

"Be careful of anyone who has to tell you who they are more than once."

The memory of what she'd said only made the match tip burn hotter. And the way she'd looked at him when she'd said it . . . She'd been angry, no denying that. Yet she'd said it so calmly, so matter-of-factly. As if she'd been giving the statement considerable thought for some time.

He leaned forward, the muscles in the back of his neck and shoulders corded tight. So Rebekah

Carrington thought him prideful, arrogant. Did it really matter what she thought about him? As long as she helped him with his symphony, what concern of his was her opinion of him?

He sighed and rubbed his temples, realizing he wasn't doing a very good job of not thinking about her.

He needed to go home again—that's what it was. And he needed to go soon. At the end of the week. Being home always grounded him, helped him see situations—and people—more clearly.

The carriage turned up a long drive and eventually stopped in front of a stately Victorian home. Tate followed a servant through the house and down a hallway into an artist's studio, a corner room, the two outside walls comprised of floor-to-ceiling windows. And it occurred to him . . .

Why would an artist choose to start his first sitting in the middle of the afternoon instead of in the freshness of morning light?

A much older man seated on a stool in the corner turned to greet him. "Ah . . . Maestro Whitcomb. This is indeed an honor, sir."

"The honor is all mine, Mr. Cooper. The remarkable reputation of your work precedes you."

The gentleman smiled. "As does yours, Maestro. I attended the performance you conducted nearly a month ago and found it riveting."

Tate smiled to hide a wince. He'd found the performance painful. The group had been made up of music teachers from the surrounding area, and he'd conducted the ensemble as a favor to a donor. And with every out-of-tune note and missed entry, he'd regretted his decision.

"Your hands were often a blur, Maestro. Either that, or my eyesight is failing." Cooper laughed good-naturedly. "But even at so brisk a tempo, the myriad individual notes emerged with remarkable clarity. You exercised such control with the musicians. Especially for being so young a man, if you don't mind my saying. It's as though each instrument awaits your slightest movement before taking its first breath."

Tate offered a brief bow in response to the praise, knowing the man was being gracious.

Cooper gestured. "If you'll sit here in this chair, we'll begin our first session. Which will consist of me sketching you, becoming familiar with the lines of your face, your stature."

Tate took a seat and suddenly became very self-conscious. All he could see in his mind's eye were the conductors in those other portraits.

"Turn toward me a little, please, Maestro Whitcomb. A bit more. There, very good. You have excellent posture, Maestro."

"Thank you," Tate responded, but all he could think about was what Rebekah might say if she were there right now, watching him sit for the portrait.

When he'd sat beside her on the bench, it had taken every ounce of willpower he possessed to keep from staring at her. She wasn't only an intelligent woman, gifted in music—she was a rare beauty. And when he'd accidentally brushed her thigh, he'd almost come off the bench. And probably should have, considering where his thoughts had taken him.

He didn't want to admit it, especially knowing how she felt about him, but he was attracted to her, and had been since the first time he'd laid eyes on her. He clenched his jaw, telling himself the same thing he'd been telling himself for years—

A relationship didn't fit with his career. It wasn't congruent with the plans for his life. And certainly not now.

People thought they knew him, when really, they only knew details about him. They didn't know the truth. And neither did Rebekah Carrington. Nor could she.

"You're telling me that you're *the conductor and I'm not."*

Recalling her pointed comment, Tate felt the pinprick within him jab deeper, and he suddenly realized what it was that Rebekah had done. She'd wounded his pride. No, she'd tried to annihilate it.

"Very good, Maestro Whitcomb. Give me that stern expression we see as you conduct. The famous look that can *wither at a glance.*"

Rebekah Carrington's thorough dressing down had been uncalled for. But . . . she'd also been right about the music. The bars leading up to the shift were lacking. He'd sensed it all along but hadn't known how to fix it. And she'd seen it immediately. She was brilliant.

And—as much as it rankled him—she was right.

He couldn't be the conductor, not with her How could she share her honest opinions with him if he was busy telling her how to play? And yet, how did he put that part of him aside? It was the very fabric of who he was.

It was his pride that had refused to let her play, to let her criticize his work. How often had he told an orchestra member who'd complained about him being too hard on them that pride was the enemy of greatness?

"Excellent, Maestro!" Washington Cooper smiled broadly. "The deep furrowed brow is perfect. The sign of a truly gifted musician. Quite Mozart-like, if you'll allow me the comparison."

But Tate scarcely heard the man. All he could think about was Rebekah. And the passion, the fire she possessed. A passion and fire he needed. It seemed to simmer in every part of her being. And he knew, if she would work with him, if he could channel her passion—and didn't throttle her somewhere along the way, or she him—he could finish this symphony in time.

They could finish it. *If* she came back.

15

Still weighing the cost of disappointing Adelicia Cheatham if she didn't agree to be Tate Whitcomb's assistant—or his *second* assistant—Rebekah pulled her attention back to the primary reason she was at Belmont. Adelicia's daughter . . . who stood close beside her.

Rebekah placed the sheet music on the stand before Pauline, and the girl began playing. It was a familiar title, one from church—that had been played in the morning service that past Sunday, in fact—and Rebekah knew Pauline knew it well.

But there was something lacking in the girl's execution, and as Rebekah listened to her play the notes, she suspected she'd guessed correctly.

Oddly enough, her *guess* had been helped along by the argument she and Tate had had yesterday in his office. And on their first afternoon of working together. That didn't bode well.

"Please stop, Pauline," she said softly after a moment.

The young girl huffed. "But I know how to play this. Why can't I simply play it?"

"Because you're not playing it correctly."

"But I am, Miss Carrington. I know I am. I've played this many times before!"

"You *are* playing it correctly, in one sense. The

problem is, Pauline, you're *not* playing the music as it's written on the sheet before you."

The slight lift in the girl's chin unwittingly revealed the truth. And confirmed Rebekah's suspicions.

"Do you know how to read music, Pauline?"

"*Yes,* Miss Carrington."

"Splendid. What is the timing of this piece?"

Pauline looked. "It's in three-four meter." Smugness tightened her tone.

"Very good. And can you tell me what that means?"

"It means . . ." The girl tossed her hair over one shoulder. "It means that the piece is written in three-four timing."

Rebekah suppressed a smile, having seen that same expression on a similar but more mature countenance in this very home.

"And would you please define what three-four timing means?"

Pauline stared at the music, her grip tightening around the neck of her violin.

Rebekah gently touched her shoulder. "I think you and I have a lot in common, Pauline. Especially when it comes to playing the violin. Something I was able to do at a very young age was to listen to a piece of music only a few times, and then play it relatively well without looking back at the notes."

Pauline chewed the inside corner of her mouth.

"That's actually a very helpful and wonderful gift to have. We call it playing by ear. The notes and the tempo tuck themselves away inside you. It almost feels magical, in a way."

"So that's a good thing," Pauline said, but her expression held question. "A gift, like you said."

"It is. But as with any gift, it can also be a detriment, as I discovered when I began learning how to play the violin after having played the piano." She thought for a moment. "Did your previous tutor teach you much about how music is written?"

The young girl shook her head, briefly looking down as she did. "He said that sort of thing was unnecessary, that I played well enough because . . . girls only need to know how to play for parlor performances."

Rebekah's face heated. "He said that to you?"

Pauline nodded.

"I had a violin tutor who said much the same to me when I was your age, Pauline. But we shouldn't allow the ignorance of certain people in this world—men included—to define what we do or what we accomplish, should we?"

Pauline peered up, studied Rebekah's face for a beat, then smiled. "No, Miss Carrington. We should not."

"Very good, then." Rebekah leaned closer. "God has given you a gift, Pauline. He gives each of His children gifts. And it's our responsibility to hone those gifts, to study to be the very best we can be using those skills. Because we only want to offer Him our very best in return. Do you understand?"

Pauline beamed. "You want to teach me how to play better than for only parlor performances."

Rebekah sought the girl's undivided attention. "I want you to give your best to God every single time you play. Whether in a parlor"—an all but defeated dream raised its weary head—"or someday . . . in an orchestra . . . in an opera house."

Pauline's smile faded. "But Mr. Fulton said women aren't meant to play in orchestras."

Rebekah swallowed. "Mr. Fulton—Mr. *Darrow* Fulton—was your violin tutor?"

Pauline nodded. "But I didn't like him very much," she whispered.

She huffed. "I can understand why."

When Pauline snickered, Rebekah swiftly turned her attention to the piece of music on the stand, not wanting to encourage more discussion on that front. If Darrow Fulton ever found out that he'd lost his tutoring position to her . . . She could already see the veins bulging in the man's neck. If she *did* decide to work for Tate, she'd most certainly see Darrow on occasion at the opera house. Not a pleasant prospect any way she viewed it.

Rebekah pointed to the sheet music. "All right, Pauline . . . You're familiar with this title, I know. But when I transcribed this last night—"

A knock on the door, and Miss Tindal, the new governess, peered in. "Please forgive the interruption, Miss Carrington. But I'm looking for

Claude so we can start his lessons this morning. Have you seen him?"

Rebekah shook her head. "No, I haven't." She glanced down at Pauline and caught a glint in the girl's expression. "Pauline, have you seen your older brother since breakfast?"

The girl briefly ducked her head. "You might want to check behind the sofa in the small study, Miss Tindal. Claude began reading a new book last night and rather likes it."

Miss Tindal shook her head, whispered her thanks, and closed the door. And Rebekah counted her good fortune that *she* wasn't the governess. Claude, soon to be thirteen, would be attending boarding school next fall, as did his four older brothers and sister. But until then, he was a handful. One Rebekah was grateful she didn't have to manage.

Returning to the lesson at hand, she pointed back to the music stand. "As I was saying, Pauline, when I transcribed this last night, I made a few changes. Hence, how I knew you were playing by ear."

Pauline's cheeks colored.

"Let's try it again. We'll start from the very beginning." Rebekah pointed to the time signature. "The number three means that there are only three beats in each measure in this piece, and the number four means that the quarter note equals one beat. So a measure in this piece can have, for example, three quarter notes, or a half note and a quarter note, or six eighth notes. As long as the notes in a measure total three beats. Does that make sense?"

Pauline stared at the music, her gaze narrowing. "Three beats in a measure. No more than that. And the quarter note gets one beat."

"Excellent!"

The lesson flew by that morning, and Rebekah had more fun than she could remember having in a long time. She almost felt as if she were teaching her younger self to play. But unlike the world she faced now, she prayed Pauline would grow up in a world that would afford more opportunities for women besides performing in parlors—

Or anonymously from second-floor landings.

Rebekah quickened her steps through town, still exuberant about Pauline's lesson that morning, yet eager to put this next errand behind her.

The bone-chilling air held the unique scent of winter, and the cold reached inside her cloak with icy fingers. She wrapped the garment tighter around herself in response.

Her childhood home loomed ahead, and she fought the urge to turn and run in the opposite direction.

But she'd made a promise. . . .

However, she *hadn't* promised to knock on the front door. Instead, when she reached the house, she slipped around to the back entrance by the kitchen, where neither her mother nor Barton would likely be. She saw no sign of the fancy new carriage and hoped that meant he was not home.

She knocked on the door, peering through the window, and saw Delphia glance back.

The woman's face lit up, and her smile looked so much like that of Demetrius that Rebekah was reminded of his laughter, his generosity, the way he'd lived so unselfishly. And she found the weight of grief at missing him eased somewhat by dwelling on what a blessing he'd been, and how much poorer her life would be if she'd never known him.

The door opened, and a rush of warm air wafted from the kitchen, pushing against the cold. It carried with it a sweet aroma wrapped in buttery goodness, and Rebekah hoped her initial hunch proved right.

"Get on in here, child!" Delphia tugged her by the hand, then pulled Rebekah into a hug. "I been lookin' for you every day, wonderin' how you gettin' along. Your mama told me you wrote her, said you got yourself a job and a place to live. But she said you didn't spell out much about either of 'em."

Rebekah breathed deeply, wondering if the scents of home would always bring back such a flood of memories. Both good and bad. "I'm doing well, Delphia. Far better than when I left here that morning. And I *do* have a job, but . . . I'd rather Mother and Barton not know where I am. At least for the time being. In fact, to keep you from being put in a difficult spot should they ask, it's probably best I not tell you either." Seeing Delphia's frown, she rushed to explain. "It's not that I don't trust you. I do!"

"You don't have to say no more, ma'am. I understand. As long as you're doin' well, that's all I need to know." Delphia gave her arm a pat and turned back to the worktable, where cookies cooled on a rack. "Just took 'em hot from the oven not ten minutes ago."

"Your sugar cookies." Rebekah's mouth watered. Her hunch had been right.

Delphia handed her a cookie on a napkin, and Rebekah didn't hesitate. The sweet comfort melted in her mouth, its warm goodness acting like a tonic. She closed her eyes, savoring the taste, certain that, if it ever came to it, she could live on tea cakes and sugar cookies alone.

"Your mama and Mr. Ledbetter, they ain't home right now," Delphia offered, as though reading Rebekah's mind. "Your mama, she gone shoppin' with two woman friends. Mr. Ledbetter said he needed the carriage, so they come by and pick her up earlier. Then he left out a while after. Don't ever say where he's goin'."

"How is Mother doing?"

"She doin' fine. Bit sick last week. Weak feelin', she said. Wouldn't eat much. But she's stronger now. And missin' you—that's for sure. But she done had lots of years to get good at that."

The tenderness in Delphia's expression convinced

Rebekah she hadn't intended for the comment to hurt. But still, it stung. "I'll come back again soon, at a time when she's here."

"And at a time when he ain't." Delphia gave her a look.

For a moment, Rebekah wondered again if Delphia knew what Barton had done to her. Then the woman smiled and returned to minding the pot on the stove, and Rebekah decided she was imagining things.

"I *can* tell you that I'm tutoring a young girl. For my job. I'm teaching her the violin," she added softly, feeling an unexpected catch in her throat. "Just like he taught me."

Tears sprang to Delphia's deep brown eyes. "Oh, Miss Rebekah, I can't tell you how good it feels to hear that. If Demetrius could know somehow, it'd sure make him proud." She stared at Rebekah for a moment, then shook her head. "I still 'member that night you sneaked down to the cabins to listen to us singin'. And I 'member the first time you picked up my brother's fiddle too." She laughed, deep and hearty. "Lawd, you made the awfulest sound, draggin' that bow back and forth 'cross them strings. Like a polecat beggin' to die!"

Rebekah laughed along with her, wishing she had her violin here so she could play for Delphia, show her what she'd done with all the love and patient instruction Demetrius had invested in her. It would almost feel like she was playing for him.

Almost.

"This youngun'," Delphia continued, "whoever she is, she got herself a good teacher."

"Thank you." Rebekah smiled. "She's quite bright and eager to learn. I believe she'll do well."

Delphia paused, wooden spoon in hand. "We had us a pig roastin' on the spit that night too. You 'member? You were just a little sprout of a thing." She chuckled. "Demetrius, he was just standin' there, turnin' and turnin', and you was just standing there, cryin' and cryin', feelin' sorry for that poor ol' mister pig. 'Til you got a taste of him—then suddenly you wasn't so sad no more."

Delphia laughed and turned back to stir a pot on the stove. Rebekah smiled at the memory too, until another recollection crowded close, and her humor faded.

After finding out about how she'd sneaked down to the slave cabins, her father had scolded her harshly and warned her never to go back. But when Mother had learned, she'd whipped her with a belt. Rebekah winced, recalling how the welts had burned on her legs. Days later, she'd seen Demetrius in the garden. "Miss Bekah . . ." His smile held welcome, like it always had. "Been thinkin' 'bout you, child. You doin' all right?"

Rebekah remembered nodding while also tugging her dress lower, embarrassed by the welts still marking her legs. "I'm good, Demetrius. You planting today?"

"Yes, ma'am, I am. Plantin' corn and green beans and okra and melons. And some sweet taters too. 'Cause somebody I know likes them *special good*!"

She giggled, loving the way his slouch hat rested just above his eyes, eyes that seemed to smile even before his mouth did. Much like her father's.

"Miss Bekah . . . you know what happened the other night," he said softly, then scooped some freshly tilled soil in his hand, dropped a seed in the ground, and smoothed the dirt back over. "When your daddy found you at the cabins."

She nodded, then quickly looked down to make sure her shins were still covered.

"Well, your daddy, he's right. Young girl like you oughtn't be roamin' round at night on her lonesome. You gotta do like your papa says. He's a good man. And good men, they's hard to come by. And he loves you somethin' fierce."

"But I like hearing you play, Demetrius. And I like all the singing too."

There went his smile again, reaching down inside her like a dose of sunshine on a gray April day.

"Well, I tell you what. . . . How 'bout I start playin' and singin' a little louder so maybe you can hear it from the swing on the back porch."

She grinned. "Or maybe from my room. If I open my window."

He nodded, gave her a handful of seeds, and moved on down the line. She followed, dropping seeds into the waiting beds like he'd taught her, and then watched as he covered them, tucking them in to sleep.

"About your mama," he said after a while, his voice extra quiet, as though someone else might be listening. But there was no one else in the garden. "I'm sorry what she done to you, child. It weren't right. You let Delphia put some of that salve on again tonight. It'll help the sting. And the healin' too."

She nodded, embarrassed that he'd found out about her getting a whipping—while also not. Because, somehow, him saying that what her mother had done was wrong . . . made it not feel so bad.

"I made you somethin', little one."

He reached into his shirt pocket, then held out his hand, wriggling his eyebrows. Smiling, she presented her open palm, and he dropped a piece of wood into it. Only, it wasn't just plain old wood. It was—

"Button!" She gave a little squeal. "It's my dog Button!"

Demetrius laughed, and even that sounded like music. "I picked up a stick of wood the other day and just saw that cute little dog of yours in there, peekin' out at me. Him with that cute, round nose. So I carved and I carved until he finally came crawlin' out."

She held the wooden dog close to her face and kissed its nose, then threw her arms around Demetrius's big, strong neck. Next to her father's hugs, his were the best.

The clank of a metal spoon on the cast-iron stove jarred Rebekah back to the present, and part of her wished she could stay back there in the garden, in her memories with Demetrius a little longer. As the years passed, she'd learned just how right he'd been about the whipping.

That incident had shown her how different in temperament her parents were from each other. She recalled Papa slipping into her room the night after her mother's whipping, and he'd kissed her forehead. The welts on her legs still throbbed, and she'd pretended to be asleep, not wanting to risk making him as angry as her mother had been—not yet understanding at that young age that such a thing wasn't possible of her father. He'd knelt silently by her bed, head bowed, and had stayed there for some time. She'd peeked at him in the dark, watching him, and—even confused and hurting—she'd felt so loved.

As she'd grown, she'd become familiar with her mother's tendency toward worry and hysterics, and she'd come to believe that her father had been praying as much for her mother that night, if not more, than he'd been praying for her. But one thing was certain . . .

Her mother never whipped her with a belt again.

"You wanna sit yourself down and have some vegetable soup, Miss Rebekah? It's all but ready."

Rebekah checked the time and shook her head. "I need to be going. But first . . ." Thinking better about what she'd said to Delphia before, she found pen and paper in a drawer and wrote down the Belmont estate address. "I want to leave you with the address of where I'm working. And living." She handed her the piece of paper. "If there's an emergency or if Mother gets sick, and you need me, simply give this to someone you trust, and they'll be able to contact me. Please, hide it in your room. Put it somewhere Mother or Barton won't find it, should they look."

Delphia studied the address as though she could read it, then she tucked the piece of paper into her pocket. "Yes, miss. I'll hide it good. But 'fore you go, let me box up some of them cookies. You can eat 'em later on and think of me." She winked and packed a small tin full.

Rebekah took the tin and hugged her tight. "Between these cookies and the lemon tea cakes a woman makes where I'm living, I'll be forced to start letting out my skirts any day now."

Delphia's smile faded. "*Lemon* tea cakes, you say?"

"Yes. Most of the time she makes them with lemon. But the vanilla are no less scrumptious."

A shadow eclipsed Delphia's expression.

Sensing she'd hurt Delphia's feelings and not wanting to appear ungrateful, Rebekah cradled the tin to her chest. "But, never you fear, your sugar cookies are still my favorite!"

"This place where you stayin', Miss Rebekah, are you—"

The telling squeal of hinges on the front door all

but leached the oxygen from the room. They stared at each other, unmoving.

"Delphia!" Barton's deep voice bellowed.

Rebekah reached for the door. "Thank you, again. I'll be back soon to check on Mother."

Delphia nodded, the unease in her features deepening. "You take good care, Miss Rebekah."

Rebekah hurried down the pathway to the sidewalk, then took the long way around the block to avoid having to walk in front of the house. With each step, the unrest she'd sensed from Delphia became more disconcerting. Until she reached the corner of Fifth and Pine, and something even more disconcerting wrestled her attention—and won.

She looked down the long thoroughfare to the opera house at the other end of the street, and knew she had no choice. In the end, whether or not she was brave enough to go against Adelicia Cheatham's wishes had little bearing on her decision. Because she needed money for whatever the future held after she prepared Pauline for the May recital, which would arrive before she knew it. And when that time came, she had no idea what she was going to do next.

But she *did* know the next step she needed to take.

With determined strides, she closed the distance to the opera house, hoping against hope that Tate Whitcomb wasn't as gifted at negotiating salaries as he was at conducting orchestras.

But she'd done her fair share of dickering at the

street markets in Vienna—she'd watched Sally and learned—so she planned on driving a hard bargain. Because she needed every penny she could get. Part of her wished she knew what Miss Endicott was being paid. Because certainly, based on what Tate had said about the young woman to Mrs. Cheatham, she should be paid at least as much.

"Get your paper, right here!" The hawking of a newsboy drew her attention. "Read all about the Grand Central Depot bein' built in New York City! Biggest in the country! Opens this fall!"

Rebekah looked across the street, hoping to see the same young boy who—

But it wasn't him.

This boy was older and dark-haired. Nothing like the slim young lad she'd met weeks earlier. Still, the chance to read about New York drew her. She crossed the street, paid her nickel, and stepped to the side to peruse the front page article about the new railroad depot.

While in New York, she'd seen the construction in progress, and the depot buildings were nothing short of magnificent. As was the rest of the city. What would it be like to live there? A place that was thriving and growing, instead of wounded and barely limping along. But New York was a world away, and beyond her grasp.

Resigned, she folded the paper, tucked it beneath her arm, and retraced her steps toward the opera house. The innocent question within her from moments earlier repeated itself. But this time, with a skitter of hope . . .

What *would* it be like to live in New York City? Far from the daily reminders of a war fought—and lost. Far from Barton Ledbetter and his lecherous designs. And where the philharmonic had recently admitted a woman into their ranks.

"Well done, Miss Carrington. That was exquisite."

She paused beside the opera hall and stared up at the aging structure. Tate Whitcomb's responses to her oboe audition returned—but in a new light.

Based on his comments at her audition—coupled with those he'd made about the mysterious violin soloist at Mrs. Cheatham's—she'd started to believe he'd meant what he'd said. He truly considered her talent worthy of playing in an orchestra, even if her gender prevented it, in his opinion. So if the New York Philharmonic hired one woman, why wouldn't they hire another? Especially if her talent proved worthy? All she needed was money enough to get there and then some to live on.

With fresh possibility fueling her determination, Rebekah readied herself for the negotiation that could change her life.

"You came back."

Upon seeing her, Tate Whitcomb immediately rose from behind his desk, astonishment—then relief—chasing across his features. His response did something curious to Rebekah on the inside, but she tried her best to appear unmoved—and to not forget her bargaining points.

She removed her cloak and placed it in a chair alongside her reticule and the tin of cookies. "You thought I wouldn't?"

"I had my doubts."

She nodded. "So did I."

"But you reconsidered." A smile barely touched his mouth.

"I did."

He held her gaze, and the relief in his expression slowly gave way to gratitude. "I'm so glad."

Thrown a little off-center by this new, more humble side, she knew better than to trust it. Tate Whitcomb needed her help—that was the reason for the change. And it was likely temporary, at best. But she couldn't fault him for it. Her reason for returning was no less selfish. She needed him. Or rather, needed his money. Speaking of which . . .

Broaching the subject felt just shy of vulgar, but if she didn't look out for her own interests, who would?

"We haven't discussed salary yet . . . Tate."

His brow furrowed. "Oh yes. I should have addressed that with you yesterday. The salary is six dollars per month."

Rebekah hesitated, certain she'd misunderstood him. *"Six dollars?"*

"Yes . . . unless you find that sum inadequate. In which case, I can appeal to the benefactor for more, but I doubt that—"

"No . . . that amount is adequate. Thank you." Six dollars a month was far more than she'd hoped for—and suddenly her dream of New York City appeared considerably brighter. And not so out of reach. So much for trying to out negotiate the man.

He moved from behind his desk. "Of course, that will include coordinating advertising and ticket sales with Mrs. Murphey and Mrs. Bixby. And the time necessary for you to transcribe the symphony—once it's finished—for all members of each section of the orchestra. Which will be quite an undertaking."

"And which gives us even more incentive to finish the symphony as soon as we can." She glanced at the handwritten sheet music on his desk, assuming that's what he'd been working on. "You told Mrs. Cheatham it's coming along well. Are you nearly finished?"

His eyes narrowed. "I wouldn't say nearly finished, exactly."

The uncustomary trepidation in his tone piqued her curiosity. "So, what *would* you say?"

He glanced away briefly, then his attention wandered back. "The first two movements are completed. And the third is partially written, but it's only—"

"You still have *two* movements to write? In five months?"

He winced. "Actually more like three months, since the new opera house will be finished earlier than estimated, and we still must leave time for transcribing and, of course, for the orchestra to practice." He gathered the sheet music and crossed to the piano. "So let's not waste another minute, shall we?"

Laughing beneath her breath, Rebekah felt a weight settling around her shoulders. Even though it wasn't *her* symphony, she'd now become yoked to this man, and therefore his success—or failure—reflected directly upon her. And her future.

She sat beside him on the piano bench, keenly aware of him. The way his rolled-up shirt sleeves revealed sun-bronzed arms, and his hands, large and strong, not the typical hands of a pianist, yet most definitely the hands of a conductor. Decisive, in control. Her gaze drifted to his profile, his dark hair and closely trimmed beard, those discerning blue eyes.

The aroma of bayberry and musk wafted toward her, and she breathed in the masculine scent, grateful beyond words that he didn't use cherry laurel.

At this close proximity, she could see the faintest flecks of silver in his bearded jawline, and it wasn't difficult to imagine how distinguished and even more handsome a man he would become as the years passed. She wondered if the portrait commissioned of him would capture the way his—

"I would suggest that we . . ." He turned to her as he spoke, and paused.

Horrified that he'd caught her staring, Rebekah

jerked her gaze to the piano keys. She felt his attention lengthen and—growing more self-conscious as it did—she began playing the opening measures of the "Ode to Joy" from the final movement of Beethoven's Symphony No. 9, a piece she often chose when warming up.

"What is it you wanted to suggest?" she asked over the music, trying for a casual tone.

"I was going to suggest that you play the first two movements of my symphony in their entirety, unhindered, then give me your opinion on what needs to be changed. If anything."

She stopped playing midmeasure, knowing Beethoven would have been furious. "And by unhindered, you mean . . ."

"That I won't stop you."

She looked over at him, doubtful.

He smiled. "Not even once."

"Do you think you can do that?"

His smile faded. "I honestly don't know. But I'm willing to try."

She laughed, then took the sheet music from him and propped it on the music rack. "May I remind you that, except for the first thirty-something measures, I've never seen this music before in my life. So please don't—"

"I will offer no criticism, Rebekah. Nor will I interrupt."

Admiring his grandiose intentions, but quite certain they would prove futile, she began playing. Reading ahead, she anticipated the first page turn, but he beat her to it, and turned at precisely the right time.

The music increased in difficulty and demanded her undivided attention. Feverishly reading, she found that to compensate she had to play more slowly through measures written at a faster tempo, which stirred her frustration. Especially because she knew how annoyed he must be.

She hit a wrong note and grimaced. "Sorry," she whispered, continuing on.

He said nothing, simply turned the pages at the exact timing required. But she sensed him playing the piece internally alongside her. Every note, every crescendo, every decrescendo. And she found it both beyond irritating—and stimulating.

He turned the next page, and she glimpsed the last few bars. The first movement ended in an abrupt coda. With pulse racing, her eyes devouring the notes and fingers flying across the keys, she built toward it, trying her best to play it exactly as he'd written, and as his right hand—unbeknownst to him, she felt certain—silently conducted at his side.

She played the last chords with solid resolve, arms aching, and looked next to her, a little out of breath. "So . . . was that as hard as you thought it would be?"

His eyes narrowed, and then he looked over—and smiled. "You have no idea."

16

A week later, Rebekah pushed Pauline especially hard during their practice, all while Tate Whitcomb's symphony played in the back of her mind. She could hardly wait to get back to the opera house to continue working on the third movement.

She and Tate had made some progress in recent days. But mainly, they'd reached a personal truce—which was an accomplishment in itself. They'd celebrated that first afternoon by eating the entire tin of Delphia's sugar cookies. She'd made a mental note to bring some of Cordina's tea cakes today, if Cordina had them ready.

Watching Pauline as the girl played, and listening closely, Rebekah determined what the issue was. "Your grip on the violin is diminishing your vibrato."

Pauline looked up at the ceiling and sighed for at least the tenth time that morning. "But I'm holding it precisely where you taught me to hold it, Miss Carrington."

Rebekah smiled. *Such a little Adelicia.* Rebekah had quickly learned the young girl was the spitting image of her mother in every way, including stubbornness. "That's true, in one regard. But you're not holding it *as* I taught you. When you hold your violin and bow, you need to do it subconsciously, without even thinking about it. As though they were both extensions of your body. For instance, when you pick up a brush to brush your hair, you don't give any thought about how to hold it. Or how you're going to work the bristles through. You simply . . . brush. But it wasn't always that way. You had to learn. Holding a violin is much the same. It isn't a natural feeling at first, I realize. Here, let me show you again."

Pauline surrendered the beautiful instrument, and Rebekah cradled it against her collarbone, then let both arms rest at her side.

"Trust your head, Pauline. It's quite heavy enough to hold the instrument without chin pressure. Do you see?"

Pauline smirked. "That means *your* head is heavy enough too!"

Smiling, Rebekah demonstrated her meaning by first playing "Twinkle, Twinkle Little Star" while gripping the violin tightly, then by cradling it correctly. "Using the right form not only frees your hands to make music, but it frees you on the inside to *feel* the music, and therefore your vibrato will come through more naturally. Does that make better sense?"

Pauline nodded. "I want to try again."

Rebekah returned the instrument, impressed, not for the first time, with the child's enthusiasm, which was such an integral part of learning. And which made the occasional sighs and ceiling glares not nearly as tiresome.

Pauline cradled the instrument and played the assigned music from Vivaldi. But this time, with a noticeable difference.

"Excellent, Pauline! Now, continue to the end." Rebekah stood back and listened, watching the girl's form as she played, and loving moments such as this—the exhilaration that accompanied actually seeing someone *learn*. Especially the violin.

Two hours later, Rebekah was thrilled that the lesson went far better than she had expected.

Before leaving for the opera house, she returned to her room, where a tray lunch sat waiting, as usual. She made quick work of the cold pork roast and cheese, along with a thick slice of Cordina's honey buttermilk bread slathered with butter, then hurried downstairs to the kitchen to ask about the tea cakes.

She'd not yet visited the kitchen—spoiled with her meals always being delivered to her room—but she'd seen the servants coming and going from the staircase across from the family dining room often enough to know where it was.

She opened the door and didn't see Cordina. But another woman stood at a worktable, kneading a mound of dough. Her back to Rebekah, the woman didn't turn, but Rebekah recognized her instantly.

"Esther." She spoke softly, not wishing to startle her.

Esther turned and, despite fair warning, still seemed a little jarred. *"Oh,* Miss Carrington."

Esther glanced at an open side door, then back to Rebekah, wiping her hands on her apron. "Is . . . there somethin' I can do for you, ma'am?"

"Yes, please, there is. I wondered if Cordina has any tea cakes she could part with. I'd like to take some with me to the—"

Only then did she notice the painted murals covering nearly every wall of the kitchen. Scenes of rose gardens with gazebos, the statues and fountains around Belmont, and the surrounding hillsides in their various seasons. There was even a scene of the servants' brick houses all clustered together. She recognized them from having seen them while out on a walk.

"How beautiful!" Rebekah felt as though she were looking through a series of windows. "Who painted these?"

Esther's gaze shot again to the door. "Um . . . I think it was a young woman who used to work here for Mrs. Cheatham, ma'am."

"Well, whoever she is, she's extremely talented. These are works of art. Almost feels like we're not even in a basement." Rebekah smiled, sensing the woman's unease and wondering if it stemmed from their last encounter, when the fire in her bedroom hearth was late being lit. "Esther, I hope you're not still—"

"About them tea cakes, ma'am. I'm sure Cordina has some. I'll get them for you right quick." Esther crossed to a cupboard, and Rebekah quickly gathered she didn't wish to talk about it.

As Esther wiped out an empty tin, Rebekah's attention fell to the counter where the woman had been working. There, near the mound of dough, sat a little wooden bunny perched on its hind legs.

Rebekah took a step closer. "That's so cute! Is it yours?"

Esther turned and looked but said nothing.

"The reason I ask"—Rebekah reached into her pocket and pulled out Button—"is because I carry a little dog that looks a lot like—"

"That's mine" came a voice from behind, and Rebekah turned to see Cordina standing in the doorway.

Cordina offered a quick smile. "Cute little thing, ain't it? Got it some time back. Didn't mean to leave it in your way, Esther." Cordina snapped up the carving and tucked it into her apron pocket. "Now . . . Miss Carrington, what brings you down here, ma'am? Your lunch tray not get delivered?"

"Oh yes, it was delivered. And was also delicious, thank you, Cordina. I simply came down to see if you had any tea cakes. Esther here was very kindly getting me some."

"Well, I'll be happy to help you with that now, ma'am." Cordina glanced in Esther's direction. "Esther, we needin' your help back there with packin' bread. I'll finish out here."

Esther dipped her head in Rebekah's direction, set the tin on the worktable, and wordlessly left the room. Rebekah watched her go, reading what appeared to be relief in the woman's expression, and feeling as though she'd gotten her in trouble somehow.

"And now for some tea cakes!" Cordina opened a pie safe on the far wall. "How many you wantin', ma'am?"

"Could you spare a half dozen?"

"You know I can. I always make extra." Cordina flashed another smile. "I just wish I knew where you was puttin' all these sweets. Lawd, I eat one of these things and 'fore it's halfway down my throat, I can feel it on my thighs."

Rebekah laughed softly. "Well, they're not all for me this time. I'll be sharing them . . . with a friend."

Cordina handed her the tin. "Anythin' else you needin', ma'am?"

"No, that's all. Thank you."

"Well, you have yourself a good day, then. And come back hungry tonight. We havin' chicken and dumplin's and sweet bread puddin'."

Rebekah crossed to the door leading to the stairs and glanced back, unable to shake the feeling that something was amiss. "Cordina . . . did I do something wrong a moment earlier? In speaking to Esther? Because if I did—"

" 'Course, you ain't done nothin' wrong, Miss Carrington." Cordina laughed. "I just need her help with the bread—that's all. We busy back there makin' extra loaves for a widows' and children's home in town, and it takes everybody's hands and more to see it done."

Rebekah nodded. "Oh, good. I feel better, then. Thank you again for lunch . . . and for the tea cakes!" She waved as she walked out. And as she climbed the stairs, she was more convinced than ever that something was amiss. And that Cordina was hiding something.

Because Cordina inquired about everything. And for the woman not to inquire about "the friend" she'd be sharing these tea cakes with was like expecting a bird to walk from Belmont to town. A bird had legs. It *could* happen. But never, in a million years, would it.

And yet, it had.

Which only made Rebekah determined to find out who Esther was. And why, apparently, Cordina had forbidden the woman to talk to her.

The moment Rebekah stepped into the back corridor of the opera house, she heard the orchestra. February had ushered in an even colder chill to the wind and, half frozen, she stood stock-still and let the warmth—and sound—wash over her.

"Beautiful, isn't it?"

Rebekah turned to see Mrs. Bixby seated behind the desk, a welcome change to sour old Mrs. Murphey.

She nodded. "It certainly is."

"Today's lunch rehearsal is running long, Miss Carrington. For the concert tomorrow night. But you're welcome to continue to the maestro's office and begin your work, if you'd like."

Rebekah glanced at the door leading to the back of the stage. "Would it be all right if I were to sneak in and listen for a moment?"

Mrs. Bixby's eyes lit. "Of course, my dear. I do the same thing on occasion—when Mrs. Murphey isn't present, of course. She frowns upon it. Says we might interrupt the 'flow of the moment.'" She winked. "Which only makes me want to do it all the more!"

Rebekah laughed, loving this woman more each time she was with her.

She stood by the backstage door, waiting for the horn section to come in again so that any squeak the door might make when opening would be masked.

She knew the symphonies the orchestra was performing tomorrow night because she'd seen the music on Tate's desk. The first, and the one they were practicing now, Ferdinand Ries's Symphony No. 5 in D Minor, opus 112. The next, Bach's Brandenburg Concertos Nos. 3 and 4 in G Major were also familiar. She followed the music silently . . .

And finally, in came the bassoons, trumpets, and French horns.

She carefully opened the backstage door, not knowing how the orchestra members were situated and wishing to remain unseen. But she needn't have worried. The orchestra was seated downstage center, several yards away, in their usual semicircle, facing the conductor, and dark curtains hung at staggered intervals in the wings providing ample places from which to spy.

She tiptoed along the back and stopped at the edge of a curtain, which afforded her a view of the entire orchestra, including its illustrious leader. It was her first time to see Tate conducting—not counting how he silently conducted her at the piano.

And he was . . . *impressive,* to say the least.

Baton in hand, he sliced the air with a vengeance, sweat layering his brow. His piercing gaze darted from one section of the orchestra to another. Sometimes cuing, other times demanding more with a ferocious look. Then yet at other moments, he insisted on less, his hands, his expressions, his entire body leading, guiding. A dark curl fell across his forehead, but he seemed oblivious to it, so focused, so consumed was he by his work.

Rebekah found herself smiling. And . . . admiring.

While she recognized the symphony by Ferdinand Ries, she didn't know it well enough to name which movement they were playing, but she guessed they were in the—

"No. No. *No!*" What started as a seething growl exploded into a roar. "How many times must I *say it!*"

In the space of a blink, the music shattered. Discordant notes slammed into each other, then into sudden silence, and the air reverberated with the shock.

Rebekah cringed and held her breath.

Tate's face flushed crimson. "Ries wrote the third movement as a forceful scherzo. Not a *dirge!*" He gripped the baton with both hands, and Rebekah feared he might snap it in two. "Violins, you were late! Horns, you were flat! And flutes"—he threw his hands up in the air and the baton went flying—"you weren't even in the house. I heard nothing from you. *Nothing!*"

Not a sound issued from the orchestra. Not a breath stirred. And Rebekah didn't dare move either for fear Tate would see her and implode right then and there.

But she'd heard the flutes just fine. They'd played pianissimo, but they *had* been playing.

She looked across the orchestra, and her gaze quickly settled on the only member she knew—Darrow Fulton. He looked anything but pleased, which aptly described every other man out there as well. Or those whose faces she could see, anyway.

She'd weighed the dreaded likelihood of running into Darrow since she was working at the opera hall now. But considering the duress under which she'd taken the job, seeing him hadn't qualified as a big enough deterrent. But if he somehow revealed to Tate Whitcomb that she played the violin—something she'd sworn to Mrs. Cheatham not to reveal—and then if Tate put two and two together about the night of the dinner party—and that information somehow got passed along . . .

That would not be advantageous for her

271

personally, nor for her relationship with Adelicia Cheatham. So Rebekah planned to give Darrow Fulton an extra wide berth.

Tate shoved a hand through his hair, not that the wayward curl paid any attention as it fell stubbornly back across his forehead. He drew in a breath, then exhaled through clenched teeth. "Gentlemen, we will start, yet again, at the beginning of the third movement. And may I remind you, lest each of your memories be as fragile as that of a small girl—"

Rebekah frowned, not caring for the analogy.

"—the final movement is a stormy finale, played in the typical rhythm of the Fate motif, and in obvious homage to Beethoven, of whom Ries was his favorite disciple, as we know. Or *should!* Hold that thought foremost in your minds, gentlemen, for it *will* alter the way you play. Whether you can hear the difference, matters not. For *I* most certainly will."

He bowed his head for a long moment, then finally looked up and lifted his hands. With military-like precision, the orchestra responded with instruments raised.

The music started, and as it progressed, Rebekah found herself watching the oboe players. Several moments passed before she became aware of the sharp rise and fall of her chest. And of what she was feeling. Remorse. And also . . . envy.

She tried to relinquish both. And managed the former more easily than the latter. She stayed through the third movement and well into the fourth, then tiptoed back into the corridor, not trusting her memory of how long the symphony lasted.

By the time Tate returned to his office, she'd filed nearly a full stack of music—that the apparently filing-challenged Miss Endicott hadn't completed. She hadn't met Miss Endicott yet but wanted to—if only to see what she was really like.

Tate walked in, went straight to his desk chair, and sat, head in his hands. She stole glances at him.

Finally, he sighed and leaned back. "Good afternoon, Rebekah."

She made a point of looking up. "Good afternoon, Tate."

"How long have you been here?"

She paused, wondering if he'd seen her backstage, and knew that honesty—or at least a version of it—was best. "I arrived a while ago. I heard the orchestra practicing. It sounded beautiful."

"It sounds as though we're not ready. Because"— he huffed—"we decidedly are not."

"Do you think that perhaps you're being too hard on yourself? And the orchestra?"

He leveled a stare. "No. I do not."

Hearing finality in his tone, as well as the hunger for a fight, she gave him a simple nod and went back to filing.

"Oh no," he said, rising. "There'll be none of that."

"None of what?"

"None of this." He bobbed his head up and down as though mimicking her, when all he did was make himself look like an utter fool. "You obviously have something to say. So why not say it?"

"Because I don't think you're in a frame of mind to discuss it."

The smile that curved his mouth held challenge. "And what frame of mind might that be?"

She set the music aside and stood. "You're frustrated because your orchestra isn't performing to your high standards. Which are extremely demanding. And understandably so," she added, giving him a look that she hoped said the statement wasn't a declaration of war. "And you're tired. I can see it in your eyes. You're likely not sleeping well because you're worried about composing your symphony. No doubt, you often stay up late into the night writing."

A muscle twitched at the corner of his eye, as if confirming her supposition, while also revealing that her words were finding their mark.

"You have three months in which to write two movements, of which the final movement is typically the most difficult—because it's the culmination of the masterpiece you've struggled and clawed and sweated to pull from the secret places inside you. And all the while . . ." She paused as her own story—different from his, yet not *so* different—subtly, unexpectedly wove its way into the moment and thieved a fraction of her voice. "All the while you're living for the time when . . . your *creation* will finally take its first breath and stand in the light of day. Then you hope with all your heart—"

The words caught in her throat as she relived the feelings she'd experienced that night as she'd played the Stradivarius, even though as an unseen, nameless ghost. And the tender intensity in his expression only made speaking more difficult.

"—that people will receive it, and will respond," she whispered. "And that maybe they'll . . . *somehow* hear a portion of the beauty you first heard when the music was merely the faintest whisper inside you."

His gaze held hers, and though she told herself to look away, she could not. An undeniable tension held her there. A tension not so much unpleasant as it was . . . unsettling. Yet also enticing.

But when his gaze dropped to her mouth and he took a step toward her, the tension snapped. And Rebekah blinked.

Her heart racing, she looked down, not completely certain that what she'd thought was about to happen had truly been about to happen. Still, she looked at her hands, then at the piano, then at his feet. Anywhere but back in his eyes.

"Thank you . . . Rebekah," he finally whispered, his voice like velvet, so different from earlier when he'd unleashed his fury upon the orchestra.

She smiled, then chanced a quick look up. A

softness in his eyes replaced the intensity of seconds before, telling her it was safe now—but also confirming that what she'd seen . . . was real.

"And just what is this?"

She looked at where he pointed, aware of the sharp turn in conversation, and grateful for it. "Those are lemon tea cakes. From Cordina."

He raised his eyebrows in question.

She nodded. "Help yourself."

Tate opened the tin and held it out to her first. She took one, then he did likewise. They ate in silence, and she loved the way he closed his eyes as he chewed. More descriptive than any words could convey.

When he opened them, there was a sliver of peace that hadn't been there moments earlier. "So what did you think of the fourth movement?"

She stopped chewing and politely covered her mouth. "You saw me?"

He smiled. "Not until you turned to leave. How long had you been standing there?"

She frowned. "A while."

His stare persisted, and she sighed.

"I arrived right before the . . . thunder began."

He laughed. "And by thunder, I take it you mean my frustration with the third movement."

"So that was you being frustrated." She nodded. "Remind me never to get on your bad side . . . Maestro Whitcomb."

"Oh, I daresay you're capable of a little thunder yourself, Rebekah Carrington."

She looked over at him and saw both amusement and seriousness in his expression—and felt that tug of tension between them again. She reached for the tin. "Another tea cake?"

He smiled and took one. "Don't mind if I do." As he ate, his gaze dropped to her dress. Gentleness moved into his features. "May I ask . . . are you in mourning, Rebekah?"

Surprised at the question and, even more, that he'd noticed and would inquire, she nodded. "I am. My grandmother passed in December."

"I'm sorry," he offered softly. "Was she especially dear to you?"

Again, his question caught her off guard, as did the tenderness in his voice. "More than I can say."

He opened his mouth as if to respond, then simply looked at her, understanding in his eyes that needed no words.

They worked for the afternoon in comfortable silence and sprinklings of conversation—Tate at the piano composing, and Rebekah at his desk transcribing the first two movements of his symphony for full orchestra with all instruments included.

She'd only played the piano version before, and a fresh copy of a full instrumentation was needed. One that incorporated the recent notations and changes he'd made in the margins in the event that this copy was—heaven forbid—lost or destroyed.

They also needed a cleaner copy from which to work together, and she appreciated the opportunity to study his work as she transcribed.

She kept her own notes in a separate notebook as she went along, referencing the specific measure in the music in a column on the left with the corresponding notation in a column on the right. She'd brought the last few sheets of staff paper that she'd prepared before leaving Vienna, and it felt odd to be using it here now, so far from where she'd drawn it.

A deep sigh from the piano bench brought her head up.

Tate played a few chords, then stopped, then played, then stopped and put pen to paper. Then played again and sighed and rubbed his temples. She could almost *feel* the creative process emanating from him, and from this perspective, it didn't seem nearly so glamorous or exciting as she'd expected.

She returned to her work with a prayer on her lips. Both for him and this entire undertaking.

Much like Beethoven's Ninth, the opening measures of Tate's first movement were dominated by the violin, viola, and cello. And as she transcribed the notes for the violin, she yearned to be able to reach for hers and play the part as written, but she settled for her imagination instead.

Right on time, Mrs. Murphey delivered afternoon tea. "Here you are, Maestro." She gave Rebekah a passing glance. "Miss Carrington."

Rebekah smiled. "Good afternoon, Mrs. Murphey. And thank you."

"Yes, thank you, Mrs. Murphey," Tate muttered from the piano, his gaze never lifting.

Mrs. Murphey looked at him and smiled with all the love and affection of a proud mother. "You're welcome, Maestro. I'll pick up your black coat and tails from the laundress tomorrow on my way in, as well as your shoes."

"Thank you, Mrs. Murphey." Again, he didn't look up.

But that didn't diminish the glow of maternal affection shining in the older woman's eyes. However, looking back at Rebekah did, and the woman departed with her usual dour countenance firmly recast.

Rebekah could only smile. She glanced at the open door to the office, wanting to make certain Mrs. Murphey was out of earshot, then kept her voice to an absolute whisper. "I think she's growing to like me." She chuckled.

But Tate didn't respond. So she spoke a little louder.

"I *think* Mrs. Murphey is growing to *like* me."

Still, nothing.

"Tate!" she said in full voice.

"Yes . . . thank you." His pen never lifted from the page.

"Are you listening to me?"

He gestured for her to give him a moment, and she shook her head. This behavior, she was accustomed to. She'd seen Mrs. Heilig have a full conversation with her husband when he was seated at the piano, him giving occasional grunts and nods. Yet Maestro Heilig would later swear it had never taken place.

Rebekah rose, needing to stretch and needing more paper. And needing *tea*. She poured herself a cup, then took it to him instead, setting it on a side table.

Brow furrowed, he wrote feverishly, eyes squinted, shoulders taut. He was certainly a driven man of strong temperament, and one often short of patience. Add to that a disposition listing toward the irritable. But what musician couldn't that describe?

She waited until he moved to play again. "Where do you keep the supply of staff paper?"

For a moment, she thought he hadn't heard her.

"Cupboard. Bottom. Oh! And write a note to Mrs. Bixby asking her to leave two tickets for a Mr. and Mrs. Barrett at the box office for tomorrow night. Complimentary."

Rebekah wrote and delivered the note and then relished a cup of tea and another of Cordina's tea cakes before going in search of the paper. She rummaged through box after box, wondering how long some of them had been in there. She opened the final lower cupboard and saw a box sitting alone on a shelf. That had to be it.

She pulled it out, but something clinked within, like glass, and she immediately stilled, hoping she hadn't broken anything. She lifted the open flap and peered inside. Bottles. At least half a dozen. She lifted one and read the label, then read it again, hoping that somehow it would read differently. But it didn't. And all the labels read the same.

Laudanum.

She stared at the bottles as everything she knew about musicians came crashing forward in her thoughts. Their weekend visits to opium dens. Specially made concoctions that purportedly increased creativity.

No, no, no . . .

Suddenly Tate banged the keys on the piano and she jumped. He said something beneath his breath she couldn't quite hear but could imagine well enough based on his harsh tone.

Disbelief and anger vied for control as she felt the dream of New York City slipping from her grasp.

Gripping the bottle in her hand, she looked up to see him rake an impatient hand through his hair. Then he leaned forward and rested his head in his hands, and she thought of his irritability, his impatience, his continually being tired—and she knew.

17

Tate felt as though his head were about to explode, and listening to the symphony tuning on the stage didn't help.

Customarily, he lived for these evenings, the anticipation as he waited in the wings, only seconds from taking the stage, the shushed susurration of the audience drifting beyond the barrier of the thick crimson curtain. He'd walk on, stop briefly to shake hands with his concertmaster, despite Darrow Fulton not being high on his list at present. Then he'd step up to the dais, grasp his baton, and do what he'd been born—and had trained nearly his entire life—to do.

Yet right now, all he wanted was to be far, far away from every jagged piece of noise that sliced at his inner ear like shards of glass rubbed against newborn skin.

The previous evening, the ache in his head had finally dulled, and he'd been so grateful. But no sooner had that pain lessened than the sensitivity began. He only prayed it would cease before he took the dais. If it hurt this much to hear the orchestra responding to the oboe's tuning note, he couldn't imagine the pain he would endure once every instrument began playing at its full—

He swallowed, the temptation to walk away almost overwhelming. But a conductor not taking the stage was paramount to turning in his resignation. Forever. No other symphony would ever—

He blinked . . . and the punishing shards of glass suddenly fell away.

His breath came quick, and he closed his eyes, his body flooding with relief at the absence of pain. He rubbed his temples, daring to hope, yet dreading taking the next swallow.

But . . . he did. And his world stayed right.

He tilted his head from side to side, only then feeling how tight his neck and shoulder muscles were. Maybe that was part of the problem. Too much work, too little rest. Hadn't Rebekah said as much to him yesterday?

Yesterday . . . He'd nearly made a terrible mistake with her.

Not that kissing Rebekah Carrington would have been terrible. Quite the opposite, he was certain. But he needed her assistance to finish this symphony on time. So doing anything that would hinder or harm that goal was out of the question.

However, thinking about kissing her—he pictured her smile, her lips, the sensuous curve of her neck—now that was a different matter altogether.

Movement to his left drew his attention, and he saw the object of his thoughts—and curbed desires—standing only feet away, looking in his direction. He closed the distance.

"Good evening, Miss Carrington." Mindful of others around them, he opted for the more formal address and kept his voice soft.

"Good evening, Maestro Whitcomb." She followed his lead, her tone professional. She peered up at him. "How are you feeling this evening?"

"Up until a few moments ago, not well." Tate caught the gesture from the master of ceremonies and acknowledged it with a tilt of his head. "But I think I'm making strides toward the better."

Rebekah nodded, but something in her eyes offered silent dispute. Yet seeing his cue, Tate had no time to address it—or tell her how beautiful she looked. Even in colors of mourning.

He walked to the edge of the curtain, stretched the muscles in his neck and shoulders, tugged on his coat sleeves, and strode on stage.

He hadn't taken four steps before the audience rose to their feet, their applause filling the rafters. And their enthusiasm buoyed his ruffled spirit.

He paused and shook hands with Fulton, noting the man's bloodshot eyes. Tate tightened his grip, with a look daring Fulton to make a mistake this evening. Tate already had his suspicions about the man's *habits* outside the symphony. And while he respected a musician's privacy, when what that musician did in private reflected negatively on the orchestra—or affected Tate's own career—he gave privacy the boot.

Which is just what he'd be giving Darrow Fulton, if the man didn't start living up to his responsibility as concertmaster.

Tate took the dais, turned briefly to acknowledge the audience's applause with a bow, and focused once again on his score on the music stand. Head bowed, he drank in the momentary silence laden with anticipation, and focused every thought on the task before him.

Already, he could hear Ferdinand Ries's symphony in his head, perfect in tempo, in pitch, and in its intended purpose to honor the master, Beethoven himself. Now to do the piece justice, as well as bring deserved honor to Bach, later in the concert.

Tate lifted his head, met the gazes of each section leader, one by one, then raised his baton. The musicians responded with instruments readied, and entered precisely on Tate's cue.

He'd all but committed the symphonies to memory through the years, especially the final movement in Ries's masterpiece, his favorite of the four. He embraced each note, certain there were fewer pleasures known to man greater than that of music, and knowing how much duller the world—and his world, in particular—would be without it.

Rebekah had intended to take her seat in the audience before the symphony began, but curiosity had prevented her. She'd wanted to see how Tate was faring, especially after what she'd discovered yesterday.

And when she'd seen him standing there, waiting to go on, she'd known something was wrong.

His grimace, the way he massaged his temples, the shadows beneath his eyes were all too familiar. And seeing the signs only further stoked her anger. She'd watched countless musicians in the Vienna Philharmonic squander money on similar addictions, risking their talent and position, throwing away opportunities she would've given her eyeteeth for. And for what?

An empty, fleeting feeling of euphoria. Or so she was told. Selfish was what it was. And idiotic.

And yet to look at Tate now—which is why she'd remained backstage, to watch him—he seemed perfectly fine. Or more than fine. He was doing precisely what he'd been created to do, and he was doing it splendidly.

Watching the passion with which he conducted—the emotion in his face, his gestures, the intensity in his gaze—drew her to him in a way she couldn't describe. And didn't want to explore, much less encourage.

The musicians responded to him too. Though conductors were famous for being stingy with their praise, and Tate certainly followed in that vein, when the music did please him, when he thought it worthy, his expression conveyed his affirmation in a way words could never capture.

And as Rebekah watched the musicians watching him, she saw sheer joy reflected in their eyes when their conductor's merest look conveyed pleasure.

The opus moved into the second movement, and she listened as the music soared and filled the opera house. Then just as swiftly, the tempo slowed, the notes caressing the listener with tones so sweet and tender, stirring the heart.

Stirring *her* heart.

The second movement concluded on a definitive, resonating chord, and the third began with equal energy, the wayward curl on Tate's forehead having long since broken free of any attempt to be tamed. Only when the third movement drew to a close and the fourth began did Rebekah notice how her feet ached.

She shifted her weight from foot to foot. That's what she got for standing for so long. Having seen a chair on her way in, she tiptoed back toward it but found it occupied by one of the stage workers.

She swallowed a sigh.

At least from this perspective she had a better view of the orchestra. And of Tate. She heard one of the trumpets go flat and, at the same time, saw Tate grimace and send the offending horn a withering stare she felt all the way from where she stood. What would it be like to be on the receiving end of such a glare? Unnerving, to say the least.

But she would risk it, and far more, for the chance to play with a group of musicians like this, to perform in front of such an audience. And to be conducted by a man like Tate. Not that she wanted him to know that.

With mastery worthy of a maestro twice his age, Tate directed the finale with vigor and precision, and Rebekah stared in slightly begrudging wonder, realizing now that everything the newspaper articles reported about him . . . was true. He really did possess extraordinary talent and musicianship, which he demonstrated yet again in the second half of the concert with Bach's Brandenburg Concertos Nos. 3 and 4 in G Major.

The Nashville Philharmonic—comprised of approximately fifty men—wasn't as large as the one in Vienna. Nor were they all professional musicians, she'd learned. The ad hoc quality of the ensemble bothered Tate, she knew. Yet the sound and energy he drew from the group—that he inspired them to deliver—was astounding, more likely proving a credit to his ability as a conductor than to the musical talent of the orchestra members themselves.

When the final note from Bach's Brandenburg Concerto No. 4 faded, Tate cast a glance over the orchestra, then lowered his arms, and the audience rose in a standing ovation.

Not looking particularly pleased, though not scowling either, Tate indicated for the orchestra to rise, then he turned, bowed, and succinctly left the stage.

Rebekah met him as he came around the corner. "Tate, that was—"

"As though we'd scarcely practiced at all, I know." The rigid set of his jaw matched the steel of his tone. "It's a wonder the audience didn't get up and march out during the second movement.

When I turned a moment ago, I fully expected to find half of the seats empty."

Rebekah frowned. "I believe you're being the *slightest* bit unreasonable. And completely unrealistic. Yes, there was a mistake or two. But the philharmonic was splendid, and you conducted masterfully."

"Says someone who knows nothing about conducting."

The remark landed like a blow, and Rebekah took a step back.

As though sensing the wound he'd inflicted, Tate moved toward her.

But she put up a hand. "Don't."

"I'm sorry, Rebekah. I didn't mean for it to come out that way. I—"

"No. You *did* mean it." She looked into his eyes, despising this side of him, and wondering how many people—if any—had ever spoken truth to the man. "You're an enormously talented conductor, Tate. But what you hoard in talent you sorely lack in perspective and temperament, and in common decency. And, obviously, in respect for others' opinions."

Struck by the magnitude of his perfectionism and stubbornness, she felt her last hope of New York fade to nothing.

"Forgive me, Rebekah." He winced and rubbed his temple. "But while I appreciate your opinion of tonight's performance, it's my own I must live with."

A laugh void of humor slipped past her lips.

"Are you listening to yourself? In the same breath, you say you appreciate my opinion while also saying it's essentially worthless."

He glanced at others around them. "May we please continue this conversation somewhere else? Later, and in private?"

"I doubt we will. But *fine*." Rebekah turned to leave.

"Miss Carrington."

Struggling to contain the wave of hurt, she looked back.

Tate gestured toward the hallway. "Would you please accompany me to the foyer?"

She blinked. "You can't be serious."

"The philharmonic board and their wives would like to meet my . . . other assistant. They've heard about you, and"—he gave a quick nod to a gentleman standing off to the side watching them—"I told them you would be here."

"You told them—" Rebekah clenched her teeth so hard her jaw ached.

"Please, Rebekah." Tate placed his hand on the small of her back and leaned close. "My head is splitting. Simply do this, and then I'll take you home."

Wanting to tell him he only had himself—and his addiction—to blame for the ache in his head, she finally nodded. "I'll do it. But I'll find my own way home."

He offered her his arm, and wishing she could wring his neck instead, she accepted.

Once in the lobby, she spotted Darrow Fulton and two other violinists moving in their general direction, and with nowhere to hide, she braced herself for the encounter, knowing it wouldn't be pleasant. And with so many other people around.

"Fulton!" a man called over the buzz of conversation and patrons exiting the hall.

Darrow turned in the direction of the man's voice and raised a hand in response, then headed toward the exit where he waited. Rebekah breathed a sigh of relief, at least for the moment.

As Tate made introductions, she smiled and graciously greeted couple after couple, forgetting their names almost as soon as Tate said them, and knowing she'd never remember all their faces. Except for one couple, and a beautiful young woman standing beside them. Instinctively, she guessed who the young woman was even before Tate made introductions.

"May I introduce Mr. and Mrs. Harold Endicott"—Tate tilted his head in polite deference—"and their eldest daughter, Miss Caroline Endicott. Likewise, allow me to present Miss Rebekah Carrington."

Rebekah curtsied, amazed that Miss Endicott could maintain a smile while shooting such daggers with her eyes. "It's my honor, Mr. and Mrs. Endicott. Miss Endicott."

"The pleasure is ours, I'm sure." Mrs. Endicott sniffed and turned her head as though catching scent of something foul, while Mr. Endicott reserved his severe countenance for Tate alone.

"See here, Maestro, I trust it's clear to you that the philharmonic will *not* be responsible for the cost of this second assistant you've seen to—"

"Rest assured, sir . . ." Tate angled his body in such a way that Rebekah couldn't see the other man anymore. But she could still hear their voices. As could others nearby, no doubt. "That fact was made immensely clear."

"And, frankly," Mr. Endicott continued, "considering the board's generosity in providing an assistant in the first place, we expect you to utilize my daughter's time in the most productive fashion. And only two mornings a week scarcely seems—"

"But you'd be amazed, Mr. Endicott, at the amount of productivity in those two mornings." Tate shook the man's hand. "Thank you again for coming this evening, sir. And for your generous support of the symphony."

With a glare, Mr. Endicott and his wife moved on, while Miss Endicott bypassed Rebekah and went straight for Tate.

In the space of a curtsy, the young woman reframed her daggers into a blushing smile, while also not so discreetly arranging her bodice to reveal even more décolletage than was already visible. Which was saying something. Rebekah watched the display, partly amazed at the smoothness of the woman's actions, while also keeping watch on Tate's line of sight. From her peripheral vision, she noticed other men growing quite still, their attention openly transfixed on Miss Endicott's plentiful assets. But Tate—

His gaze never strayed from the young woman's face.

"Miss Endicott, so nice to see you and your parents again," he said. "Thank you for your attendance this evening, and for your continued support of the philharmonic. It's most appreciated."

Miss Endicott toyed with the taut laces of her bodice. "I'm willing to support the symphony in any way you desire, Maestro Whitcomb. As I've told you, many times."

Rebekah felt her own face grow warm even as her curiosity piqued. She was accustomed to seeing women flock to musicians following concerts in Vienna. She'd simply never been so close to the actual . . . *flocking*.

Watching Miss Endicott fawn over Tate, she felt an unsettling twinge of . . . resentment. But when she realized what it was she was truly feeling, she couldn't decide which was greater—her frustration at her own jealousy, or her sudden desire to slip her hand back into the crook of Tate's arm just to see how the young woman would react.

Yet she didn't dare, not wanting Tate to misconstrue her intention.

Thankfully, the Endicotts were the last of the board members and their families, and Rebekah moved off to the side as Tate swiftly became engulfed by others seeking an audience with him.

No wonder the man thought so highly of his own opinion, with everyone clamoring after him like they did.

But what was this about the philharmonic not covering her wages any longer? Tate had mentioned a benefactor, and she'd assumed it was the symphony board. Or someone on it. But if no one from the board was paying her, who was? Or worse, what if Tate had lost that funding and simply hadn't told her yet?

Worried, weary, and ready for home, she reached down and adjusted her right boot, the soles of her feet starting to throb. She'd opted to walk to and from Belmont more often in recent days and was paying for it now.

She searched the dispersing crowd for Dr. and Mrs. Cheatham but didn't see them anywhere. Adelicia had mentioned there was a chance they might not make it to the performance tonight. Rebekah sighed. So much for asking the couple for a ride home.

"Rebekah, my dear girl. . . . What a surprise!"

Hot prickles needled up Rebekah's spine. She slowly lifted her gaze, already detecting the sickly scent of cherry laurel.

"Barton," she whispered. "W-what are you doing here?"

He smiled and took hold of her fingertips, then pressed an overly warm—and lingering—kiss to the back of her hand. Her skin crawled, and she quickly drew her hand away.

"I'm here attending the symphony, of course. As are you, I see."

His gaze shot to Tate, then back again. But Rebekah was already looking past him for her mother.

"Is Mother here with you?"

"You know better than that, Rebekah." Barton smiled, his gaze leisurely moving over her. "Your mother doesn't care for the symphony, nor does she prefer venturing out on such cold evenings."

"So you're here alone?"

Again, he smiled, a gesture that would've seemed innocent on anyone else. But on him, it looked vulgar. "At least I can tell your mother with whom you're keeping company these days. Since you obviously don't care enough to inform her yourself."

Rebekah knew better than to be drawn into an argument with him. Still, it was hard not to defend her actions.

"Miss Carrington?"

She turned to see Tate beside her and panicked as two very separate worlds were set to collide.

"Maestro Whitcomb." Barton Ledbetter extended a hand. "May I say what an excellent performance you conducted this evening. Magnificent in every way."

Tate inclined his head. "Your praise is appreciated, sir."

Rebekah felt both men watching her.

"Rebekah, dear." Barton raised an eyebrow. "Won't you please introduce me?"

Knowing it was wrong to hate someone, yet unable to equate her present emotion with anything other than hatred, Rebekah acquiesced. "Barton Ledbetter, may I introduce Maestro Nathaniel Tate Whitcomb. Maestro, Barton Ledbetter."

"Mr. Ledbetter. A pleasure."

"The pleasure is all mine, Maestro." Barton shot Rebekah a look. "May I ask, Maestro . . . Precisely how is it you know my daughter?"

"Your . . . *daughter?*" Surprise thickened Tate's voice.

"*Step*daughter," Rebekah corrected, feeling Tate's attention. "Maestro Whitcomb and I know one another because I work here. In the symphony offices."

"Ah . . ." Barton nodded, looking between them as though having heard something more than what she'd said. "Well, it's good to finally know where you're working, at least. I'll be sure to tell your mother. She worries about you so, Rebekah. It hurts her that you visit so infrequently."

Rebekah narrowed her eyes. "I bid you good evening, Barton."

The man hesitated, then bowed, the gesture looking foolish on him. "Good evening, my dear. Maestro."

Feeling sick to her stomach and eager to wash the scent of cherry laurel from her hands, Rebekah watched Barton exit the door, a rush of cold wind entering as he did. He joined a group of men waiting outside, and she could hear their laughter as they walked away.

"Rebekah?"

The way Tate spoke her name, softly, and with a question wrapped around it, made her wish she was already back at Belmont and safely in her room. "My father died when I was twelve," she whispered so only he could hear. "My mother was grief stricken, as was I. But . . . she apparently couldn't cope with the pain and loneliness. So five months later, she married *him*."

Silence stretched between them.

"It must have been difficult to see someone else take your father's place."

"That man will *never* take my father's place."

"No, of course not. I didn't mean to insinuate that—"

"If we're finished here for the evening, Tate, I'll take my leave."

He held her gaze. "Certainly. I'll call for the carriage."

"No need. I'll arrange for my own transportation."

"No, I'll take you home as I said."

"Thank you, Tate, but—"

"I'll be right back."

He strode to the front door and stepped out. A waiting carriage pulled forward. Rebekah shook her head. The man scarcely had a need before it was already met.

Tate returned. "Did you wear your cloak this evening?"

Remembering, she glanced behind them. "I left it in your—"

"I'll fetch it. Again, wait here for me. Please," he added, as though sensing her frustration.

Feeling ordered about and resenting it, yet not wishing to walk for blocks looking for a carriage willing to travel all the way to Belmont and back to town, she did as he said.

He returned moments later, helped her into her cloak, then assisted her into the carriage. The compartment, luxuriously furnished and smelling of fresh cedar, provided shelter from the wind. But still, the air was frigid. Her breath puffed white, and she pulled her cloak about herself and kept her gaze confined to the window.

He claimed the opposite bench, his long legs taking up more than a passenger's fair share, and she angled hers so as not to touch him.

He leaned back and closed his eyes, but she sensed the tension coming from him. It was his own fault, though, his addiction to laudanum. So she felt no pity.

They rode in silence, and at times, she sensed him watching her in the darkness. She wanted to ask him about the money. If he couldn't pay her, she deserved to know. But she hadn't even earned a full month's salary yet. So how could she? Yet how could she not? She needed to be earning.

Only after they reached the turnoff to Belmont

did he rouse fully. He leaned forward and angled his head from side to side, a gesture with which she was becoming familiar.

The carriage stopped in front of the mansion, a soft glow illuminating the multicolored glass of the foyer sidelights, and she reached for the door latch. But he beat her to it.

"Rebekah . . ."

How was it he could say her name and something inside her went soft?

"You're right. I can oftentimes lose perspective when it comes to the caliber of my orchestra. And my temperament can, on occasion, be . . . mercurial. My expectations of my musicians and of myself are enormous. And while I won't apologize for that, I do apologize for speaking to you in such a cavalier manner tonight. It was my own frustration with myself that fueled what I said to you . . . Words I should never have spoken. And while you are correct, again, in saying that I don't give much weight to others' opinions, I do, however, hold yours in the highest regard."

Though darkness hid the precise definition of his features, the sincerity of his tone tempted Rebekah to believe him. Even more, she found herself *wanting* to believe him. "I wish you could hear the music as others heard it tonight. As *I* heard it. It was . . . magical, Tate. Transforming, luminescent."

He said nothing for a moment, then sighed. "I appreciate that. But it could have been better."

She stared at him, sensing him doing the same to her, and the shadows in the carriage seemed to grow deeper. Finally, he opened the door, exited, and took her hand as she descended. His own hand was large and warm and strong, yet capable of such demonstrative grace, as she'd witnessed earlier that evening.

He walked her to the door, then reached into his pocket and pressed a tiny velvet drawstring bag into the palm of her hand. "Here's your first month's salary."

Her hand closed around it. "But I've only worked—"

"I know. But I'm also aware that I frustrate you. Greatly, at times. And I want you to keep coming back, Rebekah. I need you to keep coming back."

"So by your reasoning, if you pay me in advance, you think I'll feel obligated to return."

"You're a woman of integrity. If I pay you, I *know* you'll return."

She stared at the velvet bag in her hand. "I overheard what Mr. Endicott said to you tonight. That the symphony isn't willing to pay my wages."

"Don't worry about that. Another benefactor has guaranteed your wages."

"May I ask who that is?"

"You may. But I'm not at liberty to say."

She eyed him. "This is a lot of money, Tate. For which I'm grateful. But are you certain that—"

"Don't worry about your wages, Rebekah. They're guaranteed. I give you my word."

He bowed and waited as she opened the door. She stepped inside, the foyer dark except for a single lamp burning on a side table.

He returned to the carriage, and Rebekah pushed the door almost closed, still watching him, feeling admiration and a smidgen of—though she was loath to admit it—*sympathy* for the man.

She watched the carriage until it disappeared from sight.

Bone weary, she hurried through her nightly rituals and was asleep almost as soon as she laid her head on the pillow.

Sometime during the night, a persistent knocking awakened her, and she sat up, her thoughts foggy, the room cold. The knocking grew more insistent, and she fumbled for her robe, managing to slip it on as she reached the door.

She turned the latch and found herself squinting into lamplight.

"Hurry and come quick, Miss Rebekah. It's Missus Cheatham. She's hurtin' somethin' fierce!"

18

Rebekah followed Cordina across the darkened grand salon to the staircase, the chill in her own bedroom nothing compared to the cold in this part of the house. "Is it the neuralgia, Cordina?"

"Yes, ma'am." Cordina glanced back. "And it's painin' her bad. It come up right before dinner. And she'd planned on goin' to that opera house tonight. I told her I'd send to town for the doctor, but she won't have it. I made her some tea, but | she ain't drinkin'. And I'm not knowin' what else to do. You said your mama suffers from it, so I's thinkin' you might could help."

Not certain she could, Rebekah hurried to keep up. "Isn't Dr. Cheatham home?"

"No, ma'am. He left early this mornin'. Missus Cheatham, she supposed to meet him in Murfreesboro tomorrow with the children. But I ain't sure that's happenin' now."

Cordina held the oil lamp aloft as they ascended the stairs, and the shadows scattered before them. But with renewed bravado, they swiftly returned and enveloped the staircase below. Silver-spun moonlight filtered through rectangular windows spanning the length of the second-floor landing, and a ghostly light painted the gallery setting, reminding Rebekah of the night she'd played the Stradivarius.

Cordina paused beside Mrs. Cheatham's closed bedroom door. "I already give her a powder about half past one. It helped for a time, but now the achin's back. Worse than before, she says." Cordina set the lamp on a table in the hallway. "The light hurts her eyes," she whispered as she turned the knob.

Darkness blanketed the bedroom, its only

contender a low-burning fire banked in the hearth. The embers glowed white-hot, and Rebekah quickly closed the door behind them to sequester the warmth.

"Missus Cheatham?" Cordina whispered. "I got Miss Rebekah here with me, ma'am."

Rebekah moved around to the other side of the bed, feeling awkward about entering her employer's bedchamber without a proper summons, yet wanting to help, if she could.

"Miss Carrington" came a surprisingly weak whisper. "I'm sorry my troubles . . . have become a bother to you."

Rebekah leaned closer, taken aback by how much smaller and less intimidating this strikingly impressive woman seemed in this setting and circumstance. "It's no bother, Mrs. Cheatham. Is there anything I can get—or do—for you, to help relieve the pain?"

"I assure you"—a long sigh—"if there were, I would not hesitate to command it of you, Miss Carrington. No matter the hour."

Rebekah couldn't help but smile. *This* was the woman she knew and had swiftly grown to respect.

"I done tried rubbin' her head earlier, but that ain't helpin'," Cordina whispered, gently smoothing the covers on the bed.

"Have you tried drinking a little wine, Mrs. Cheatham?" Rebekah couldn't remember ever having seen the woman partake, but she did remember that her own grandmother, God rest her, sipped muscadine wine, on occasion, when she had an especially bad headache.

"No," Mrs. Cheatham said softly, yet with a definitive note. "I have not. But I certainly will . . . if you think it might help."

Cordina was out of the room before Mrs. Cheatham even finished the sentence. Eyes closed, Mrs. Cheatham never moved her head— or anything else—in acknowledgment of Cordina's response. She lay perfectly still.

Not knowing what else to do, Rebekah *did* know better than to talk.

She moved to sit in a chair off to the side when she noticed an open door leading to another room. Curiosity trumped her better judgment, and she peered around the corner.

It was another bedroom, smaller, and decorated in a more masculine feel than the bedroom in which she now stood. In the space of a second, her thoughts leaped ahead. Did Dr. and Mrs. Cheatham not share a bed? Though she was hardly an expert on the subject, she knew there were couples who didn't share a bed. Or a bedroom, for that matter. And though she didn't care to dwell on the *why*s behind their reasoning, she found it sad and rather counterproductive to the whole theme of matrimony.

Or at least what she perceived it to be.

But one thing was certain. . . . When she married—*if* she ever married—she wanted to share her husband's bed. She wanted to share everything.

She glanced back at the bed to make sure Mrs. Cheatham wasn't watching her. She wasn't. Nor had she moved.

Rebekah yawned and pulled the collar of her robe closer around her throat, reminded of her early days in Vienna. She had awakened about this time nearly every night, her hands cramping due to having practiced the violin for upwards of six hours a day—a nonnegotiable demand from the Viennese tutor Nana had miraculously procured. But besides her hands hurting, her heart had ached for home. And for her grandmother, after Nana had returned home to Nashville.

Sally had risen with her during those early hours and would rub her hands and forearms, gently kneading out the kinks and soreness, and singing to her in that deep, soulful voice until the aches in Rebekah's hands—and in her heart—eventually subsided so she could gradually find sleep again.

Sally's mother had been a healer and, like her mother, had long held to the axiom that the head, hands, and heart were somehow connected. And that in massaging the hands, the soothing of those muscles encouraged the heart and mind to let loose of their worries. What a gift those middle-of-the-night moments had been.

The memory of them warmed Rebekah's heart even now—and gave her an idea. She crossed to the fire and warmed her hands over the flames, rubbing them together, then moved back to the bed.

"Mrs. Cheatham . . ." she whispered. "If you'll allow me, I'd like to try something I think might be of help."

"Please . . . Miss Carrington. Anything."

Rebekah gently took hold of her hand—it was cold to the touch—and pressed it between hers, as Sally had done. Then she applied slight pressure to the palm, massaging, working outward to each finger, pressing a little more firmly as she went, before moving upward to the wrist and forearm. Mrs. Cheatham's hand and arm were stiff at first, but gradually relaxed until Rebekah supported their full weight.

Rebekah moved to the other side of the bed just as Cordina returned with the glass of wine. With assistance, Mrs. Cheatham sat up and managed a few sips, then lay back down. Cordina set the wine aside, and Rebekah continued massaging, sensing her employer's trust in the limpness of her arm and wrist.

After several moments, Mrs. Cheatham sighed. "Where did you learn to do that?"

"From Sally, the servant who—"

"—accompanied you to Vienna," Mrs. Cheatham whispered. "I remember you telling me about her."

Rebekah shared about the nights she'd awakened with her hands hurting. "I quickly became convinced that Sally was right. Although, I still don't claim to understand how one's hands are connected to one's head."

"*Hmmm . . .*" Mrs. Cheatham took a deep breath, then exhaled. "Well, whether it's the wine or what you've done, or both . . . the pain has lessened considerably. Thank you, Miss Carrington. And thank *you,* Cordina. Now please, both of you . . . find rest for yourselves. As I will gratefully do."

After Cordina added another log to the fire and they made certain Mrs. Cheatham had everything she needed close at hand, Rebekah followed Cordina from the room. She was closing the door behind her when she heard her name and paused.

"Yes, Mrs. Cheatham?"

"There *is* one last thing you could do for me . . . if you're willing."

Rebekah stepped back inside the bedroom and closed the door. "If I'm able, I'm willing."

"The Stradivarius," Mrs. Cheatham whispered, her tone considerably more relaxed. "It's in my trunk room. Light the lamp there, on the dresser."

Both honored and delighted, Rebekah did as she was asked and found the distinctive red case. When she opened the lid, it felt a little like seeing an old friend. A *very* old friend. Appreciating the feel of the instrument—and its history—tucked against her collarbone, Rebekah quietly tuned the strings.

"Is there something in particular you'd like for me to play, Mrs. Cheatham?"

"Anything soothing, my dear."

Rebekah didn't have to think long. She drew the

bow across the strings, and all the love and appreciation she felt for Demetrius quietly reverberated as the lyrics filled her mind.

"Come, thou fount of every blessing, tune my heart to sing thy grace . . ."

Whether it was the darkness, or the stillness of the room, or the quiet brush with these oft unvisited hours of night, she felt as though the confines of the bedroom suddenly fell away, and she was playing to a much larger audience. Her throat tightened, and her eyes watered as she wondered if Demetrius could somehow hear her now. Or her father, who had managed to leave so much of himself behind when death had taken him.

Tears ran down her cheeks and onto the violin, and while she felt protective of the instrument and didn't wish to harm the finish, an almost tangible presence told her not to worry, that her tears would merely blend with those already shed upon the instrument through the years, and that the music would somehow be all the sweeter for it.

Having sung all the verses in her mind, she played through the music one last time, more slowly, the vibrato of the instrument so pure, so clear, she still felt the resonance inside her chest after the last note faded.

Quiet enveloped the room, and though she thought Mrs. Cheatham might have fallen asleep, a soft sniff revealed the truth.

Rebekah returned the instrument to the protection of the case, pausing briefly to check for any residue of her tears—and finding none. She wiped her cheeks and went to stand alongside the bed.

Mrs. Cheatham peered up, her expression thoughtful. " 'Tune my heart . . . to sing thy grace,' " she said softly. "Such a beautiful thought . . . for such a difficult undertaking."

Rebekah nodded, recalling something she hadn't thought about in a very long time. "I once heard a minister say that every morning when he awakens, he asks himself, 'Will I serve myself today? Or will I serve my Savior?' "

"And do you ask yourself those same questions?"

Rebekah glanced away, embarrassed to admit the truth. "Not nearly as often as I should."

Mrs. Cheatham laughed softly. "Sadly, that's the response that could be given for most of our souls' pursuits. Mine included. And yet, as more years gather behind me than before, questions such as those occupy more of my thoughts . . . and my heart."

Rebekah smiled, sensing no judgment in the statement, yet still feeling a firm tug on her conscience.

"You were born to play that instrument, Miss Carrington." Mrs. Cheatham looked in the direction of the violin. "I believe that with all my heart, and have since the first time I heard you. Talent such as yours is rare. And . . . is a gift. Not that you haven't worked hard to hone that talent. I wouldn't say that for a moment. But . . . someone else could spend her entire life learning how to play and not come close to the beauty you create at such a youthful age."

Rebekah bowed her head. "Thank you, Mrs. Cheatham."

As much as she appreciated the compliment, and didn't doubt its sincerity, the sentiment left her feeling a little hollow when she thought of what she wanted to do with that talent, with her gift. And New York City . . .

Movement on the bedcovers drew Rebekah's attention, and she felt the warmth of Mrs. Cheatham's hand on hers. "I know that playing like this, for me, and for yourself, is not your heart's desire." Her grip tightened. "But you must trust that the Lord has your best at the center of His heart, and whatever His plans are for your life, for this talent He's given you, He will bring them to fruition in time."

She laughed softly and tucked her hand back beneath the covers. "The problem, as I have learned, is that His timing and His plans often do not coincide with my own. But even in that, Miss Carrington, I have discovered immeasurable and . . . unexpected blessings from His hand. And I've learned patience." She sighed. "Patience beyond what I would've thought possible for such a stubborn soul."

Rebekah smiled.

"Seek His desires, Miss Carrington, above all, no matter what you will have to surrender. And you *will* have to surrender. We all do. It's part of the soul's refinement. I wished I'd learned that earlier in life. That when we surrender . . . or when He takes something from us, His motivation always stems from love." Mrs. Cheatham closed her eyes once again, her features relaxing. "Listen for His voice, for He *will* speak to you. And be ready when He does. Because oftentimes"—her lips firmed and the lines of her brow briefly knit— "not only is the cost one you need to have counted beforehand, but the opportunity He brings . . . will likely never come again."

Rebekah studied her expression, certain from Mrs. Cheatham's tone that she was referring to a missed opportunity in her own life, and Rebekah could only wonder what it was. Then with her very next breath, she wondered if God truly did pay such close attention to the details of a person's heart. Of *her* heart.

Sadly, she'd never heard His voice in the way Mrs. Cheatham described. And she felt bereft because of it.

"Now . . ." Mrs. Cheatham exhaled. "I believe I'll finally be able to sleep, and would suggest you do the same. I'm planning to travel to Murfreesboro tomorrow and will likely be gone for a few days. But Cordina, Eli, and, of course, Mrs. Routh are here to assist you, should you need anything."

"Thank you, Mrs. Cheatham."

Rebekah turned down the lamp she'd lit and

closed the door noiselessly behind her. Her cloth slippers were silent on the carpeted stairs, and she hurried back to her room, unable to get the word *surrender* out of her mind.

The fire in her hearth burned brightly—thanks to Cordina, she guessed—and she snuggled back into bed, glancing at the clock as she did. Only two hours before she needed to awaken again.

She nestled deeper into the feather mattress and cradled the pillow to her cheek. What might God call her to surrender, as Mrs. Cheatham had suggested? New York City was the first answer that came to mind, but she immediately rejected the possibility. Not simply because she didn't welcome that intrusion into her life. But, more importantly, because—thinking about it on a grander scheme—it made no sense.

Why would God demand the very dream he'd given her years ago? The dream her father had nurtured and that she held most dear. That was contrary to logic, and contrary to the doors that had recently opened in her life—*if* she could only manage to keep Tate Whitcomb from throwing away his own opportunities, to which hers were uniquely and inseparably linked.

Thinking again about the bottles of laudanum she'd found in his cupboard and the telltale signs of his addiction—moodiness, irritation, headaches, short temper—she determined to help him. Albeit, her motivation wasn't altogether altruistic, but in the end, he would thank her.

He would have completed his symphony on time, and she would be on her way to New York City.

Moments passed, and finally, she grew blessedly warm beneath the covers, and her thoughts drifted on a wave—about composing the symphony with Tate, about home and her mother, and about what Mrs. Cheatham had said in regard to listening for God's voice.

And the last thoughts she recalled, as though they moved toward her from a far-off shore . . . What if the cost of hearing God's voice lay in surrendering what was most dear to her? Was that a price she would be willing to pay? And even more . . .

Would God give her the choice?

"You're *late*, Rebekah." Frustrated at her for cutting into their workday—a day already shortened due to his needing to leave for the train station in less than two hours—Tate didn't bother looking up from the piano when she finally arrived to his office.

But his real frustration lay in the fact that he'd been working since early morning and had little to nothing of consequence to show for it. The music simply refused to come, no matter how he tried to force it.

"I know, Tate. I'm so sorry." She tossed her cloak and reticule into a chair. "I sent word earlier. Did you not receive it?"

"I did. But that doesn't change the fact that you're late."

"Again, I apologize. I was up during the night, then had trouble going back to—"

"You marked the opening six measures on page four in the first movement as needing to be more focused, more concise. What do you mean by that?"

She stilled. "You're reading my notes?"

"Yes. You left them on the table there." He motioned, pencil in hand.

"I intended to go over those notes with you personally. And I'm fairly certain I conveyed that to you."

"You did. However, that was before you were nearly three hours late."

"Which I explained in the note I sent, and which I'm attempting to tell you now"—she pinned him with a look—"was due to my being up a good portion of the night. Then, following Pauline's lesson this morning, Mrs. Cheatham asked me to help her with something before she and the children left today, so—"

"Taking the time to explain why you were late, Rebekah, is only taking up more of our time together. Could we please simply get to work?"

She opened her mouth as though to respond, then promptly closed it and took her place beside him on the bench. He sensed her frustration, but it didn't come close to rivaling his.

"First of all . . ." She turned to him. "Good afternoon, Tate."

He stared. "Good afternoon . . . Rebekah. Or good evening, as soon will be the case."

The smile she aimed was anything but sweet. "As you'll see in my notes, my first comments are about the beauty of the first two movements you've written. I've made several notes about both movements, of which I'm guessing you're already aware. But the main observation I have at this point, and which I'm referring to in the notes you're referencing, is that I'd like to see your primary symphonic theme, which is quite beautiful—"

She turned to the piano and played the opening measures of his symphony. By heart. And flawlessly. Impressed—and a little moved—he tried not to show it when she turned back to him.

"—woven more intimately throughout the first and second movements. As we're writing the third and fourth, we'll work to be cognizant of maintaining that fluidity." Her eyes suddenly brightened. "Something I thought of this morning during Pauline's lesson was this . . ."

Her hands moved over the keys and resulted in a brief—yet engaging—interpretation of the music she'd played a moment earlier. And he felt his irritation at her, and at himself for his lack of productivity, diminishing.

She'd worn her hair up today, though he actually preferred it down. At least when she wore it this way, he could enjoy the slender lines of her throat and the way the tendrils of her hair teased the nape of her neck. He caught a whiff of lavender and vanilla and—whether it was the evocative scent or how soft he imagined her skin would be—he found it impossible not to imagine what it would be like to—

"Now, I realize, Tate, that you may not like it. It might seem too . . . *feminine* to you. But imagine it with the timpani and horn, then the double bass." She played the notes again as she referenced the various instruments. "Then the first and second violins come in, then the oboe, and cello. I think the variance could add great depth and movement to the entire piece. What are your thoughts?"

He stared at her, knowing he dared not reveal to her what he was truly thinking about. "I think"— he cleared his throat—"that you've been working on this outside of the time you spend here."

She smiled. "Well, you *have* already paid me for the first month."

He laughed, the warmth in her expression vanquishing whatever irritation remained. His gaze dropped to her pert little mouth, and her lips parted as though she intended to say something further. Yet she didn't. She just stared at him, same as he was doing to her. And the thought of those lips on his stirred him in a way he hadn't experienced in a very long time.

Knowing better, he indulged the fantasy, and his imagination proved most prolific where she was

316

concerned—despite having failed him miserably that morning as he'd struggled to compose.

He'd considered Rebekah Carrington beautiful the first moment he saw her. But the more he'd come to know her—and realized what depth of talent and character she possessed—the more attracted he'd become. And right now, all he could think about was taking her in his arms and—

Suddenly aware of the lessening distance between them—and the potential cost of what he was about to do—he caught himself and turned back to the piano, seeing the keys, yet unable to focus on them. Writing this symphony took precedence before all else. It had to. Or all he'd worked for would be for naught.

Steeling himself against his own desires, he cleared his throat. "Let me hear that rendition again, if you will . . . please."

She immediately did as he asked, acting as if nothing had happened, but the flush of her cheeks hinted at a different story.

She played the rendition again with such feeling. And the second her hands left the keys, he reached over and repeated what she'd played, but changed the tempo slightly, and ended on an E-flat instead of a G.

She nodded enthusiastically. "Yes. Good! That's a much more heroic key—majestic." She reached for her notebook and a pencil.

Tate looked on as she expertly drew a staff and the notes, capturing what they'd just written together, and admired her skill. Admired *her*.

For reasons unknown to him, the image of her with her stepfather last night came to mind. There certainly seemed to be no love lost there, which made him wonder about that situation, and if the lack of warmth between the two of them hindered Rebekah's relationship with her mother. How could it not?

He had no plan to share his opinion with Rebekah, but the man had definitely rubbed him the wrong way. Nothing that he could pinpoint exactly. More a feeling he had, which he quickly decided was best kept to himself, despite her obvious dislike of the man.

Tate watched her as she made notes. "Where did you learn to do this?"

She finished writing before she responded. "While I lived in Vienna, I served as governess to the conductor of the Vienna Philharmonic."

Tate knew he did a poor job of masking his surprise. "The conductor of the Vienna Philharmonic taught you?"

"I wouldn't say that . . . exactly." She set aside the notebook and pencil. "Over time, I came to help him in his office at home, and musicians from the orchestra would often come to him for lessons. And when they did"—she gave a little shrug—"I listened."

He laughed. "I think you did more than listen. Was this conductor Herr Heilig, by chance?"

She frowned, and he gave her a sheepish look.

"When your trunk came open that day and the contents spilled out, I noticed his name on several of the pieces of music."

"Ah . . ." She nodded. "He's an extremely talented man. And though I'm certain he has no idea, Herr Heilig taught me a great deal. For which I'm most grateful."

With effort, he kept his gaze from wandering from her eyes. "As am I, Rebekah. As am I."

The remnant of the afternoon flew by, proving far more productive than he could've imagined. And before he knew it, he heard the clock on the mantel chime five times.

Five times? He jumped up. "Forgive me, Rebekah, but I have to go."

She looked at him. *"Go?* Go where?"

He grabbed his bag from the corner, along with his satchel. Thirty minutes to get to the train station. And this was the last train of the day. If he missed it—"I'll be back on Monday afternoon, by the time you come in. Or shortly after."

She stood. "Monday afternoon? But where are you going? And for the entire weekend?"

She looked from him to his baggage, then back again, suspicion coloring her features. But he had no time to explain. About where he was going, or when he'd be back.

"If I remember correctly, Tate, Mrs. Cheatham told you in no uncertain terms that she—and the symphony board—didn't care for the weekend trips you've been making. So, naturally, I assumed, since you're serious about your position here and finishing this symphony, that you would have canceled your—"

"Rebekah, I don't have time to explain. I have to catch a train. I'll see you on Monday."

"But, Tate, I really wish you would—"

He raced out the door.

Left standing midsentence, Rebekah could only stare as Tate strode from the office. He'd left. Simply left. Without a backward glance. Too stunned at first to feel anything other than surprise, she quickly learned how swiftly her emotions could flip.

Her body flushed hot as she thought about where he was likely headed. To an opium den, perhaps. Or maybe a gentlemen's club, where "creativity-boosting" libations flowed and where morphine was administered like candy. And where there was never a shortage of *those* kind of women.

The more she imagined it, the angrier she became.

Hoping against hope that she was wrong, she crossed to the cabinet, knelt down, and opened it. Gone.

The box of laudanum was gone.

"Of all the *confounded*—" She pushed out a breath through clenched teeth, that word not customarily a part of her vocabulary. "If you think for one minute, Tate Whitcomb, that I'm going to allow you to throw away my opportunity the way you're throwing away yours . . ."

She grabbed her cloak and reticule and headed for the train station, not knowing what she was going to do. She only knew she had to do something.

Outside on the street, a biting wind whipped at her cloak, and she regretted not wearing her gloves that afternoon. But she hadn't planned on walking any great distance, much less racing across town to the train station.

She tucked her chin to the wind and covered ground as fast as she could, determined not to let Tate board that train. He'd be throwing away so much. For them both.

Working with him that afternoon had been pure pleasure. Actually having a hand—albeit a small one—in writing a symphony was . . . She could hardly find the words to describe it. The experience was one of the most exhilarating she'd ever known, and they'd only just begun. Speaking of exhilarating . . .

That moment on the bench, when he'd stared at her, then had briefly leaned in . . . She'd been attracted to men before. And though she'd never been kissed, she was still no novice in matters of the heart. But how could she be so moved by a man when he hadn't even touched her? But oh, how she'd wanted him to. In that moment, anyway. Looking back on it now, she was so thankful he hadn't.

Because that would have changed everything. And she couldn't allow anything to interfere with this opportunity. Because an opportunity like this wouldn't come again. She'd done her best to appear as though she'd been oblivious to his attention. When really, her heart had all but hammered straight out of her chest.

Almost twenty minutes later, she reached the train depot, winded, throat raw from the cold, lungs and legs aching. She climbed the stairs to the crowded platform—and spotted him boarding the forward-most passenger car. But . . . why would such a well-to-do man purchase a third-class ticket?

She called out his name. But the train whistle blew, masking her words. Tate didn't look back.

"All aboard!" a porter yelled above the noise and foot traffic. "Train to Knoxville with the final stop in—"

Another whistle blast drowned out the last of the announcement. But . . . *Knoxville?* She tried to push her way through the crowd to get to Tate, but her efforts proved useless. She'd never reach him in time.

"Two tickets, please!" a frantic voice said behind her, and Rebekah turned to see a couple buying tickets.

She looked back at the train and thought of Tate first, then of New York, and shoved her way to the ticket office. "One ticket, please."

The clerk eyed her through the grilled window. "Miss, this train is leaving."

"And I'm going to be on it, sir!" She slapped a bill on the counter.

"To Knoxville or to the end of the line?"

She thought quickly. "End of the line." She had no idea where Tate was going.

As the man counted back her change, she spotted a telegraph behind him.

"How much to send a telegram, sir?"

"Miss, you ain't got time to—"

Rebekah grabbed a pencil and blank slip and wrote hastily, grateful Mrs. Cheatham was gone for the weekend.

With a dark look, the clerk took the message and shoved the coins and a ticket toward her. "Sure hope you can run, lady."

She narrowed her eyes. "Just watch me."

Feeling the train slowing down again, Tate awakened with a start.

He looked out the window, expecting to see only darkness as they rounded a curve. But instead he saw the faint lantern glow from the depot at Chicory Hollow—and a flurry of white.

Finding it difficult to believe he'd slept the brief leg from Knoxville, he stifled a groan at seeing the snow. Inclement weather always made his trek more arduous, especially in the dark, but at least it wasn't sleeting. And knowing how excited Opal would be to see the snow somehow made the large, fluffy flakes seem less burdensome.

Tate looked beside him at the old-timer who'd asked to share his bench seat back in Knoxville. The man was scrunched up against him, head on his shoulder. Tate shifted in the seat, but the man didn't budge. Seems he wasn't the only one who'd been dog tired.

Tate nudged him again. "End of the line, sir," he said softly. The man finally roused, along with the other few passengers in the train car whose business took them to Chicory Hollow—where civilization ended and another world began.

The train car was cold, despite the wood stove situated in the center. As usual, as he'd come to learn, the fire had been allowed to die out soon after they'd left the station in Nashville. Traveling in third class was not for the faint of heart. Nor those wishing to stay warm.

But it *was* for Nashville Philharmonic conductors who wished to remain unrecognized.

He stood and stretched, his back and neck muscles aching from being too long in one position, and an awkward one, at that. Despite the rest he'd gotten on the way, he still felt tired, and looked forward to going to bed later that night.

What he wasn't looking forward to, however, was apologizing to Rebekah when he got back home. The woman was probably livid, and likely still would be come Monday, based on her tone when he'd walked out. But under the circumstances, he'd had no other choice.

Not that she would understand. And not that he could tell her the truth about where he'd been this weekend.

Weary within and without, he grabbed his bags and made his way up the aisle, waiting for the slow-moving passengers in front of him to disembark. He'd been in such a hurry to leave Nashville, he hadn't had the chance to change clothes, but he would before he started out.

A rush of cold air greeted him as he stepped from the train, and he breathed deeply, welcoming the fresh air after the ripe odors that had permeated the passenger car. It felt good to stretch his legs, and he headed to the public privy—when he looked up and saw a familiar face stepping off the next car.

Shocked for an immoveable instant, he quickly ducked behind the nearest billboard, his pulse escalating. What were the odds that Rebekah's stepfather—Tate tried to remember his name. *Ledbetter, wasn't it?*—would be on this train?

Tate waited a full two minutes after Mr. Ledbetter passed before daring to venture from behind the sign. What business did the man have in Chicory Hollow? Tate had no idea, but if he were a betting man, he would've wagered no business fit for a gentleman.

Still, he didn't plan on hanging around to find out. Not when he had such a hike waiting for him, and not when he remembered what Virgil and Banty Slokum had tried to do to him a couple of times ago when he'd arrived this late. But tonight, he was ready for them.

Not wasting another minute, Tate made a beeline for the public privy.

"Miss? Hello?"

Eyelids heavy, Rebekah struggled to awaken and saw an older gentleman staring down at her. For a moment, she couldn't remember where she was. Then the enormity of her mistake hit her and she threw off the lap blanket and shot to her feet.

"Miss! Watch your—"

With a *thwack,* her head met with the above compartment of the passenger car, and she sank back down again, briefly seeing stars.

"I'm sorry, miss. I tried to warn you."

The porter wore an apologetic look.

"It's not your fault," she whispered, grimacing and rubbing the tender spot on her head while peering through the dirt-smudged windows looking for Tate. She'd fallen asleep? She'd battled drowsiness all the way from Nashville to Knoxville, where she'd briefly disembarked and had watched for Tate to do the same. When he hadn't, she'd gotten back onboard. She'd been so cold from standing outside that she'd reached for a blanket . . .

And that's the last she remembered. She exhaled. Staying up the night before with Mrs. Cheatham had proved costly.

Rebekah steadied herself on the seat in front of

her and rose again, squeezing her eyes tight as the pounding continued. "How long have we been here, sir?"

"Oh, not long. Five minutes at the most. But this is the end of the line, ma'am. Train doesn't leave again 'til morning."

She nodded and looked around her feet for her reticule. It was gone! She dropped to her knees and—

There. Beneath the bench seat.

She grabbed the purse, checked the contents and found them, to her relief, as she'd left them. She stood again, more mindfully this time, and thanked the porter, then quickly made her way down the aisle and outside—disembarking to a cold rush of air hitting her face.

Fat flakes of snow swirled and danced in the wind like little fairies before draping the evergreens in white. The scene looked like a picture someone might paint on a card sent at Christmas. Only, at the moment, she failed to fully appreciate the beauty.

She pulled her cloak more tightly about her and searched the nearly empty platform, wishing again that she had her gloves. The clerk at the station in Nashville had sold her a first-class ticket for the ladies-only car, which meant she hadn't been able to move from car to car as she'd hoped. But she knew Tate hadn't disembarked in Knoxville, and this was the next—and last—stop. Still, she marveled at the idiocy of her plan. Or lack thereof.

What had she been thinking? Simply buying a ticket and getting on a train? What woman did that? It certainly wasn't in character for her to do so.

Chicory Hollow.

She read the worn shingle hanging at odds from its chains. Nice to know where she was, even if knowing didn't help much. She looked for the porter, but the platform was empty. A CLOSED sign hung in the window of the ticket office. Same for the telegraph office adjoining it. Then she spotted a man walking away from her at the far end of the platform. A local, judging from the simple cut of his trousers and worn overcoat.

She started to call out to him, then stopped, recognizing his confident gait, those broad shoulders and that lean waist, even if she didn't recognize his homespun clothes. She stared, certain Tate had been wearing a suit when he'd left Nashville.

So why on earth had he changed? And into that? Debating whether or not to approach him now, she quickly decided not to.

She'd come this far, so her best option was to follow him and find out, for certain, what he was doing and then confront him about it—when he couldn't deny his actions or try to talk his way out of it.

She followed him from the train depot, keeping her distance. But when he suddenly veered off into the woods, she stopped, not knowing what to

328

do. Why on earth was the man going into the woods? And at this hour of night?

One possibility came to mind, but she'd seen privies back at the station. Privies she now wished she'd made use of. Plus she was hungry. Lunch seemed forever ago.

Imagining all the grief she was going to give that blue-blooded blackguard when the time came, she followed him through the prickly maze of pine and poplar, and almost immediately lost her sense of direction.

Snow and pellets of ice bullied their way through the thick stand of evergreens, and the wind sent them swirling this way and that, which only added to her confusion. But she quickly gathered her wits about her. Because Tate Whitcomb needed to be back in Nashville writing that symphony. For his future, as well as hers.

She heard something *crack* behind her, and spun. Yet saw nothing. But she knew she'd heard something.

"Tate?" she called out. Seconds passed and, dread rising inside her, she called his name again. Telling herself not to panic, she turned in a slow circle, searching the world of bare tree limbs and shifting shadows for any sign of the train station, or civilization in general.

But it was as if the train station had never existed.

A noise, like the crackle of leaves, sounded somewhere behind her, and she turned again.

"Who's there?" Her heart beat so loudly in her ears, she could scarcely hear anything else. "*Tate, is that you?*"

Feeling the frosty tendrils of actual fear, she shivered, sensing she wasn't alone. But before she could call out again, a hand reached from behind her and clamped an ironlike grip over her mouth.

20

Rebekah tried to scream, but the strangled attempt never left her throat. She fought and kicked, scratched and tried to scream again, doing everything Sally had taught her to do if something like this ever happened.

"*Whoo-wee!* You and me, we gots us a real wildcat here!"

A high-pitched cackle to her right told Rebekah there were at least two of them. The grip on her mouth shifted just enough and—

"*Ow!*" A string of curses left her assailant. "She done bit me! *Bit* me!"

Nearly gagging from the vile taste, Rebekah let out a scream and continued to fight as a band of steel encircled her waist.

"Hold on there, you pretty thang. I hain't gonna hurt you none. Just wantin' me a little bit a—"

The unmistakable ratchet of a shotgun severed the night—and Rebekah's struggle. She stilled, her body shaking.

"Let her go."

"Tate!" She turned in the direction of his voice but saw only endless night and shadows.

"Aw, come on, Witty!" The hold around her tightened. "We's just havin' us some fun—that's all. We hain't gonna hurt her none. Maybe just steal us a kiss or two."

"Yeah." Another high-pitched cackle. "If she don't bite your nose off first, you dumb little—"

"I said, *let her go,* Virgil."

The shadows to the left moved, and Rebekah made out the barrel of a shotgun, then saw him. His name left her in a throaty whisper, and the man holding her loosened his grip.

Rebekah turned and shoved him hard, but the effort only earned his laughter. She quickly joined Tate at his side.

"Witty, you oughtn't let your woman go a-wanderin' the woods on her lonesome. 'Specially followin' the aidge of dark."

"Then again," the second man piped in, "you Whitcomb boys hain't always been the brightest."

"Are you all right?" Tate whispered down to her.

"You *know* these men?"

"Just answer my question, Rebekah."

"*Yes,* I'm fine. Scared, but fine." Though she didn't care for his corrective tone, or the way she couldn't stop shaking.

"Virgil, you and Banty get on out of here before I remember you're on Whitcomb land."

Virgil stepped forward. "This here land belonged to my grandpappy long 'fore—"

"He lost it to mine," Tate finished. "In a poker game. I know the story. And telling it again won't change the ending. Go on and get, Virgil. You too, Banty." Tate raised the shotgun. *"Now!"*

After leveling glares, the men did as he asked, stepping through an opening in the pines and disappearing into the night.

With the threat diminished, Rebekah's fear swiftly melted to anger. "*What* are you doing out here, Tate? In the middle of nowhere!"

"You *followed* me, Rebekah? All the way from Nashville? Have you lost your mind?"

"Me? Lost *my* mind? *You're* the one standing here conversing with those two . . . imbeciles—who you apparently know!"

He lowered the shotgun, his gaze swiftly scanning the tree line before he faced her. "Seriously, Rebekah. What are you doing here?"

"What are *you* doing here? Other than throwing away everything you've worked so hard for, all the years of study, of practice. You've been given so much, Tate. Opportunities others will never have. That *I* will never have. Yet you're willing to trade it all for a few days of laudanum and . . . debauchery."

He stared. "*Debauchery?* What are you talking about?"

"I'm talking about your addiction." She swallowed, the emotion threatening to choke her. "And whatever else it is you're planning to do out here. *Oh,* I've read about what musicians do, Tate. I've seen it firsthand. In Vienna. Going to your opium dens and drinking your . . . cocaine elixirs. You think it broadens your creativity. But it does just the opposite." She sighed. "You're in danger of losing all you've gained if you continue doing this."

He said nothing for the longest time, only looked at her. Then he laughed. *Laughed.* "My *addiction?* You think I'm addicted to . . ." He turned away from her, shaking his head. "Oh, Rebekah, you couldn't be more—"

"I saw the laudanum, Tate! Days ago. In the cupboard. Then after you left today, I looked . . . and it was gone. *All* of it."

He turned back, his expression firm, all humor having vanished. "Yes, it was gone. I took it because—"

Something moved in the brush beyond the trees, and Tate lifted a finger to his lips, then took hold of her hand. She followed him, working to keep up with his long strides as a thousand questions ran through her mind. Foremost being where were they going? And who was this man she knew but apparently didn't know as well as she thought she did?

She made so much noise compared to him, her boots crunching over fallen limbs and leaves, her skirt catching and pulling on branches and underbrush, while he moved through the woods with scarcely a whisper.

A loud *crack* sounded somewhere off to their right, and Tate stopped short. He pressed his mouth to her ear. "We're going to be fine," he whispered. "But we have a hard hike in front of us. Up into the mountains. Usually an hour or so. But with the snow, it'll be closer to two. Maybe more. Can you do that?"

Without hesitating, she nodded, not really knowing whether she could or not. And still needing to use a privy.

"Tell me if you need to stop." He glanced beyond her. "Just don't need to stop until we cross the ridge, all right?"

She nodded again, the cold working its way into her bones.

She followed him, staying as close as she could, wishing he would take hold of her hand again. Not only because it had felt so nice, so safe, but because he was warm. Yet he didn't.

No matter how deep into the woods they walked, or how high they climbed—Tate occasionally stopping to help her over the larger boulders—she couldn't shake the feeling that they were being watched. Or maybe hunted.

Neither possibility appealing, both sent shivers up her spine.

Along with the uncertainty about their surroundings came fresh misgivings about him too. Whitcomb land? Won by a grandfather in a poker game? But that couldn't be true. Everyone knew Nashville's new symphony conductor hailed from back east . . . somewhere. New York or Boston or Philadelphia. One of those cities known for their lineages of blue bloods.

She tried to remember whether, in the numerous articles she'd read about him since arriving in Nashville, anyone had mentioned where he'd been born. She'd thought she'd figured out who Nathaniel Tate Whitcomb—or *Witty?*—was, and would've sworn she knew the truth.

But now . . .

His bags in one hand and the shotgun tucked into the side of his satchel, Tate took hold of Rebekah's hand with his other and helped her over a fallen tree. He held on to her a little longer just because he could, and also because she didn't seem too eager to let go. Not a bad discovery, considering her earlier character assessment of him.

He still couldn't believe she'd followed him. The woman was certainly full of surprises. Problem was, he had a few surprises of his own. Ones he would've preferred to have kept hidden. Surprises that could cost him his job, his career. And he wasn't altogether certain he could trust her with them.

But what choice did he have? Leave her out here on her own? There wasn't another train until morning, and the temperature was already below freezing and only getting colder.

He glanced back. "We're almost to the ridge. Then we can rest for a minute."

She nodded, her breath coming hard. Yet she hadn't complained once.

The snow had tapered off over the past half hour and the night sky was clearing. The patches of white dotting the ground would be gone by tomorrow afternoon, but for now, they made climbing in the dark a challenge. And in Rebekah's heeled boots, particularly, he guessed. Still, they'd managed to cover a good distance.

Addicted to laudanum. Visiting opium dens. That's what the woman thought of him? What she'd traveled all this distance to prevent him from doing. And *debauchery?* He'd laughed earlier, but the more he thought about it, the less humorous it seemed.

He'd come to admire and respect her, both personally and in regard to her musical talent. And he'd hoped she felt somewhat the same about him. But instead . . .

She'd decided he was an addict. And a rogue.

A while later, they crested the ridge, and his beloved Appalachian Mountains fanned out across the night horizon, layered one after another in the distance, their tree-lined peaks draped in deep lavender robes. And the stars, thousands upon thousands of them, dotted the night sky, their pinpricks of light paying homage to the thumbnail moon. It was a view he never tired of seeing. And never would. He only hoped the view would be here for years to come. Which he'd come to doubt would be the case with all the mining companies moving in.

Rebekah paused beside him.

"It's . . . so beautiful," she whispered, winded, hands on her hips.

"Yes, it is."

They stood in the silence, drinking in the beauty of the night, cold though it was, and he felt a peace within him that he hadn't felt in a very long time. A peace he missed.

She turned to him. "Are we safe now?"

"More so than before."

"Why? I mean, why now that we've crossed the ridge?"

"Because this land is watched."

She went perfectly still. *"Watched?"*

He held out his hand, knowing the less she knew, the better. "We don't have that far to go."

Acting more than a little wary, she slipped her hand in his, and he felt how cold she was. He set down his bags and took both of her hands between his palms, and rubbed.

She shivered. "How are you still so warm?"

"It's all that laudanum. And cocaine."

She ducked her head and looked away. But with his finger beneath her chin, he lifted her gaze back to his.

"I'm sorry, Tate," she started, but he pressed a finger to her lips. The warmth of her breath stirred him. He traced a feather-soft line across her lower lip, his imagination filling in the blanks he wished he could fill in himself.

"Rest is over," he said softly. "Time to get moving again."

"I hope wherever we're going has a privy," she said almost shyly.

He smiled. "It does. Come on."

The trek downhill was tricky, and she slipped once, but he caught her. She was strong and quite agile for a woman. Although he knew she wouldn't appreciate him phrasing it that way.

They reached the old log bridge, and he felt her tense beside him. Winter melt had swollen the partially frozen creek, and the water ran higher than usual, and swifter. Water sprayed over the boulders in the middle of the stream where it wasn't yet frozen, almost as if daring them to take a plunge.

"I'll cross first, leave my bags, then come back for you."

She nodded, her arms wrapped around herself, and he could well imagine her thoughts at the moment, though she was too proud to admit her fear. The "bridge" consisted of two uneven logs with an occasional board nailed roughly each step or two along the way. He'd crossed it a thousand times or more and had never stopped to really look at it. But he did now, seeing it through her eyes, and could only imagine what her reaction was going to be when she saw what was yet to come.

He crossed the logs quickly, then came back for her.

He took her hand. "It's not too slippery. Just follow close behind me."

She didn't move. "I . . ." She shuddered, a cloud of white ghosting her face. "I don't know how to swim."

Her voice sounded so small, so fragile.

"Well, that's good. Because I don't plan on us going in."

She didn't laugh. Her hold on him tightened.

He led her forward, and halfway across, still holding his hand, she gripped the back of his coat as well. He didn't relish her being afraid, but this more dependent side of her wasn't altogether unattractive, and a protectiveness rose within him that rivaled any he'd felt before.

Once on the other side, she exhaled a deep breath and relinquished her hold on him, much to his disappointment.

Half an hour later, they reached the copse of oak and chestnut trees, and he paused, wondering again if he was doing the right thing. Bringing her here. If they hiked for another hour or so, they could make it to the old hunting cabin. There should be blankets and food stores laid up, if someone hadn't already used them. He could build a fire, and they could pass the night there. Then come morning, he could take her back down the mountain and put her on the train.

If she would even board the train once he got her there, which was doubtful, considering how strong-minded she was.

But weighing the prospect of spending the night with her in a cabin, alone, in the deep woods, he knew it wasn't an option. There was her reputation to consider. And even though it was a different world up here, some things didn't change. So since he had no intention of compromising her in any way . . .

He was forced to compromise himself and his world instead—and what precious little time he had left before that world changed forever. He only hoped she wouldn't look at him differently after tonight, or judge those he loved most.

Because despite the years that had passed since he'd first moved to the conservatory and into the world of the *foreigners,* he hadn't forgotten the terms people had used to describe the community who lived in these parts—mountain folk, salt-of-the-earth people, highlanders. And the considerably less kind names—inbreds, simpletons, yokels.

She *had* called Virgil and Banty imbeciles earlier, which wasn't too promising. But those two brothers *were* imbeciles, so he could scarcely fault her for that.

Looking over at her—her hair and cloak damp clean through, her hands near freezing, her breath coming quickly, puffing white in the cold—he knew there was only one thing to do.

"We have a lot to talk about, Rebekah. And I'm sure you have questions. And will have even more, after tonight. I'll do my best to answer them, later, as much as I can." He hesitated. "You need to know . . . I never pictured sharing this place with you. Or with anyone else, for that matter. I didn't think it possible. And I still don't think it wise. But . . ."

He took hold of her hand and led her through the all-but-hidden path in the trees and stopped on the other side when the cabin came into view. "Welcome . . . to my home."

21

Shivering from the cold, Rebekah stared at the rudimentary cabin, then back at him. For the past near two hours as they'd trekked up and down heavily wooded mountains, she'd struggled to keep pace with him while also struggling to sort the fragmented pieces of events and details from this evening, trying to make sense of it all. And though what Tate just said had danced at the edge of her thoughts, she hadn't been able to make it align with what she knew to be true about this man. And yet . . .

"This is your home," she repeated softly. "This is where—"

"I was born and raised," he finished for her.

A dull ache started somewhere near the vicinity of her heart as awareness set in. She shook her head, her chin trembling. "I didn't realize," she forced out, suddenly finding it difficult to breathe as the enormity of the mistake she'd made—by following him, by trespassing into this part of his life, a place she wasn't welcome—pressed down hard inside her. "I didn't know. Or I would never have presumed to—"

The front door of the cabin opened, and light poured onto the front porch, then trickled down onto what appeared to be stone steps. A woman stepped out into the night, her ankle-length skirt backlit in the soft glow of lantern light. Her form appeared so small in contrast to the vastness of the night and the surrounding mountains.

"Witty?" she called into the night, the intonation of her voice almost musical. "That be you, son?"

Instinctively, Rebekah took a backward step. "I shouldn't be here."

Tate's hand tightened around hers. "Rebekah, it's all right. Or will be, soon enough."

She tried to pull away, but he held her fast.

"Where are you going to go, Rebekah? Believe me, I've tried to think of another option. There isn't one."

"This was so wrong of me. So . . . presumptuous." She winced. "But based on how you were acting—the headaches, the irritability, how I found those bottles of laudanum in the cabinet—"

"The headaches and laudanum I can explain. But the irritability, I guess that just comes naturally."

Unexpected tenderness softened his voice, which somehow made her feel even worse. He was looking down at her, and though she couldn't see the precise definition of his features, she somehow knew he was smiling.

"Tate, I'm so sorry."

"Come on," he whispered, tugging her hand. "My mother already knows someone's here. So unless you want her to get the Winchester, we'd better make ourselves known."

But Rebekah didn't budge.

He leaned closer. "Come on now. I promise they won't bite. Although . . . apparently I can't promise them the same of you."

Humored, she gave him a little shove, but apprehension still ruled. No longer able to feel her toes in her boots, Rebekah knew he was right. There was no other option.

Tate held her hand until they got closer to the cabin. Then he gave it a quick squeeze and let go.

"Mama!" he called out, then ran the rest of the way, taking the steps in twos. He wrapped his mother in a hug, her feet briefly leaving the porch. The woman's laughter seemed to light up the darkness.

The display was so full of affection, so natural—yet so foreign to Rebekah—that she couldn't look away. Not even when the woman's gaze trailed to where she stood in the yard.

"Mama," Tate said quickly, descending the steps. "I'd like to introduce Miss Rebekah Carrington. She's my personal assistant at the symphony in Nashville. And she's also . . . my friend."

Tate placed a hand on the small of Rebekah's

back and urged her forward. She felt warmth and forgiveness in the act. And in the title *my friend*. He'd said it so sweetly. Still shaking from the cold and damp, she gathered her wet skirt and cloak and climbed the stone steps.

"Rebekah, may I present my mother, Mrs. Angus Whitcomb. But I can already tell you, she'll insist you call her by her given name . . . Cattabelle."

Rebekah curtsied, feeling awkward and embarrassed and hoping it didn't show. She knew her appearance must be horrendous, and shame chided her over intruding into such a private setting. "It's a pleasure to meet you . . . Cattabelle."

"Howdy do, Miss Carrin'ton." There was a quiet dignity and grace to the greeting. Mrs. Whitcomb stepped to one side, and lantern glow from the cabin revealed a kind, expressive face. "Best get yourselves on inside. Looks like it's weatherin' up to snow agin. Gettin' worse us just standin' here."

Rebekah glanced back and, sure enough, the snow had begun a reprise. Giving Mrs. Whitcomb a smile, she stepped across the threshold of the cabin and was greeted first by warmth. Her body shuddered in response, and she wondered if she would ever be fully rid of the chill in her bones. A discordant mixture of scents greeted her next— coal oil, leather, bacon fat, and tobacco—followed by the simplicity of the setting.

The cabin was crudely built, made of roughhewn logs chinked with mud, and the initial furnishings she glimpsed were sparse at best, save for a gleaming black cast-iron wood stove hulking in the center of the far wall. Atop it, pots simmered and spewed. She caught the scent of meat cooking, and her stomach clenched with hunger. She couldn't decide whether it was pork, chicken, or beef she smelled. But whichever it was, it smelled delicious.

Pegs pounded into the logs held cooking utensils and various other pots and pans. A long wooden table with benches on either side crowded the area in front of the stove, and in the center of the table sat stacks of wooden bowls and plates.

If she didn't know better, she might have thought she'd traveled back in time, into another world. She remembered seeing the austere drawings of her great-great-grandparents and had heard the stories about how they'd been among the first to settle the land around Nashville. How they'd lived in a cabin. This reminded her of those retellings, and of the pioneer spirit credited to them.

Contrasting this austerity with the opulence of Belmont Mansion nearly overwhelmed her senses. It truly was like living in two different worlds. Then she turned—

And her gaze stopped cold.

Just behind a sofa and two chairs, three beds—all crafted from pine and adorned with patchwork pillows—lined the wall, side by side. Apparently the living area doubled for sleeping as well. She tried not to stare, but everywhere she looked—be it at the beds, or to the long-barreled rifle balanced atop what appeared to be an elk-horn rack, or to the multiple pairs of overalls hanging on a peg by the door—she felt as if she were staring at something she shouldn't.

So she looked back to Tate instead and saw him closing the door, then putting his bags aside. He watched her the whole time, an earnestness in his expression.

He gave his mother another hug. "It smells good in here, Mama. I should've written ahead, though, to tell you I was bringing a friend. I'm sorry."

"No, it's my fault." Rebekah spoke up quickly. "I'm sorry for barging in like this, Mrs. Whitcomb. Cattabelle," she corrected, seeing the woman's telling smile. "I'm afraid I . . . surprised your son at the train station. I simply didn't think through what an imposition my presence would pose. So, please, forgive me." She shot a quick glance at Tate, hoping he knew the apology was intended for him as well.

Warmth filled Cattabelle's expression. "Miss Carrin'ton, hain't no friend belongin' to Witty be a stranger in this home. You's as welcome here as any kin."

Touched more than she let on, Rebekah smiled. "Please, I'd prefer if you would call me Rebekah."

Mrs. Whitcomb beamed. "Rebekah, it be then. Now take off that coat of your'n. Wet as water, it is."

Rebekah relinquished the cloak, noticing Cattabelle's faded calico shirtwaist and skirt, a stain-spattered apron cinched about her waist. Rebekah smiled her thanks, her own dark gray skirt and simple shirtwaist seeming extravagant by comparison.

Tate's mother appeared younger than Rebekah would have imagined, and was petite, a good four or five inches shorter than Rebekah. Cattabelle Whitcomb possessed clear, beautiful features, yet despite their delicateness, nothing about the woman seemed fragile or easily broken. Quite the contrary. She exuded a quiet strength. A strength Rebekah had seen before. So it wasn't difficult for her to imagine from whom Tate had inherited that particular quality.

Mrs. Whitcomb motioned. "Now set yourself down by that fire and dry out. I'll have supper ready in no time a-tall."

"Actually . . ." Tate motioned. "I'll show Rebekah to the privy first."

"Thank you," Rebekah mouthed and followed him down a short hallway. He opened a door, and she was pleasantly surprised to see an earth closet. No having to go outside in the freezing cold and snow. A basin of water, soap, and a towel occupied a rustic table in the corner. Astounding how something so simple could swiftly become so appreciated.

She returned minutes later and joined Tate by the fire. She relished the warmth, along with the mother and son's back-and-forth about Tate's orchestra and life in the "big city."

"Before supper, Mama . . ." Tate glanced at the only other door, located opposite the one they'd entered through. "How is he doing?"

The light in his mother's eyes dimmed. But before Cattabelle could respond, the front door burst open and, along with a blast of cold air, in came what Rebekah assumed to be the rest of Tate's family—three brothers, all younger, judging by their youthful looks, and a much younger sister, a beautiful little girl. They chattered and greeted Tate all at once, hugging him and clapping him on the back.

But all greeting and conversation fell away when eyes turned to Rebekah.

Cattabelle moved to stand beside her. "This here be Witty's friend. From Nashville-way. Miss Carrin'ton be her proper name. These be my sons. Emil . . ." Cattabelle pointed to the tallest and oldest-looking of Tate's brothers. And the one who favored him most. "Then Rufus and Benjamin. And this little thang here, all o' eight years, is Opal. She's the least 'un." Maternal pride colored the woman's voice, her tone softening a degree when she said her daughter's name.

The siblings' stares, already appraising, turned more so, and Rebekah found the attention a tad unnerving.

"H-hello," Rebekah said softly. "It's a pleasure to meet all of you."

"She talks purty," the young girl said. "Just like you do, Witty."

"Witty *does* talk mighty purty, don't he?" Rufus ribbed, and Tate's other brothers quickly joined in.

"Purty as a flow'r come spring." Emil made a silly face, which only encouraged the youngest brother to laugh all the more.

Cattabelle smiled at Tate, who seemed to take it all in stride. Then she aimed a look at the boys. "Stop bein' so fool-headed and give Miss Carrin'ton here a proper welcome."

A staggered chorus of howdy-dos followed, the boys ducking their heads almost in unison while Opal's smile reached full bloom.

Rebekah noticed Emil watching her in particular. He smiled at Tate, wriggling his brows, then gave his big brother a grin and a not-so-discreet shove in the back, to which Tate frowned and gave a subtle shake of his head in response.

"Miss Carrington is also my personal assistant at the symphony in Nashville. She's helping me prepare for the big performance this spring."

"Them's fine wearin' clothes," the girl said, looking at Rebekah's skirt and shirtwaist. "Is they boughten?"

"Opal Nettie Whitcomb!" Cattabelle scolded. "Hain't right to be makin' such talk. You and your brothers get dinner done while we go thither to the other room."

Cattabelle motioned for Tate and Rebekah to follow her, but Rebekah hesitated. She was none too eager to lag behind and make conversation with Tate's brothers, but she also didn't wish to intrude. And she had a sinking feeling that the reason for Tate's possessing so much laudanum lay just beyond that door.

"Tate," she whispered, "perhaps I should stay here and let you—"

"You're here now, Rebekah. He'll want to meet you. And . . . I'd like for you to meet him."

Sensing deeper meaning in the words—*I'd like for you to meet him . . . while there's still time*—Rebekah nodded reluctantly. All while yearning for the moment she could board that train and give Tate Whitcomb back his privacy.

Which she never should have trespassed upon.

Tate braced himself as his mother opened the bedroom door, uncertain what lay beyond it. He could feel Rebekah's trepidation beside him as well, yet he was grateful, in that moment, that she was there with him. Her shock over what she had followed him into still showed clearly in her expression and demeanor—to him, at least—and he was eager to speak with her alone, to explain why he'd chosen to keep this part of his life hidden.

And why she *had* to agree to do that as well.

A single oil lamp rested on his parents' bedside table, and his eyes swiftly adjusted to the dimmer lighting. The lamp's meager flicker cast a burnt-orange glow about the small room, and his father, once a mountain of a man, lay still in the bed beneath a layer of quilts.

He looked even older than the last time Tate had been home. How could someone age so much in a matter of weeks?

"Angus?" Cattabelle cooed softly, laying a gentle hand to his father's brow. "Witty come home to see us agin." When his father didn't stir, his mother glanced back. "Your pa, he's been sleepin' most of the day. I been feedin' him the potion like you told me, son." She glanced at the nearly empty bottle of laudanum on the table by the bed. "And he hain't been hurtin' near as bad, which be a blessin' to us all. That last 'uns almost done for, but I been stretchin' it out."

"I brought several more bottles this time, Mama. And can get as much as you need. So give him the full dose if he's hurting." He reached for his father's hand, so large and callused, yet absent its customary strength.

His father's fingers gently tightened around his, and Tate realized his father was watching him. Seeing all the love and respect in his gaze caused a knot to form at the base of Tate's throat.

"Witty," his father whispered, and it came out sounding more like a question.

"I'm here, Pa." He tried to swallow, and couldn't. "H-how are you feeling?"

His father gave a semblance of a smile. " 'Bout like common, I reckon."

Tate felt a tug in his chest at the familiar response. "Are you in pain right now?"

A slow shake of his head. "That potion you give me . . ."

"The laudanum," Tate supplied.

His father sighed. "Makes me feel somethin' akin to . . . floatin' on a cloud, I guess."

Tate smiled. "That doesn't sound half bad. I might need to try some myself." His father laughed softly, and unable to resist, Tate cut a quick look at Rebekah.

Her shy smile did his heart wonders, and he wished he could tell her that he bore her no ill will for having followed him. Not anymore. In fact, a part of him was almost relieved. It was nice for someone to know the truth about him. Made him feel more . . . real, in a way. Less like a fraud.

He tried to continue speaking with his father, wanting to introduce him to Rebekah. But the laudanum did its work well, and his father quickly drifted back to sleep.

They returned to the next room to find dinner on the table, and Tate's mouth watered. His mother was a fine cook. But without question, this family meal would not fall anywhere on the scale of Rebekah's usual fare, and he worried how she would react when she discovered what she was eating.

Seated directly across the table from her, he spotted her eying the stew, then the hot corn pone, and he felt a twinge of discomfort, then guilt, when he realized it was shame he was feeling. Having been gone from these mountains for over half of his life now, he would've thought he'd moved beyond the struggle. This was his family, and this was his home. His upbringing here in Chicory Hollow had greatly contributed to the man he was now, and to the life he had. So how could he be even the least bit ashamed? Along with that thought rose a defensiveness within him against anyone who might make these people, who he loved so much, feel like less. Which he didn't believe Rebekah would do.

At least not on purpose.

"Witty." His mother's blue eyes sparkled. "Won't you raise up our thanks tonight, son?"

Tate nodded and took hold of Emil's hand, then reached for Rebekah's across the table. As she took hold of Opal's, he bowed his head, grateful his mother didn't know how long it had been since he'd prayed aloud.

"Heavenly Father, we thank you for this bounty and for a warm place from the cold. Thank you for the people gathered around this table, and be with the rest of our loved ones who aren't. Be with Pa. Bring him healing . . . please, we ask. Through Jesus, our Lord and Savior . . ."

Hearty amens sounded around the table, and then the usual frenzy of filling bowls and plates ensued—Emil, Rufus, and Benjamin taking the lead. Tate noticed how his brothers kept sneaking glances at Rebekah. Worse, Rebekah noticed too. Tate could tell by the blush in her cheeks.

She had to be cold yet. Her clothes, like his,

were still damp. Having brought nothing with her, she'd need to borrow something from his mother, which churned up yet another concern—the sleeping arrangements.

"You ever been on land so uptilted before, Miss Carrin'ton?" Rufus asked, eighteen years old and a man, yet still a boy in many ways. Much as Benjamin, who'd only recently turned fourteen.

"'Course, she hain't, you half-wit!" Emil, the eldest of the three at twenty, shoved Rufus beside him. "She's a level lander. Hain't that right, Miss Carrin'ton?"

Rebekah's attention shot to Tate, question in her gaze.

"Level lander," Tate explained, "is how we sometimes refer to people who aren't from these mountains."

"We got us other names for y'all too!" Benjamin smirked.

Everyone laughed, and even Rebekah smiled. But thankfully, no one went into detail.

"You're right, Emil." Rebekah held her bowl as his mother ladled a hefty portion of stew. "I'm not from the mountains, but I have been in them before. Not these, but . . . others."

Tate looked across the table, knowing how she could have responded—having lived in Vienna all those years, traveling in Europe—and his affection for her grew tenfold. She took a bite of stew, and he held his breath.

She chewed slowly, as if attempting to decipher

what it was she was eating. And he wished she would just chew, swallow, and not think about it.

Opal tugged on Rebekah's sleeve. "Corn pone, Miss Carrin'ton?"

"Why, yes. Thank you, Opal."

"Gotta have ya some plum butter with it too, ma'am," Opal chimed, motioning for Benjamin to pass the jar. "Mama makes the best in all the holler!"

Tate relaxed, grateful for Opal's unintentional distraction while he seized the opportunity to change the subject. "So tell me the news. What's happened since my last visit?"

"Accident last week." Emil's expression sobered. "Two miners got 'emselves near killed. It was bad, but it weren't their fault. An explosion. Fuse burned too fast. Cheap line some of the coal minin' companies are usin'."

"Are the men neighbors of ours?" Tate asked, looking beside him.

Emil shook his head. "Don't know 'em personal. They's some of the outsiders who live in the company town."

Benjamin leaned forward. "I heard tell one of 'em got his leg blowed off. The other lost a hand and then—"

"No coarse talkin' at my table, son!" Cattabelle's soft but serious tone brooked no argument. "You boys find out for me if them injured men got families, mouths to feed, and we'll do our best to be of help to 'em."

355

Benjamin nodded, head bowed. "Yes, ma'am."

"Now . . ." Cattabelle turned her attention to Rebekah. "I wanna hear 'bout what all you do at that music hall with my Witty. He said you're his . . ."

"Personal assistant." Rebekah smiled. "Which means that I help him with . . ."

"Tate," Emil whispered.

Tate looked to his brother as Rebekah continued.

" 'Member me tellin' ya 'bout the new mine that opened last spring? To the east of here?"

Tate nodded, still half listening to what Rebekah was saying.

"That's where the accident happened," Emil continued. "The men who run that 'un are worse than the others. Don't care a wit for their workers." Emil's voice dropped lower. "They just bought the mine where Rufus and me work. We hain't told Mama yet. Or Pa, of course. And we don't aim to."

Tate glanced at his mother, who hung on Rebekah's every word, and to Opal, who seemed equally enthralled. "I guess that's best, considering," he whispered. "But have the new owners said yet how things are going to change?"

"Miners who live in the company town"—Emil lifted his cup to his mouth but didn't drink—"part of their pay's gonna start bein' doled out in *scrip,* the bosses call it. Some kind of . . . minin' company pay. Not even real money. And it's gotta be spent at the company store that just hikes up the prices. New bosses say we all gotta bring our own tools now too. They won't be supplyin' 'em anymore. It's plain thievin', and it hain't right. It's hard work we do, and dangerous. Miners are gettin' fed up with it. Some of 'em threatened to stop workin' 'til the bosses make it safer. And more fair. Bosses told 'em they'd just fire 'em and hire all new workers. Now some of the miners are threatenin' to take it out on the bosses themselves."

Tate hated that his brothers had started working in the mines in addition to running the farm. He already sent a good portion of his salary home as it was. But Emil and Rufus were of age—Emil to be married soon—and his brothers wanted to make their own way. Understandably. But that took money. Even in Chicory Hollow.

"Have you and Rufus been in any accidents?" he whispered.

Emil didn't answer immediately. "Not as bad as that one."

Tate looked at him, and noticed the black coal dust embedded in the creases of his hands and under his nails.

"Had a cave-in a few days back. Just down from where me and Rufus were. But we got all the men dug out. It's just . . . the new owners are known for cuttin' corners every way they can. Usin' weaker beams to hold up the shafts, cheaper explosives. If they start runnin' our mine like they do that other'n"—Emil drained his cup—"more bad things are gonna start happenin'. To us, for sure. But maybe to them too."

"Listen to me, Emil." Tate leaned closer. "You and Rufus are smart. Too smart to get drawn into any violence against the mineowners. That'll come to no good. But don't be afraid to stand up to the bosses if they start asking you—or any of the other workers—to cut corners. Don't do it. It's not worth it."

"*What* are you two boys whisperin' 'bout down there?"

Tate looked up to see his mother eying first him, then Emil. Her eyes narrowed, and he wondered if she'd overheard part of their conversation.

"You boys best not be connivin' to sneak moonshine behind the barn. Like ever'one of you done before!" A telling twinkle lit her eyes, followed by a grin. "You may all be bigger'n me now, but I'll still tan your hides!"

Grinning, Emil pointed at Tate. "He's the one tryin' to get me in trouble, Ma. Said he bought some good white lightnin' off Virgil and Banty on the way up the mountain." Emil's gaze slipped to Rebekah. "Said Miss Carrin'ton liked it so much she bought her some too."

Tate smiled across the table at Rebekah, who laughed along with everyone else. And with that, the table banter fell into full swing again.

Tate noticed Rebekah spreading plum butter on her bread. She tasted it, and her smile said more than words ever could. "This is delicious, Cattabelle. The stew is too."

His mother's expression softened with gratitude.

"Glad it's to your likin'. I sent the boys out this mornin' and they got two gooduns."

"I helped with the skinnin'!" Opal added, then shoveled in a mouthful of stew.

"Pass the corn pone, please," Tate said quickly, eager to change the subject again. "Have any of you had a chance to read that last book I—"

"Skinnin' hain't worth nothin' without there bein' somethin' to skin," Benjamin retorted, always determined to put his younger sister in her place.

Opal's brow knitted, never a good sign.

Rufus huffed and shot Emil a wink. "Like you did anythin' to help, Ben. You missed everythin' you shot at this mornin'. Was me and Emil who got them squirrels, and you know it."

"Was not!" Benjamin's face reddened. "I's the one who . . ."

Tate watched Rebekah pause midchew, her face going pale. His older brothers egged on the younger, but his mother seemed not to notice, smiling through it all, accustomed to this after years of raising boys.

Please, Rebekah . . . If he could've escorted her from the room right then, so she could spit out the bite of stew discreetly, he would have. Because he understood what she was experiencing. He knew both worlds. And squirrel stew was definitely not part of Rebekah's.

She coughed, reached for her cup of water, and drank, then refilled it from the jar on the table and drank again.

"Too much pepper for ya?" his mother asked, smiling from down the table.

Rebekah took a quick breath and met his mother's gaze, and the moment seemed to freeze as Tate watched, helpless to intervene between the two women and knowing that neither would hurt the other for the world. Yet one could very easily hurt the other with a single word.

Rebekah swallowed. "Not at all, Cattabelle. I think I . . . simply ate it a little too quickly."

"Well." His mother nodded. "It do my heart good, seein' you like it so well. Now get yourself some of that potlikker. It's good for soppin'. And like my Granny Austin always said, *'Eat for the hunger that's comin'.'* "

Rebekah's expression was awash with emotion, and Tate couldn't begin to guess what she was feeling, or what she would do next.

Seconds passed—his brothers still arguing amongst themselves—before Rebekah looked across the table at him, and a slow smile turned her beautiful mouth. She picked up her spoon, dipped it into her bowl, and continued eating.

Tate thought his affection for her had swelled moments earlier, but that was nothing compared to the gratitude—and desire—he felt for her now.

A while later, after enjoying a second helping of Cattabelle's homemade dried apple pies and savoring every delicious bite, Rebekah watched

Emil retrieve a banjo, Rufus a dulcimer, and Benjamin a mandolin.

More than a little intrigued—and wondering why Tate wasn't playing anything—she watched the brothers tune the instruments as Cattabelle excused herself to check on Angus. Meanwhile, Opal climbed into Tate's lap, a quizzical look on her face.

"Did ya bring it agin this time?" Opal pressed a slender hand to Tate's cheek, her blue eyes nearly identical to his in color, though her blond hair set her apart from him and the rest of her brothers.

"Do you even have to ask?" Tate whispered, and brushed a kiss to her forehead. He gestured toward his shirt pocket while looking at Rebekah.

An expression she couldn't read clouded his handsome features and seemed to deepen the blue of his eyes. She had no idea what he was thinking, but somehow, she thought—or at least hoped—that it had something to do with her. But whatever it was, she was certain nothing else this man could say or do would surprise her after the past few hours.

But when she saw what he pulled from his shirt pocket, she was proven wrong. Yet again.

22

Rebekah didn't even try to hide her surprise when Tate slipped the tiny instrument between his teeth. Nashville's illustrious conductor—playing a *mouth harp?* Or Jew's harp as she'd heard Yankees occasionally refer to it. If only Adelicia Cheatham were here to see her beloved conductor now. Rebekah couldn't help but laugh at the thought of it.

But her laughter soon fell silent as his playing, along with his brothers', when they joined in, earned her admiration instead. They were good— *very* good—and possessed a skill in timing and rhythm that only came from musicians who played together often.

As she watched them laughing and smiling, giving each other encouraging nods, or making faces when one of them slipped on a chord or note, she couldn't help but wonder . . .

What must it have been like to be raised in this setting? With so little in one regard, and yet so very much in another?

As she listened to the song they were playing, a lively tune, she felt so thankful she was here. Yet a part of her wished, again, that she hadn't boarded that train earlier today. Tate had wanted to keep this part of his life hidden. And knowing the workings of symphonies and conductors, she understood why.

There was nothing shameful about being from a place like this. And there was certainly no reason to hide it—unless you were one of the most lauded symphony conductors in the United States. After all, symphony board directors and their distinguished patrons wanted only the best. The *crème de la crème*. And that meant prestigious schools and a pedigree worthy of boasting rights.

And Chicory Hollow . . . Well, this place wasn't quite on par with the Oberlin Conservatory of Music or the Peabody Conservatory of Music in Baltimore. How she wondered, having now seen *this* side of him, had he ever been afforded those opportunities.

How did a boy from Chicory Hollow become the conductor of the Nashville Philharmonic?

Grateful her clothes had finally dried, she watched Tate and his brothers as they played, her foot tapping along with the music despite the late hour and her growing fatigue.

No sooner did the first song finish than they started another. Opal jumped up as if on cue, and Rebekah soon learned why.

" ' 'Twas in the merry month of May,' " the girl sang, her voice clear and bright, so lyrical, natural, " 'when green buds were all a-swellin', sweet William on his deathbed lay, for love of Barbara Allen. He sent his servant to the town . . .' "

Rebekah found herself wishing she had her violin so she could join them. Yet she knew she couldn't, even if she'd had it. Because to Tate's knowledge, she only played the oboe and the piano. And for her sake, and Adelicia Cheatham's, that's the way it had to stay.

Opal took a bow at the close of her song, then scooted close beside Rebekah on the sofa.

Rebekah slipped her arm around the little girl's shoulders. "That was beautiful. What's the name of that song?"

"That there was 'Barbara Allen.' The afore one be 'Arkansas Traveler.' This un's"—Opal smiled at her mother, who had joined them again and was already singing—"named 'Lord Thomas and Fair Ellender.' It's one of Mama's fav'rites."

Cattabelle's voice was lower-pitched than her daughter's and could drift toward the melancholy, but it was just as unfettered and beautiful. Rebekah admired their courage in singing. It was as though they sang without thought of being heard, simply poured out the contents of their hearts, so at peace with themselves and who they were—and with the people listening to them—that no thought of criticism or lack of acceptance ever entered their minds.

Rebekah had always been self-conscious about her own voice. It was breathy and soft, nowhere near worthy of an operatic soprano or mezzo, or of any other part. Perhaps that's why she'd worked so hard to perfect her skills on the instruments she played. But . . .

What would it be like to grow up with the kind of acceptance and contentment they possessed? To sing—or play or compose—without that heavy-handed inner voice whispering like a disheartening metronome, *"That's not good enough. That's not good enough. That's not good enough."*

As Tate played, that tousled curl of his fell across his forehead, and Rebekah smiled. He caught her watching him—and winked. And a part of her heart responded to this man she'd thought she knew so well as they worked together in Nashville. Now enjoying the chance to observe him unhindered, she found her thoughts taking a more intimate turn and was grateful he couldn't read them.

The songs Tate and his brothers played were challenging instrumentally, and Rebekah realized she was attempting to transcribe the notes in her head as they played. But the livelier tunes were far too quick-paced and intricate for her to have any success, and the lyrics of the slower ballads drew her in so much with their stories that she couldn't concentrate, for wanting to know what happened next.

The music was so beautiful. It bore a faint resemblance to the music she remembered Demetrius and the others singing when she was a child. The structure and tempos were different, but the soul of the music itself—the lyrics, the undercurrent of emotion—possessed the same depth of feeling . . . and sense of loss.

She heard Angus coughing again and looked around for Cattabelle, only to hear the woman speaking in low, comforting tones from the next room. At dinner, Cattabelle told her they'd been married for almost thirty-four years. Such love filled the woman's eyes when she spoke of her husband.

"Ya know any ballads, Miss Carrin'ton?" Emil asked as the final chords from the last song hung in the air. "We can play 'bout near anythin'."

Surprised at the question, Rebekah shook her head. "No . . . I . . . I'm afraid I'm not a singer."

"Miss Carrington plays the oboe and the piano," Tate volunteered, more than a hint of pride layering his voice. "And extremely well, I might add. She's a most gifted musician."

Rebekah warmed at his compliment.

"What's a . . . *oboe?*" Opal asked.

Rebekah smiled. "It's a kind of horn—a woodwind instrument—that's shaped like a tube, about this long." She held out her hands to indicate the length. "And you play it by blowing into a mouthpiece at the top."

Opal slipped her hand into Rebekah's. "Shore 'nough, Miss Carrin'ton, you gotta know some kind of song. Everybody be totin' a song inside 'em. Leastwise, that's what our pa says. And he hain't never been wrong."

At the girl's mention of her father, Rebekah felt a tender thread tie itself around her heart—and pull tight. But did she dare sing in front of these people? In front of Tate?

She hadn't sung in front of anyone since her mother had caught her singing in her bedroom years ago. And that had been enough. *"Singing is not your strength, Rebekah."* The displeasure in her mother's expression had spoken even louder than her words. *"Far better for you to cultivate a talent that sets you in a favorable light, and then pursue that to the fullest."*

So that's what she'd done. Only, her mother hadn't approved of her final choice either. But seeing the innocent hope in Opal's eyes, and the earnest anticipation in the others', Rebekah gave a gentle shrug. "I honestly don't know any of the songs you've played thus far."

"What about 'Purty Polly'?" Rufus asked. "Bettin' you know that 'un."

Rebekah shook her head.

"'The Cuckoo'?" Emil tried, and strummed a few chords on the banjo.

Again, Rebekah shrugged.

Opal leaned in. "What about 'Wayfarin' Stranger'? Everybody knows that'un."

Even before Rebekah could respond, Tate's brothers started smiling.

"Ah . . . she knows that'un!" Rufus laughed. "I can tell it from her eyes!"

Her stomach already in knots, Rebekah forced a smile. "A man very special to me used to sing that song when I was a little girl. But . . . I'm not sure I still remember all the words, so perhaps I should simply—"

Opal leaned close. "If ya go and forget some, I'll come alongside ya."

"That un's one of Angus's fav'rites," Cattabelle said from the doorway of the bedroom. "Mine too. Why don't you play on Pa's fiddle, Witty? He's wakeful right now, so maybe he'll hear it."

Seeing the tenderness in Tate's expression, Rebekah gathered that playing the instrument belonging to their father was a privilege and something not often done.

Tate retrieved an old leather case from a high shelf, opened it, and withdrew a beautiful fiddle. And a well-played one too, judging by the worn finish on the instrument's body and neck.

As he tuned it, his gaze kept returning to Rebekah, and the intensity in his eyes warmed her more than a mere look should have. She only hoped she wouldn't make a fool of herself. And of him, in turn.

Tate began playing, then Emil, Rufus, and Benjamin gradually joined in, and the familiar strains felt like a welcome visit from a dear old friend, yet her midsection was doing somersaults. She was half afraid she might lose the dinner she'd just eaten, and considering how hard she'd worked to get—and keep—that stew down the first time . . .

She took a deep breath.

Tate and his brothers played through the verse once, then Tate nodded her way. Rebekah closed her eyes and opened her mouth.

"'I am a poor wayfaring stranger, while traveling through this world of woe . . .'" Her voice shook, but she sang on, imagining that she was sitting in her bedroom by the window again, listening to the voices drifting toward her from the cabins toward the back of the property. " 'But there's no sickness, toil, nor danger . . . in that bright world to which I go.' "

Anticipating the next words, she felt a catch in her chest.

" 'I'm going there . . . to see my father. I'm going there . . . no more to roam. I'm only going over Jordan . . . I'm only going over home.' "

She took a much-needed breath and opened her eyes to see Tate's own so full of emotion that tears rose in hers.

"Ya sing real purty," Opal whispered.

Cattabelle nodded. "Like a spring rain comin' down all gentle-like."

Rebekah smiled, then realized the next verse was coming up. But she didn't remember the words—

Opal took a breath. " 'I know dark clouds'll gather roun' me,' " the young girl sang. " 'I know my way be rough and steep.' " Her voice wrapped itself around the notes, lifting and falling with such ease for one so young. " 'Yet beauteous fields lie just b'fore me . . . where God's redeemed their vigils keep.' "

Remembering the rest, Rebekah joined in and sang along with her.

" 'I'm going there to see my mother, she said she'd meet me when I come. I'm only going over Jordan . . . I'm only going over home.' "

Opal grinned and scrunched her shoulders, obviously pleased, and Rebekah hugged her tight.

Cattabelle walked closer as she began singing. " 'I soon be free from earthly trials . . .' " The woman's voice, so rich and raw, held a yearning that Rebekah's heart identified with and responded to. " 'My body rest in the ol' churchyard. I'll drop this cross o' self-denial . . . when I go singin' home to God.' "

Feeling almost carried along by the music, Rebekah joined in again, as did Opal and all of Tate's brothers.

" 'I'm going there . . . to meet my Savior. Dwell with him and never roam. I'm only going over Jordan . . .' "

The rest of the voices fell away and Rebekah—as though they'd practiced this time and again—sang the last on her own.

" 'I'm only going . . . over home.' "

Half singing, half whispering the last words, Rebekah could scarcely draw breath, her heart felt so full. Slowly, the banjo faded, then the dulcimer, then the mandolin, until, finally, only the strains of the fiddle remained. And then . . . silence. For a moment, no one moved. Then—

Smiles and laughter swept through them all.

"That's the best we ever done on that'un!" Emil clapped Tate on the back.

"Miss Carrin'ton." Rufus eyed her. "Ya can't be sayin' you hain't a singer no more. That song just proved ya are!"

"Land sakes, it did!" Cattabelle's eyes shone with emotion. "Ya got such a honeyness to your singin', ma'am. So soft and sweet." The woman's eyes went wide. "Ya gotta come back this summer for the annual singin'. Everybody in the holler comes. We got food and singin' and dancin'. All the women, they bring what they made, whether't be sewin' or bakin'. We can do 'Wayfarin' Stranger' for all them folks!"

"Oh!" Opal sprang up. "And we can teach ya lotsa songs 'tween now and then, Miss Carrin'ton!"

Feeling slightly overwhelmed, but in a good way, Rebekah laughed as the comments continued back and forth, bracketed by laughter and enthusiasm.

And—though it saddened her, in a way—she realized she'd never been in a setting where the love the family members had for each other was so evident. Though this family could certainly spar with each other—she'd witnessed that at dinner—she knew without question they would also walk through fire for each other, if the situation ever called for it.

Thirsty after all the singing, she retrieved her cup from the table and drank the remains, then filled it again from the pitcher.

"Be it present time yet, Witty?" Opal asked softly.

Tate gently tousled her hair. "I reckon it is. Run on and grab my satchel and bring it here."

For the first time, Rebekah caught a trace of the twang in his tone. As she sipped her water, she wondered how hard he'd had to work to rid every trace of the holler from his voice.

His sister did as he asked, and he opened up the satchel. "For you, Mama . . ." He pulled out a paper-wrapped bundle and handed it to her. "Maybe you can make something for the annual singing this summer."

Cattabelle unwrapped the package and her mouth slipped open.

Rebekah's did, too, when she saw the beautiful floral material along with a coordinating fabric in a lovely cobalt blue.

"Oh, Witty, it's so purty!" Cattabelle hugged him tight. "But it's too fancy for the likes 'a me."

"Nonsense," Tate said, kissing her forehead. "Besides, once Pa's feeling better, he'd appreciate seeing you in a dress made from this. His favorite color on his favorite gal. Isn't that what he always says?"

Cattabelle's eyes watered. She nodded.

"Next . . ." Tate cleared his throat. "For my brothers."

"The ones that're here, anyway." Benjamin laughed.

"There are *more?*" Rebekah asked, thinking better of it once she had.

Everyone laughed.

Tate nodded. "I have three more brothers. Older than these, but all still younger than me."

Opal held up her hand. "There's Tucker, who's wed to Sudie. They live just over the mountain.

They got three young'uns and another on the way. Then there's Elisha, who's wed to Nadi. They got two lil' girls. They live on land her papa give 'em. 'Bout a day's walk from here, over Trover's Ridge. Then comes Clyde, who got tied last year to Mollie. They had 'em a baby boy last month and got 'em a cabin down the mountain a ways."

Rufus punched Emil in the shoulder. "And don't be forgettin' Emil here, who's weddin' Effie this spring. You shoulda seen him afore he asked her pa for her hand. He was scare't as a young pup."

"Was not!" Emil punched his brother back, but truth reddened his cheeks.

Rebekah did a quick count. So seven boys, then Opal. All raised, she assumed, in this small cabin. She couldn't even begin to imagine.

Tate pulled out three rectangular boxes and handed them to his brothers.

They opened them and—contrary to the responses Rebekah anticipated—their expressions sobered.

Cattabelle leaned close. "Oh, Witty, them's beautiful."

"Looks just like Pa's," Emil whispered, fingering the pocketknife.

"I looked all over Nashville and couldn't find the ones I wanted. But a lady who lives there gave me the name of a jeweler in New York, and he made them special to order. They have mother-of-pearl handles just like Pa's."

"Thank you, Witty." Emil grabbed him in a hug, as did Rufus and Benjamin in turn.

But watching Tate, Rebekah knew he was getting far more pleasure from the giving than they were in the receiving, which was saying a great deal. And once again, she glimpsed a side of this man she hadn't seen before.

"Last but not least . . ." Tate reached into his bag and felt around. Then his expression went slack. "I must've forgotten yours, little one."

Opal giggled, and Rebekah quickly gathered that this was part of the fun.

"Oh, wait . . . Here it is!" Tate's smile slid back into place. He handed Opal a small gold box. "I saw this and thought you'd like it."

Her eyes sparkling, she hugged his waist tight.

Benjamin shook his head, grinning. "Hold on, bean sprout. Ya don't even know what it be yet. Ya might not like it."

Everyone laughed again, then Opal slowly lifted the lid from the box.

Her delicate chin began to quiver. "Oh, Witty . . . it's the purtiest thing I ever seen."

Rebekah peered over, and felt her own heart do a little pitter-patter. An opal pendant set in gold—the gemstone sparkling blue-and-green fire—threaded on a delicate gold chain.

"You bein' too good to us, son," Cattabelle whispered.

Tate looked at his mother, then at the rest of his family. "That's simply not possible, Mama."

Rebekah drank in the scene as everyone commented back and forth on what the other had gotten, when she heard Tate whisper her name. She looked over.

He wore a sheepish grin. "Sorry I don't have anything to give you."

Wanting to tell him how much this evening had meant to her, or better yet, wishing he would take her in his arms and kiss her the way she wanted him to do in that moment, she smiled. "You *have* already given me something, Tate. And it's more precious than you can imagine."

The look in his eyes set something aflame inside her, and her face grew warm with the heat of it.

"Time for beddin' down," Cattabelle announced, and Rebekah caught a flicker of mischief in Tate's expression before she quickly looked away.

She checked the clock on the mantel, not surprised to see it was nearing two o'clock in the morning. Her gaze drifted to the beds lined up against the wall, and as good as they looked, she wondered exactly what the sleeping arrangements would be. She'd never slept in the same room as a man before.

But she had a feeling she was about to.

23

W hat be your front name?" Opal whispered in the dark.

Rebekah smiled and told her. "And you're welcome to call me by my front name, if you want to."

"I'm wantin' to."

"All right then. Rebekah it is."

Opal giggled. "I like ya bein' here."

"I like being here too," Rebekah whispered, wondering if they were keeping the others awake. But the soft snores from nearby beds told her that was unlikely. Except for the silence coming from the sofa—where Tate was sleeping.

"You're right high-stocked with brains, hain't ya, Rebekah? Just like Witty be."

Charmed by how the girl phrased things, Rebekah also heard a note of uncertainty, and longing in her voice. "Your oldest brother's very smart, yes. But you are too, Opal. I heard you tonight, singing and telling stories with your songs. And the questions you asked at dinner, about Nashville, about life outside of Chicory Hollow . . . I think asking questions is a large part of becoming 'high-stocked in brains,' as you say. I've learned so much from asking questions. So . . . you're already well on your way."

Opal let out a satisfied sigh, and Rebekah

reached over and gave the girl's arm a squeeze.

Moments passed, and the *ticktock* of the clock on the mantel counted off the seconds, and Rebekah wondered if she'd ever get to sleep.

"My feet are cold. What about your'n?"

"Mine are too," Rebekah whispered, feeling the cold air seep in around the edges of the loose-fitting window by her head. Her fingers and toes were like ice, despite having worn her stockings to bed.

When Cattabelle learned she hadn't brought a "go-away" satchel with her, the woman had kindly offered the loan of her flannel nightgown. But Rebekah, fearing it might be the only one the woman owned, had politely declined. But when Cattabelle insisted—and after catching Tate's urging nod—Rebekah had accepted.

The gown hit her about knee length, but she was grateful. Even if she was about to freeze to death.

She smiled to herself, picturing how Cattabelle had ordered "the boys" onto the porch while she readied for bed. Rebekah had changed swiftly. First, because she was chilled to the bone. And second, because no curtains draped any of the windows. Only once she was abed did Cattabelle allow her sons entry again.

Opal stirred beside her. "Do you favor spoonin'?" she whispered, her tone tentative.

It took Rebekah a minute to comprehend what the little girl was asking, but when she did, she smiled again. "I certainly do," she said softly. "Do you?"

Not bothering to voice a response, Opal scooted over, giggling as she did, and curled up against Rebekah. Rebekah pulled the girl close, tucking the covers around them both.

Opal whispered, "Mama said I'd best not ask 'bout spoonin' 'cuz she hain't sure about level landers. So I'd be much obliged if ya didn't go tattlin' on me."

"Not to worry. It'll be our secret."

Opal snuggled closer. "Night, Rebekah."

Rebekah kissed the crown of the girl's head. "Good night, Opal."

Within minutes, the child's soft, even breaths told Rebekah she'd drifted off. But even being bone weary herself, sleep still felt far, far away.

The room was quiet, save for the continued snores, the creak of snow-laden branches outside, and the gurgling of a nearby stream under its blanket of ice. Finally starting to get warm, she yawned and closed her eyes, doing her best to lure sleep nearer.

Her thoughts turned to Nashville and she hoped the telegram had been delivered to Belmont as she'd requested. She didn't want anyone worrying about her. Even though she was only four or so hours from Nashville, she couldn't escape the feeling of being another world away.

Here, in this cabin, it was still the eighteenth century, a world frozen in time, a hundred years behind the rest of civilization. And this was Tate's home, as fantastic and unbelievable as that fact was.

Lying there in bed, thinking about him and about the evening she'd spent with his family—even after all the regret she'd experienced over having boarded that train—she couldn't fathom *not* being here. Not knowing about this side of his life. Even more, she couldn't imagine not knowing him.

And not having him in her life. . . .

Rebekah awakened some time later, warm in her cocoon, thanks to spooning with Opal, who didn't appear to have even moved. Unable to see the clock on the mantel in the dark, Rebekah slowly raised her head to peer outside. She didn't want to waken the child. Or anyone else.

Nighttime still ruled beyond the window, but the faintest cheery-morning twitter of a bird gave hint that dawn was on its way. The fire in the hearth burned low, the embers glowing white and red, and Rebekah thought she caught a whiff of coffee but quickly decided it was only her wish for it instead.

A stirring from the direction of the sofa drew her attention, and she stilled. "Tate?" she asked softly. "Are you awake?"

"Yes" came back the definitive whisper.

So definitive, she got tickled and was afraid she might awaken Opal. But the child slept on.

Rebekah raised her head again and saw the outline of Tate's form. He was sitting up.

She kept her voice low. "Can you not sleep?"

"I did for a while, finally. Then I woke up and couldn't go back. Want some coffee?"

"So I *did* smell coffee. I'd love some. Thank you."

He rose, crossed to the cupboard, then to the hearth, then . . . returned to the sofa?

She eyed his silhouette. "You're going to make me get out of bed?"

"Only if you want coffee."

Hearing unmistakable teasing in his voice, she also sensed challenge, yet was a little confused. "Tate . . . I'm not properly—"

He stood again, and she smiled smugly—right before he tossed a blanket toward her. It landed on the foot of her bed. This time, she felt an indisputable dare.

She stared at the blanket, then at him, then slipped from bed, tucked the covers back around Opal, and draped the blanket around her shoulders. After all, she was wearing his mother's flannel gown, which left *everything* and more to the imagination.

She moved to join him on the sofa, but a soreness in her calves and leg muscles from trekking up the mountain made the effort almost painful. She ran her fingers through her hair, doing her best to make it presentable. She sat beside him—though not *too* close beside him—and covered her feet before the chill could set in, then wrapped her hands around the mug he offered.

She shivered in response to the warmth and drank, relishing the heat and strength of the brew. "This coffee could have served itself."

He laughed. "Everyone's a critic."

She smiled and took another sip. "It really is good. But how did you get up and make it without me hearing you?"

"I typically wake up early, so I get everything ready the night before. All I have to do is slip the pot over the fire and add the grounds."

She studied him over the steaming cup, his face cast in shadow. "You have trouble sleeping at home too?"

He shrugged. "On occasion." Then he sighed. "Too often, I'm afraid."

"Thinking of the symphony?"

"Thinking of everything," he whispered.

The melancholy in his voice tugged at her. "Anything I can do to help?"

He turned and looked at her. "You already did."

Despite the soft snoring of his brothers across the room, and Opal asleep nearby, Rebekah suddenly felt as if they were very much alone. They'd been alone before. Often. In his office. In a carriage. But this felt different. *They* felt different.

"I'm glad you're here." His voice was soft. His tone, honest. "Which is saying a lot, compared to how I felt when I first saw you in the woods. Or . . . *heard* you."

"You were angry with me. And with reason. But those men—Virgil and . . ." She couldn't remember the other's name.

"Banty." Tate shook his head. "The younger of the Slokum brothers . . . You know why he's named that, don't you?"

She waited.

"It's the way he laughs. He cackles like an old banty hen. Has for as long as I can remember."

Recalling that sound, Rebekah cringed a little, remembering what had happened. "Well, the name certainly fits."

As they sipped their coffee, the room, the cabin, being in these mountains, still felt so surreal.

"You worry about your brothers working in the mines."

"I do. But with my father sick, and with the future so unknown, plus with Emil getting married . . . they need to work. We had the hog killing just before Christmas. That brought in a good amount. And come spring, they'll have some crops again and the honey to sell. The symphony pays me well and my needs are few, so I help as much as I can."

Rebekah knew he helped far more than he let on, and in more ways than with money alone.

A soft groan came from the next room, followed by Tate's mother murmuring words of comfort that Rebekah couldn't make out, but she sensed the tenderness and love in them all the same.

"Thank you, Rebekah, for accepting my family the way you have."

"They're wonderful, Tate. All of them. I've enjoyed every minute."

"Even the squirrel stew?"

She rethought her declaration. "*Almost* every minute."

The first wink of dawn shone through the bare window, and she could see his face—and the way he was looking at her.

He set his cup aside. "Thank you, too, for caring enough to follow me yesterday. That means a great deal."

She gave a nod. "You're most welcome."

But a twinge of discomfort needled at her. And she realized why. Because she knew the real reason she'd boarded that train in Nashville. Yes, she'd been concerned about him, but she'd been more concerned about New York.

"Although," he continued, "next time, you could save a lot of effort by simply asking if the medicine you find hidden in my cabinet is mine or not."

"Yes, that *would* be easier." She attempted a playful tone but didn't quite manage it.

He reached over and covered her hand on the sofa between them, and though it was a moment she would've more than welcomed hours earlier, the discomfort inside her only deepened.

"Tate," she began. But he wove his fingers through hers, and all desire to tell him the truth fled, replaced by another, much stronger, longing.

"I haven't told you what a help you're being to me in writing this symphony. I never thought actually collaborating with someone on this would work, much less be something I would choose to do. You keep surprising me, Rebekah Carrington." He reached up and fingered a curl on her shoulder. "And I'm not easily surprised."

She tried to think of something to say, but couldn't. Which was just as well, because her heart was in her throat. He leaned closer, and she could all but feel his lips on hers, his hand cupping the side of her face as he—

A loud snore erupted from the other side of the room.

Rebekah jumped and quickly put distance between them, thinking that one of his brothers was playing a trick on them, and perhaps had even been watching. The very thought made her go hot and cold. But Tate only laughed.

"Don't worry," he said softly. "They're still asleep, I assure you. If they weren't, we would've already heard from them. They're not the least bit shy in that regard—as you've already seen."

"Yes," she smiled, feeling a little foolish, and embarrassed. "I learned that early on. But they're nice, not to mention talented. And they certainly seem to think a lot of you."

"As I do them."

He leaned back and rested his head on the back of the sofa, and she did the same. They stared out the window, watching the distant horizon gradually move from dark gray to purple, splashed with hints of pink and gold.

"There's a saying around here," he whispered. " 'Never move so far away that you can't see the smoke from your parents' chimney.' "

As if on cue, the fire in the hearth crackled and popped, and sparks drifted upward as wood succumbed to flame.

"But you did. Move far away."

He didn't answer.

"How did you ever come to leave Chicory Hollow?"

He looked over at her. "What you're really wondering is how does a boy born here, in this place, end up becoming a conductor for a symphony? Even a newly formed one."

She found herself unable to argue.

"It's simple, really. It's all due to my father, who shared his love of music with me and taught me how to play the violin and piano. And to a missionary by the name of Jacob Marshall. On one of Mr. Marshall's early trips into the mountains, he heard me play the piano in church. We never had one at the house, of course. But the church I grew up in did, and I started playing at a very young age."

She didn't know why, but she hadn't figured him for a boy who'd grown up going to church. Or at least, she wouldn't have before last night.

"I was fourteen when Mr. Marshall met with my parents about me going away. He'd been visiting Chicory Hollow for several years, so they knew and trusted him. He said he'd recognized my talent early on and had spoken with a wealthy benefactor who had no children and who was eager to support 'a poor but promising young musician.' I was the same age as Benjamin is now."

"That's when you left here?"

He nodded. "I came home every chance I could. At first. Then as the years passed, as school and schedules grew more demanding, the trips got less frequent. Until about five months ago."

Instinctively, she knew. "When your father became ill."

He nodded. "I've made it home at least once a month since, sometimes twice. Before coming to Nashville, I had several offers to consider. I chose this one because it is closer to home."

Suddenly, it all made sense to her. "The weekends, and guest conducting. But you weren't guest conducting, were you?"

"I have actually guest conducted a few weekends, but as for the others . . . Well, if conducting my family counts, it wasn't exactly a lie." He sighed and gave her a look that said he hoped she would understand. "You know the world of orchestras, and how these things work. I could scarcely tell Mrs. Cheatham that I was traveling to Chicory Hollow to see my family, could I?"

She studied his features, the fine crisscross of lines at the corners of his eyes. "It's not right, Tate . . . how things work, as you said. But no, you couldn't."

"Mr. Frederick Mason, my benefactor, died

nearly five years ago. And Jacob Marshall, the missionary, passed on soon after. They were the only ones, besides my phonetics professor"— he laughed softly—"who knew where I really hailed from. And that professor is gone now too."

"Which made it easy to pretend."

"It was never easy, Rebekah. It's still not."

"I'm sorry. I didn't mean to—"

He took hold of her hand again. "It's all right. I know what you meant. I just want you to know it hasn't been easy . . . pretending to be someone I'm not, in that regard, while also trying to live up to people's expectations. Especially when those people are greatly responsible for my being where I am, for my having the success that I do. It's almost impossible for people to see the truth— much less embrace it—when they're so intent on the truth looking and behaving a certain way."

She threaded her fingers through his. "Now *that's* something I know a great deal about," she whispered.

He lifted her hand to his mouth and kissed it— once, twice, his lips lingering—and her skin tingled from the warmth of his breath.

"I don't think you realize how much it bothered me, Rebekah, that I had to say no to you that day when you first came to my office. I haven't always felt this way, but if it were up to me, and if things were different, if the times were different, I'd welcome you to the symphony. I'd more than welcome you, I'd pursue you. Just as I've tried to pursue whomever the gentleman was who played at Mrs. Cheatham's party that night. He was magnificent. I've asked Mrs. Cheatham about him numerous times, but she continues to insist she doesn't know."

"And you don't believe her?" Rebekah knew to tread carefully.

"No, I believe her. I simply want—no, I *need*—that talent in my orchestra."

Guilt pricked her conscience again, and Rebekah briefly closed her eyes. She was bound by an oath not to reveal what she'd done at the party that night. But only her pride bound her in the other case.

"Tate . . . I need to be—I *want* to be—honest with you about something."

He turned and looked at her.

"While I *was* concerned about you and your . . . addiction"—even saying it now sounded foolish—"my motivation for following you wasn't only to keep you from throwing away your career. . . . It was also to keep you from throwing away *mine*."

Wishing he weren't watching her so closely, she rushed on to get the words out before he could say anything.

"Once you and I have completed the symphony, and we've had the grand opening of the new hall, and Pauline, Mrs. Cheatham's daughter, has performed in her recital . . . I'm going to New York. To audition for the philharmonic there. It's what I've always wanted to do. To play. And they've already accepted one woman, so . . . I figure, they might be willing to accept another. And oddly, considering how things have worked out here"—she smiled but felt sad all the same—"you're the one who's given me the courage to do it."

Saying nothing, he looked back to the window, but his hand tightened around hers. When he finally spoke, his voice was husky with emotion.

"So we're in this together, then. You help me achieve my dream . . . and I'll help you achieve yours. I'll even write a personal reference, if you wish." He looked at her and smiled.

And she did her best to offer her own in return. Because she was getting what she wanted . . . wasn't she? Her dream was coming true.

But if that was the case, why did she feel as if she was casting aside the most precious part of her life?

24

Tate sat by his father's bedside, willing him to awaken, willing his pale complexion to regain color and fervor again. Tate could hear Rebekah and his mother talking in the next room, getting breakfast ready, while Opal and his brothers were outside doing their chores.

"Pa," he whispered, thankful for this time alone with him, a rare commodity in such close quarters.

Especially with the rest of his brothers and their families coming over that afternoon. There were things he needed to say to his father, and a distant ache inside him whispered that time to give them voice was running out. "Can you hear me?"

His father's eyelids fluttered. His hand stirred atop the covers.

Tate gripped it and leaned closer, holding on to his father much like a drowning man would clutch a lifeline. Because, despite his father's failing health, Tate felt like the one who needed saving. "It's me, sir. It's Witty."

His father sighed, and a gradual smile crept into his face. "Witty . . . *son*." His breath came hard earned, a deep rattle in his chest. "I dreamt . . . you was visitin'."

"It's not a dream, Pa. I'm here. I came for the weekend. But . . . in a way, I'm always here. With you, and Mama, and the family. I think about you all so much, and I—" His voice threatened to break, and he paused. "I carry the mountains . . . and home inside me, wherever I go."

His father's hand tightened around his, feeble though his grip was, and he slowly turned his head to look at Tate. "Don't wanna be . . . hearin' contriteness in your voice, son." His father's eyes watered. "You're doin' what the Almighty . . . fashioned you to do." His father took a deep breath, wincing as he did. "Don't ever be sorry for that."

Tate nodded.

"She's a pretty thing, that woman you brung with you. Your . . . *friend*."

Tate smiled. "She is a friend, Pa. And my assistant. But nothing more." Not that he wouldn't have welcomed more if the situation were different.

His father shifted in bed, gritting his teeth when he did.

"Are you in pain, Pa?"

"A mite, I guess."

Which Tate knew meant a lot. He poured some water into a cup and added laudanum, then held the cup to his father's lips.

"No," Pa whispered. "Not yet. I like havin' my wits about me for a change."

"But I don't want you to hurt."

"There's far worse things than hurtin', son."

Tate returned the cup to the bedside table, feeling guilty for not insisting his father drink the medicine. But it'd been so long since they'd had time like this with each other.

"I don't mean to sound like I regret my decision, Pa. But sometimes I do wish I could have lived both lives. The one here . . . and the one outside the hollow."

His father sighed. "The good Lord give us each a race to run, Witty. He be the one to . . . mark it out. It be your'n to run where He pointed. And I know you're runnin' well, son."

Tate looked at the well-worn Bible on the bedside table and recognized the verse his father was referring to. He was grateful now—more so than in previous years—that his parents had thought it important for their children to hide the Word of God in their hearts. "'Wherefore seeing we also are compassed about with so great a cloud of witnesses, let us lay aside every weight, and the sin which doth so easily beset us, and let us run with patience the race that is set before us.'"

His father smiled. "'Lookin' unto Jesus,'" he continued softly.

Tate nodded. "'. . . the author and finisher of our faith . . .'"

"'Who . . . for the joy that was set before him . . .'"

"'. . . endured the cross, despising the shame, and is set down at the right hand . . .'"

"'. . . of the throne'a God,'" his father finished, pleasure in his voice, his grip a bit stronger than before. His gaze turned earnest. "The Lord . . . He always keeps His vows, Witty."

"I know He does, sir."

They sat in silence, Tate watching his father as he looked out the window at his beloved mountains rising in the near distance, the sun brilliant in the cerulean sky, quickly burning off the ragged wisps of gauzy clouds that shrouded them each morning.

"How's it comin' along?" his father asked, not looking away from the view.

Tate shrugged. "It's . . . coming, sir. I'm still working on it. I have a ways to go yet."

His father sighed and closed his eyes. "You'll get there soon 'nough."

Tate bowed his head, willing his voice to hold. "You're going to get better, Pa. And you and Mama are going to be there that night . . . to hear it. In person. It's . . . it's for you, after all. For all you taught me. All you gave me. I'm writing this symphony for you."

"I know ya are, son. And I'm *mighty* grateful." His father slowly turned back, his gaze clearer than it had been in a long time. "And I'll be hearin' it too. Whether't be in that"—he grimaced and gritted his teeth—"fancy music buildin' over Nashville-way or in that great cloud'a witnesses." His lips trembled, his eyes awash with tears. "Whatever way my race takes me, son . . . I be listenin' for your music."

Tate nodded and reached for the medicine.

"In the chest over there." His father gestured. "In the top drawer. Would ya get my papers? There's somethin' I want you to read."

Tate put the cup back down and did as his father asked. He withdrew a stack of papers loosely tied with twine.

"Should be near the top there. Just look through 'em, son. You'll see it."

Tate flipped through various receipts for farming supplies and tools, dog-eared pages ripped from a farmer's almanac with passages either circled or underlined—but as soon as he saw his father's handwriting and read the first sentence, he knew this was what his father wanted him to read.

Tate looked up.

"It's not fancy, son, I know. But it's what I want read . . . when my time comes. That and some Scripture your mama and I already picked out."

As Tate scanned the poem, his vision blurred.

"I penned it a long time back, Witty." His father's voice fell away. "For my own pa . . . after he died. I'd like to hear you read it, son . . . just this once."

Tate heard question in his father's voice and tried to smile. Then he cleared his throat, doubting he'd get far, and started softly.

> "I grew up on a farm, but it did me no
>   harm.
> We just plowed and we planted and we hoed.
> We hauled bundles of hay, throughout the
>   long day.
> I kept hoping"—

Tate swallowed hard.

> —"to haul the last load."

His father sighed. "You 'member, son? That's what you and your brothers used to always ask me too . . . 'Pa, is this the last load?' Same as I did with mine."

Tate nodded, the soft smile on his father's face all that was keeping his emotions in check. He continued.

"I learned lots from my mother,
bonded strong with my brothers,
took pride in our humble abode.
And I'm still here alive, 'cause I learned
    how to drive,
with my pa as we hauled one more load.

I learned by observing, Pa's method of
    serving,
in silence and calm as we rode.
And while feeding the cattle, no jabber,
    no prattle . . .
Just thinking, 'Is this the last load?'"

As Tate read, he found himself smiling over memories the poem painted of his grandfather who'd died many years back.

"Now he lived a long life, on the farm
    with his wife,
who was happy to share the workload.
You would not see him frown, though the
    years wore him down.
He kept hauling and hauling that load."

Tate glanced at the last two stanzas, and it felt as though a cord tightened swift and fast around his heart.

"We fought off the gloom, in his sickbed
    room,

Pa was nearing the end of his road.
He just eyed me and said, as I stood by
   his bed,
'It's time . . . to haul the last load.'"

A single tear trailed down Pa's cheek, but he nodded for Tate to continue.

Tate firmed his jaw, and a moment passed before he could finish.

"What a sobering thought, to be careless
   and caught,
without tending your row to be hoed.
So I challenge you, friend, to be true to
   the end,
'til it's your time . . . to haul the last load."

His father reached for his hand and Tate gripped it tightly. They sat for several minutes, neither speaking. Then Tate held the cup of medicine to his father's lips and sat quietly beside the bedside as his father slipped into slumber, his breathing even and deep.

The words of the poem and the verse they'd quoted filled his heart, and Tate bowed his head and thanked God for making this man his father, for making Chicory Hollow part of his earthly race. *Help me, Lord, to run well. To run better than I ever have. And please . . .* He wiped the moisture from his cheeks as he studied the weathered lines of his father's face. *Give him more time.*

●　●　●

The train whistle blew in the distance, and Tate knew they'd have to hurry in order for Rebekah to board on time. Not that getting a seat from Chicory Hollow would be a challenge, but securing one on the connecting leg from Knoxville to Nashville later in the day often could be. And he didn't want her arriving into Nashville past dark.

Following breakfast, she and his mother had sat talking at the kitchen table for far too long, and this after they'd all visited with his father. Yet he wouldn't trade that time with her, and them, for anything. He certainly wasn't old at thirty-two—though some days he felt like it—but he'd learned not to rush certain moments in anticipation of those yet to come, no matter how urgent they seemed.

Because some opportunities, once passed, never came again.

Seeing Rebekah struggle to navigate her way over a boulder in her heeled boots, he lifted her by the waist and set her down before him.

She laughed, a little winded. "Well, that's one way to do it."

The confession she'd made earlier that morning, before sunrise, about moving to New York stuck in his thoughts like a burr. Add to that, just as they'd left the cabin, one of his headaches had come on, and every step down the mountain felt like a sledgehammer inside his head.

Glad he'd made an appointment for Monday

morning in Knoxville, he dreaded it all the same. He'd experienced headaches from time to time in recent years, but these were different. And were increasing in frequency. The spells made him feel off-balance and sent the sounds around him swirling, like it was coming toward him through a tunnel.

Rebekah looked up at him, the light in her eyes fading slightly. "Are you all right, Tate? Or, should I call you Witty now?"

He heard her voice, only from far away, like he had cotton stuffed in his ears. He managed a smile. "I'm fine. Just a little tired. As are you, I suspect."

He held out his hand, and she threaded her fingers through his. They walked the path together until it narrowed again, then he resumed the lead.

"Tate?"

He turned back, not sure if she'd spoken.

She wore an odd expression. "I just asked you . . . Where did the nickname Witty come from?"

"Isn't it obvious?" he said quickly, trying to cover for not having heard her. "It's because I'm so funny."

She laughed. "Of course, how did I miss that? I suppose it's better than Banty, though."

"I would hope so."

She studied him. "Are you certain you're all right?"

"I'm fine. Just . . . had a headache come on earlier."

Her brow furrowed. "I'm sorry."

He waved off her concern. "My head feels a little stuffy right now, is all."

They continued on. The air was cold with the bite of winter, but the sunshine and blue skies portended a dry day, which he welcomed after yesterday's trek.

"I enjoyed spending time with your father this morning," she said after a while, walking beside him again. "He seems like a fine man."

"He is. The finest."

"He has a quick wit about him. Much like his oldest son."

Tate smiled. "He's always had a way of seeing the world a little differently. But the laudanum dulls his mind, and that troubles him—I can tell."

"He's been seen by a doctor, I take it."

"Several. They all say consumption, and that there's nothing left to be done."

The silence lengthened.

"I'm so sorry to hear that."

He hesitated to share his latest endeavor regarding his father's health, not having shared the news with anyone yet. But maybe part of his hesitation was because he didn't want to get his own hopes up, only to have them dashed.

"I've written numerous letters to physicians in Boston, New York, and Philadelphia, inquiring if they know of any new treatments or procedures for consumption patients."

"That's wonderful. Have you heard back from any of them?"

"It's been almost three months. And not one reply."

He maneuvered through a thick cluster of pine, the scent pungent and fresh. Then they came upon the clearing where the Slokum brothers had confronted her the night before.

Rebekah slowed her pace, as though recalling the event. "Those men . . ." She paused. "Virgil and Banty. Do they really sell moonshine?"

"They do. They make it themselves too. And they're proud of their 'recipe,' as they call it. They caught a man spying on them once, as they were stilling. He was trying to figure out how they made it." Tate laughed, remembering. "That earned him a seat full of buckshot and a fast trip down the mountain."

Rebekah smiled, then quickly sobered. "I've heard of blood feuds in these mountains before. Is there truth to those tales?"

"Absolutely. Although, I'm grateful to say, none in my family since at least two generations back. But these people, like Virgil and Banty . . . They're stiff-necked and strong-minded. A credit, in one sense, to their strong Scotch-Irish roots. It's bred an iron will into them—which isn't all bad. It takes that kind of bullheaded determination and strength to live in these mountains. The weaker ones don't make it, I learned early on. These people, *my* people . . . they possess a proud sense of self-reliance and an intense love of freedom. But they don't like anyone coming in here telling them what to do or how to live, or trying to take advantage of them. That's the best way to get yourself killed in these mountains, underestimating a highlander. Or trying to cheat them. It'll come to no good. Every time. You have to understand . . . Most folks around here, like Virgil and Banty, still live by the old mountain creed."

Her expression clouded.

"People in these mountains have their own law. Sometimes it meshes with the one out there in the world, sometimes it doesn't. It's been a couple of years ago now, but three highlander men were shot and killed for running illegal stills."

"Moonshining."

He nodded. "The government's fine with people running stills, as long as those people pay the tax on that liquor to the government. Revenue agents ride these mountains looking for those who don't. An agent rounded up three of those men. They were unarmed and refused to go with him. So the agent shot them. Right there in front of their wives and children. Days later, that revenue agent—at the risk of being indelicate—was found some miles from here. With his throat slit."

Rebekah winced. "Did they ever find out who killed him?"

"No. And they never will."

"Too much time had passed, I guess."

"It's not about time passing, not here in these mountains. It's about loyalty. And about being an outsider."

"An outsider . . . like I am."

"Yes." He smiled. "You're most definitely an outsider, Rebekah. But also . . . no. Because you're not demanding that the people here change their ways—that they surrender the life and livelihood they've known for over a century or longer. Viewing it from a highlander's perspective, that revenue agent killed three of their men in cold blood. Three fathers, three sons, three husbands. And these people never give up their own."

"Even if their own have done wrong?"

He eyed her. "Sometimes *wrong* isn't always so straight-edged. After all, those three men died unarmed. Unable to defend themselves. And I knew all of them. They were fine men, Rebekah, who left behind wives and children."

She considered that for a moment. "But . . . surely your family doesn't condone moonshining?"

"Not at all. You heard what my mother said at the table." He smiled. "The Whitcombs put that behind us years ago, long before I was born." He motioned for them to continue on down the path. "But for some of these people, moonshining is part of who they are. It's a sacred skill their parents and grandparents handed down to them. It's how they provide for their families. Selling to outlanders. I'm not saying what those three men did was right. But I do know it's not easy to carve out a living back here, especially when you've got lots of mouths to feed."

A whistle blast pierced the air, and they hurried

on toward the train station. As they approached, Tate remembered something, and he searched the platform and the boarding passengers.

"One more thing, Rebekah, before you go . . . With all else that happened, I haven't given this any thought since yesterday. But . . . I saw your stepfather getting off the train. Here, in Chicory Hollow."

The surprise in her expression rivaled his own at the time.

"Did he say what he was doing here?"

"I didn't ask. In fact, I made a point for him not to see me. I simply thought you should know."

Same as he'd done, she searched the platform, her features a mixture of dread and concern. "Thank you for telling me."

Despite her protests, Tate purchased her ticket at the window, then slipped it into her hand. Part of him wished she wasn't going back just yet, while the greater part of him knew she didn't belong here. Although, for not belonging, she certainly had won his family over.

He walked her to the first-class passenger car. "Do you have money for the trip home?"

She smiled up at him, nodding, looking lovely in the morning light. "I've already begun praying that you'll hear from one of those physicians, Tate. And that your father's health won't worsen in the meantime."

"Thank you," he whispered, wondering precisely when her features had become so cherished to him. The soft hollows beneath her cheekbones, the way her brows arched over kind eyes, how her hair framed her face when she wore it pinned back, as she did now. Even the delicate slope of her nose and her hazel eyes drew him. And those lips . . .

He reined in that particular thought, unable to do anything about it at the moment. "I'll be back Monday afternoon. Please see if you can have the third movement completed by then. That would be a great help."

She gave him a mock salute. "Why not the fourth as well, since we're dreaming."

"I don't know—I think you can do it." He eyed her, keeping his smile in check. "Since you're so high-stocked with brains and all, like me."

Her mouth slipped open. "You were eavesdropping on me and Opal last night!"

He laughed. "I was. What little I could hear, anyway. You *were* whispering, after all."

Her laughter washed over him as her gaze briefly slipped from his eyes to his mouth, then slowly inched back upward, and he read desire in the act. He glanced at the men still loading the bags at the far end of the platform, took her by the hand, and led her behind the ticket office. She came willingly, matching him almost step for step.

They rounded the corner, and he took her in his arms and kissed her. Her arms came around his neck and pulled him closer, tighter. He deepened the kiss, and she melted into him, her body pressed so close he was certain he felt the beat of her heart in his own chest.

The final whistle blew, and he reluctantly drew back, smiling a little when she resisted letting go of him. As quickly as he'd led her back here, he returned her to the platform, pressed a quick kiss to her forehead, and put her on the train.

Heaven unleashed the storehouses of rain just as Tate stepped onto the platform in Knoxville. The train had left Chicory Hollow thirty minutes behind schedule that morning, which meant now he was thirty minutes behind as well. Sometimes he hated traveling.

He checked his baggage with the porter, turned up the collar of his suit coat, and plunged into the fray of street traffic.

He'd never visited this physician before. In fact, he hadn't required a doctor's services in years. But he was familiar enough with Knoxville to know the part of town in which the man's office was located.

Contrary to the opinion Rebekah had held, he wasn't one to take unnecessary medications or tonics. But if medication is what the doctor prescribed, he would take it. Or if surgery was necessary—following the grand opening of the opera house—he would agree to it, as soon as his schedule allowed.

He hadn't slept much the past two nights in Chicory Hollow, thinking about today and the increasing recurrence of headaches—and his hearing. He told himself the problem would improve significantly once he'd finished composing the symphony. *Simply get past May and the stress of the grand opening, and it will get better.*

Twenty minutes later and all but soaked, he located the appropriate shingle hanging on the exterior of one of the handsome redbrick buildings lining both sides of Maple Street. He checked his pocket watch. Ten minutes until his appointment, which meant he was already five minutes late by his book. He'd soon learn whether the physician operated his practice on a similar schedule.

Tate opened the ornate wooden door and was greeted by the off-putting antiseptic scent. A young woman seated behind a secretary's desk met his gaze with a subdued smile.

"How may I help you, sir?"

"Mr. Whitcomb to see Dr. Hamilton."

"Thank you, Mr. Whitcomb. Please have a seat. The doctor will be with you shortly."

The woman pulled one of several cords located on a signal board on the wall behind her, and Tate claimed a chair in the small but nicely furnished waiting room. He checked his pocket watch again. The doctor had five minutes.

Not two minutes later, an interior door opened and a distinguished-looking older gentleman stepped out. "Mr. Whitcomb, I'm Dr. Ronald Hamilton. Please, come in."

Considering the appointment off to a good start,

Tate preceded him into the room and took the offered wingback chair.

"Your letter intrigued me, Mr. Whitcomb." Dr. Hamilton closed the door and seated himself behind the desk. "You were quite thorough in your explanation and charting of your headaches—or . . . episodes, as you referred to them—and I'm eager to discuss that at greater length. But before we begin the examination, I want you to know that I greatly appreciate the trust you're placing in me, and I assure you I will do everything medically possible to diagnosis and treat your ailment."

"Thank you, Dr. Hamilton. And I appreciate not only your stellar reputation here *and* at Boston Medical for so many years, but your confidentiality as well."

The doctor tilted his head in acknowledgment. "As I explained in my missive, we all tend to take our various senses for granted. Only when one of those senses is impinged upon in some way do we realize how precious a gift it truly is. You've done well not to allow this to progress any further without seeking medical attention. Sometimes the remedy is as simple as draining fluid from behind the eardrum. Other times, the treatment, if one exists," he added with a hint of caution, "can be far more involved. We shall hope it's the former."

Tate nodded, eager to move past discussion and on to discovery.

As though sensing his impatience, Dr. Hamilton rose. "Per our exchange, following my examination today, I will share the findings with my colleague in Boston who also specializes in auditory maladies. Then I'll detail our recommended course of action to you in a letter. Unless, of course, you'd rather return to Knoxville to receive the diagnosis."

"A letter will suffice."

"Very well, then." The doctor paused, briefly looking down at his clasped hands. "I saw you conduct in New York, two years ago now, I believe. I've heard Beethoven's Ninth many times, but never like that. Your talent and ability to inspire musicians is nothing short of masterful. Especially for one so young, if you don't mind my saying."

Tate tried not to hear finality in the man's voice. "I don't mind at all. And I thank you, sir, for the compliment."

"Well then, let's get started. Shall we?" The doctor crossed to a side door and opened it to reveal an examination and surgical room. "After you . . . Maestro."

hat had Barton been doing in Chicory Hollow?

All day Monday Rebekah worked in Tate's office, anticipating his arrival that afternoon, but she couldn't get the question out of her mind. Had Barton seen her getting onto the train in Nashville and followed her? It made no sense. How could he have known? She hadn't even known herself until the very last minute. She'd kept watch for him on her return trip to Nashville Saturday, but hadn't seen him.

Something else that made no sense was Tate not showing up when he'd said he would. She was eager for him to return so they could begin working on the symphony again. But that wasn't the only reason she wanted him back. The way he'd swept her behind the ticket office and kissed her breathless before seeing her off also figured into it. Were all kisses like that?

If yes, she understood even more why men and women married. Because her first kiss was absolutely . . .

Remembering Tate's mouth on hers, his arms around her, his hands on her back—she grew flushed all over again. And with that thought ever vivid in her mind, she returned to her task. Or tried.

She'd half expected to run into Miss Endicott that morning, but the young woman hadn't showed. Which suited her more than fine.

Finally, after five o'clock came and went, Rebekah left a note for Tate on the piano, more concerned now than frustrated. She detailed what she'd accomplished for the day, along with proposed changes for the third movement—on the off chance he came in to compose later that evening.

She met the carriage at the appointed place and

settled in for the ride to Belmont, suddenly wishing—after the wonderful time spent with Tate's family—she could stop and see her mother on the way. To perhaps begin trying to heal the rift between them. But being so late in the day, Barton would likely be home—*if* he was back in town. And as much as she wanted to see her mother, she didn't want to risk seeing him.

The carriage turned onto the drive leading to Belmont, and situated atop the hill, the mansion glowed rosy pink in the fading afternoon light. But she missed having a place to call home. Belmont was lovely. Exquisite, actually. And she was grateful to be here, given the alternative. But it wasn't *home*. Not for her.

The driver guided the carriage up the final turn, and Rebekah spotted Eli and Zeke, a young groomsman who worked in the stables, waiting out front. As the carriage drew closer, Zeke took off running around the side of the mansion—quick as a flash—as she'd seen him do on other occasions when carriages arrived. On some errand for Eli, she guessed.

"Good evening, Miss Carrington." Eli greeted her as he opened the door. "Hope you had yourself a good day of working in that music hall, ma'am."

Rebekah accepted his assistance. "I did. Thank you, Eli. But it's also nice to be back here."

"It's always good to get home, ma'am. No matter where home is, that's where the heart is rooted."

"Yes." Her smile faltered. "That's so true."

The mansion was unusually quiet, same as the evening before. Dr. and Mrs. Cheatham and the children had extended their stay in Murfreesboro, which meant she had more time to work on the symphony with Tate—which she would be happy to do, especially after their time in Chicory Hollow.

And in light of the hasty telegram she'd sent before boarding the train—which Mrs. Routh confirmed they received—Rebekah again counted herself lucky that the family had been traveling that weekend. Fewer questions from Adelicia Cheatham, the better.

She discovered her dinner tray waiting in her room, somewhat irritatingly so, considering her memorable encounter with Esther and Cordina. It would've bothered her far less if Cordina had simply been the type of head cook who didn't like others "trespassing" in her kitchen. Herr Heilig's head chef hadn't allowed *any* nonculinary employees to step foot in his areas of the home. But Cordina wasn't like that. This was something else completely. Something more. Only, Rebekah didn't know what.

And that troubled her.

Not bothering to light a lamp, she pulled up a chair and ate by the window, as she usually did, dusk swiftly descending over the rolling hills that comprised the majority of the Belmont estate. She ate the hot split-pea-and-ham soup as her gaze settled on a tree line in the distance—maples, she'd discovered on a walk—and she imagined how beautiful they would be all leafed out with spring.

But spring felt a long way away tonight. As did her future in New York City.

She finished dinner, and as she stood to put the tray outside her door, she glimpsed someone walking from the direction of the servants' houses toward the mansion. A man, judging from his clothes, and an older man at that. Because he walked with a cane, his limp pronounced. She might not have paid him any mind, except that he walked with such purpose—straight toward a towering old oak. Where, upon reaching it, he stepped into its shadow and vanished.

Rebekah squinted. If she hadn't already known he was there, she never would have been able to see him. But someone else did.

Because at that very moment, a woman walked hurriedly from the back of the mansion directly toward the tree. One of the servants, Rebekah assumed. And just as the man had, the woman disappeared into the shadow of the massive tree.

Rebekah waited. For what, she wasn't certain. Only, she found she couldn't look away. Then, as seconds passed, she began to wonder if perhaps she *should* look away. For propriety's sake. But . . . she knew better. The man was old, and something about the woman had struck her as mature as well. So she was certain nothing—

The couple stepped from the shadows, and the woman reached up and—Rebekah frowned— struck the old man on the shoulder! What on earth was she . . .

Rebekah leaned closer to the darkened window, her breath fogging the pane. The woman hadn't intended for her gesture to be hurtful at all. But rather . . . playful. Rebekah could tell by the way she leaned into him, as though laughing, their foreheads touching. Moved by their obvious affection for each other, Rebekah watched them walk arm in arm back toward the servants' houses.

Until finally, the night enveloped them both.

For what seemed like a long time, she stared at that empty slice of darkness, surprised to find herself smiling even as her eyes filled with tears. She turned away from the window, struggling to rein in her thoughts. One thought, in particular. And she found the needed distraction in transcribing a portion of notes she'd brought home with her.

But as she crawled into bed a while later, weariness overtook her resolve, and she hugged her pillow tight against her cheek, hoping that someday—if it was in accord with God's desire for her life—that she, too, would be able to grow old with the man she loved.

Eight o'clock the next morning, the carriage let Rebekah off near the side alley of the opera house, and she heard the orchestra as soon as she opened the back door. She liked arriving this early and wished she could make it a regular occurrence. No sign of Mrs. Bixby or Mrs. Murphey, so she continued on to Tate's office, stashed her things, and sneaked in through the door leading backstage.

Tate had chosen Mozart, yet again. Symphony No. 31 in D Major. The Paris Symphony, as it was also known. Maestro Heilig had conducted this as well, many times.

What she remembered most about this symphony was Maestro Heilig's amusing, but true, comment. *"It simply contains too many ideas, too much variety, too much content. And therefore, wins over practically everyone who hears it!"*

She walked to the edge of one of the side curtains and saw Tate, and her heart did a tiny flip. She watched him, recalling every detail about their kiss and wondering if he'd had similar recollections of the moment. Or did men not think about such things as women did?

He conducted with such boldness, such masterful grace. With the slightest movement of his hand, the rich tones of the horn section swelled and floated upward, their dominant note ruling the moment. Then the woodwinds—clarinets, flutes, oboes, and bassoons—then the strings, every section in turn seeming intrinsically tied to Tate's merest whim. All he had to do was look and they responded. She'd observed enough conductors in her lifetime to know that he was, indeed, special. And she felt, maybe for the first time, at least at this level, how fortunate she was to work so closely with such a man, much less to feel this way about—

Even though she didn't want to finish that sentence, even in her mind, she knew that her choosing not to give it voice didn't make it any less true. She loved him. She knew it. Maybe she'd known it for a while now but had ignored it.

Tate never looked her way, but she suspected he already knew she was there. Nothing seemed to escape his—

"Stop!" he thundered, the anger in his voice harsh, even for him. And like crystal glasses knocked from a tray, the music—only seconds earlier beautiful and soaring—crashed against an imaginary brick wall and plummeted and shattered onto the floor of the stage.

"Why are you not responding to my cues?" he yelled. "Horns, are you asleep? I cued you and you did nothing. *Nothing!* Just kept playing. Flutes, you . . ." He ran both hands through his hair and threw his baton to the ground. "We're done for the day." He stepped from the dais and strode offstage—straight toward her.

Rebekah darted out the side door and ran as fast as she could back to the office. She plunked down on the piano bench and opened the music where she'd left off yesterday—only to discover huge Xs slashed through most all of her changes.

No . . . correction. Through *all* of the changes she'd suggested.

Heavy footsteps portended the storm, and she suddenly wished she hadn't come in early after all. Had something happened in Chicory Hollow following her departure that had—

Oh, no . . . his father.

Something had happened to Angus. That had to be it. Her heart ached as she imagined the grief that Tate, his mother, and siblings must be enduring at his passing. And, of course, Tate *would* choose to dive back into his work, using anger as a shield and distraction.

He entered the office and slammed the door behind him. "Don't even pretend you weren't there. I saw you the moment you arrived."

Rebekah rose, tears threatening. "Tate . . . I'm so, so sorry."

"I doubt that, otherwise you wouldn't do it repeatedly."

She stared, stunned, and thrown a little off-balance. But she knew how difficult he could be at times, so she reached for patience, and tried again. "Tate, I know you're angry right now. And hurting. But what I'm trying to convey to you is my sympathy over your—"

"I need your sympathy like I need another . . . Darrow Fulton." He exhaled. "With him for a concertmaster, I'm doomed. We all are." He cut her a look. "You accused *me* of being addicted to laudanum? To morphine? Look no further than—"

416

"Tate!" she interrupted.

He fell silent.

"If you'll stop ranting for five seconds—" Heart pumping, she crossed the room to stand before him. She took a quick breath. "I'm trying to express to you how sorry I am about your father."

"My father," he slowly repeated.

She nodded.

His eyes narrowed. "What about my father?"

"About his—" Then she hesitated, wondering now if she'd misread the situation. "Wait. Is Angus . . ."

Confusion clouded his features, and she suddenly shared the same uncertainty.

"Tate, is your father still alive?"

His eyes widened. "When I left Chicory Hollow yesterday, yes. He was. Why, have you heard something?" He paused, his confusion swiftly overrun by concern. "Did a telegram arrive?"

"No," she said quickly. "No telegram. I haven't heard a thing. I simply thought that since you were so upset, something must have happened." She stopped and briefly firmed her jaw. "Tate, what is it that has you so angry? That has you in this . . . state of mind?"

An inexplicable emotion flickered behind his eyes. Then he looked at her as though she were touched in the head. "You were there just now, Rebekah. You *heard* them. There are no crescendos. No decrescendos. The entire orchestra ignores my every cue. It's as if I'm not even standing up there conducting. And you have to ask me what's wrong?"

She backed away, so angry with him in that moment that she thought her hands might act of their own volition, wrap themselves around his throat, and *squeeze*. "Tate"—she managed a civil tone—"you're telling me that all of this anger, this yelling and baton throwing is because of—"

A sharp knock on the door jarred the already fragmented moment.

"Come in," Tate finally said, still staring at her.

Rebekah returned to the piano bench, sat, and picked up the music, but saw only a haze of red as the door opened.

"Excuse me, Maestro Whitcomb. I'm here to get the music, as you instructed during the rehears—"

Recognizing the voice, Rebekah wished she could disappear. But she lifted her head. Judging from the disapproval on Darrow Fulton's face, his feelings about her had changed about as much as hers had about him.

Tate motioned. "The music is on the piano, Mr. Fulton. Have it ready by Friday. And please, for Chopin's sake, learn the meaning of *adagio*."

Darrow crossed to where Rebekah was seated, his eyes never leaving hers. She resisted the urge to look away first, knowing it wouldn't do for him to sense her unease. If he did, he would go for the jugular, like he always had.

Tate motioned, as though having had an afterthought. "Allow me to make introductions. Mr. Fulton, this is my assistant, Miss—"

"Rebekah Carrington," Darrow finished for him, smiling an enemy's smile. "Yes, I already have the pleasure of knowing Miss Carrington. She and I . . . grew up together."

Tate stilled. "Well . . ." His tone revealed surprise. "That's an interesting bit of news of which I wasn't aware."

"Yes, it's true, Maestro Whitcomb." Rebekah hurried to fill the silence. "Although . . . those childhood years feel quite distant these days. Do they not, Mr. Fulton?"

Darrow's smile only widened, the effect like venom, and Rebekah readied herself for the bite.

"Have you played for the maestro yet, Miss Carrington? After all, as I recall, it always was your *dream* to become part of an orchestra, wasn't it?"

Pulse rapid, breath trapped at the base of her throat, Rebekah tried to think of a response. Darrow was referring to her playing the violin, she knew. And yet, if she answered *No* to his question, that would be a lie, and Tate would know it. Because she'd played the oboe for him.

But if she answered *Yes,* then Darrow might question her further, thereby revealing she played the violin—and then what she'd vowed to keep hidden would be revealed. Either that, or her *Yes* might in some way divulge that she actually *had* auditioned for Tate, which could put Tate in a most awkward position with the symphony board.

She looked past Darrow to Tate's appraising gaze and thought again of how important this job was to her. To her future. How important *Tate* was to her. And of how quickly all of that was about to fall—

"Miss Carrington is my assistant, Mr. Fulton." Tate joined them. "So *of course* she's played for me. Do you think I would hire someone who wasn't familiar with music?"

In an instant, Darrow's smugness fell away. "Well . . . no, Maestro, of course not. I . . . I wasn't implying that. I only wanted to see if she'd—"

"Here's your music." Tate picked it up and handed it to him. "Will there be anything else?"

It was then that Rebekah noticed the slight tremor in Darrow's hand as he took the music. She thought of what Tate had just said, and though it hadn't registered at the time, it did now. And putting two and two together . . .

"No, Maestro Whitcomb." Darrow ducked his head. "Thank you for the music, sir."

Rebekah sensed Darrow's parting glance. But pencil in hand, she feigned immersion in the sheet music, and only once the door had closed did she breathe and look up again.

Tate was watching her. "Childhood sweethearts, I presume?"

She stared. *"What?"*

"You. And Darrow Fulton. His discomfort was obvious. So therefore, I'm assuming there was some sort of . . . romantic connection between you. Albeit, as youths."

She scoffed, then shook her head. "You really are something. Do you know that?"

"So you're saying that you and Mr. Fulton—"

She stood. "Darrow Fulton would no more look at me in a romantic sense than I would him. The man was the bane of my childhood existence. His goal was to torment me. And he was good at it! So what I am telling you, *Maestro* Whitcomb, is that Darrow Fulton and I have never been—"

Tate took her in his arms and kissed her, his lips gentle at first. Then slowly, deliberately, as he wove his hands into her hair, his kiss grew more insistent, his breath quickening as did hers. Rebekah had thought the moment they'd shared behind the ticket office had robbed her of composure, but this—

She felt herself melting into him, keenly aware of where she ended and he began, but her desire for him begged her to lessen that distance. She wrapped her arms around his neck just to make certain she stayed upright.

"Rebekah," he whispered against her mouth.

He tasted of mint and something else sweet.

"What," she said softly.

"Are we still arguing?"

"Yes . . ." She grinned. "And I'm winning."

He laughed. "If this is how we argue . . ." He kissed her again. "Then I'll let you win every time."

She broke the kiss and drew back slightly. "You'll *let me* win?"

The gleam in his eyes told her his comment had been intentional.

She laughed softly and searched his gaze. "I'm glad you're back. I missed you."

"I missed you too. But why are you here so early?"

"The Cheathams extended their stay in Murfreesboro, so I came in to get a jump on things. I managed to get a lot accomplished yesterday afternoon, but"—she turned and reached for her notes—"imagine my surprise when I came in and found this."

She held up the pages of notes that he'd X'd out.

He stepped back. "Rebekah, I was frustrated when I came in and saw that first thing this morning."

"If you don't agree with a change or suggestion I make, all you have to do is say it. You don't have to—"

"I know. I'm sorry." He reached for the notes. "Let me look at what you wrote again."

He did, rubbing his right temple as he read through her comments, and she wondered if it was wise for her to return to their previous conversation.

"As for the orchestra earlier, Tate." She chose her words carefully. "I know you strive for perfection . . . and I don't fault you for that," she added quickly. "It comes with the territory, as they say. But I do think that, at times, you could listen more carefully. Because there *were* crescendos and decrescendos. I heard them."

His expression hardened, almost as if a door had been slammed shut between them.

"Now," she continued, "perhaps the escalation in volume is not to your standards, which are high. As they should be." She softened her tone, thereby trying to soften the words. "But I do believe the orchestra is attempting to follow your lead. That's all I'm trying to—"

The door suddenly opened.

"I'm sorry I'm late, Maestro. But to celebrate your return from guest conducting this weekend, I made breakfast for us again. Including your favorite muffins and—" Miss Caroline Endicott looked up and stopped stone-cold, her expression swiftly turning likewise.

26

O h . . ." Miss Endicott looked at Rebekah and affected a laugh that came out flat and unconvincing. "How wonderful to see you again, Miss Carrington. I didn't realize the maestro and I would have company this morning." The sparkle in the woman's eyes narrowed to a glint. "What brings you in so early?"

Rebekah forced a smile. "Good morning, Miss Endicott." Knowing she should say more, the comments "made breakfast for us *again*" and "favorite muffins" struck a shrill note inside her, and it took effort to coerce some kindness into her expression while also trying to make it appear genuine.

After all, she'd kissed Tate *twice*—she could still feel his lips on hers, for heaven's sake—and she didn't know the man's favorite muffin! Much less had she made breakfast for him. Working to form a response, she opened her mouth, but Tate beat her to it.

"Good morning, Miss Endicott! Miss Carrington's usual morning tutorial was canceled. So she very graciously came in early. Which is good, because there's plenty of work to do."

"Well!" Miss Endicott's grip tightened on the baskets. "How marvelous for us all."

"It's very kind of you to bring breakfast . . . again." Tate's voice gained a gentility it lacked before. "But as I've told you, that's not necessary."

"I know it's not." The young woman turned her full attention—and charms—toward Tate. "But I like taking care of you, Maestro. And I know you don't eat as well as you should. So why don't I set this up on your desk, like we did last time." She threw Rebekah a look. "I'm certain Miss Carrington won't mind. She has plenty of work to do, as you said."

"Miss Endicott . . ." Tate stepped forward. "I don't believe that's—"

"Of course, I don't mind." Rebekah didn't know

whether or not her smile looked genuine, but the jealousy twisting her insides certainly felt real enough. And she didn't like it. The jealousy. Or the fact that Tate spent two mornings a week with this woman. She'd known Miss Endicott was a flirt. But she hadn't known to what extent those flirtations reached. Or perhaps she simply hadn't thought it through. Either way, she hadn't cared that much.

Until now. But *care* she did. Yet she tried hard not to show it.

Tate caught her gaze, and his eyes communicated something she couldn't quite comprehend. So she simply smiled, then plunked back down at the piano and looked at the page where she'd left off. She saw, for a second time, the huge Xs he'd slashed through her suggested changes, and she wished she could slash through something of his at the moment. Instead, she busied herself with transcribing, doing her best not to listen to the conversation going on six feet behind her.

"You just sit right down, Maestro. There you are! And I'll do everything for you." A twitter of laughter resembling that of a drunk magpie interjected the woman's sickening sweetness. "Here's your napkin. Let's tuck that in. And I brought the bacon you liked so much last time. Fried all nice and crispy."

"This is very nice, Miss Endicott. But I *really* have a lot of work to do, so perhaps—"

"And I'll help you get every bit of that work

done, Maestro. Once you've had a good breakfast."

Rebekah was going to be sick. Right there. On the piano. And it would serve Tate right. Letting the woman fawn over him like that. *Ridiculous!*

"And here's your muffin. Buttermilk spice. Buttered just like you like it."

Buttermilk spice was his favorite? Rebekah vowed never to eat another one again.

"Once you're finished with breakfast, Maestro, if you'd like for me to rub your shoulders like last time then—"

She'd rubbed his shoulders?

"Miss Endicott, that will *not* be necessary, I assure you. As I've told you before."

A simpering sigh. "Whatever you say, Maestro. As long as you're still coming to dinner this week. Mother and Father are looking forward to spending time with you again. Mother's asked our cook to make the braised lamb you liked so much last time. And I'll make sure to give you a personal tour of our winter garden as well."

Having heard all she could stomach, Rebekah rose. "If you'll both excuse me, I need to play these measures aloud. So I believe I'll use the piano down the hall."

"Rebek—" Tate started. "*Miss Carrington.* There's no need to . . ."

But Rebekah was already out the door. She hurried down the hall, despite not hearing any footsteps pursuing her. She spotted Mrs. Bixby at the desk at the end of the hallway.

"Mrs. Bixby, would it bother you if I were to use the piano in the back room?"

"It wouldn't bother me a bit, dear. But I'm afraid it hasn't been tuned in ages. However, the grand on the stage is available." The woman leaned forward, a conspiratorial gleam in her eyes. "Why not play that one? No one will mind. At least, no one who's here right now." She winked. "Mrs. Murphey is gone for the morning."

Rebekah smiled. "Remind me to hug you later."

Mrs. Bixby frowned. "Why wait for later?"

Rebekah laughed, skirted about the desk, and hugged the woman tightly. But it was the way Mrs. Bixby rubbed and patted her back—much like a mother would her daughter—that coaxed her emotions to the surface.

"Thank you, Mrs. Bixby," she whispered, finally drawing back.

"Oh, my dear . . ." Mrs. Bixby looked into her eyes. "Is everything all right?"

Rebekah nodded. "It will be. Once I start playing that grand."

Mrs. Bixby nodded and squeezed her hand.

Rebekah let herself onto the stage via the side door. All the wall sconces had been extinguished, but the high-arching windows at the back of the aging hall let in ample light for her purposes.

She sat on the bench, arranged the music on the stand before her, and placed her hands on the keys, her thoughts firing at rapid speed. What kind of man was Tate Whitcomb, truly? The man she knew here in Nashville? Or the man she'd seen in Chicory Hollow? Or were they both Tate Whitcomb, and he merely adapted to his surroundings? Or to the various *women* surrounding him?

But she knew better than that. . . . Didn't she?

Wanting to silence the questions, she began playing, but something entirely different from the music on the page flowed from her fingertips. A piece she'd committed to memory years ago, shortly after moving to Vienna. And as she played, she let the beloved music soothe the hurt—and the jealousy, which she detested in herself.

Herr Heilig had happened upon her playing this piece late one evening on the family's piano in the central parlor. He'd given her permission to play the beautiful instrument as often as she wished. So she had. He'd paused briefly inside the doorway. "Do you know, Fräulein Carrington, that Chopin wrote this when he was no more than twenty? Splendid talent that man possessed. And gone too soon from this world. You honor him in your playing. He would be pleased."

"You knew him, Herr Heilig?"

"*Ja*, I did. It was many years ago that we met."

As Rebekah played, she again thought of that night and of Chopin, and of the insights Herr Heilig had shared into the brief life of the gifted composer.

Finishing the short piece, she played it again. But this time, she played as though Chopin himself were seated beside her, listening. And she tried to see and feel the music through his eyes.

His opening measures contained graceful upward leaps, which became increasingly wide. But years of midnight playing made them effortless for her. The melody, occurring thrice more during the piece, varied with each repetition by more elaborate, decorative tones and trills. Her favorite parts.

Yet Chopin's unassuming genius lent the piece an almost waltz-like accompaniment that gave it a dreamlike quality.

Masterful . . .

Nearing the end of the opus, Rebekah played it as Chopin had written, his passion pouring onto the page, the final melody beginning softly, then ascending to a higher register. She played the octaves the same, and the music swirled and lifted around her, filling the empty opera hall. But she played as though every seat were full. Because she wasn't playing for herself.

"I want you to give your best to God every single time you play." That's what she'd said to Pauline. And she'd meant it.

As the notes softened once again and the excitement in the music ebbed, Rebekah concluded the opus as calmly and serenely as it had begun. She sat in the silence until the final, fading note slipped into the past, then she played the opus again and again, finding fresh peace and wonderment not only in the familiar notes, but at the power within a composer's pen.

"Nocturne in E-flat Major, opus 9, number 2," a voice said softly behind her. *Close* behind her.

She didn't turn when Tate eased in next to her on the bench. He said nothing, simply watched her play.

After a moment, she chanced a look over and found his eyes closed. How had she allowed herself to begin loving this man? When had it started? And . . . *how* did she stop? If all went as planned—though it didn't look fully promising at the moment—she was going to New York. And he was . . .

She wasn't quite sure what his plans were. To finish his symphony and then to build an exemplary orchestra—sans females—here in Nashville. Or it was more likely that one of the nation's prominent symphony orchestras would lure him away from Nashville in no time. Whatever his plans were, though, she doubted very much that they included her.

In fact, she realized now that, other than his kissing her—which might not have meant as much to him as it had to her—he'd never so much as even hinted at having any lasting feelings for her. Much less any sort of commitment. Oh, she'd been such a fool, even knowing musicians as she did!

"Did you know that Chopin wrote this by the age of twenty?" he said softly.

She looked beside her. "I did. Did you know he had a fear of being buried alive?"

His blank expression was answer enough.

"Prior to his death," she continued, playing as she did, "he requested that his body be opened and his heart returned to Warsaw, where it now rests at the Church of the Holy Cross."

"Are you serious?"

"Completely."

"How do you know this?"

"Herr—"

"Heilig," he quickly filled in. "Of course. I'm certain Herr Heilig's social circle encompassed many of Europe's great contemporary composers." He sighed. "What a life you must have lived in Vienna."

Rebekah said nothing. She simply began the opus over again for the . . . She'd lost track of how many times she'd played it thus far.

"Rebekah . . ." He leaned closer. "You know Caroline Endicott is a notorious flirt."

"I gathered as much the first time I met her."

"She also has a very . . . enthusiastic imagination. And she's my assistant only because it's—"

"Political." Rebekah hid her heart behind a look of nonchalance. "Her father is on the philharmonic board and you must keep the board happy. I know how these things work, Tate. You don't have to explain them to me."

"But I want to. And from the tone of your voice right now—and before—I believe I need to."

She hated being so easily read. "Tate, truly, you don't owe me—"

He took hold of her right hand and a dissonant chord sounded even as the way he touched her, the way he wove his fingers through hers, felt more right than anything she could remember.

"Rebekah, I'm sorry for what happened. Yes, it's political and I need to keep the board happy, and Harold Endicott is a major donor to the symphony. But in no manner are you any less important to me in all of this. Quite the contrary, in fact."

He brought her hand to his mouth and kissed it, then held it against his chest. She searched his face. Could it be that he felt for her what she felt for—

"I want you to know that"—he briefly looked away—"I'll be writing the conductor at the New York Philharmonic. I know him. Crawford Leplin. Not an easy man to get along with, by any means. But your talent will be more than enough to impress him. He's a seasoned conductor. And a good one. And since Leplin's already admitted one woman into his orchestra, I'm certain your place is all but assured."

Rebekah stared, fighting back a knot of tears. So he cared for her. But . . . not enough. Or at least, not in *that* way. She was reminded again of what Mrs. Cheatham had said about seeking God's desires for her life . . . no matter what she had to surrender. *"And you* will *have to surrender. We all do. It's part of the soul's refinement."*

So was this *her* surrender? She had to give up Tate in order to get New York? But how could that be, when he'd never been hers to begin with?

She nodded, barely able to find her voice. "Thank you, Tate. I'd be most grateful."

"And, of course, I should add . . . I *do* want you to finish here. Before you go." He gave a weak smile.

She returned it. "Yes, of course. That's understood."

He looked down at their hands, then relinquished hers.

And just like that, he opened the door to her dream while closing the one to his heart.

Rebekah knocked on the kitchen door but didn't see Delphia inside. Yet there was no sign of the carriage either, which meant Barton was most assuredly gone. The door wasn't locked, so she let herself in.

"Delphia?" she called out softly, feeling like a stranger in her own home. Or what had been her home. The stove still radiated warmth as she hurried by, the lingering scent of maple syrup hovering in the kitchen.

She checked the remainder of the downstairs. No one. Then she crept silently upstairs to the bedrooms. Empty. All of them. Better than she'd hoped. Although she did want to see her mother again, she'd come here today with a different purpose in mind.

She wanted to know what Barton Ledbetter had been doing in Chicory Hollow.

She hurried back downstairs and to her father's—or Barton's—office and tried the knob. Locked. She tried it again, more aggressively, but without success. Her father had always kept the key in the drawer in the foyer table. She very much doubted Barton kept it there. Still, she checked.

Nothing. However . . .

She hurried back to the kitchen, hoping that what she remembered being in one of the cupboard drawers all those years ago might still be there.

The drawer stuck when she pulled it out, as it always had. She rummaged, feeling toward the back, but no keys. Delphia had had a set at one time, she was certain. The ring had held a key to her father's office, to the larder and the sugar chest, and then the second house key. She knew because she used to sneak the key to the sugar chest on occasion. A moistened finger dipped in the corner where no one would see was a sweet treat on any day.

Rebekah shoved the drawer closed—and heard a telling jingle.

She tugged the drawer out again, all the way this time, and pulled out a rumple of dishcloths wedged in the back. She smiled. *Bless you, Delphia.*

Keys in hand, she hurried back to the office . . . but the clomp of horses' hooves sounded out front. Heart in her throat, she crossed to the foyer and peered out the window by the door. A carriage stopped in front of the house. To her relief, it wasn't Barton's. But . . .

A man got out. And started up the front walkway.

Rebekah quickly stepped away from the window, knowing he could see her if he was looking. Same as he would see her if she crossed to the hallway now. She had no intention of receiving the man. This wasn't her house, after all. And what if he was an associate of Barton's? Any friend of his was someone she wanted nothing to do with. Thoughts racing, she pressed back against the door, keys in her grip.

He knocked and it suddenly occurred to her, she didn't even know if the front door was locked. What if he tried to—

He knocked again, more forcefully this time, and she clenched her jaw, wondering now why she'd ever thought sneaking into the house was a good idea. But when Tate left early that afternoon for another of his portrait sittings, she'd seen her chance. And frankly, after what he'd told her yesterday, about providing a letter of recommendation to the conductor in New York—making his lack of meaningful feelings for her more than clear—she welcomed a few hours away from the office. Besides, she *had* to know what Barton was—

A shadow darkened the window beside her, and she realized the man was peering in. Stone-still, she didn't blink, she didn't move, she didn't breathe . . . as an eternity crept by.

Finally, retreating footsteps. And she exhaled in a rush.

She waited for the creak of carriage wheels before peering around the edge of the window. Nothing distinctive about the carriage that she could see. Or the man, for that matter. He'd been about Barton's age, she guessed. Maybe a few years younger. But he was gone now. Which is exactly what she needed to be. Soon.

But first . . .

She hurried to the office, shaking off the jitters. The second key she tried gained her entrance, and she grimaced at the odor that greeted her when she opened the door—days-old cigar smoke and something sour. Stale sweat, perhaps, or bourbon. She looked around, the curtains open on the windows, the room awash in light. Yet the space was so much darker than she remembered.

A decade had passed since she'd stepped inside this office. Back then, before Papa died, this had been a haven for her. The room had smelled of books, freshly sharpened pencils, her father's sweet pipe tobacco . . . and love. But the years had erased every trace of that. Only the memories remained.

Setting aside those memories, Rebekah set to work.

What she was looking for, she didn't know. Anything that would tell her what Barton was up to. What he'd been doing in Chicory Hollow. She started by looking through the papers on his desk, careful to return everything to its place. A bill of sale from a mercantile in Knoxville. Then another from Memphis. Yet the receipts didn't list what was purchased, only the total amounts spent.

She raised an eyebrow. Nearly two hundred dollars for each. What was he buying? If she were to ask him, he would most assuredly give her the same song and dance about his career being in "acquisitions and trade."

She found several bills of sale from a lumber company in Nashville, along with freight receipts from a railroad. But the first hint of any tangible evidence came when she uncovered a stack of scrawled IOUs written on scraps of paper, an amount of money listed on each, followed by a signature that was barely legible. She sighed. Well, those IOUs likely explained Barton's evenings.

But she could find nothing that included any mention of Chicory Hollow.

She moved next to the desk drawers. Her father had kept them so neat. Everything in its place. How Barton ever found anything in this mess was beyond her.

Finally, the bottom right drawer revealed loose bank receipts. Deposits and withdrawals for an account belonging to *Barton P. Ledbetter,* the name handwritten at the top by various bank clerks. Rebekah paused, seeing the amount of one of the deposits. Nearly seven hundred dollars. She looked at the date. Scarcely two months ago. And another deposit receipt dated two weeks earlier for nearly that same amount. Then multiple withdrawal slips.

But she didn't see a pattern of any sort. Where had all this money come from? And what was Barton doing with it?

She flipped through more receipts, then reached for another batch when her attention fell to the receipt staring up at her atop the pile in the drawer. For an account belonging to *Mrs. Ellen Carrington.* A withdrawal of . . . over five thousand dollars! Rebekah read the date of the transaction and felt a punch to her gut. December 2, 1870.

The day after her grandmother died. *Oh, Nana . . .*

Rebekah could scarcely breathe. So that's what had happened to Grandmother's money. Just as she'd thought, Barton had taken every last—

"Sarah, as I told you on the way home, you need to *rest!*"

Rebekah froze at the sound of Barton's voice coming from the hallway. How had she not heard them return? She had to hide, but—

The office door. She'd left it open!

Keys in hand, she raced to close it, and engaged the lock as noiselessly as she could. She returned to the desk and shoved the receipts back into the drawer, wincing at the creak as she pushed it closed. She scanned the room. The only place to hide was behind the door. And if he came in and closed it, then she would be—

"But, Barton, dearest . . . I'm feeling some better now."

Her mother's voice, muffled through the door, held an earnestness that tugged at Rebekah's emotions.

"Sarah, you said in the carriage that you were dizzy."

"Well, yes . . . I was. Earlier. But now—"

"Have you taken your powder yet today? The one your doctor prescribed for your nerves?"

"Not yet. But I will . . . if you think I should."

Rebekah squeezed her eyes tight, loathing the devotion and trust in her mother's voice.

"I do, Sarah. It will calm your nerves so you'll feel stronger for this evening."

The clink of a glass. Where were they? In the parlor, perhaps?

"But what's happening this evening?"

"Sarah." An exasperated sigh. "How many times must I tell you? We're going to enjoy an evening out together. We'll dine at a fine restaurant I've been wanting to share with you."

"Oh, Barton! That will be *wonderful.*"

Rebekah sensed her mother's sincerity, and it pained her that her mother couldn't see what kind of man she'd married. Rebekah held her ear to the door, straining to hear more, when she heard footfalls from the other side. She pressed back against the wall, holding her breath. But when a key slipped into the lock, her lungs emptied completely.

The door opened and every nerve in her body went taut.

"Barton?" her mother called. "I can't find my powders."

Barton paused just inside the office, so close Rebekah could smell the cherry laurel on him. He cursed beneath his breath. "Coming, dearest . . ." And with a sigh, he closed the door.

Rebekah bolted for the window, flipped the latch and shoved. It didn't budge. *Oh please . . .*

She tried again, crouching lower and pushing with all her might. The window inched open, complaining loudly as it did. But she paid it no mind. She pushed until her arms and shoulders burned, then climbed through the narrow space. She turned and, with her last ounce of strength, pulled it closed again, then crouched behind the shrubbery and checked the street, in hopes no one had seen her.

Heart hammering, she waited long enough to catch her breath and then sneaked back around the house to the kitchen, mindful of the windows.

She saw Delphia by the stove and quietly opened the door. Delphia turned at the sound, but Rebekah shook her head and pressed a finger to her lips. She placed the keys on the worktable and whispered, "His office. Lock the window, please."

Delphia looked at the keys, then at her, and

concern darkened her eyes. "You best be careful, child," she whispered as Rebekah closed the door.

Later that night, Rebekah lay in bed reliving every moment of being in that house that afternoon, and one thought rose above the rest. To her surprise, it wasn't about her grandmother's inheritance—the money was probably long spent anyway—or even what Barton had been doing in Chicory Hollow. It was about her mother.

She had to find a way to get her mother away from Barton Ledbetter. The man had a hold on her somehow. Rebekah didn't know what it was, or how he did it, but she was determined to find out. And to break the spell.

Tate watched her as she sat at the piano playing and transcribing, grateful his desk chair afforded him an unobstructed view. She reached to rub her neck, and tendrils of her hair slipped loose from the pins, as most always happened by this time of the afternoon. She was easily one of the most talented musicians he'd ever known, and without question the most talented female.

But something had changed between them over the past couple of weeks, ever since that day he'd joined her on stage as she'd played the grand. She'd looked so *right* sitting there on the bench, an entire opera house focused on her. And that's when he'd known. What he was doing—allowing himself to grow closer to her, and her to him—wasn't wise.

Neither was it fair to her, considering all the unknowns in his future.

Since then, they'd managed to recapture some of the ease with which they worked together. But in those moments when their hands happened to touch, or their thighs brushed as they sat together on the bench, he found it next to impossible not to show her how much he truly cared for her.

She'd spoken twice in recent days about going to New York City, and he half wished he could retract his offer to pen her a letter of recommendation. Yet he knew he could never intentionally stand in the way of her achieving her dream.

Not when she was the reason he was about to achieve his.

They'd finished the third movement of the symphony, and he knew the accomplishment was largely due to her. She helped him in ways she didn't even realize. Through hours and hours of transcription, and by playing back what he'd written, letting him hear how the music flowed—or didn't. And her suggestions were always on the mark. Her years of study in Vienna had served her well.

But even more than benefitting from her talent, he found her mere presence calming, reassuring. Having her in his life made him feel less alone as he faced a future that once held such undisputed promise, a future he'd never questioned being able to attain. He was Maestro Nathaniel Tate Whitcomb, after all. One of the most prominent conductors in the United States.

A rueful smile tipped his mouth. One of the most prominent conductors in the United States—who might well be going deaf.

He hadn't said anything to her about it yet. But recalling what she'd said to him a while back, he wondered if she might suspect. *"I do think that, at times, you could listen more carefully."* But she wasn't one to hold back. If she suspected, she would ask him.

She sat straighter on the bench, stretching her back, and her womanly curves drew his eye with little coaxing. He loved seeing the pout in her lower lip as she looked at the music on the stand, then at the stack yet remaining to be transcribed. Then, as always, she refocused her attention and returned to the task.

Likewise, he stared at the empty page of sheet music on his desk. He'd had a headache earlier that morning, less aching in his temples this time and more ringing in his ears. And he still felt as though he were hearing through a tunnel.

No word yet from Dr. Hamilton. But it had only been a little over two weeks. Tate told himself that the longer it took to hear back from the man, the better. But deep inside, another voice whispered something far different.

Suddenly needing to move, to get out of this office for a while, he had an idea and rose from his desk. His chair creaked loudly as he did, but Rebekah didn't look back.

Sometimes, like now, she became so engulfed in the music that she seemed to forget he was even here. He walked up behind her and gently touched her arm. She nearly came off the bench.

"Tate!" She peered up at him. "You scared me to death!"

"I'm sorry." He laughed, finding her reaction comical.

"You don't sound sorry." She gave him a dark look, but her smile shone through and told him he was forgiven.

"Could I tempt you to quit for the day? Or at least, for a while?"

"But it's only"—she checked the clock on the shelf—"half past three."

"I know, but it's a beautiful day. I need to get out . . . and I want you to come with me. There's something I'd like to show you."

She narrowed her eyes. "Does it involve rubbing your shoulders or making buttermilk spice muffins?"

He laughed. "Are you ever going to let me live that down?"

"No." She shook her head. "I'm not."

"All right then. Good to know where I stand."

She stretched her shoulders. "Does this outing involve stopping by a bakery for a doughnut?"

He frowned. "A doughnut?"

"I was speaking with Mrs. Cheatham's niece,

Eleanor, yesterday, and she told me about a bakery here in town that makes the best doughnuts she's ever had. And I *love* doughnuts."

A while later, on a mission, they located the recommended bakery, and Tate ordered four doughnuts, along with two coffees. Amidst the aroma of freshly baked bread and the thrum of conversation, they ate them at a table by the window.

The laughter of a little girl drew his attention, and he looked at what appeared to be a mother and daughter seated near them. The child's gaze was centered on a doughnut on a small plate before her, and her high-pitched giggle was almost contagious. Was it really possible that a day might come when he couldn't hear that simplest of sounds?

The jingle of a bell sounded on the door as people came and went, and the rumble of carriages and wagons slipped inside from the street each time they did. Dr. Hamilton was right. Only when one of the senses was impinged upon did a person realize how precious a gift that sense truly was.

He only hoped he wouldn't have to learn that lesson firsthand.

"Penny for your thoughts?"

Rebekah's voice broke through his reverie from across the table, and the light in her eyes, in her smile, somehow eased the heaviness in his heart.

But it was her voice—the lilt of it, its warmth—that he found himself wanting to memorize and never forget.

"I was thinking of how beautiful you are, Rebekah Carrington, and of how grateful I am that you came out with me today" was what he wanted to say . . . but didn't. "I'm thinking we need to be on our way."

Once outside, he started to offer his arm. Then it occurred to him that if they were seen this way together, people might begin to talk. He didn't care about it for himself, but he did for her.

"Where are we going?" she asked, walking beside him.

"You'll see soon enough."

Conversation came easily, and when they'd nearly reached their destination, she turned to him. "Oh! I know where you're taking me! I've seen the outside but not inside. It looks like something straight from Vienna!"

He smiled. "It seems only right that with all the work you do for me, and for the symphony, you deserved to see the interior before the general public does."

They turned the corner and the new opera house came into view. While the exterior of the structure was impressive with its stone archways and Palladian windows, it was the interior of the building that he considered a true work of art.

They entered via a side door, the front doors still locked to discourage curious passersby. Rebekah's mouth slipped open as they wound their way to the front of the opera house.

Tate spotted Marcus Geoffrey, the Austrian architect, across the marble-tiled foyer, and waved him down.

Geoffrey's handshake was firm. "Good to see you again, Maestro."

"Mr. Geoffrey." Tate gestured beside him, knowing Rebekah would enjoy meeting this man and hearing the hint of Austria in his voice. "I've brought my assistant with me today. May I present Miss Rebekah Carrington."

Rebekah curtsied. "Mr. Geoffrey. It's an honor."

"The honor is mine, Miss Carrington. But I feel as though I already know you. Mrs. Cheatham, my wife's aunt, speaks very highly of you, ma'am. And that doesn't happen with everyone, I assure you."

Rebekah laughed. "Thank you. That means a great deal. Please pass along to Eleanor that we found the doughnut shop she recommended. And her counsel was excellent."

Geoffrey smiled. "Ah . . . Mr. Fitch's. I buy the man's pastries by the dozens. I don't think this building would be standing now without them. The crew has come to expect his doughnuts almost every morning."

"Would you mind, Mr. Geoffrey, if I give Miss Carrington the nickel tour?"

"Not at all. But if you want the quarter tour, I have a few moments and would be happy to show you around myself. We completed the stage area yesterday, and I'm eager for you to see it, Maestro."

Tate gestured. "Lead the way!"

Tate savored Rebekah's excitement as Marcus Geoffrey showed them first the foyer with the grand staircase, then the side halls, and finally the stage area and auditorium. It made him feel as though he were seeing it all again for the first time.

A break came in the conversation, and Tate took advantage. "Mr. Geoffrey assumed management of this project after the original architect was . . . relieved of his duties. And what was once a 'functional but rather sterile building project,' in Mrs. Cheatham's words, now has the appearance of something plucked from the streets of Vienna."

"Oh yes . . ." Rebekah nodded, her head tipped back. "You've replicated the Vienna Baroque style in such an exquisite manner. And the frescos on the ceiling. Beyond beautiful!"

"Mr. Geoffrey," Tate interjected, "Miss Carrington actually lived in Vienna for several years."

Marcus Geoffrey stopped in his tracks. "You *lived* in my homeland?"

"I did." Rebekah tipped her head back as she took in the vastness of the auditorium. "I lived not far from the Schönbrunn Palace, the summer residence of the Habsburg monarchy."

"The . . . Schönbrunn Palace," Geoffrey repeated, looking a bit flustered.

If Tate didn't know better, he would think Rebekah had alarmed the man.

"But, of course," she continued, her voice turning a touch dramatic. "I was never invited to said palace. So, alas . . . I have yet to meet any of the illustrious Habsburgs."

Marcus Geoffrey laughed. "Well, I hear it's not nearly as exciting as one might imagine."

They laughed along with him, and then Geoffrey continued the tour. Eventually, he led them onto the stage, where they stood facing the seats.

"As some say," Geoffrey continued, "this is the best seat in the house."

"Oh," Rebekah whispered. "It's *so* beautiful. My deepest gratitude, Mr. Geoffrey, for building such a magnificent venue in which to showcase music in this city. And my congratulations to you and your workers. You truly have brought the timeless beauty of Austria, of *Europe,* to Nashville."

Tate estimated that roughly half of the opera house's almost four hundred and fifty gas lamps—which Geoffrey had told him earlier— illuminated the horseshoe-shaped auditorium, and their golden glow cast a softness over everything within reach. Tate's gaze drifted over the sea of empty burgundy seats to the luxury promenade seating, and up to the balconies, tiered four high, all draped in shades of burgundy and gold.

One thousand six hundred and thirty-six seats in all, Geoffrey had told him.

Tate walked to the area on the stage where he imagined he would stand when conducting, and he could see, in his mind's eye, each section of the orchestra—the instrument *he* played. First and second violins seated on his left. Oboes, clarinets, bassoons, and flutes directly before him. Violas to his right, flanked by the cellos. And behind the cellos, from right, curving back to left, the basses, tubas, trombones, trumpets, the hauntingly beautiful French horns, the majestic timpani, percussion, harp, and finally, the piano, nestled behind the first violins. He could see all of the faces behind the instruments as well.

But mostly, he could hear each section, the rise and fall of each sound created as they joined together and became the music comprising the first movement of his symphony, then the second, and third.

"The seating in the auditorium is slightly inclined, Miss Carrington," Geoffrey explained behind him, "to ensure optimal visibility from all seats. In similar fashion, the stage walls slope slightly inward to help focus the sound toward the main house. Be careful what you say up here, because the acoustics are quite good. The auditorium's horseshoe design allows even a whisper-low tone of voice from the stage to be heard in any part of the hall."

"Truly amazing." Rebekah's tone mirrored her admiration. "I especially love the balconies."

"We intentionally designed them to be shallow,"

Geoffrey continued, "to avoid trapping or muffling the sound. The coffered ceiling and statue-filled niches—the statues chosen and purchased by our lovely Mrs. Cheatham, of course—also help provide excellent acoustics." Geoffrey gave a seemingly satisfied, if not reflective sigh. "I've only been working on this building for roughly two years now. But in a way, I've been working on it all my life."

The last comment brought Tate back around. That was a sentiment he could echo himself.

"The grand opening will be here before we know it, Maestro Whitcomb." Geoffrey nodded his way. "But no cause for worry. The opera house *will* be ready come May! A month earlier than planned."

Tate forced an excitement he didn't fully feel. "Yes, that's a night we're all looking forward to, Mr. Geoffrey."

Tate caught the discreet look Rebekah sent him, and knew he wasn't fooling her. But she only knew a part of what was bothering him. Yes, they still needed to finish the fourth movement—which weighed heavily enough on him—but the question that haunted him most at the moment . . .

Even if he *was* able to finish the symphony in time, would he be able to hear it? Much less, conduct it?

When he arrived home that evening, he flipped through the mail waiting for him on the sideboard, and the return address on one of the envelopes jabbed him like a stab to the heart. DR. RONALD HAMILTON.

Tate stared at the name, and his hand began to shake.

Mrs. Pender, his housekeeper, had dinner prepared, and he ate a little, not remembering it. Later, in the privacy of his bedroom, he sat on the edge of the bed, the still-sealed envelope in hand, trying to sort out the tumult of thoughts ricocheting inside him—the *what if*s, the *might have been*s—until finally, he rose, envelope in hand, took the oil lamp from the bedside table, and went downstairs to the study.

The hour was late, well past eleven, and he closed the door behind him, not wanting to awaken his housekeeper. But Mrs. Pender slept soundly, the older woman claiming she never heard his midnight sonatas.

So he played. First Mozart, then Chopin, Vivaldi, Handel, Haydn, then his beloved Beethoven, the ivories cool and smooth beneath his fingers, the music wrapping itself around him like the faithful love of an old friend—all the while lifting his unspoken petitions to his heavenly Father, who held every moment of his future in His loving hands.

He drank in the chords, both the dissonant and harmonious, knowing both were required to create music worthy of stirring the soul, music that would last beyond a lifetime.

Not knowing how much time had passed, only knowing that he'd played until he had nothing left within him, he reached for the envelope, slid his finger beneath the sealed flap, and opened the letter.

T hat's *not* what I wrote, Rebekah!"

Hearing Tate's frustration, something she heard often these days, Rebekah felt her own annoyance rising to match it. "Yes, it *is*. I'll play it again for you."

Reading his notations on the sheet music, she repeated the measures exactly as he'd written them. Albeit, pounding the eighth notes a little harder than necessary.

He said nothing for a moment, then blew out a breath. "Well, that's not what I intended to write." He shoved a blank score sheet toward her, the wick in the oil lamp beginning to smolder atop the piano. "The following is what I meant to write. Make note of it, please."

Biting her tongue, she listened, scribbling the notes frantically onto the staff while working to commit the rest to memory.

He finished. "There. Did you capture all that?"

She paused, pencil on the paper. "Does it look like I captured it all?" She glanced at the paper, then back at him. "Do you really think I can transcribe that quickly?"

At least he had the decency to give her a somewhat sheepish look.

Every afternoon for over the past two weeks, she'd finished her violin lesson with Pauline—who was improving at a rapid rate—only to rush to the opera house to find Tate already neck deep in composing. And in a very sour mood.

But regardless of the hours and hours they'd spent working in recent days, they'd accomplished very little on the fourth movement. And each day it seemed Tate grew more tense. And restless.

When they worked individually, she would glance over at times and find him staring into space, a look of near desperation on his face. At other times, when they worked together at the piano, as they were now, she could *feel* the tension pouring from him.

Twice, she'd asked him if anything was wrong between them, if she'd done something to upset him. But he simply scowled and said, "No, of course not," and went on.

She was grateful that—except for times like these—they had again reached an amiable place in their relationship. Her feelings for him had not changed. If anything, they'd grown stronger. But since he hadn't given her any reason to hope for more, she continued to look for reasons not to love him.

It didn't help that the more she got to know him, the more she realized she'd misjudged him at the start—in some areas. But in the areas of stubbornness and an unyielding proclivity toward perfectionism, she'd greatly underestimated his thresholds.

When Tate thought he was right, it was like moving a mountain to get him to change his mind. Fortunately—or *un*fortunately, depending on the momentary perspective—his instincts in composing were right most of the time, which kept her mountain moving to a minimum. And rarely was anything ever good enough for him. So she kept writing and playing and writing and playing until her head and shoulders ached and the joints in her fingers burned.

But when they finally composed something he loved . . . those moments were golden. And she carefully wrapped the memory of each one and tucked it deep inside her.

He squeezed his eyes tight and massaged the back of his head. "How late can you stay today?"

She studied him, worried. "Are you having another one of your headaches?"

"Yes. Now, how late can you stay?"

"You ask me that every day. And every day, I answer the same."

He gave her an annoyed look she knew by heart.

"I can stay until close to nine o'clock. Then I need to return to Belmont and prepare Pauline's lesson for tomorrow."

"Today's Friday. You don't give Pauline lessons on the weekends."

She blinked. "You're right. But I still need to be home by nine o'clock."

"Why?"

"Because I'm exhausted!"

He managed a smile, and she did too, which helped ease the moment.

So tired she could scarcely hold another thought, she angled her head from side to side in an effort to loosen the taut muscles in her neck.

He sought her gaze. "I have an idea."

She waited.

"Actually . . ." he hedged, "I have a plan."

"A plan is most certainly more definite than an idea."

He checked the time, then smiled. "Grab your cloak and reticule. I'll pack up the music and notes."

As they readied to leave, Mrs. Bixby knocked on the door, her smile exuberant.

"Maestro Whitcomb, a package arrived for you earlier but I didn't want to disturb you while you and Miss Carrington were working. It's something special I believe you'll want to see."

"It will have to wait, Mrs. Bixby. We're leaving for the day."

Mrs. Bixby blinked. "Of course, sir. I . . . I'm sorry for having interrupted you."

Rebekah shot him a look, and he stilled.

"I apologize, Mrs. Bixby. It's been a long day. *Please* . . . do share it with me."

The woman's eyes softened, her excitement

returning. "Since the delivery man told me who sent it, I took the liberty of opening it for you." She held up a beautifully framed certificate. "Isn't it handsome? It's a gift from the assembled orchestra in Charleston, the one you guest conducted in the fall. And see here"—she pointed—"the mayor of the city signed it himself and extended his personal gratitude. I'll have it hung for you next week with your other commendations." Mrs. Bixby turned to admire the wall covered with accolades of one sort or another.

Tate tugged on the sleeves of his suit coat. "I think we've hung enough of those already. Why don't we put that one—"

"In the hallway?" Mrs. Bixby volunteered.

"I was going to say in a drawer somewhere. But . . . the hallway would be fine." A boyish smirk tipped his mouth. "However, the drawer would be my personal preference."

"Oh, *Maestro* . . ." The woman playfully swatted his arm. "You're far too humble."

Rebekah watched the two of them, wondering how he did it. One minute he could push the limits of a person's patience to the brink and beyond. Then the next, he could be as kind and generous as any man she'd ever known. Well, except for one man, perhaps.

She'd missed Demetrius so much recently. Odd, how those moments would sneak up on her, catching her unaware.

She'd been to see her mother three times in

recent weeks—aided by Delphia, who quickly let her know when her mother was home and when Barton Ledbetter was not. But each visit had been worse than the one previous. Her mother seemed to grow more reclusive and spiteful toward her by the week. Rebekah couldn't figure out why, but she determined to continue the visits. And to get her away from Barton. Because she knew what kind of man Barton was, but also because after meeting Tate's family and experiencing their love and acceptance, she wanted that between her and her mother. And as dear Demetrius had once told her, *"As long as there's breath in a body, a person can change."*

As Tate escorted her from the office, she glanced back. "So no more additions to the Great Wall of Tate?"

He frowned. "The Great Wall of Tate?"

She shrugged. "I believe there's some room on the opposite wall by the grand piano. We could begin another collection over there, if you like."

"What I'd like is to finish this symphony before the new opera house opens."

His sarcastic tone warned her to leave the subject be.

A carriage was waiting on the street, part of his *plan,* she guessed, and he assisted her up the step. She arranged her cloak to cover her legs from the chill. March had arrived like a roaring lion, bringing colder temperatures and bouts of ice.

She only hoped the month would depart like the proverbial lamb, leaving spring in its wake.

She leaned her head back to rest, pleased when Tate claimed the space on the bench beside her. "Where are we going?"

"Patience, Miss Carrington. Patience."

Smiling, she gripped the seat as the carriage lurched forward, the last vestiges of daylight begrudgingly giving way to dusk. "Only one more movement in the symphony, and then you'll be done."

"Then *we'll* be done. But the last movement, as we know, is always the most difficult."

She again wondered why that was. The old adage "Save the best for last" came to mind, and she guessed that figured into it. No composer—or writer, for that matter—wanted to weave a story only to have it fall flat at the end.

They'd finished the third movement in two weeks. Two *arduous* weeks—working well into evenings and on Saturdays. Yet they'd worked equally as hard over the past two weeks and still had so little to show for it.

A deep sigh left him. "The new opera house opens exactly two months from tomorrow. Nine weeks. Sixty-four days."

"Not that you're counting."

A moment passed, and he leaned forward and rested his elbows on his knees. "I need to get back home again soon too," he said softly, almost so softly she couldn't hear over the squeak of the carriage wheels. "I've let an entire month go by this time."

She leaned forward. "I know. But your family understands you're busy. And that what you're doing is important, and takes time. That it's *urgent*. And as you alluded, time is flying by."

He nodded, staring out the window. "Which is all the more reason to get back there as soon as I can."

Moments later, the carriage slowed to a stop, and Rebekah peered out the window. She wasn't familiar with this part of town, nor did she recognize the street. Parkwood Lane.

"Since you've seen my home in Chicory Hollow," he said softly, then climbed from the carriage and assisted her down.

She'd never inquired about where he lived here in town. She'd never given it much thought, really. But looking up at the modest two-story brick home, she realized this wasn't what she would've expected, based on his position with the symphony and her first impression of the man.

Then again, having gotten to know him better in recent weeks and discovering how misleading first impressions could be, perhaps this did fit. The residence sat nestled between two larger, much more stately homes that all but threatened to dwarf this one, making it somewhat the wallflower of Parkwood Lane.

Yet the home certainly wasn't without its charms.

A massive oak tree that had weathered at least thrice the winters Rebekah had seen in her lifetime stood the proud sentinel in the small front yard. Its impressive limbs, leafless still, stretched upward and out, portending an impressive canopy come summer, and was a perfect companion to the white porch swing that swayed to and fro in the chilling breeze.

On the front door hung an evergreen wreath, a simple adornment, absent any decorative ribbons or berries. The exterior of the home lacked any sign of a woman's touch. And oddly, that discovery pleased her greatly.

Tate opened the front door. An older woman, her gray hair swept into a knot atop her head, shawl caught about her shoulders, greeted them in the narrow front hallway, oil lamp in hand.

"Miss Carrington"—Tate closed the front door behind them—"May I present Mrs. Pender, my housekeeper, cook, and a woman without whom I could not leave the house every morning. Or at least, leave it in somewhat presentable fashion."

Rebekah nodded. "A pleasure to meet you, Mrs. Pender."

"Pleasure be all mine, Miss Carrin'ton. I been hearin' so much about you of late."

Rebekah shot Tate a questioning look.

"Now, now . . ." His expression wasn't so much bothered as it was a shade embarrassed. "Let's not bore Miss Carrington with unnecessary details."

The woman's cornflower-blue eyes sparked with

humor. "Dinner be all ready for you, sir. So come on into the dinin' room when you see fit. Oh, and the mail's waitin' there on the sideboard for you."

As the woman made her way down the narrow corridor, Rebekah didn't have to wonder why Tate had chosen her as his housekeeper. She was a touch of home for him, and a welcome reminder of Chicory Hollow for Rebekah as well.

Tate casually flipped through the envelopes, until he came to the last one. He paused.

"Another commendation for the Great Wall of Tate?" Rebekah smiled.

He looked over at her, and an emotion she couldn't define flashed across his face. "It's from a Dr. Clarkston in Philadelphia."

"Someone you know?"

He tore open the envelope and scanned the letter, a smile the likes of which she hadn't seen in a long time coming to his face. "He's answering the letter I posted to him last fall. About my father."

Rebekah heard the hope in his voice. "What does he say?"

A laugh escaped him. His eyes grew misty. "He says there's a procedure he performs on patients with consumption. And he's had great success. It's not a cure, he says. It's a relatively simple treatment that drains pleural effusion from around the lungs, and he says it usually prolongs a patient's life. Sometimes for months, sometimes years."

"Oh, Tate, that's wonderful. Does he say if he's willing to come to Chicory Hollow?"

Scarcely had she gotten the words out when the light faded from his face. "He says he performs the procedure in his office in Philadelphia, and that he'll happily see my father there." Tate shook his head. "My father wouldn't live through a trip like that. He's scarcely been out of bed in weeks. The letter from my mother a few days ago said breathing has become even more difficult for him."

"Perhaps you could write to this . . . Dr. Clarkston again, and ask him to make the trip."

"I did that in the first letter. And this was his response."

Sharing his heartbreak, Rebekah touched his arm. "Tate, I'm so sorry."

He nodded and gestured for her to precede him down the hallway.

A dinner of roast beef with potatoes, both cooked fork-tender, along with field peas and buttered corn bread with honey inspired Rebekah's meager appetite, and she ate more than she thought she would.

But she could hardly say the same for Tate. He was quiet, and sullen.

Mrs. Pender served dessert, and though the cake—apple butter cake, the woman called it— was delicious, Rebekah ate enough to satisfy etiquette, then set her fork aside.

Mrs. Pender returned with the coffeepot and refilled their cups.

"Dinner was delicious, Mrs. Pender." Rebecca

sipped her coffee. "And the cake was divine."

The woman beamed. "Got the receipt from my grandmama when I's just a girl. 'Twas my fav'rite cake'a hers."

Tate tucked his napkin by his plate. "Yes, thank you, Mrs. Pender. Your roast beef was legendary, as always."

The older woman smiled her thanks, then eyed his place setting. Her expression conveyed concern, but the firming of her mouth said she'd keep those thoughts to herself. "If there be anythin' else you needin', sir, just call for me."

Once the door closed behind her, Tate looked across the table. "Shall we get to work?"

He started to rise, but Rebekah didn't move.

"Tate . . . something is wrong. I know it. I mean, besides your father. I wish you would confide in me. Maybe it would help . . . whatever it is."

He looked at her and for a fraction of a second, she thought she saw him waver, that he was going to open up to her.

"Nothing's wrong, Rebekah. I'm simply ready to get back to work. After all, this last movement isn't going to write itself."

Hurt, yet doing her best not to show it, Rebekah rose.

A grand piano took up the majority of space in the study, and though smaller than the instrument in Tate's office at the opera house, it appeared to be of equal quality, and, therefore, she assumed, would possess a similar quality of sound. Maestro

Heilig had always claimed that composing on a grand piano was a necessity. Apparently, Tate agreed.

After warming her hands over the fire in the hearth, Rebekah took her place on the bench and began playing the "Ode to Joy" from Beethoven's Ninth. She played it with less gusto than usual, the emotive chords feeling more melancholy than joyous at the moment.

"Do you *always* warm up to something from Beethoven's Ninth?"

Rebekah stopped and looked over at him. "Is there something else you would prefer I play?"

When he said nothing, she pulled their notes for the fourth movement from his satchel and spread them atop the piano. She read them through to refresh her memory with what little they'd written thus far.

Deciding it best to move on, she propped the sheet music on the music stand and played the opening measures. "The beginning still doesn't feel quite right, does it?"

He sat down beside her on the bench. "It's lacking something. But I still don't know what."

He reached to play, and she scooted over a bit. He played the measures over and over again, eyes closed, and Rebekah watched his expression, almost able to feel the music moving within him. She recognized the concentration, the reaching deep within for something that lay just beyond his grasp. Though she didn't fully understand the breadth of the process involved in writing an entire symphony, she could offer feedback, and occasionally had success with bridging measures and building tension within the score, but she wasn't the composer. He was.

At heart, she was a violinist. No other instrument, for her at least, could capture the strains of the soul's deepest yearnings and desires, its bitterest disappointments and losses. If only she could lend her expertise in that area, then perhaps she would be more of a help—

He stopped abruptly, rose, and stepped to a cabinet a few feet away. He withdrew a case, and Rebekah instantly knew where his instincts were taking him. The same place her own had taken her.

He withdrew a violin, tuned the instrument, and began playing the opening measures. Only, he played them in C major, instead of C minor—and the notes took on a life of their own. It felt almost as if the veil between this world and the next lifted ever so slightly, and heaven, with the subtlest of breaths, shared a melody from a distant world awaiting. The beauty of it trapped her breath tight in her chest.

The thrill of watching music being born tingled up and down her spine, and the tender strains of the violin—the emotion with which Tate played, determination in every movement—gave meaning to notes that had, until now, been dull and lifeless on the page.

Warmth rose to her eyes as she watched him.

Help him, Lord. Give him what he needs to do this. To finish well. For himself, yes, and his career, but far more, for you.

The prayer hadn't formed so much in her mind as in her heart, and as she listened to him play, she thought of New York City and of the world of possibility awaiting her there. And though she enjoyed contemplating that life, she could scarcely imagine leaving him behind.

"Timpani," he said, and she instinctively knew what he wanted. She found the correct sheet music with the timpani score and played the coordinating keys on the piano, imitating the deep, resonating drum.

"Now the cello."

Reading the music, she played the cellos' part.

"And the clarinets."

She worked to keep up, wishing there were a way to capture what they were both playing as they were playing it, so they could go back and listen to it together later.

"And again." He started over from the beginning.

She followed his lead, playing the various parts, as she could, then—

The violin went sharp. Just a little. Tate kept playing, his brow furrowed, jaw tense with determination. Then it happened again, and he grimaced. Then lost the tempo.

A knock sounded on the door, and Rebekah stopped playing. But Tate ignored it, continuing as though determined to find his way back.

A second knock, more insistent, sounded.

Tate stopped, strode to the door, and jerked it open. "*Yes,* Mrs. Pender! What is it?"

The older woman, already slight in stature, appeared even more so with the darkness from the hallway framing her from behind. She held out a piece of paper. "This just come for you, sir. Man said it be urgent."

Tate stared for a beat, then his gaze dropped to the telegram. He took it from her, opened it, then slowly turned back, his face drained of color.

Rebekah rose from the piano. "Tate, what is it?"

"It's from Emil . . . about Pa. He says to get home as quickly as I can."

29

Tate paused briefly when the cabin came into view. At least half a dozen horses were tied up at the posts, and dread settled heavy in his chest. Even at this distance, he could see through the windows to the people gathered inside. And he took it as a bad sign.

He looked at Rebekah beside him. "Thank you," he whispered. "For coming with me."

She touched his arm. "There's nowhere else I'd rather be."

"I meant to ask . . . What did you tell Mrs. Cheatham? When you left?"

Her smile came softly. "I told her I had a friend who needed me."

Tate's love for her deepened even as they stood there. How was it he'd finally met the woman he wanted to spend his life with at the precise time when the life he'd wanted to share with her was being rewritten?

Before they could reach the stairs, the door to the cabin opened. He saw his mother's tearstained face, and his world shifted. He hurried up the steps, dropped the satchels in his grip, and pulled her close.

"Pa's still with us, Witty. Lord only knows how, but he is." She let go of him only to pull Rebekah into a tight hug. "Good to be layin' eyes on ya again, sweet girl. Kind of ya to come all this way with my son."

"It's good to see you too, Cattabelle. Though . . . I'm so sorry for the reason."

His mother nodded. "Yesterday we's all thinkin' he was done for, but he just kept on breathin', like he hain't ready to go yet." Fresh tears fell. "I hain't ready for him to go neither. Never will be." She wiped her cheeks. "Come on in now. He's been askin' after ya, Witty. Your brothers and they wives, they's all here earlier, but they done taken their leave." She grabbed Tate's hand, then motioned for Rebekah to follow.

The main room was full. Mostly women and babes in arm, but some husbands had come along. Tate nodded to Trudy Robertson, Lilly Tatum,

Harriett Javis, Mr. and Mrs. Coburn, and the O'Fallons and the Morrisons. Emil, Rufus, Benjamin, and Opal, her blue eyes red rimmed, sat at the kitchen table, dish after dish of food spread out before them. None of them eating.

Opal got up and ran to him, and Tate hugged her tight. He kissed the crown of her head, wanting to tell her everything would be all right. But he couldn't. It would've been a lie.

Trudy Robertson's newborn began to cry, and the girl—all of fifteen now, he thought—unbuttoned her shirtwaist, pulled out a breast, and began nursing her child. He saw Rebekah look over, then just as swiftly look away, her cheeks reddening. No one else in the room paid it any mind.

"Come on into the bedroom, son." Her mother tugged his hand. "You too, Rebekah. Time for swappin' names can come later."

They entered the bedroom, Rebekah a few steps behind. His father lay beneath the covers, his head propped up on two pillows, and he looked much the same as the last time Tate had seen him, except his breathing was noticeably more labored, and his face more ashen.

Determined to hold on to a little hope, Tate had brought additional laudanum, but he wondered now if they'd need it.

"Angus," his mother whispered. "Can you wake up, darlin'? Witty be here with his woman friend, Rebekah. They come to see ya."

His father stirred, then coughed, the deep rattle in his chest making Tate's own lungs ache. Tate moved closer and leaned in to be in his father's line of sight, the ache in his own chest fanning out.

"Hey, Pa. It's good to see you again, sir."

His father blinked in the dimly lit room, then reached for his hand on the covers. "Be it . . . time for the last load, son?"

Tate gripped his hand, not wanting that time to be here. Not yet. "No, sir. I don't think it's quite time."

His father sighed, a soul-weary sound that all but broke Tate's heart. He knew he was being selfish. But he wasn't ready to say good-bye yet. He was so close to being able to honor his father in the way a man like Angus Whitcomb should be honored—by sitting front and center in the new Nashville Opera House and hearing the symphony his son had written for him, inspired by him and the life he'd lived, and all he'd given.

Tate heard a shaky breath behind him and turned to see tears streaming down Rebekah's cheeks.

Later that evening, once neighbors had taken their leave, the family sat down to dinner—what little everyone ate. The cabin felt more spacious, certainly, but also emptier somehow, and sadder, as Angus Whitcomb's struggle to breathe filled every corner of the home.

And that's when Tate knew what he had to do. . . .

He walked back into the bedroom and took his father's hand. "Pa," he whispered, tears in his eyes.

His father's eyelids fluttered open, and it seemed to take a moment for him to focus in the soft glow of lamplight.

"Pa . . . I might have been wrong earlier."

A frown creased his father's brow.

Tate steeled himself against the wave of emotion cresting inside him. "Like you've always taught me . . . the Lord calls each of us to run a race, a race meant only for us. And when your race is done"—his voice broke as tears pushed past his reserve—"Jesus will make that known. So listen for him, Pa. And when you see that finish line, whenever it comes, you run for Him with all you've got."

Tears slipped from the corners of his father's eyes and trailed down his temples. "Ya been . . . a good son, Witty."

"And you've been the best and most loving father I could have ever asked for."

Tate stayed by his father's bedside all night. Until, finally, dawn broke and the sun edged up over the mountains. Each time his father took a breath, Tate expected it to be his last. Yet even as he sat there, he found himself thankful that he could hear his father breathing, that he could hear the creak of the cabin, the slow-burning crackle of the fire in the hearth, and the first warble of a songbird calling for the world to awaken.

Staring out the window, watching the smoke-colored clouds drift slowly over the highest peaks, he felt a hand on his shoulder and looked up to see Rebekah, her hair tousled from sleep, her eyes full of care and concern. He brought her palm to his lips and kissed it, breathing in her sweet scent, so grateful she'd come with him. So grateful she was in his life, for however long.

"Witty . . ." Voice soft, his mother walked up from behind. "Coffee be on the stove. You and Rebekah go get yerself some. I'm gonna sit with Pa awhile."

Tate stood, his muscles stiff from having sat in the chair so long. In the kitchen, he poured two cups and handed one to Rebekah. "Let's grab blankets and go sit outside. I want to talk to you about something."

They settled on the front steps, and Tate draped a blanket around her, then another around them both. They huddled close, the steam from the coffee rising to their faces, the crisp mountain morning offering fresh hope after the dark of night, and he thought . . . this wouldn't be a bad way to spend one's life.

None too eager to chase away the silence and peace of the moment, Tate drank his coffee and tried to think of a way to tell her what he needed to tell her. He'd brought the letter from Dr. Hamilton with him, had it in his pocket even now. He'd intended to tell her night before last when he'd invited her to his house for dinner. Then the response from the Philadelphia doctor had arrived, followed by the telegram . . .

But there was something else he needed to tell her first. "As I was sitting by my father's bedside through the night, I kept thinking about the fourth movement and what it's lacking, and why it's been so difficult to write."

"What you did, though, with what you've written so far, changing from C minor to C major, that was masterful."

"What *we've* written so far." He gave her a look. "And yes, I think that helped. But as I've composed this symphony, I've tried *so* hard to write something worthy of the European masters—Haydn, Mozart, Beethoven. And while I'm pleased, for the most part, with the first three movements, I want the last one to reflect more of who I am. More of . . ."

He lifted his eyes to his beloved mountains, which boasted shades of green too numerous to count, their rugged beauty incapable of being described by words alone.

"This," he said softly. "My world in Chicory Hollow. Because while I'm writing this symphony for the opening of the new opera house, the *real* reason I'm writing it, Rebekah . . . why it's been so difficult and frustrating and maddening at times, is that I'm writing it . . . for my father." He felt her watching him, her body warm against his beneath the blanket. "I want this music to be not only a celebration of his life, but a reflection of my love and admiration for him."

Without words, she slipped her hand through the crook of his arm, and he pulled her closer.

"Which, I finally realized early this morning, means that the fourth movement *must* include a violin solo. I'd use the fiddle, if I could, but I doubt my esteemed colleagues would appreciate it."

Her soft laughter echoed his.

"However, I have one small concern," he continued. "By incorporating a violin solo, that means that Darrow Fulton, the first violin and my concertmaster—and a man upon whom I'm not at all certain I can depend—will be the one to play it. Then, of course, there's the *slight* challenge of adapting mountain music into the fourth movement of an orchestral arrangement."

Finger to his chin, she gently turned his face toward hers. "If there is any composer in the world who can do this, Tate . . . it's you. I could not believe in you more than I already do."

Her words like a balm, they also opened up a place inside him where he didn't want to go—and where he didn't want to take her. He hadn't yet come to grips with the diagnosis himself. How could he invite her into that place of chaos and uncertainty? And how to tell her the truth when she believed in him so unwaveringly?

"Rebekah, you've asked me, numerous times, in recent weeks if . . . something's wrong. Or if something's happened." Dread, both of her reaction and of an unknown future, knifed his gut. "And . . . it has."

She frowned, and he instinctively started to pull away, but stopped himself. Moving away from this woman was the last thing he needed—or wanted— to do right now. Soon her assistance in composing would become more vital than ever. And then, after the symphony was completed and the grand opening behind them—the knife twisted inside him a half turn—he would do everything in his power to pave her way to New York City where a new life awaited her. But first, to get through this. . . .

"You remember the weekend you followed me to Chicory Hollow?"

She nodded, studying him.

"The reason I didn't return Monday afternoon as planned was because . . . I had an appointment with a doctor in Knoxville that morning, and the examination went longer than expected."

"Tate . . ." She placed a hand on his arm. "Is everything—"

"I'm going deaf, Rebekah." Saying it aloud for the first time jarred him. He couldn't look at her. "Based on his examination, the doctor said I've already lost a considerable amount of my hearing. He wanted to consult colleagues and sent his prognosis in a letter that said, based on the few patients with similar afflictions they've treated . . . I can expect to suffer full hearing loss over the course of a year, maybe a few months more. Maybe . . . a few less."

"How . . ." She cleared her throat. "How long have you known?"

"About two weeks. The day I showed you the opera house."

He finally turned to look at her beside him, and she nodded, her face pale, lips pressed firmly together.

"I returned home that night and the doctor's letter was waiting." He sighed, feeling a bitter smile. "I didn't open it at first. I couldn't, even though I knew not reading it wouldn't change anything in the long run. I think I simply wanted to live a few more hours without knowing for sure. So I went to my study, and I played. I don't know how long I was there at the piano. But when I finally stopped, I opened the letter, I read it . . . and have been trying to come to grips with it ever since."

She wove her fingers through his. "Tate, I . . . I'm so sorry. I knew something had changed, that something was wrong, but . . . I never suspected."

The shock in her expression, the disbelief, were familiar to him. They'd been his constant companions for days on end.

"Did the doctor say anything else? Are there treatments? Are there other doctors, perhaps, that you could see? Ones with more experience in this area?"

"Dr. Hamilton is the leading physician in the field of hearing maladies. He served as director of medicine at Boston Medical for over thirty years. The doctors he consulted are also experts in that field."

Tate had thought the burden inside him might ease a little once he told her, but it hadn't. The sadness in her eyes tore at him. "So you see now," he continued, needing to fill the silence, "why the prospect of writing a violin solo will be even more of a challenge."

"Tate . . ." She wiped the moisture from her cheeks, her eyes earnest. "I can help you do this."

"I know you can, Rebekah. You've already helped me more than you'll ever—"

"No, you don't understand." She briefly closed her eyes. "I haven't been completely—"

"Witty?"

Tate turned to see Emil standing in the doorway.

"Ma says ya need to come. Pa's askin' for ya."

Giving Rebekah's hand a gentle squeeze, Tate rose and started for the door—when the planked porch shifted beneath him. He reached out for the wall of the cabin as the ringing in his ears grew thunderous. He found it difficult to breathe, much less remain standing.

From a long distance away, he heard Rebekah's voice.

"Tate, are you all right?" *You all right . . . you all right . . . you all right . . .*

Her voice echoed down a long tunnel toward him, each reverberation more painful than the last.

"I'm fine," he heard himself say, his voice traveling back toward her. But even as he said it, he realized how foolish it sounded. How foolish he must look to her.

A muscular arm came around his shoulders.

"Brother, ya okay?"

Emil.

As quickly as the episode came on, it subsided, but equilibrium was slower to return. A dullness filled his ears, as if sound was passing through a wet blanket before it reached him.

"I'm fine," he said again, holding the side of his head. "I . . . must've gotten up too quickly." He looked at Rebekah, whose expression was pained.

"Ya better not be sneakin' any moonshine behind Mama's back. She'll skin ya alive." Emil laughed.

Rebekah didn't.

With effort, Tate walked inside of his own accord and continued to the bedroom. Rebekah and Emil followed. Everyone was gathered— Rufus, Benjamin, Opal, his mother. Her face lit when she saw him.

She held out Pa's fiddle, her eyes glistening. "He's wantin' to hear ya play, son. Done told us hisself. And we already knowin' what he wants to hear."

His mother's voice was distant and muffled. Tate looked at his father, saw the ghost of a smile on his face. Tate reached for the fiddle, careful not to look at Rebekah.

He plucked the strings, tuning as he went, the simple task he'd done countless time now proving a challenge. But what if this was the last time his father would ever hear him play? What if *this* would have to suffice instead of his symphony?

"This be Angus's fav'rite church song," he heard his mother telling Rebekah. "He learnt it to Witty when he was just a boy."

Tate tucked the cherished instrument against his collarbone and drew the bow across the strings. The resulting notes were familiar to him, but still sounded distant, and distorted in a way.

Please, Lord . . . For him. Let me do this for him.

Tate closed his eyes, concentrating, and played, the notes and cadence of this song having been woven into the fabric of who he was long ago. But oddly, the lyrics—which he knew but didn't dwell on as much—were what rose in his mind this time, and the words all but drowned out the music. *"Come, thou fount of every blessing, tune my heart to sing thy grace . . . Streams of mercy never ceasing, call for songs of loudest praise . . ."*

He squeezed his eyes tight, struggling to find the melody, but the ringing in his ears returned. And by the time a note finally registered, another soon piled in upon it, then another, and another, until the notes were more a jumble inside his head than a tune.

Realizing the futility, he lowered the bow to his side and slowly lifted his gaze. His father's eyes were still closed, but furrows knit his brow. In the faces of his family, Tate read confusion. But in Rebekah's, he read heartache. And understanding.

"I'm s-sorry," he stammered. "I seem to be

having another one of my headaches. Perhaps, I can try again later and—"

Wordlessly, Rebekah crossed the room, gently took the fiddle from his grasp, and with tears in her eyes, began to play.

30

Rebekah didn't dare look at Tate as she played the beloved hymn, yet she could think of nothing and no one else. *Tate . . . going deaf.* She could scarcely wrap her mind around what he'd told her and what that would mean for him. And yet, it explained so much. His erratic behavior in recent days and weeks, his irritability and frustration. It all fit—

And it broke her heart.

She tried to imagine how she would react if she'd gotten that news, losing the ability to do what was most dear to her. A cold stab of fear caused her to grip the fiddle more tightly than she should, and with effort, she consciously relaxed her hands.

From the corner of her eye, she spotted Opal inching forward and quickly realized the young girl's intentions. The glistening in Opal's eyes made her own tears start afresh.

" 'Here I raise mine Ebenezer . . .' " Opal sang, joining in the middle of the second verse, her tender love for her father evident in her voice.

"'And I hope, by thy good pleasure, safely to arrive at home. Jesus sought me when a stranger, wanderin' from the fold'a God. He, to rescue me from danger, interposed His precious blood.'"

The fiddle's chin rest, worn on one side, felt especially smooth against Rebekah's skin, the instrument having been well loved and well played. And how precious that *this* song meant so much to two men she and Tate had loved so dearly in their lives.

The rest of the family—except Tate and his father, whose eyes remained closed—joined in on the third and fourth verse. Then Rebekah played the melody again, one last time—slower, softer—the uniqueness of this family's vocals and their way of expressing themselves in song influencing the vibrato and trills she played. The fiddle reminded her of the one Demetrius had owned and upon which he'd first taught her to play.

The image of Demetrius and how he'd looked the last time she'd seen him—his smile, the way he'd stood in front of the house waving good-bye—brought to mind again the last words of the fourth verse. . . .

Here's my heart, O take and seal it, seal it
   for thy courts above.

Thy courts above . . . where Demetrius was now. Along with her father, and soon . . . Tate's father. All believers. Men who had trusted in Christ. As the last note faded, the soft look of contentedness in Angus's rugged features made her heart swell, as did Cattabelle's tears as she closely watched him.

But when Rebekah sneaked a look at Tate, she couldn't decipher the emotion in his sober expression and quickly looked away again.

"What ya be sayin'?" Cattabelle leaned closer to her husband's face, then looked up, her composure wavering. "Pa says ya fiddled nice as ever, Witty." She gave him a soft wink. "Says he's real proud."

Tate nodded once and bowed his head, and Rebekah felt for him, grateful Angus still thought his son had been the one playing.

"You done real good," Emil whispered to her as he left the bedroom.

Benjamin nodded, following after. "'Twas real nice, Miss Carrin'ton."

"Ya done Pa's song mighty proud, Rebekah." Opal touched the neck of the fiddle as she passed, Rufus on her heels.

"Thought I's hearin' angels playin'," he said softly.

"Thank you," Rebekah whispered to each as they passed.

Cattabelle wiped her eyes. "Think I'll just set here'a spell with him, just the two of us, if ya hain't mindin'."

"No, ma'am." Tate spoke up. "We don't mind. Rebekah and I . . . we're going for a walk. We'll be back directly."

Cattabelle nodded, and then her eyes narrowed. "Worries me somethin' fierce, Witty. Them aches in your head."

"I'll be fine," he whispered, hugging his mother tight. "We'll be back in a while."

Hearing his decisive tone, Rebekah surrendered the fiddle, and he returned it to the case atop the chest of drawers. She followed him outside and down the front steps, the sunshine so bright after being indoors that she had to shield her eyes for a moment, yet she drank in the uncustomary warmth for March.

Tate turned to her. "It was you. That night. At Mrs. Cheatham's dinner party." His blue eyes were bright with emotion. But what emotion, Rebekah couldn't tell.

"Yes." She nodded.

"Yet you never said anything. Even when you *knew* I was trying to find out who it was."

"I was going to tell you earlier, before Emil came out. And the reason I didn't before now is because I made a promise to Mrs. Cheatham the night of the party that I wouldn't. We agreed not to tell anyone."

"But why?"

She looked at him. "You know why. A woman playing the violin? In public? At Adelicia Cheatham's party? We both know it's not to be borne." She shook her head. "I never should have done it. The main reason I did"—the truth stuck fast in her throat—"was to spite *you*."

His expression darkened, and she rushed to explain.

"You had said no to me after my audition, and I wanted to do something that would rankle you like you'd rankled me. And . . . I also wanted to know what it was like to play in front of an audience. A *real* audience. What I didn't plan on, however, was you coming upstairs afterward."

"You saw me?"

She briefly looked away. "I was hiding in the shadows in the children's bedroom."

For a moment he said nothing, and she finally looked back to find him staring. Then a tiny smile tipped one side of his mouth.

"Rebekah Carrington . . . you truly are a most unconventional woman. And . . . a masterful violinist."

She hesitated. "You're . . . not angry with me?"

"Angry? I might have been, if I'd found out earlier. But now . . ." His gaze softened. "Recent discoveries have caused me to view life in a slightly different light."

He reached for her hand and drew her into his arms. She went without hesitation.

"I'm sorry," she whispered, head against his chest. "For not telling you, and . . . for what's happening to you."

He pulled her closer. She felt so at home in his arms, safe and cared for. And she tried not to think about what her life would be like without him in it.

"Thank you for playing for my father. There are times, like what just happened a while ago, when a ringing starts in my ears. It's almost overwhelming and makes playing all but impossible."

She drew back slightly. "But the ringing isn't there all the time."

"No. Not yet anyway. It's unpredictable. Right now, I can hear without any reverberation. But earlier . . . It feels like the sounds are traveling down a tunnel. Then, typically, once the pain leaves, everything is muffled for a while. Like I'm hearing through a wall. But it's considerably better now."

They walked a path that led around the cabin and down the hill, neither of them speaking. Beside them, filling the comfortable silence, a stream trickled and tumbled over a rocky bed, its melody ancient but never old.

"You're certain the doctor who examined you is the best in his field?"

"I'm certain." Tate pulled a piece of paper from his pocket and handed it to her. "It's the letter from Dr. Hamilton. He explains what he believes is happening to me."

The letter looked well read for one so recently received, its edges crinkled, a corner torn. Rebekah paused and silently read the doctor's findings, scarcely starting the second paragraph before her hopes for Tate's healing were dealt a heavy blow.

It is my conclusion that you suffer from an aggressive and degenerative malady of which my colleagues and I have witnessed only a handful of times, and never before in a person of such youth and vitality. There is an abnormal, microscopic growth of bone in the walls of your inner ear that is causing the stapes bone to become fixed in place. In a normal ear, the stapes vibrates freely to allow transmission of sound into the inner ear. But when it becomes fixed to the surrounding bone, as in your case, it prevents sound waves from reaching the inner ear fluids and hearing becomes increasingly impaired.

I told you I'd seek consultation from a colleague in Boston, and I did. But burdened by the nature of your illness—and you being so gifted by the Almighty—I took the liberty of seeking additional counsel as well, while keeping your identity concealed. You must know, Maestro Whitcomb, I have never been more eager to have my findings proven false.

Rebekah found herself not wanting to continue. She wanted to rewrite this doctor's conclusion. Give it a different ending.

While we have made enormous strides in medicine in recent decades, there is yet so much we do not know. So it is with the greatest regret I inform you that there is no known treatment or cure for your condition. And while the time frame I'm about to share can vary, you should expect to suffer full hearing loss over the course of the next year. Perhaps a few months less, perhaps more. I am earnestly praying for more.

Rebekah couldn't blink back the tears fast enough, and the stationery trembled in her grip. The words on the page ran together, and she could no longer read them. Tate slipped an arm around her shoulders and took the letter.

She pointed to where she'd left off.

"'My deepest regrets to you, Maestro'"—he read softly—"'for the diagnosis I have had to deliver. Know that you have my continued prayers as well as an open door to my practice—and to my home—whenever you are in Knoxville. If you require anything additional from me, all you need do is ask. My best to you and yours always. Sincerely, Dr. Ronald T. Hamilton. P.S. I have already secured tickets to the grand opening for the new Nashville Opera House, and have never anticipated an event more.'"

He refolded the letter and returned it to his pocket. "Walk with me?"

Rebekah looked at his outstretched hand and knew he was offering it as a friend. And she accepted, still wanting so much more.

Dappled sunshine sneaked through the trees overhead and cast lacy shadows on the path. The twitter of birds in the branches and the sweet smell of fresh pine in the breeze made her wonder if there was any more beautiful place on earth. Or anyone else she'd rather be with right now.

Tate pulled something from his shirt pocket. It was about the size of a hickory nut, wrapped in paper, then twisted on both ends. He unwrapped it and held it to her lips. "Bite off half."

She eyed it. "Tell me what it is first."

He smiled. "It's not made with moonshine. Or squirrel."

Smiling, she did as he asked and the chewy, buttery sweetness on her tongue made her instantly glad she had. "It's like a caramel, only . . . different."

"It's Mama's molasses taffy. I thought you'd like it." He popped the other half into his mouth. "Come on. I want to show you something."

Farther down, the path opened into a meadow. And there, nestled among prairie grass and winter wheat, sat a little church building, its white steeple stretching tall and proud. Rebekah paused to take it in.

"Idyllic," she said with a sigh.

The door to the church was open, the inside orderly and swept clean. Wooden pews, six on each side, were arranged neatly in rows. A simple pulpit adorned a raised dais at the front, and to its right, a piano.

"Men on that side." Tate gestured. "Women on this side."

She looked over at him. "You are joking."

"I am not. It's the rule of the highlanders. But not to worry . . . There are plenty of barns and wagons around here where a boy and girl can spark mischief."

She gave him a little push, not liking the idea of him *sparking mischief* with anyone else but her. He walked to the piano bench and sat down, leaving room for her beside him.

"This is where I first learned to play."

"Here? On *this* piano?"

He nodded, and began playing. She was pleased to discover the piano in tune, except for middle C, which was slightly flat.

She smiled at the song he played. "Brahms's 'Wiegenlied: Guten Abend, Gute Nacht.' Translated," she continued, "Brahms's 'Lullaby: Good Evening, Good Night.' I actually had the honor of hearing Johannes Brahms perform this in Vienna."

Tate looked at her and shook his head. "Pitiful little thing."

Smiling, she gave him a nudge. "He and Maestro Heilig were colleagues, and Brahms would visit him often. Maestro Heilig once said that Brahms had acquired the reputation for being a *grump,* and not without reason. But he also said that few could ever be as lovable as he."

Tate paused in his playing. "What was it like? To live there."

"Quite lonely, at first," she answered honestly. A little too honestly, judging from the uncertainty in his expression. "I was scarcely thirteen when I moved there with my maid, Sally."

"That was . . . after your father had passed." His voice held a hint of question. "And shortly after your mother remarried."

"That's right."

"Do you see her often? Your mother?"

Wondering how they'd wandered into this part of her life, she gave a small shrug. "I try to. She and I don't share the same kind of affection you have with your family, Tate."

She looked down at the keys, determined to change the subject. She continued the lullaby where he'd left off, the sweetness of the music a helpful transition. "Living in Vienna was also exciting." Scenes rose in her mind. "To walk the streets where Mozart and Beethoven walked. To sit in the same cafes and symphony halls. I've walked by Mozart's home countless times, and by the Schönbrunn Palace where he gave his first performance for the Hapsburg family. At the age of six, which is so amazing when you think of it."

"I envy you having lived there. In the City of Music."

"I'm grateful for my years there. But I'm also grateful"—her hands paused on the keys—"for being back here."

"As am I. Far more than you know."

He held her gaze, and she would've sworn—not

that she was an expert at such things—that he wanted to kiss her. And she wished he would! But . . .

He finished the Brahms instead. And before the last chord faded, he began the opening measures of the fourth movement from his symphony. Only, he continued past where they'd written. The music was beyond splendid, and different than what he'd composed in the first two movements, and from what they'd written together in the third. She heard traces of the European masters they both loved, but she could also detect the faintest influence of . . . mountain music?

The discovery brought a smile.

"This would be the violin solo," he said. "Or the start of it."

The chords and rhythm of the piece slowly transitioned, his fingers expert on the keys—no trouble for him hearing at the moment, she noticed—and she could perfectly imagine the music being played on a violin. Oh, she wished she could be the one to play it. But that was impossible, she knew. Darrow Fulton would play it. And with his talent and practiced skill—minus his meanness—the solo would be superb, the perfect climax and finish to a symphony that was, in her estimation, brilliant.

"Where did *that* come from?" she asked once Tate finally paused.

He shrugged. "I have no idea. I was awake last night, composing in my head, and then again on the path with you on the way here, but I couldn't get anything to make sense."

"Quite the contrary, I'd say." Yet she understood what he meant by composing in his mind. Melodies would come to her at the oddest times.

He smiled. "Let me play it again. And perhaps, between the two of us, we'll remember most of it."

Wishing she had pencil and paper, she worked to commit the chords and tempo to memory. Tate played it again and again, then they hurried back to the cabin, laughing and humming as they went.

They quickly gathered pencil and paper, and with Tate playing his father's fiddle, they sat on the front porch steps, so as not to bother Angus, and worked to re-create the chords. Rebekah transcribed them as hurriedly and accurately as she could, making suggestions and comments as they went. Then they played the measures from the page and made yet more notations.

As dusk crept in, they finished their task and were pleased to have a solid beginning to both the opening of the fourth movement and also the violin solo. They ate a bite of dinner, then Tate asked to sit with his father for a while. Angus's breathing, a labored chore, hurt them all to hear.

In the family's faces, Rebekah saw both love for their father and a desire that he stay with them. Yet a love that hated to see him hurt, to struggle for every breath, the rattle in his chest sounding even more pronounced than when they first arrived.

She stood in the doorway of the bedroom and

watched Tate as he sat by his father's bedside, elbows on his knees, head bowed, and she imagined what he must be praying. She knew he wanted his father to stay alive long enough to hear the symphony he'd written for him. The son longed to honor the father.

And yet Tate had already honored him in the life he'd lived—and would continue to live.

And though now wasn't the time to tell him this, she believed—no matter what happened—that Angus *would* hear that symphony Tate had written for him, the symphony that would be played that first night in the new hall, whether Angus was still here with them to attend . . . or not.

Later, cuddled beside Opal in bed, Rebekah awakened to the soft shuffle of steps on the plank floor. She peered up, recognizing Tate in the soft glow of lamplight coming from the bedroom, and also Cattabelle, who'd been asleep on the sofa.

"Bless you, Witty, for lettin' me get some rest," Cattabelle whispered, patting his arm as she passed.

Tate nodded, heading toward the sofa, then glanced back. "If it's all right with you, Mama," he said softly, "I might stay on a few days. Until . . ."

He didn't finish the sentence. Didn't need to.

"I's hopin' you would, son." A deep sigh left her. "I's hopin' you would."

The door to the bedroom closed, and darkness enveloped the room again. Tate added another log to the fire, and the wood crackled and sparked as the flames renewed their vigor.

Soft snores from Tate's brothers combined with Opal's gentle breaths to crowd out the silence. Rebekah lay still, knowing Tate had to be exhausted and needed rest. She didn't know what time it was, but it was still dark out, so she closed her eyes again and soon drifted off.

But she awakened again some time later, not by a noise, but . . . by a feeling. She looked over at the sofa. Tate was lying down.

And yet she knew he was awake.

Not bothering to whisper his name, she rose, slipped her arms into her robe, wrapped a blanket around her shoulders, and padded softly across the floor. Wordlessly, he sat up and made room for her beside him. She was chilled after leaving the warmth of the bed and pulled the blanket close about herself.

"Can't sleep?" she whispered.

He shook his head. "The quiet is deafening."

It took a moment for his meaning to become clear. But as she listened—beyond the soft breathing of his siblings, beyond the muted sounds of his father's struggle—there was absolute stillness. As though the night around them were a vacuum absorbing every speck of sound. Not an owl hooted, not a breath of wind stirred. Even the rhythmic *tick-tick-tick* of the clock atop the mantel was silent, the routine effort of winding the mechanism forgotten in the shadow of death.

Sensing he needed to talk, she waited. And prayed.

"I know I should say I'm not scared," he whispered. "That I haven't . . . lain awake at night wondering if I have weeks or months, or another year. Or if it will happen before the grand opening. But I can't. Because, the truth is, Rebekah . . . I can taste the fear. I can feel it pulsing inside me. As steady and strong as my own heartbeat. I begin thinking of all the things I'll never hear again. And then I wonder if, over time . . . I'll forget them all."

The muscles in his jaw went rigid, and the honesty in his confession wrapped itself around her throat, making it difficult for her to speak.

"Tate, it's only right that you should be afraid. Anyone would be. *I* certainly would be."

He looked toward the window where darkness lay beyond, the night skies black and star studded. "I've been lying here trying to imagine what the rest of my life is going to be like. Will I be able to remember what Beethoven's Fifth sounds like? Or his Ninth? Or Mozart's Oboe Concerto in C Major? Or . . . 'Rondo alla turca' played by a lovely ghost on a second-floor landing."

Tenderness softened his voice, along with uncertainty, and she reached for his hand and held it tight. What to say that would give him hope?

"Right now, if you concentrate," she said after a moment, lowering her voice, "can you hear the way the rain sounds as it falls on a tin roof? Or the

496

cry of an eagle as it soars high above in the cloudless blue?"

He looked over at her.

"Even after so many years," she continued, "I can still hear my father telling me he loves me when he used to tuck me in at night. I can hear the singing drifting up over the hill from the slave cabins behind my childhood home. And Demetrius, a slave in my father's house and . . . actually, the man who first taught me to play the fiddle"—she sensed Tate's surprise—"was very special to me. There are moments when I close my eyes, and I promise you"—her voice caught—"I can *hear* his rich baritone and the way he could make his fiddle sing. And will, I think, for as long as I live."

She paused, the memories thick around her. "So while I in no way mean to make less of the burden you've been given to bear, Tate, I do believe you'll remember. I believe the music that you love, that you've studied and learned, and have brought to so many other lives will always be inside you. Just as *your* music will always be inside me."

He didn't speak for the longest moment, and then he brought her hand to his lips and kissed it. "Thank you . . . Rebekah." His voice was husky, and halting. "Not only for . . . being here right now, but for everything you've done for me. You've . . . inspired me in ways I never expected. And could never have begun to imagine."

She looked at him, the shadows playing across

his face. "You've inspired me too, by allowing me to get a glimpse of what you do. I love what music gives back to me when I play. But playing is so different from composing, which is something I'll never be capable of."

"I beg to differ. You've shown you are more than capable."

"No, Tate. I've been a . . . sounding board for you. I've helped bridge the gaps here and there. But the real inspiration has come from you. And your love for your father shines through every note. I see that so clearly now."

He reached up and fingered a curl on her shoulder. "What would I have done without you?" he whispered.

She stared. "You speak as though I'm already gone. I'm still here. Right beside you."

He cradled the side of her face, and his touch fanned her desire for him with a fierceness she'd not experienced before.

"I know you're here, Rebekah," he whispered. "And I appreciate all you've done. More than you know."

Wondering if what she was about to do was completely proper, she realized that, at the moment, she didn't fully care. Not when hearing the worry in his voice. She leaned close and kissed his cheek. She *knew* he cared for her. She felt it in his touch. In his voice. Even now, in the way he looked at her. Growing bolder, she kissed him on the corner of his mouth and caught the sweet scent of molasses on his breath. He'd had another of those candies.

"Rebekah, we—"

"Shhh," she whispered, and brushed her lips against his, softly, slowly, as he'd taught her. And with something akin to a sigh, he angled his mouth to meet hers and kissed her deeply, slowly, as though trying to memorize what that was like too, so he wouldn't forget. And faced with such an unknown future, she found herself doing the same. His lips held yearning she understood. And shared. She slipped her hands around his neck, and pressed closer to him.

Suddenly he drew back, breaking the kiss. He looked at her, his breathing overloud in the silence, his features lost to the shadows.

"Is . . . something wrong?" she whispered.

He raked a hand through his hair. "It's late, Rebekah. We'd better get some rest. Morning will be here soon."

She stared. "Tate, if I did anything—"

"You didn't do *anything* wrong, Rebekah. I'm just . . . tired. And we both need to rest."

His tone was curt, almost dismissive. She finally managed a nod and returned to bed. But couldn't shake the feeling that she'd done something she shouldn't have.

"Wait here for me?" Tate caught Rebekah's eye. "I'll send the telegrams and be right back."

At her nod, he crossed to the telegraph office.

She'd been quiet that morning, and no wonder as to why. He'd hurt her feelings last night. He never should have allowed that to happen between them. But when she'd leaned close and kissed him . . . at first, he'd been too surprised to move. Then as she'd grown bolder, he hadn't wanted her to stop. If she only knew how hard it had been for him to distance himself from her, she might feel differently toward him. Then again, she might not.

But it was only due to loving her as much as he did that he'd been able to do it.

He penned the first telegram to Mrs. Cheatham and handed it to the clerk, then started on the next. What to tell Mrs. Murphey when he didn't know what was going to happen himself? Before leaving Nashville, he'd informed her about his father's illness and told her he was "headed east" to be with his family. Best word the telegram as vaguely as he could, while communicating the necessities.

Father's condition worsened. Little hope. Assure board opening night on schedule. Returning soon.

He handed the second telegram to the clerk and counted out the coins. "The first goes to Mrs. Adelicia Cheatham at Belmont Mansion in Nashville, Tennessee. The second to Mrs. Murphey at the Nashville Opera House."

"Got it, sir. I'll send 'em right away."

Tate thanked him and rejoined Rebekah by the

passenger car, aware of the lingering hurt and question in her eyes. But he consoled himself, again, with the knowledge that what he'd done—and would do from this point forward—was for her best.

"Thank you again, Rebekah, for coming with me this weekend. And for delivering the notes to Mrs. Bixby. She'll get them to the various section leaders."

"You're welcome." She shifted the basket dangling from her arm. His mother had insisted on sending her with food, and he'd managed to slip in a little something himself. "Promise me you'll let me know . . . about your father."

"I will."

"And, Tate . . ."

The sudden blast of the train whistle sounded, and he welcomed the interruption, sensing she was about to press him for more.

"Once you've finished transcribing the first two movements," he continued, "we'll distribute them to everyone." He walked her closer to the door, able to tell by her expression that she knew exactly what he was doing. "I'll review the third movement when I return, likely later this week, then you can get started on that. We have seven weeks before we need to begin rehearsing as an orchestra. Which means, considering the time each section will require to learn their parts before assembling as a group, I have roughly three weeks to finish the fourth movement." That thought caused the weight in his chest to double in size. "I'll continue to compose while I'm here, as I can, at the church."

"And I'll continue to work on the violin solo. You already have a wonderful start. It's going to be a difficult piece, but Darrow Fulton can do it, I know he can. He's quite brilliant when he puts his mind to it."

Tate wished he had the same confidence in the man's ability that she did. "One more thing . . ."

He pulled the envelope addressed to Maestro Leplin from his coat pocket and handed it to her. She looked at the name, then back up at him. He steeled himself to the injured look clouding her expression.

"I promised you a reference letter, Rebekah. As I said before, I know Maestro Leplin and can all but assure you that you'll get an audition. But once he hears you, know that everything that comes your way from that point forward is due to your talent alone. Not to anything I will have said or done."

He thought again of what she'd told him last night. That she'd first learned how to play the fiddle from a slave. It would seem that the seeds of their mutual love for music had both been planted and nurtured in similarly improbable ways.

"All aboard!" a porter called, his voice nearly drowned out by the final whistle blast.

Tate pressed a quick kiss to her forehead, and she looked up at him.

"I wish you'd tell me what's wrong, Tate."

The hurt and uncertainty in her eyes threatened to dismantle his resolve. "As I told you, nothing's wrong. I . . . simply have a lot on my mind right now." He stepped back to allow her to board.

And as the train pulled away, she looked out the window and he smiled, doing his best to hide the fact that she was taking his heart with her.

He could already picture her playing in the symphony hall in New York, could see her walking out onto the stage. She wanted—and deserved—the opportunity to play in an orchestra. And her best chance for that was in New York. In time, if life were fair, she would earn the position of first chair. Politics would delay that for several years, perhaps a decade or two, but Rebekah was young. Not even twenty-four yet. She had her entire life before her, and he refused to be the one to stand in the way of her living it.

A stab of regret accompanied his recollection of first considering her too soft, too genteel to handle the company of a group of male musicians. While that might be true for most women, it was decidedly *un*true about her. She could hold her own with any musician he'd ever known. And she deserved so much more than he could give her now. He was going deaf. Be it weeks or months, it was going to happen. Which meant he would lose his job, of course. Who wanted to hire a deaf conductor?

His career was ending just as hers was beginning.

The train now a distant spot on the ribbon of rails, he started back up the mountain, mindful of the gray skies overhead. He scaled a rocky climb, recalling how much more easily she'd managed the trek this trip. She was strong and intelligent, unafraid in the face of challenge. And stubborn. The way she'd questioned him about whether or not he'd sought out the best physician . . .

Nearly an hour later, having hiked hard and fast, his heart pumping, he paused by a stream and drank his fill, then rested for a moment on a felled tree. The last ascent to the ridge awaited, then home . . .

To wait for his father to die.

The heaviness inside him slowly worked its way from his chest to his throat and made it nearly impossible to breathe. He bowed his head as emotions he'd stuffed down deep for far too long refused to stay there any longer.

The sun broke through the clouds, and he lifted his face to the warmth, aware of the wind through the pines, the cry of a hawk somewhere off in the distance, and the beat of his own heart.

As he'd done countless times, he withdrew Dr. Hamilton's letter from his pocket and read it again, as if the doctor's words might somehow read differently this time. He paused toward the end, his focus catching on a phrase, and he read it again. *"If you ever require anything from me, all you need do is ask."* So kind an offer.

Tate stood and tucked the letter back into his

pocket, then started up the ridge. There was nothing the doctor could do for him, he knew. If only there were something Dr. Hamilton could do for his father.

Like silk catching on barbed wire, the thought snagged. *If you ever require anything from me, all you need do is ask.*

Tate searched his memory. What was it Dr. Clarkston, the specialist in Philadelphia had said? A treatment that helps prolong a patient's life. But he'd used the word *simple,* Tate felt certain. And it had involved . . . draining the area around the lungs. Dr. Clarkston wasn't willing to come all the way to Chicory Hollow. But Knoxville was scarcely an hour away by train, so perhaps—

He made it back down the mountain in record time.

Rebekah disembarked the train in Nashville feeling as though she'd left half of herself back in Chicory Hollow. She'd cried most of the way to Knoxville, then had opened the basket and found the piece of wrapped molasses taffy Tate had stuck inside. She knew it was from him because he'd drawn a picture of a squirrel on the wax wrapper.

She'd spent the remainder of the trip trying to figure out why he was acting the way he had. And the more she thought about it, the more it came down to two possibilities.

Either he truly didn't feel about her the way she thought he did—the way she cared for him—or he was distancing himself from her because of the doctor's diagnosis. If the former, she would somehow find a way to accept that, and move on. And the sooner she got to New York, the better.

But if the latter were true . . .

If Nathaniel Tate Whitcomb thought he was going to be rid of her so easily, the man clearly did not possess the intelligence with which she'd credited him—and he didn't have an inkling as to how much she loved him.

Crowds pressed together on the station platform, trains arriving and departing, and passengers hurrying to reach their destinations. Someone bumped her from behind, and Rebekah tightened her grip on her reticule, having learned the hard way about pickpockets in Vienna.

"Miss Carrington, ma'am!"

Nearly to the steps exiting the platform, she heard her name being called, and turned. Armstead, Mrs. Cheatham's personal driver, stood waiting by one of the estate's carriages.

Bless you, Adelicia Cheatham.

Rebekah waved and made her way toward him when someone off to her right, a young boy, caught her attention. She looked over in time to see him reach into an older man's coat pocket and relieve him of his wallet. The man continued on, none the wiser, as indignation heated her from top to bottom.

"You there!" she called, starting toward him, and the boy turned.

Rebekah froze. Recognition shot through her like an arrow striking its mark. For him, too, judging by the widening of his eyes.

His meager frame appeared even slighter than when she'd first met him upon her arrival to Nashville months earlier, and his threadbare coat now sported a rip at the collar and along the sleeve. The shrewdness she'd recognized—and even admired—in him had deteriorated to desperation, and seeing the fear and hunger in his eyes broke her heart.

"Stay there," she called to him, trying to sound authoritative. "I want to talk to you."

The boy looked down, expertly riffled through the man's wallet, withdrew the money, then dropped the wallet and ran.

Rebekah gave chase.

She dropped her satchel and basket at Armstead's feet—"I'll be back!"—and kept running, mindful of the surprise in the man's face.

Her only goal was to catch that boy.

31

Skirts hiked, Rebekah fought to keep up, reticule bouncing on her wrist. But maneuvering her way in and out of the crowds took her longer than it did the boy. He simply ducked and ran, squirreling his way through the sea of passersby like a streak of lightning. He'd had more practice at this, no doubt. But she wasn't giving up.

On open ground, she would've given herself fairly good odds of catching him. But like this . . .

She spotted him about fifteen feet ahead of her, then saw him slip down an alleyway. Trying to think like a boy of seven or eight might, she knew she had only one option.

Winded, she doubled back to the alley she'd just passed and ran as hard as she could, heart pounding—when she heard the sound of someone else running equally as fast. She braced herself.

They reached the corner at the same time.

The boy, clearly shocked, his face all eyes, tried to slow down enough to turn when Rebekah grabbed him by the arm and held on. He fought and kicked, nearly landing a blow to her shin, but she moved just in time. And never let go.

"I'm not going to hurt you! I only want to talk."

He struggled and tried to kick her again. She slipped behind him and grabbed him by his upper arms. They were so thin, even through the threadbare coat, that her fingers nearly encircled them. She held him with his back against her.

"If you kick me again," she warned, "I'll give you such a wallop!" Knowing she wouldn't, she hoped she sounded like she meant it.

The boy stilled, but hardly relaxed. He was like a caged animal ready to strike. Or take off running.

"If I let go of you, do you promise not to run away? Or try and kick me again?"

He said nothing, but she sensed his keen little mind spinning.

The smell of his unwashed body and filthy clothing nearly overpowered her at this close proximity. "I promise I won't hurt you. And I won't turn you over to the authorities. I *only* want to talk to you for a moment."

Finally, he relaxed a little.

"I've thought about you, you know," she continued. "Several times, since first seeing you that day." She turned him around to face her, keeping ahold of his arm while mindful of his feet. "My name is Rebekah Carrington. What's yours?"

He hedged. "Name be William. But everybody calls me Billy."

She smiled. "Then Billy it is. Are you hungry, Billy?"

He eyed her. "This a trick to get my money?"

"First off, it's not your money."

He tensed.

"But I'm not going to take it from you. That would be much the same as me doing to you what you just did to the gentleman back at the train station. However, if I knew that man and could return his money to him, I would demand you take it back. But since that can't happen—"

"I *need* this money. More'n he does."

"While that may be true, it doesn't make stealing right. There are ways to earn money. Like you do when you sell your papers."

He grimaced. "Ain't got that job no more. Got all my papers stole, so they won't gimme no more to sell. And ain't nobody hirin'. Leastwise, that's what they say."

"I'm sorry to hear that."

She glanced around them, gaining her bearings and wondering how she could help him. Then she had a thought. Armstead was still waiting for her, but this wouldn't take long.

"Are you hungry?"

His gaze lit, then just as swiftly darkened with suspicion, and Rebekah's heart responded.

"There's a mercantile not far from here, Billy." She glanced in that direction. "Let me buy you some food, and we can talk for a minute."

Biting his lower lip, he cut his eyes to the right as though considering her offer, then looked back at her as if weighing whether or not she was trustworthy. Meeting his shrewd gaze, Rebekah prayed he would say yes.

He gave a simple nod, and then his eyes narrowed. "You run good for a girl."

She laughed, pleased at the grin tipping his mouth. "I told you I could run."

She pointed the way, and he followed.

The mercantile didn't appear to be crowded for a Monday afternoon, but Billy seemed hesitant to accompany her inside. Rebekah caught him eying the owner through the window of the front door and swiftly guessed why.

"Why don't you wait for me out here, and I'll be

right back." Opening the door, she prayed he wouldn't bolt.

Minutes later, she exited and didn't see him. Her heart fell—until she spotted him standing down by the corner. Billy gave her a quick nod and joined her on a bench beneath a large oak tree.

He tore into the bread and cheese, his little jaw working to get the food down to his belly. She handed him a bottle of milk, and he looked at it as if he held a treasure.

He gulped and gulped, the milk running down his chin. Then he wiped his mouth with his sleeve and tore off another hunk of bread.

"Where do you live, Billy?"

He shrugged. "I got plenty'a places."

She nodded. So much heartbreak in so few words. "And your parents?"

"Gone." He spoke around a bite of cheese in his mouth. "War took my Pa. But I ain't never knew him. I's only two when he died. And my ma . . ." He took another swig of milk, then paused and stared at something off in the distance. "The cholera got her last year." He blinked and went back to eating.

He said it so matter-of-factly that Rebekah could only stare, and think of how far removed her own experiences in life had been from this boy's. They'd both lost their fathers, but that's where the similarities ended. How she wished she could give him an alternative. Or at least a job.

A sharp whistle split the air and made them both jump.

Rebekah looked in the direction of the sound and saw an officer running toward them, one hand on his cap, the other wielding a wooden club.

"You there! *Hold up!*" he yelled.

Rebekah looked around to see who he was addressing, then realized he was looking at them. She turned to Billy beside her, only to find the boy gone, the half-drunk bottle of milk on the bench in his place.

A week came and went, and still no word from Tate.

Seated at the piano bench in his office, Rebekah stretched her tired neck and shoulder muscles and told herself not to worry. It was a long way from his parents' cabin to the telegraph office at the train depot, and he was going through a very difficult time, but she wanted to know how he was coping with it all—the loss of his father, the stress of finishing the fourth movement, all while dealing with his own personal tragedy. Had he told his family about his diagnosis yet?

Somehow, she doubted it. Knowing him, he wouldn't tell anyone else until he had no other choice. And would she do any differently?

She'd nearly finished transcribing copies of the first movement for each of the fifty orchestra members. She'd started the process two weeks ago, but her trip to Chicory Hollow had slowed her progress. And since returning, she'd done little else. Four more to go and the task would be complete, then she'd start on the second movement straightaway.

By now, she felt as if she could play the first movement—including each of the various instrumental parts—by heart.

She looked at the clock. Three thirty. She usually worked until closer to five. Then she looked at her hands—her fingers stained with ink, her joints aching—and she decided she'd had enough transcribing for one day. The last four copies could wait until tomorrow morning, then they'd be ready to distribute to the orchestra. She looked over at Tate's desk.

When was he coming back?

She retrieved her coat and reticule, extinguished the oil lamps, and closed the office door behind her, missing him, and wondering if he missed her.

"If you can't be in the orchestra, I guess you become the conductor's assistant. Or one of them. That's certainly the closest you'll ever come to it."

Already knowing who it was, she turned and met Darrow Fulton's condescending gaze, feeling his ever-present animosity for her simmering just beneath the surface. It occurred to her that this was the very spot, only steps away from Tate's office, where she'd first seen him again after so many years.

Up until now, she'd managed to avoid any personal confrontation with him, mostly by ducking into doorways when she was alone and saw him coming. The other times she'd seen him, Tate had been present. And Darrow Fulton didn't dare do anything to cross the *maestro*.

"Hello, Mr. Fulton. Is there something with which I can help you?"

He looked her up and down, not in a lascivious manner. More as though he considered her as something to be scraped off the bottom of his shoe. "Is the maestro back yet?"

"No, he isn't."

"When will he return?"

"I'm afraid I don't know."

A slow smile tipped his mouth. "But you *do* know I'm playing the violin solo for his symphony. At the grand opening. Mrs. Bixby gave me a note from the maestro himself."

She looked at him. Really looked at him. And realized he hadn't changed much through the years. All the girls she'd grown up with had thought Darrow Fulton so handsome, such a catch. Outwardly, to someone who didn't know him, she guessed he could be considered such. But he'd shown her the truth about himself early on, and she'd never seen him as anything but cruel. And undesirable.

"Yes, I know you're playing the solo. You *are* the concertmaster, after all."

"Something you will never be, Rebekah."

Tempted, in a way, to tell him about her plan to go to New York after the opening of the new opera hall, she didn't dare. Mainly because entrusting that kind of information to a man such as Darrow Fulton would be like casting pearls before swine. But also because—despite Tate's repeated assurances—she wasn't at all certain that Maestro Leplin of the New York Philharmonic would consider her good enough to warrant an invitation to join them.

"I'm going to take my leave of you now, Mr. Fulton."

She attempted to step past him, but he blocked her way.

She sighed. "Are you also planning to follow me home and break my bow again, Darrow?"

"I didn't care, you know, about your taking the tutoring position. It was a waste of my time anyway. I was only doing it for the money."

"Yes, I'm well aware of why you were doing it. Thankfully, you didn't do any lasting damage. Pauline is progressing wonderfully."

His eyes narrowed. "You were always so uppity, Rebekah. So confident and sure of yourself. You never did know your place."

"My *place?*" She didn't know what possessed her, but she laughed. "Do you have any idea that it was *your* spitefulness and cruelty, your arrogance, the way you tormented me all those years ago, that *pushed* me to work harder than I ever would have . . . simply to be as good as you were?"

"And yet you never measured up."

She didn't answer immediately. "Perhaps not.

But at least I grew up, Darrow. And I learned that while competition can, for a time, motivate you to become a better musician, it's only when you truly fall in love with the music—when it nurtures you, regenerates you, and when you learn to respect the gift you've been given—that a door finally opens, and you get the chance to become the musician you're capable of being. But you won't ever be that musician until you step aside and become second. Because in the end, it's not about the musician. It's about the music. And honoring the One who gave it."

He laughed beneath his breath. "Says a woman who will never know what it means to be a member of a philharmonic."

"I wouldn't be so sure about that. New York recently admitted their first female."

"And we all know how she managed to do that too." A disgusting smile tipped his mouth. "And what . . . *position* she was playing."

Rebekah slapped him hard across the face. She wasn't sure which of them was more surprised, him or her. Her hand stung, but the pain was nothing compared to the anger roiling inside her. "You've always been such a coward, Darrow. I didn't realize it all those years ago. But . . . you were afraid. Afraid of being bettered by a female. And . . ." She searched his gaze, his own features mottled with anger. "I think you still are."

She pushed past him, her body shaking, blood rushing in her ears. She bid Mrs. Bixby and Mrs.

Murphey good day, attempting to act as normal as possible, and started walking in the direction of Belmont.

She'd declined use of a carriage this morning and was glad now that she had. She needed to burn off some frustration. What a pompous, condescending—

She clenched her jaw, not proud of losing her temper with Darrow, but she couldn't bring herself to regret it either.

The man had had it coming—for the last fifteen years!

Late March skies boasted a cloudless robin's egg blue, and the temperature hinted of spring. It felt good to walk. With each step, she felt her pulse returning to normal.

She passed the street that led to her mother's house and slowed. She hadn't been by to see her in several days, so a visit was due. Although she dreaded the cool reception her mother would likely give her, returning earlier in the day to Belmont meant Mrs. Cheatham would likely be there. And though Rebekah wasn't exactly avoiding her, she could tell Adelicia wanted more information about where she'd traveled the weekend prior, the weekend spent in Chicory Hollow.

But Rebekah could hardly admit to it. Not when Tate had gone to such lengths to keep that part of his life private. So visiting her mother won out.

With every corner she turned, she found herself

searching for Billy, watching for a worn red cap. Though he'd left the half-drunk milk behind that day, he'd managed to take the bread and cheese with him. She hoped he wasn't going hungry.

Passing shop after shop, she couldn't help but contrast life in Nashville with life in Chicory Hollow. Tate's childhood home was another world away—and definitely a step back in time. Yet she liked it. Or at least liked parts of it. The natural beauty, the quiet. How in early morning the clouds hovered over the highest peaks and looked more like an artist's rendering than reality. And she liked Tate's family too. How they interacted and loved each other.

But life in Chicory Hollow held a brutal quality too. Especially in light of what Tate had told her about the highlanders having their own ways of meting out justice. It didn't take much imagination for her to picture what men like Virgil and Banty Slokum would do to someone who crossed them. It wasn't a pleasant thought.

She slowed as she approached the house. No sign of the carriage, which usually meant Barton was gone. As she always did, she opted to walk around to the back. Not seeing Delphia inside, she knocked on the kitchen door. Then Delphia stepped from the pantry and peered around the corner. The instant Rebekah saw her troubled expression, she knew something was wrong.

Delphia opened the door. "Come on in, child."

"Is he here?" Rebekah whispered.

"No, but the po-lice has been."

"The police? Why?" Rebekah stepped inside and closed the door behind her.

"They come askin' 'bout Mr. Ledbetter this mornin'. Wantin' to talk to him. But he ain't here, I tol' 'em. Then your mama, she tol' 'em the same. They left right after. Didn't say nothin' more."

"Where is he?"

Delphia shrugged, stirring a pot on the stove. "Mr. Ledbetter, he comes and goes to the tune'a what pleases him. Don't answer to nobody."

"When's the last time you saw him?"

"Two days ago, I reckon. But I heard him come in late last night. He done gone again 'fore I's up this mornin'."

Rebekah wished the man would go away and never come back. While she had no idea what the authorities wanted with him, she wasn't at all surprised he'd done something worthy of their attention. "Do you think mother's in a frame of mind to see me today?"

"She might be . . . if she was here. She gone to have lunch with her women friends. One of 'em came by and got her, and she ain't home just yet. But I'm glad you come by." Delphia's smile held a sparkle. "I got some things to give you. Letter come the other day. One of the gals who helps during the day, she reads—right good, too—and said it be for you."

Delphia handed her an envelope.

Rebekah read the return address. "Oh, it's from

Sally! She told me she would write once she knew the plans for her and Sebastian's wedding."

Delphia laughed. "Still can't believe she went and got her a foreign man. Here's the other thing." She opened a cupboard drawer. "Found these when I's cleanin' the dinin' room hutch last week. Stuck way in the back, in a servin' dish we use only once a year, at Christmas. Only this past year, we didn't do any celebratin', seein' as how your precious grandmama had just . . ."

Delphia let the words fade as she pulled out a thick bundle of envelopes. She handed them to Rebekah. The envelopes, several dozen at a glance, were tied with a festive red ribbon, like something that might have once been used to wrap a gift.

Rebekah's eyes widened. "These are my letters . . . to Nana."

"I know." Delphia winked. "Could'a blowed me over when I found 'em. You know I can't read none, but I know a person's mark. And I know yours right good. Plus that fancy stamp on the front always tol' me your grandmama had gotten a letter from far away. Used to make her so happy. *Mmmhmm* . . . She'd read it time and again. Even read it to me. Least some of it. I come in late at night and find her asleep with one of your letters in her lap."

Rebekah thumbed through the envelopes, then paused. "You said they were in the dining room. What were they doing in there?"

"That's what I don't know. Lessin' they sprouted legs and walked 'emselves on in there. Mr. Ledbetter, he got rid of everythin' from your grandmama's room right after she died. If I'd known he was doin' that, I'd'a got some things for you. Bless your grandma Ellen's sweet soul," she added softly, then gestured to the letters. "I knew you'd be glad to have 'em."

"Yes, I am. Thank you so much." Rebekah opened her reticule to slip the letters inside when she noticed some writing on the back of the bottom envelope. She pulled the envelope out, and recognized her grandmother's elegant script.

Jesus, please help Rebekah learn the difficult piece of music Herr Vandal is teaching her. I don't yet believe she realizes how much talent you've given her. And I think she's scared, Lord. I can hear it behind her words. Give my granddaughter the courage she needs to embrace your will for her life, no matter where it leads her. November 26, 1866 (Psalm 18:2)

Rebekah's eyes filled with tears.

"What is it, child? Somethin' wrong?"

Rebekah shook her head. "Grandmother wrote a prayer on the back—along with a Scripture reference." She looked at the next envelope, which also bore her grandmother's familiar handwriting. As did the rest. "It looks like she wrote something on the back of all of them, including the date." She held them out for Delphia to see.

Delphia ran a finger over the script. "Well, I'll be . . . Almost like a visit from heaven, ain't it?"

"Yes," Rebekah whispered. "That's exactly what it's like." She slipped the bundle into her reticule, grateful, but still wondering how the letters had gotten into the dining room hutch.

And who put them there.

"Miss Carrington . . . is that you?"

Hearing Mrs. Cheatham's voice wafting from the small study, Rebekah paused in the foyer. She'd hoped to sneak in unseen, eager to spend the evening reading the notes her grandmother had written on the backs of the letters. Yet she knew she had no choice.

"Yes, ma'am," Rebekah answered, and laid her reticule on the side table. She walked through the library to the small study, a fire blazing in the hearth. "How are you this afternoon, Mrs. Cheatham?"

Her employer glanced toward the window. "Or perhaps we should say *evening,* Miss Carrington. It's nearly dark."

"Yes, I had some errands to run after I left the opera house." She'd quickly learned it was best to avoid the subject of her mother—or her home here in town. It only led to more questions.

Mrs. Cheatham motioned for her to sit, the

gesture more of a decree than a request. Rebekah sat.

"Have you been avoiding me, Miss Carrington?"

Adelicia's frankness caught her off guard. "No . . . of c-course not, Mrs. Cheatham. I've simply been keeping long hours."

"And most of them away from Belmont."

"Yes, ma'am. Transcribing Maestro Whitcomb's symphony is taking far more time than I imagined." Rebekah held out her ink-stained hands as though offering proof. "But I'm almost finished copying the first movement, then will begin on the second."

Mrs. Cheatham held her gaze, and Rebekah felt as though the woman could read her every thought.

"As I'm sure you know by now, Miss Carrington, I value straightforwardness in people, and especially in my employees. Hence, I will be straightforward with you. And I want an honest answer. I believe I deserve that much."

Rebekah felt a slight shudder up her spine, wondering if this was about what she thought it was about. If Mrs. Cheatham pressed her for details about that weekend, wanting to know where she'd gone and with whom, Rebekah knew she'd have to tell her at least part of the truth. That she'd gone with Tate . . . somewhere.

But telling only part of the truth would make the situation appear the exact opposite of what it had been—which was completely innocent. They hadn't done anything wrong. But to anyone else looking on, it might appear as though they'd chosen to compromise their character.

Which, judging from Adelicia Cheatham's penetrating gaze, was precisely what the woman thought.

32

"Miss Carrington, is the Nashville Philharmonic in peril of losing Maestro Whitcomb?"

Rebekah blinked, the question from Mrs. Cheatham *not* being the question she'd expected. Thankfully so. Yet she still kept her guard up. Because with what she knew about Tate's situation, she walked a fine line in how she responded. "Is the Nashville Philharmonic in peril of *losing* him?" she parroted, and instantly realized that was not a wise choice.

"I have never considered coyness an attractive quality, Miss Carrington. And, before this very moment, have never witnessed it in you. May I say, it is not becoming." Her gaze, already stern, only grew more so. "I will rephrase my question. To your knowledge, does Maestro Whitcomb intend to accept a position as conductor elsewhere?"

"No! Not at all, Mrs. Cheatham." Relieved, she tried for a smile. "I give you my word . . . he is not.

Please, ask himself yourself. He'll be more than happy to allay any fears you have in that regard."

"I would ask him, Miss Carrington, if he would ever return from . . . wherever he is!"

Knowing Mrs. Cheatham had a point, Rebekah found herself at a loss for what else to say without revealing Tate's confidence.

After a moment, a single dark brow rose in arched perfection. "Do *you* know where he is, Miss Carrington?"

Rebekah hesitated, weighing her options, then realized her hesitation had already revealed her answer. Weary of secrets and of having to watch every word she said, she sighed. "Yes, ma'am. I know where he is."

"And?"

"And . . . it's not mine to tell you, Mrs. Cheatham. But . . ." Seeing the storm gathering behind her employer's deceptively calm demeanor, she hurriedly added, "I can assure you it's precisely where you would be if you were in his situation."

Adelicia regarded her for a moment. "And what situation is that, Miss Carrington?"

Rebekah glanced down at her lap. *Tate, please forgive me.* "Maestro Whitcomb's father is dying."

The air in the room seemed to grow thinner. Even the pendulum's *ticktock* in the grandfather clock seemed to fade into hiding.

"I see," Mrs. Cheatham whispered, then looked away. "And . . . the maestro . . . he's with his father now? And with his family?"

"Yes, ma'am."

The silence stretched between them.

"And would I be correct in assuming, Miss Carrington, that *he* was the *friend* who needed you the weekend you were gone?"

Rebekah felt her face heat, remembering what she'd told Mrs. Cheatham before she'd left, and how it must appear to her now. "Yes, ma'am, you would. But I can assure you that neither Maestro Whitcomb or I have undermined our integrity in any way. I simply happened to be with him when he received the news. And I volunteered"—she paused—"or rather, I *insisted* on going with him. But I give you my solemn vow, nothing untoward has happened between us."

Mrs. Cheatham held her gaze and—after what seemed like eons—the hint of warmth gradually slid into her features. "Your latter assertion, while greatly appreciated, was never a concern for me, Miss Carrington. The strength of your character and moral fiber was solidified in my eyes the night you played the violin at my dinner party."

Rebekah frowned. "I'm . . . afraid I don't understand."

"With a word, you could have claimed responsibility for the performance that night, a performance that was talked about at teas and dinners for days and weeks following. Or you could have stepped forward when the maestro himself continued to seek the identity of the *master violinist*. But you did not. You did not seek fame in the moment, nor did you push yourself into the limelight for your own glory. You honored your word and kept the confidence I requested that you keep. And now, in return, I shall keep yours."

Retiring to bed early that night, Rebekah untied the ribbon from around the letters she'd written to her grandmother. She'd looked forward to this moment since Delphia had given them to her earlier in the day.

She glanced at the hand-stamped dates on the envelopes and noticed they weren't in chronological order. She considered taking a moment and reordering them, then decided to read them as Nana had bundled them instead. At least, she assumed it had been Nana.

> Dearest Lord, my precious Rebekah is still homesick. And my knowing that her heart is breaking, is breaking mine as well. Vienna is for the best, I know. I don't doubt your guiding hand in that decision for a single moment. Especially knowing what I know now.

She paused from reading. Knowing what she knew now . . . what had her nana meant by that? Wondering, Rebekah continued.

> You are Lord of Vienna same as you are Lord of Nashville. I know that. And my

heart knows it too. Still, both Rebekah and I are hurting. Comfort and keep us close to you, Jesus. May 28, 1861 (2 Corinthians 1:3–4)

Rebekah withdrew the letter from that envelope and read what she'd written nearly ten years ago now. She didn't recall writing the words so much as she recalled the loneliness behind them. And she smiled at how she'd phrased her thoughts—most definitely like those of a young girl—and also at the tiny heart she'd drawn by her name at the bottom. Same as Nana had always drawn when closing her letters.

Rebekah folded the stationery, slipped it back inside, and then paused, noting the Scripture reference. She did a quick scan of the envelopes. It appeared as though her grandmother had included one at the end of each prayer.

Rebekah retrieved her Bible from her desk and flipped to the book of Second Corinthians. She scanned down.

Blessed be God, even the Father of our Lord Jesus Christ, the Father of mercies, and the God of all comfort; Who comforteth us in all our tribulation, that we may be able to comfort them which are in any trouble, by the comfort wherewith we ourselves are comforted of God.

Rebekah ran a forefinger over the verses, appreciating them more now than before, since they'd been special to her grandmother. She glanced back at the first envelope she'd read when Delphia had presented the bundle to her, and looked up that reference as well.

Her gaze hovered over a portion of the verse.

> The Lord is my rock, and my fortress, and my deliverer; my God, my strength, in whom I will trust . . .

Again, the Scripture mirrored her grandmother's prayer, and was a good reminder for Rebekah in her circumstances. Grateful for these insights into her grandmother's heart, she moved to the next envelope.

> Dearest Lord, thank you for being with Rebekah during the recital. I can tell she's pleased with how she performed, and that gladdens my heart in ways she will never know. But you do. She has so much of her father in her, which is good in one sense, yet troubling in another. Even from a young age, my beloved son hesitated to undertake anything he could not do well from the outset. While, as a mother, I appreciated his dedication and drive, I am now of the mind that this attitude greatly narrows one's choices in

life. Help my granddaughter to stretch herself, to reach beyond the comfortable. Give Rebekah the courage to risk the possibility of failure. And when she fails, be there for her. Because in those moments, perhaps more than any other, we are more prone to hear your voice and sense your presence. April 12, 1865 (Romans 8:28)

Once again, she read the letter within. And reading it, she felt a touch of the original thrill she'd experienced over the recital she'd written to Nana about. She remembered that day so well. Because on that day, for the first time in her young life, she'd begun to believe that she was truly good at playing the violin.

Already familiar with the Scripture reference Nana had noted, she didn't take the time to look it up.

The next envelope looked especially worn and well handled.

Father, please bring a special man into Rebekah's life. A man who loves you first, before anyone or anything else, and who will love my precious granddaughter as he loves himself. A man like her father, who will encourage Rebekah in her music. A man who will help her take steps closer to Christ, like my sweet Robert did for me. I

miss him, Jesus, even after all these years.
Please tell him I love him, until I can
tell him again myself. August 8, 1868
(Proverbs 3:5–6)

Tears welled in her eyes. *Oh, Nana . . .*

Rebekah pressed the envelope to her chest.
Hadn't she found a man just like that? Hadn't God
brought them together? She saw it. Now if only
Tate would.

She read the letter within, and wondered how her
grandmother had ever been prompted to pray
for her future husband. The letter Rebekah had
written contained nothing about a young man, or
love, or that facet of life.

Deciding to leave the Scripture references for
another time, she read on, enjoying the insights into
Nana's thoughts and prayers, as well as the
occasional prayer Nana included for herself
and the minor aches and pains she lived with.
Growing older seemed a challenge, to say the
least.

Halfway through the stack, Rebekah yawned, the
events of the day and week catching up to her.
She'd honestly thought she would read every one
of the envelopes that night. But as she looked at
the bundle and thought of what they represented—
visits from heaven, as Delphia had said—she
decided to savor them.

Because after she read them, there would be no
more.

• • •

A few days later, seated at the desk in her bedroom, Rebekah finished transcribing the seventh copy of the second movement in Tate's symphony. Only forty-three to go.

Never would she have guessed that all the transcribing she'd done during her years in Vienna—both for herself and Maestro Heilig—would have prepared her to assist a conductor in actually composing a symphony that hundreds, if not thousands, of people would someday hear. If only all of life's twists and turns were that transparent.

If only she could somehow peer into the future and see that what she was experiencing in the present—especially amidst a sorrowful time—was all in preparation for something yet to come. How differently she would view her life then, witnessing God's sovereignty with such clarity.

Determined to remember that, she paused to let the ink dry, enjoying the satisfaction that came with finishing each copy.

A knock sounded on the bedroom door, and she checked the time. Nearly half past seven. Hardly late, especially considering Dr. and Mrs. Cheatham were attending a dinner party and wouldn't be home until well past midnight. Still . . .

In her stockinged feet, she opened the door.

"Miss Carrington, a telegram come for you, ma'am." Cordina stood in the darkened hallway, oil lamp in hand, an almost mischievous look on her face.

Rebekah grinned. Tate! It had to be from Tate. *Finally*. She waited. "And . . . where *is* the telegram?"

Cordina blinked. "Oh . . . You got to come and get it, ma'am. The man, the one who brung it, he's . . . waitin' at the front door. Said he got to give it to you hisself."

Odd but . . . "All right, let me put on my boots. I'll be right there."

Rebekah grabbed her boots and shoved her feet in, then hurriedly laced them, missing eyelets as she went and not caring. Tate had finally sent word! And it was about time. Though she understood, with all he must've been through in recent days. Cattabelle too. And the rest of his family. She wished she'd been there with them, wished she could have done something to help.

She bustled down the dark hallway and across the grand salon, not bothering to bring an oil lamp. She now knew the house almost as well in the dark as she did in the light.

She crossed the foyer and gave *Ruth Gleaning*— Mrs. Cheatham's lovely, if not eyebrow-raising statue—a quick pat on the arm, then opened the front door. But . . . saw no one. She stepped outside to look, the night wind feeling especially chilly as she stood there in only her day dress.

"Personal telegram for . . . Miss Rebekah Carrington."

Hearing his familiar voice behind her, she felt a rush of emotion and turned to see him standing in the doorway of the library. Half hidden by shadows, he could've almost been a figment of her imagination. But when she closed the distance between them, and he pulled her against his chest, the solid feel of muscle and man told her he was real.

"I'm sorry," he whispered, cradling her head, "for taking so long to get back, and for not sending you word as I promised I would do."

"I've only thought about you constantly. About your mother, Opal, everyone. All you've been through." Rebekah drew back slightly. "My deepest condolences on your father's passing, Tate. When . . . did it happen?"

To her shock, he smiled and glanced past her. "Is there a place we can talk?"

33

T ate followed her into the small study, wanting to take her into his arms again, but resisting the temptation, remembering his promise to himself. He shed his coat and added wood to the waning fire in the hearth, then stirred the embers until the flames sparked to life again.

He joined her on the sofa, eager to answer the questions in her eyes. "I'm pleased to report that— thanks to you, Rebekah, and to Dr. Hamilton—my father is very much alive and regaining his strength."

"Tate," she whispered. "That's wonderful! But . . . how? What happened?"

"After seeing you to the station that day, I started back up the mountain and began thinking about Dr. Hamilton's letter. Then I thought of Dr. Clarkston, the physician who wrote me from Philadelphia about the treatment for consumption—"

Rebekah nodded. "I remember."

"And it struck me . . . If the procedure was, indeed, that simple, why not ask Dr. Hamilton if he would come and do it himself? I sent him a telegram on Monday afternoon, then went back down Tuesday to find he'd already responded and was on his way."

Rebekah's watery smile said it all.

"I know." Tate recounted the events of recent days, feeling a tug of emotion himself. "Dr. Hamilton performed the procedure there in my parents' bedroom, then stayed with us for two days following."

"In the cabin?" she asked.

He nodded. "He slept right there on the sofa. I shared a bed with Benjamin. An experience I hope to never repeat again."

She laughed, and the sound was precious to him.

"So the doctor knows, then. About—"

"My family." He nodded. "And as it turns out, the prestigious Dr. Hamilton was born in a small town about ninety miles south of here, in

Fayetteville, Tennessee. He and his parents and six brothers and sisters lived in a two-room cabin similar to ours. Yet he also understands how . . . complex the world of the symphony can be."

"So he, too, has agreed to keep that part of your life private."

"Precisely."

Her expression radiant, she simply looked at him and shook her head, and the effect was like a tonic.

A rap on the door, and Cordina peered inside. "Got a pot of tea and some warm tea cakes if y'all's hungry. After that . . . telegram."

"Are we ever." Tate rose and pulled the door open the rest of the way. "Thank you, Cordina, for cooperating with me earlier."

"My pleasure, sir." Her eyes sparking with humor, the woman poured them each a cup, then closed the door as she left.

"And following the procedure, your father's health improved," Rebekah prompted.

"Not immediately." Tate popped a warm tea cake into his mouth, then washed it down with a cup of tea. "Even though Dr. Hamilton removed a lot of fluid from around his lungs, my father's health was weakened from the long struggle . . ."

They sat by the fire in the small study and talked. An hour passed, and the conversation never waned. He only knew that he didn't want to leave. And she didn't seem in any hurry to be rid of him. He'd missed her more than he could have imagined, yet still held to his decision—painful as it was—that she deserved so much more than he could give her.

"And though you haven't asked me about it yet . . ." He reached for his coat, pulled the stack of sheet music, folded lengthwise, from his pocket, and held the pages out to her. "I finished it."

Her eyes lit. "The violin solo?"

"The entire fourth movement."

Her mouth slipped open. "You didn't!"

He laughed. "I did."

She took the pages and began reading, her fingers tapping, counting off the time on the edge of the sofa cushion, her lips moving silently. She glanced up, her eyes wide. "This is . . . splendid!" Then she went back to reading.

Tate watched her, enjoying the chance to look at her, grateful for the opportunity to be with her. For as long as he could.

"Tate, how did you do this? And so quickly?" Seriousness swept her expression. "I realize you've been working on this for months. It's been simmering inside you. Still . . ."

"I know it needs work. But being back in the mountains gave me the inspiration I needed." *As did being with you,* he wanted to add, but didn't.

She straightened the sheet music, then held it to her chest. "I can't wait to hear it. And the violin solo . . ." She flipped back a few pages. "Already, I can hear your father's fiddle in it, and echoes of his *favorite* song. I'm reminded of Vivaldi, too, in the more grueling measures . . ." Her brow furrowed as she studied the notes more closely, as though hearing them in her head.

"I admit, I was inspired by his *Four Seasons*."

"You've written some extremely challenging runs, Tate."

"Do you still believe Darrow Fulton can do it?"

She looked up, and an odd expression flickered over her face. "Yes." She nodded. "I believe he can. While aspects of his personality can be . . . challenging, he's still one of the most gifted violinists I've ever known."

"I agree with you. On both counts." He winked. "But before we give it to him, I'd appreciate your playing it through several times. I'm sure you'll have ideas that will improve it."

She smiled. "I'd be honored."

The fire crackling and popping in the hearth drew her gaze, but then she looked back at him. And Tate knew what she was going to say before she said it.

"How are you feeling?" she asked softly.

"Overall . . . I'm well. I've had a couple of . . . episodes since seeing you last. Much as the ones before. But at least nothing seems to be getting worse."

A knock sounded again, tentative this time, before the door opened.

Seeing who it was, Tate immediately rose and offered a bow. "Dr. and Mrs. Cheatham. Good evening, sir. Ma'am."

The couple stood in the doorway looking rather astonished, and with good reason, Tate knew. Especially when a glance at the mantel clock told him it was well past midnight. Mrs. Cheatham was the first to speak.

"Maestro Whitcomb, how pleasant, though surprising, to see you again. You've returned from . . . being gone."

"Yes, ma'am. I'm sure it is a surprise. It's truly good to be back again. And to be here, at Belmont. I've missed . . . so much in my absence."

Dr. Cheatham shook his hand. "My wife and I are looking forward to May, and to hearing your symphony, Maestro."

"Thank you, sir. I'm looking forward to it, too. Especially now that it's finished."

Mrs. Cheatham smiled. "That's certainly wonderful news, Maestro. Some gloriously wonderful muse must have inspired you to that end."

Not missing the subtle nudge in her tone, Tate smiled and reached for his coat. "Yes, ma'am. Both glorious *and* wonderful. But now, if you'll all excuse me, I'll take my leave so you can retire. Miss Carrington, until tomorrow."

Rebekah handed him the stack of sheet music, and her fingers brushed his as she did. Even that slightest touch moved him.

Later that night, as he lay in his bed in the dark, he prayed for her future in New York. Then prayed for his own, without her.

• • •

"There! That's it!" Rebekah set down her bow and quickly penciled in the final notations on the music for the violin solo. "It needed a double, then triple stop in those first measures on page three. That helps build the tension." She blinked, her eyes so fatigued that the notes were all but blurring in her vision. "And the arpeggios we added in measures sixty-two through seventy-eight, like the previous sets, must be fast but clean. That makes all the difference."

Tate played a few measures again on the piano. "And the section you noted at the first that should be played pizzicato, that was a very nice touch as well."

She took a tiny bow.

He grinned. "You know what we say when someone plays pizzicato back home in Chicory Hollow?"

She shook her head.

"We say, 'Ya done some mighty fine pluckin' on that there fiddle.'"

Rebekah laughed, still surprised at how quickly he could slip back into the cadence of a highlander.

She'd made a point of telling Mrs. Cheatham about Tate's father's procedure and his improving health. It only seemed right, under the circumstances. She couldn't allow Mrs. Cheatham to continue thinking Tate's father was on the verge of death.

A knock on the door drew their attention, and she laid the violin on the piano in front of Tate. They'd agreed it would still be best for appearances—Mrs. Cheatham's primarily—if Rebekah's ability to play the violin wasn't made public. Anyone passing by in the hallway would simply think it was Tate who'd been playing.

"Come in," he announced.

Adams, one of the violinists, peered inside. He held up his copy of the symphony. "May I say *bravo,* Maestro Whitcomb. I can't tell you how thrilled we all are to have this opportunity, sir. The men send their gratitude."

"The honor is mine, Adams. Please pass that along to the others."

"Yes, sir. I'll do that, sir."

The door closed and Rebekah's heart swelled with pride. Did Tate have any idea how talented he was? And how beloved by these men, no matter how demanding and harsh he might be on occasion. Though those occasions were becoming more rare as the weeks went on.

"You still hold that Darrow Fulton can do this, correct?"

Not for the first time, Rebekah noticed how his gaze dropped to her lips as she readied a reply. It was happening more and more as the days passed. But the gesture was far from romantic on his part. She knew what *that* looked like, and this was entirely different.

Opening her mouth to answer, she briefly

considered sharing with him about what Darrow had said to her. Yet she didn't wish to add to Tate's load. He already had enough to bear. "I know he can do this, Tate. I grew up watching him play. He mastered Paganini by the age of eleven. He's brilliant."

"And what age were you? Nine?"

She gave him a look. "One thing I think could help would be for you to give him a word of encouragement." Seeing his frown forming, she hastened to continue. "He greatly respects you. That's clear to see. And when someone you respect takes the time to affirm you—sincerely, of course—that can make a world of difference."

His frown was slow to fade. "To the man's credit, he does seem to be doing better these days."

She smiled. "Darrow Fulton will do splendidly on the solo. Don't worry."

But despite her assurances, he did look worried. And weary.

The last three weeks had been the busiest and most rewarding she could remember. She'd recommended very few changes to the fourth movement, for the simple reason that it was already a *tour de force*. All movements had been transcribed and distributed to the orchestra members. Now all that remained was to transcribe a final copy of the violin solo for Darrow Fulton, and she would do that today.

She looked over the music spread out atop the piano and hoped Darrow realized what a privilege and honor he was being given. An honor that usually came along only once in a violinist's lifetime.

Tate rose from the piano, rubbing the back of his neck. "I have half an hour before orchestra rehearsal. I think I'm going to lie down for a few minutes."

She noted the furrows in his brow. "Another headache?"

"I don't think so. I'm simply tired. And thirsty."

He crossed to the table on the far wall and poured himself a glass of water. Meanwhile, she fetched a fresh supply of staff paper from the cupboard.

"Tate, did you remember to ask Mrs. Bixby to secure seats for your parents?"

When he didn't reply, she looked back at him. His back was to her.

"Tate?" she said again in a normal voice, trying not to go where her fears were taking her. "Tate, can you hear me?" She stared at his back, loving him, afraid for him, wanting to be so much more to him than she was—and that he would allow her to be. "I love you, Tate Whitcomb. With all my heart. And have for some time now. It doesn't matter to me that you're—"

He turned back. And for a moment, she thought he'd heard every word.

"If I happen to go to sleep, Rebekah, would you mind waking me up in time for the rehearsal?"

She nodded. "Certainly."

He lay down on the sofa in the corner and, as she'd anticipated, was asleep within minutes. She made note of the time and when to awaken him.

He hadn't touched her in an intimate way since they'd kissed on the sofa that last night in Chicory Hollow. And she'd been the one to instigate that. She sighed, the root of hurt and disappointment reaching deep. Perhaps that *had* been a mistake on her part. And perhaps he really had been trying to give her a hint that morning when she'd boarded the train.

Unwilling to give in to that possibility—not yet—she reached for a fresh pencil and paper, when her gaze fell to the updated rehearsal schedule Tate had distributed that morning.

Individual section rehearsals were already under way, and going well. Next Monday, only four days hence, the entire orchestra would begin practicing together. Then four weeks and two days from tonight the new opera house would open, and Nathaniel Tate Whitcomb would take the stage for what was, in a conductor's career, his finest hour.

Please, Lord, please . . . don't let it also be his last.

Later that night, Rebekah crawled into bed, the bundle of letters beside her on the bedside table. In recent days she'd taken the time to look up all the Scripture references she'd skipped while reading the letters. What an encouragement that had proven to be.

Now only two envelopes remained. It had taken all of her willpower last evening to save them.

Soon she would have read them all. No more "heavenly visits" with Nana. Even as she held the last two envelopes, the melancholy of something being lost to the past was foremost in her mind. And she felt a sense of disappointment too. She'd hoped her grandmother might have written something about Barton, perhaps left behind a clue as to whether she'd feared for her life with him. Or perhaps indicated she had known that the man was planning to steal her money.

Rebekah sighed, realizing she'd likely read one too many novels in her youth. She turned over the top envelope and read the first sentence.

And her grandmother's words pricked her heart.

I fear for my granddaughter tonight, Lord. I don't know why, but I do. I wish I could talk to her. Hear her voice. If only for a moment. Simply to know she's well. And safe. The letter I wrote to her today will take at least a week, if not more, to reach her. The one that I received from her yesterday was written almost two weeks ago. I feel . . .

An indentation following the word *feel* pressed into the envelope significantly more than the handwriting had done. As though Nana had paused, the tip of her pen pressing down hard as the next thought formed.

Rebekah stared at the spot and brushed her fingertip over it. She'd never thought about her grandmother being afraid for her when she lived in Vienna. After all, the danger had been back here. With Barton.

She read on.

> . . . cheated of knowing her as well as I would if she were still here. I want to share her life, instead of an occasional letter and a handful of months every two years. Pardon my complaining, Lord. I have so much for which to be grateful, I know. Why do I always seem to . . .

Nana had run out of room and continued the prayer angled up the side of the envelope, her handwriting cramped and narrowly spaced.

> . . . focus on what I don't have instead of what I do? Keep her safe, Lord, and guard her heart. As much as I love her, I know you love her more. So please, hold her close while I cannot. May 29, 1869 (Genesis 31:49)

Rebekah felt a familiar stinging behind her eyes. She looked at the date again. May twenty-ninth.

She searched her memory for any significance that date might have held for her but came up short. She sighed. She wished she'd written Nana more often than she had.

Seventy-one.

That was the number of envelopes in the bundle. Was that all the letters she'd written to her grandmother over the past ten years? It couldn't be. She was certain she'd written more. At least one per month. And yet, why would Nana have saved some of the letters and not others?

Seventy-one.

She'd worked the math. That wasn't even one letter per month. More like seven letters per year with an extra one thrown in every now and then. She'd consoled herself by subtracting the months when Nana came to visit every two years. Because, of course, they hadn't exchanged missives then. Still . . . What was it Delphia had told her? That at night she would come into Nana's bedroom to find her reading and rereading the letters.

Yet—Rebekah fingered the envelope—the best she could do with disappointments from the past was to learn from them. So vowing to do that, she reached for her Bible on her bedside table, then remembered she'd left it in the small study earlier that morning.

Cozy and warm in her bed, she decided to leave the verses for later and turned over the last envelope.

Her gaze went to the date first—November 24, 1870—and she sat up a little straighter. Only days before her grandmother had died.

She couldn't read the words fast enough.

Thank you for my precious granddaughter, Lord. For her exuberant spirit, for her talent, for her life in Vienna, and for her love for you. She has grown up into a beautiful young woman. Thank you for Sally, who went willingly when I asked her to and who has so faithfully abided by my wishes all these years. Thank you for walking with me every step of the way, even on those occasions when I haven't followed you as closely as I should have.

Rebekah looked at the date again. *Thanksgiving.* The twenty-fourth of November had been Thanksgiving. The prayer made more sense now.

Lord, I don't know why things sometimes happen the way they do, or why you allow them to. While I've never doubted your power that I can recall (granted, your memory is better than mine) . . .

Despite the seriousness of her grandmother's thoughts, Rebekah had to smile. Because she could *hear* Nana saying that.

. . . I have often doubted your ways. And so it is again. I realize it is wrong to do such, yet to deny it with you is senseless. You see my heart laid bare, even the parts I would beg be kept hidden from you. These past ten years have been the longest and most arduous of my life. How often I have questioned if I made the right decision all those years ago. But after sifting through the bits and pieces again and again, I realize I would make the same choice. I suppose that is worth something. But what I find most difficult to reconcile, Lord, is how you force those you love to walk roads that we would never force our own loved ones to walk. And yet, I am closer to you now than I have ever been. Your intent, no doubt. And, above all, my heart's deepest desire. November 24, 1870 (Joshua 2:21)

Chin trembling, eyes moist, Rebekah turned the envelope over, feeling bereft, wanting more, yet knowing there wasn't any. She read the prayer again and again, then turned down the flame in the oil lamp, holding tight to the memory of Nana's voice. And to the kindred struggle of wanting to believe even when she didn't understand.

34

"Have you seen him again? This . . . Billy?"
Tate forked another bite of ham, glad
Rebekah had agreed to have lunch with him.
The cafe was a small one, tucked away on a less
crowded thoroughfare. So it was quiet, even over
the noon hour.

For the past two weeks, he'd spent every waking
minute at either the old opera house or the new
one. Rehearsing, moving, rehearsing, moving.
Rebekah had done much the same, except for
the time devoted to tutoring Mrs. Cheatham's
daughter. Getting away for a while would do them
both good.

"Yes, his name is Billy. And no, I haven't."
Rebekah paused as the waitress refilled their
coffee cups. "Although I find myself looking for
him everywhere I go. You should have felt his
arms, Tate. So thin. And he's so young to be living
on the streets, both parents gone."

"I know you believe what he told you, Rebekah.
About his parents and his situation. And I want
to as well," he added hurriedly, sensing an
objection forthcoming. "But these kids who grow
up on the streets are crafty."

"I understand what you're saying, and I agree.
But something about him makes me certain he
was telling me the truth. I've asked around town

about him. I talked with a few of the other newsboys, and even some of the shop owners. And while several of them claimed to know him, or are familiar with him—"

Her expression told him that not all the reasons for being *familiar* with Billy were positive.

"—none of them knows where he lives."

"And like I said before, I want to believe him too. If only for your sake." He smiled. "But my run-ins with these kids haven't been as positive as yours. Last time I tried to help one, he kicked me in the shin!"

Rebekah laughed. "Billy tried to do that with me. But I saw it coming."

Tate frowned. "Exactly what are you implying?"

She scrunched her shoulders and smiled, a very feminine gesture on her. "You *are* a few years older than me."

He gave her a look that drew a smile he wished he could capture and keep. "If you do find him again, you know there's a widows' and children's home here in town. They might have room for him."

"Yes, I've passed by the building before. You know it's managed by Eleanor Geoffrey."

Tate looked up. "The architect's wife?"

"Who is also Mrs. Cheatham's niece."

"Well, with those connections I'm *certain* you'd be able to secure a place for him there."

Tate helped himself to another yeast roll from the basket, waiting for her response. But she merely nodded and sipped her coffee.

He glanced at the clock on the wall. They had about an hour before the next rehearsal started. As of nine days ago, he'd combined all sections and the full orchestra had been practicing together in the new opera house—two four-hour sessions per day—and they'd made enormous strides.

Maybe it was the acoustics of the new auditorium or everyone's excitement about it, but the music sounded so full and rich. Yet, as usual, he still saw much room for improvement.

And only two weeks until opening night.

"I keep intending to ask you . . ." Rebekah tucked her napkin by her plate. "You said Mrs. Bixby set aside tickets for your parents. Where are they sitting?"

"They're front and center. Second row, on the aisle."

"Not box seats?"

"All of the box seats were spoken for long before I even got to Nashville. Those went to symphony board members and donors who made generous contributions to the new building." He forked the remaining piece of ham from Rebekah's plate, which earned him a shake of her head. "But they'll be fine sitting down front. Honestly, it won't matter to my parents where they sit. And for me, I'm simply grateful they'll be there. Emil's coming with them too. To help them on the train and to get around town. So it'll be the three of them. Emil's the only one of my siblings who's ever been off the mountain."

About to take a sip of coffee, Rebekah paused. "They've never traveled outside Chicory Hollow?"

He smiled. "I hadn't either, before I left. And I might've been there still, if not for Jacob Marshall and Frederick Mason."

"The missionary and your benefactor."

He nodded, wishing the men were still alive so they could attend opening night. Not only to hear the symphony, but because Tate wished to thank them again for the difference they'd made in the course of his life. He looked across the table and wondered whether or not he would have ever met Rebekah if not for Mr. Marshall's heart to share the goodness of Christ and to leave lives better than he'd found them. And also if not for Mr. Mason's generosity to share his financial wealth.

"Your father . . . he's continuing to improve?"

Tate found himself watching the curves of Rebekah's mouth as she spoke, how her lips drew into a bow when pronouncing certain words, or the way her tongue lightly touched her teeth. And, sometimes, how she paused and pursed her lips when searching for the right thing to say. How he was ever going to let her go, he didn't know.

But he also knew he'd never wanted someone else to succeed and to be granted the desires of their heart as much as he wanted that for her.

"Mama's last letter said he's slowly getting stronger. He still has days when he feels weak. But as Dr. Hamilton told us, those days are to be expected, particularly since my father was ill for so long. In the next few weeks, there's a chance the fluid could return more swiftly than anticipated, and the doctor warned of the dangers should that happen. And of how quickly my father's condition could deteriorate." He fingered the rim of his cup. "But once he's past that hurdle, his constitution should improve markedly. So . . . we're choosing to be more optimistic in our outlook."

"I'm so glad, Tate. And so happy for you all."

He couldn't be certain, but he wondered if she was thinking about her own father in that moment. And perhaps her mother too.

A jingle of the bell above the door drew his attention, and a second glance at the clock told him it was time for them to get back. He paid the bill and they walked outside.

He offered Rebekah his arm, but she hesitated.

"Actually . . ." She glanced in the opposite direction of the new opera house. "I'd planned to go see my mother this afternoon. But I'll be back soon to help with anything you or the orchestra members need."

"Take your time. I'm glad you're going to visit her. After all, we never know how long we'll have our parents with us . . . do we?"

Her smile came slowly, sadly. "No, we don't."

Seeing the house ahead, Rebekah prayed for her current frame of mind. Sitting with Tate over lunch, she'd found herself comparing his family to hers, and hers had come up so short. But no use in dwelling on that now. Things were what they were. But as Demetrius would've told her, and she believed . . .

They didn't have to stay that way.

She saw no sign of the carriage out front and continued on around back to the kitchen door. No Delphia inside either.

Rebekah knocked, waited, then checked the doorknob. It turned easily in her grip. She stepped into the kitchen, a bit wary, as she always was when Barton might be near.

"Delphia?"

No answer. Large pots of water sat steaming on the stove. But it was the plate of cookies on the counter that truly drew her attention.

Then she heard the distinct murmur of female voices—her mother's and Delphia's—and, marking the cookies for later, followed the sound upstairs to her mother's bedroom. She paused in the doorway and watched Delphia and her mother arguing over a shawl.

Her mother pushed the garment away. "I don't want to wear that old thing. I want to wear my new coat."

"You wanna wear your new coat in the *house,* Miss Sarah? That don't make no sense."

Rebekah curbed a smile. Her mother seemed more alert today than she had been during their last few visits. Although her mood . . .

"I want to look nice for when Barton comes

home. He always notices what I'm wearing. And that shawl is . . . shabby and dowdy looking. Something an old woman would wear!"

Her mother said it as though she were repeating someone else's words, and Rebekah didn't have to think long about who that someone might be.

Rebekah knocked on the open door, announcing her presence, and both women looked up, their reactions telling. Her mother's features turned icily cool, while Delphia's warmed in welcome.

"Come on in here, child!" Delphia briefly widened her eyes as if trying to send Rebekah a warning.

Rebekah's mother simply sniffed and looked off in the opposite direction.

"Hello, Mother," Rebekah offered. "Delphia." She returned Delphia's look with one of her own. "How are you today, Mother?"

"I'm cold and near freezing to death, but Delphia refuses to get me my coat."

Delphia, hands planted on hips, heaved a sigh, to which Rebekah responded with a discreet wink.

"Here . . . Is this the coat you want?" Rebekah retrieved a beautiful royal blue coat hanging on a peg by the wardrobe. "I'm happy to get it for you."

Apparently, her mother had ceased wearing mourning garb. But Rebekah wasn't about to criticize. She brought the coat to her mother, who promptly turned away.

"I've changed my mind, Delphia. I *would* like to wear that shawl."

Shaking her head, Delphia slipped the garment around her mother's shoulders while Rebekah returned the coat to its peg, recalling the wise counsel from beloved Demetrius. *"As long as there's breath in a body, a person can change."*

She claimed the chair opposite her mother's. "The last time I stopped by, you were out shopping. Did you have a nice time with your friends?"

Her mother waved off the question. "That's been so long ago, I can scarcely remember." She reached for a cup of what looked to be hot tea from the side table and drank liberally.

Courting a smile, Rebekah determined not to be drawn into an argument. "I'll do my best to come by more often. I've simply been so busy lately that I—"

"I know what you're doing. You're working at the opera house. Barton told me." Her mother grimaced. "Do you know how that made me feel? My own daughter doesn't even tell me where she's working."

Rebekah opened her mouth to defend herself, then promptly closed it, recognizing the slippery slope. Meanwhile, her mother drained the teacup and filled it again from the matching pot resting on the side table.

Not even close to giving up, Rebekah tried again. "May is almost here, Mother, and I know how much you love spring. Perhaps you and I can plant some flowers out back this year, like you and Father and I used to do when I was a little girl."

Unexpected warmth slipped into her mother's eyes, as if a cherished memory, all but forgotten, had resurfaced, and her mother smiled. *Actually smiled*. Rebekah watched in amazement at the transformation.

Then her mother blinked and her gaze reconnected with Rebekah's, and in the space of a heartbeat, the chill returned.

"Flowers don't grow very well back there anymore. It would all likely be for nothing!"

Weighing the negative-spirited woman before her with the glimpse of a woman she remembered, Rebekah realized her mother was still there, behind a wall of some sort. Grief, perhaps? Bitterness? Regret? Whatever had built the wall, all Rebekah needed to do was find a way to scale it.

"Miss Sarah," Delphia interrupted. "I'm gonna fetch the rest of your bath water, ma'am. I be right back."

Rebekah's continued attempts to engage her mother in conversation proved fruitless. So they sat in silence, her mother staring off into the distance, her eyes almost closing at times before she would snap them back open and glare at Rebekah again, as though suddenly remembering she was still supposed to be angry.

Delphia finished filling the tub in the adjacent room, then helped her mother out of the chair.

Rebekah stood but knew better than to offer her assistance.

"Good-bye, Mother. I'll come by again soon."

Her mother simply turned her head the other way. "Delphia, I hope the water's not too hot."

"It's not too hot, ma'am."

"And do you have that soap I like? The pink one?"

"You know I do."

"And my robe, I like to have my robe."

"Done got it in there, Miss Sarah."

Rebekah caught Delphia's eye and mouthed a silent *"Thank you."*

Delphia tossed her a reassuring look. "You be sure and get some of them cookies in the kitchen," she said over her shoulder.

Waiting until the door had closed, Rebekah finally gave release to the heavy sigh that had been building inside her. As she turned to leave, she could barely make out the muffled voice of her mother as she continued to ply Delphia with questions, and Delphia's as she answered.

Rebekah closed the bedroom door and hurried downstairs and to the kitchen, eager to get to rehearsal. She quickly searched the drawers in the worktable for a sack or tin for the cookies, and found Delphia's stash of cinnamon candies, a stack of clean, starched aprons, and Grandmother's set of butcher knives. But not a sack or tin anywhere.

So she wrapped half a dozen cookies in a napkin and stuck them in her skirt pocket. As she turned to leave, she heard the back door open.

35

"R ebekah, my dear." Barton closed the door behind him, a suitcase in his hand. His gaze traveled leisurely up and down her body. "What a pleasant surprise."

Rebekah smelled the cherry laurel from where he stood, and her stomach turned. Seeing the look in his eyes, she quickly gauged the fastest way out of the room and ran, screaming for Delphia.

He caught her before she could get out of the kitchen, his grip viselike around her upper arm. She fought and kicked and screamed.

"Now, now, Rebekah . . ." He shoved her hard against the worktable, then pinned her from behind. "Is this any way to greet your *loving* stepfather?"

Rebekah reached for a cast-iron skillet atop the table, but he shoved it away. She fought him, tried to scratch and bite, but she was no match for his height and strength.

"Mother and Delphia"—she could hardly breathe—"are in the parlor."

"Oh, I doubt that." He laughed. "Or they'd be in here by now. No, your mother's typically upstairs this time of day. I know her schedule better than she does."

He leaned close and smelled her hair, and bile rose in the back of her throat. She screamed again

560

and looked for anything to use as a weapon . . .
then remembered.

"I was drunk that night," he whispered in her ear.
"But not so drunk that I don't remember what you
tasted like, what you felt like beneath my hands."

The drawer wouldn't budge.

"And looks like nobody's coming to your aid
this time. Especially not that two-bit nigger friend
of yours. Oh, I took care of him, Rebekah." He
laughed. "You should've seen him after I . . ."

She tried to open the drawer again, but at this
odd angle . . . *Oh, God, please* . . . Her hands were
shaking so badly, she could scarcely—*There!*
The drawer budged.

Barton grabbed her by the shoulders and whirled
her around. Rebekah spit in his face, and the
veins in his neck corded tight. He lowered his
mouth to hers, and she turned away—just as her
grip closed around the wooden handle. She
brought the butcher knife up with as much force
as she could muster.

He cursed and let go of her and clutched at his
arm. Rebekah dropped the knife and ran.

Tate stayed after the rehearsal and met with
several members from various sections of the
orchestra, answering questions and discussing the
music. Afternoon rehearsal had gone relatively
well, except for the fourth movement. All sections
were still struggling with it, as was Darrow Fulton
with the violin solo. But something had occurred

to him in recent weeks that had somewhat altered his outlook in this regard.

A great deal of his harshness with the orchestra had, no doubt, been influenced by his hearing loss. Meaning the fault—at least at times—had been his, not theirs. It was a humbling realization. So as he answered every one of their questions, he again committed to being more patient and slower to become angry.

And as the minutes ticked by, he watched for Rebekah.

She'd said she would only be an hour or so at her mother's, yet it had been much longer. He'd already gathered that she and her mother weren't close, which might have explained the apprehension he'd sensed in her before they'd parted ways. But perhaps the visit had gone better than she'd anticipated and that was the reason she wasn't back yet. He hoped that was the case.

He took the back hallway to his new office to retrieve his suit coat, and to see if Rebekah was there. She wasn't. Boxes and crates littered the floor—so much to be done yet. Moving was a wearying business. But between them all, it would get done.

He and Rebekah had discussed finishing up in the old office together after today's rehearsal. Perhaps she'd gone there instead.

On his way out of the building, he heard his name and turned. And when he saw who it was, he felt himself tense but then remembered what

Rebekah had said to him days earlier about offering encouragement. But . . . how to make it sincere?

Darrow Fulton approached, violin case in hand. "Maestro Whitcomb, a moment to discuss the violin solo, if you could, sir."

"All right, Mr. Fulton. But first, let me say that your arpeggios today . . . showed improvement. I can tell you've been working on those measures."

Fulton blinked, and stood a little straighter. "Thank you, Maestro. I appreciate that. And I have been, most vigorously. It's a difficult piece."

"Yes, it is. But I trust you're up to it." Tate didn't wait for the man's response, eager to be on his way. "Now, your question?"

"Yes, sir. . . ." Fulton briefly glanced away. "It's about the interlude. In my solo. I'm simply wondering . . . and please know, before I say this, that I admire your work greatly. This doesn't alter that in any way."

Tate sensed a *but* coming.

"But . . . the interlude doesn't seem to share the same *nuance* as the rest of the symphony."

"Yes, Mr. Fulton. That's why it's an interlude."

"Yes, Maestro." Fulton laughed nervously, his upper lip glistening. "But what I'm trying to say—"

"Would, perhaps, be easier to say if you would simply come out and say it."

Fulton took a breath, then glanced about them as though making certain no one else was listening.

"Part of the interlude sounds a little like . . . yokel music to me, sir."

Tate didn't even attempt to smile. "Yokel music, Mr. Fulton?"

"Yes, sir. Or . . . backwoods, as some people call it. It's similar to the music you might hear played on a street corner by commoners. Or even"—sweat beaded on the man's forehead—"a little like . . . Negro music, Maestro," he whispered, repugnance in his tone. "I don't mean to be offensive, sir."

"Why would I be offended, Fulton? You're simply comparing my music to that of commoners and Negroes."

Tate enjoyed watching the man's face pale.

"No, sir! Not the symphony as a whole. Only . . . the violin solo does possess a quality reminiscent of that. And I'm simply wondering if that's for the best, considering the caliber and prestige of our patrons."

Tate stared, able to see through the man as clearly as a paned window without glass. Not only was Fulton clearly still struggling with the violin solo, as was proven in rehearsal earlier, but it also appeared as though he was embarrassed to play it. And although Fulton appeared to be less jittery and on edge lately, Tate still wasn't convinced the man wasn't an addict on some level.

Tate narrowed his gaze. "You were right to come to me with your . . . concerns, Mr. Fulton. Now allow me to allay them, not in part, but in full. The interlude in the violin solo is the heart of this symphony. It is the inspiration from which the very seed of this music was born. And if the interlude sounds like the music of *commoners* to you, then I find deep satisfaction in knowing I have achieved my goal in that regard. Because while this symphony is about the complexity and diversity of music, from Bach to Beethoven, it is also about the struggle . . . and triumph of the common man. The sort of people of which"— Tate felt a warmth in his chest—"I am most proud."

Nearly half an hour later, Tate opened the back door to the old opera house and stepped inside, willing his frustration with Darrow Fulton to fade in the silence and calm. If only women could play in symphonies. Correction—if only women could play in the Nashville Philharmonic.

He smiled at the thought, and the fact that *he'd* had it.

The waning afternoon sun stretched fading beams of light through the upper windows and illuminated a thousand dust motes as they drifted and danced across the dusky corridor. He recalled the first time he'd ever seen Rebekah, standing there in the hallway outside his office, her eyes bright with determination, the depth of which he'd sorely underestimated.

He'd never met anyone as driven as he was . . . until her.

A lamp still burned bright on Mrs. Murphey's desk, telling him that she or Mrs. Bixby, or both, were still there. Bless those women. What would he do without them?

He continued to his office, not melancholy over leaving this building so much as he felt a deep sense of gratitude for the purpose it had served through the years. He turned the corner and paused, disappointed to find his office door still closed and the slit beneath it dark.

Where was she?

He opened the door and crossed to his desk, fumbled for matches, and lit the lamp. The soft glow fell across stacks of boxes and crates, revealing a chaos similar to the one he'd left in the other building. He was eager to get—

Sensing more than seeing something move in the shadows in the corner, he held up the lamp. And saw her, sitting on the sofa in the corner.

"Rebekah, what are you doing sitting here in the dark?" He set the lamp aside and went to her, then saw her red-rimmed eyes.

36

Rebekah, what's wrong?" he whispered.

Her earlier tears having dried, Rebekah felt her fragile, pieced-together composure beginning to slip. "I . . . I didn't know where else to go." She swallowed past the lump in her throat.

Tate slipped an arm around her shoulders. "*Rebekah* . . . tell me what's wrong."

She leaned into him, the tenderness in his voice nearly her undoing. But how to tell him . . . And how would he react?

"You remember . . . meeting my stepfather." Even in the dim light she saw his jaw go rigid, and she squeezed his hand tight, thinking of Chicory Hollow and their kind of *mountain justice.* "Before I tell you what happened, Tate, promise me that you won't leave this room until we're both ready to leave together."

He held her gaze, his own pained and conflicted. But finally, he gave a consenting nod.

"When I went to see my mother today . . ." She paused, realizing she needed to start at the beginning. "I told you how, after my father died, my mother married Barton Ledbetter soon after. *Too* soon after."

He watched her closely.

"I always knew there was something . . . different about the man. But it wasn't until one night, when he found me alone in the barn . . ." She felt Tate tense beside her. "He'd been drinking, and he . . ." She closed her eyes as she recounted to him what had happened. Sensing the tension within him building, she hurried to finish. "But Demetrius, the man I told you about, the slave in my father's house who taught me to play the fiddle . . . He heard me screaming and broke through the door. He threw Barton across the barn

. . . then took me inside to my grandmother." She wiped her eyes. "My grandmother moved me into her bedroom that very night, and then a month later, we were on our way to Vienna."

He took hold of her hand. "And today?" he whispered, his deep voice husky.

"Today as I was leaving the house, h-he came home. He cornered me in the kitchen. Against the worktable. I . . . fought and screamed. Mother and Delphia, our housekeeper, were upstairs. So they couldn't hear me."

He leaned forward, forearms on his knees, her hand clasped so tightly between his it was almost painful. Yet she didn't want him to ever let go.

"Then the next thing I knew, I'd managed to open one of the drawers in the worktable. Where the butcher knives are kept."

Tate looked back at her, his expression inscrutable.

"I stabbed him. In the arm. And then I ran. And I came here."

He opened his mouth to speak but exhaled a ragged breath instead. "So . . . he didn't . . ."

She looked at him and quickly gathered his meaning. "No. He didn't."

Tate bowed his head, whispering something she couldn't hear. He brought her hand to his mouth and kissed it, then drew her close.

"I want to kill him," he whispered.

"Tate, I told you—"

She tried to look up at him, but he held her close.

"I said I *want* to, Rebekah. Not that I will. And be it right or wrong, thinking about the former helps me at the moment."

She slipped her arms around his waist. The protection of his embrace and the solid beat of his heart poured peace and healing into her that she wouldn't have thought imaginable at the moment.

"Once you left your mother's house today, you didn't go back."

She shook her head. "But I know he wouldn't hurt my mother. He'd have to get past Delphia first."

"This Delphia . . . she's a formidable woman, I take it."

"She is. Demetrius was her older brother. He meant so much to me. In fact, in my heart, the parts of the violin solo I helped with in the fourth movement—"

"Are for him," he finished softly.

She nodded, and he cradled her head against his chest.

"What I wasn't told, Tate, until I returned from Vienna, is that Demetrius was killed shortly after I left all those years ago. And what I didn't know for certain until today was that—"

"Ledbetter killed him."

Soft sobs rose in her throat. "Because of me . . ."

They sat together on the sofa, and he held her as she cried, the ache in her chest much like that she'd experienced when her father died.

The lamplight cast undulating shadows against

the bare plaster walls, and Rebekah gradually realized that, while what Barton had done today— and what she'd done to him—was harrowing, it was what he'd done to Demetrius all those years ago that was breaking her heart in two.

She was mourning the loss of Demetrius like she should have been given the opportunity to do all those years ago.

"Rebekah?"

The soft voice drifted toward her from far away. Rebekah blinked her eyes open and saw Tate standing over her. She looked around, slowly gaining her bearings.

"It's all right." He took her hand. "You fell asleep for a while. But I've been here the whole time."

He helped her sit up, and she ran a hand through her hair.

"Thank you . . . for staying with me."

"You don't have to thank me, Rebekah. I . . ." He briefly looked away. "I wouldn't be anywhere else." He helped her stand . . . only, he didn't let go of her hand. "Do you feel well enough to leave?"

"Of course." She started gathering her things.

"I'm going to take you to Belmont first, and then I'm stopping by your mother's house to—"

"Tate, I'm not sure that's a good idea."

"I simply want to make sure your mother and Delphia are safe. And then locate your stepfather."

"And if you find him?"

"We'll have . . . a discussion."

She looked at him.

"I can take care of myself, Rebekah. Have you forgotten . . ." His smile was both tender and telling. "I'm a highlander . . . first and always."

"I haven't forgotten," she whispered, but then she did remember something she hadn't shared with him. "Delphia told me recently that the police had come to the house wanting to speak with Barton. But he wasn't there. Delphia said he comes and goes a lot. And travels quite often. In fact, he had a suitcase with him today when he came in the door."

"Did he mention anything about going somewhere?"

She shook her head. "But I wish he'd leave and never come back."

The carriage rounded the tree-lined curve, and the lamplit windows of Belmont Mansion came into view. Tate peered down, Rebekah soft and warm beside him, her head on his shoulder, moonlight on her face. And as he had since the moment she'd told him what happened earlier that day, he thanked God again that nothing worse had occurred.

He'd wanted to bring her to Belmont earlier, but she'd insisted on waiting at his house with Mrs. Pender while he went to see her mother and Delphia. As it turned out, Rebekah's mother had been asleep, but Delphia was exactly as Rebekah described her. *Formidable* was almost too gentle a word for the woman.

Delphia had a protective streak a mile wide for Rebekah's mother, and for Rebekah too. When he'd relayed to Delphia what Barton had attempted that afternoon, shock slid into the woman's eyes followed by a fury the likes of which Tate wouldn't ever want aimed at him. Delphia's opinion of Barton Ledbetter was clear. And scathing. It was clear she held the same opinion of the man as Rebekah.

Delphia said she hadn't noticed anything different in the kitchen at first. Until she spotted drops of blood and noticed a drawer open—and a butcher knife missing. One from a set that had belonged to Rebekah's grandmother.

A butcher knife . . . Tate looked down at Rebekah, her eyes closed. The woman was fearless.

Delphia had been confused and concerned but hadn't been certain what to do about what she'd found, so she was relieved when Tate told her Rebekah was safe and secure at his home. She had found no sign of Ledbetter at the house. By her calculations, and Tate agreed, the man had likely taken off. Tate had no idea where he'd gone, but having seen him in Chicory Hollow, he planned to contact the authorities there first thing in the morning and let them know to be watching for him.

The carriage slowed to a stop in front of the mansion.

"I don't want to get out" came a soft whisper beside him.

He smiled, feeling much the same, and wishing again that his future was as secure as it once had been. He leaned forward to open the door, when she touched his arm.

"Tate, I've been wondering about something."

He paused.

"My grandmother was scarcely ill a day in her life. Yet she died in her sleep. Do you think that Barton could have . . ."

Understanding what she was asking, Tate wasn't sure how to answer. He wouldn't have put it past the man—Ledbetter appeared to lack even the thinnest thread of moral fiber—and yet . . . "I don't know," he whispered. "But I do know what Angus Whitcomb would say. *'We won't be leavin' this earth one minute before the good Lord wills it, nor one minute past.'*"

Her eyes watered. "Thank you for that."

He walked her to the front door, and made a suggestion he hoped she would heed, yet somehow already knew she wouldn't. "You've been through so much today, Rebekah. Why don't you take some time and rest. Don't worry about the symphony or opening night, or any of those details. Mrs. Murphey and Mrs. Bixby can—"

"The last thing I need, Tate, is to sit in a parlor for days on end and think about what happened. I want to work. I *need* to work." Her gaze was earnest. "I've allowed Barton Ledbetter to overshadow far too much of my life already. I'm not about to let him ruin all that you and I have worked for—all we've done to honor two very special men in our lives. So . . . I'll see you tomorrow, right after Pauline's lesson."

He waited for the front door to close and latch behind her, then climbed into the carriage.

On the way home, he mulled over what she'd said. Though he guessed they'd likely never know the truth about whether or not Barton was responsible for her grandmother's death, he couldn't deny that there was a certain poetic justice in how Rebekah had defended herself today.

Perhaps that was answer enough in itself.

Later that night, unable to sleep, Rebekah rose and lit the oil lamp, then wrapped a blanket around her shoulders. She drank the remaining now-tepid tea Cordina had delivered earlier that evening. But the tea cakes, for the first time she could remember, remained untouched on the delicate china plate.

She felt such a restlessness inside.

Maybe it stemmed from what had happened earlier that day with Barton—understandable—or maybe it was nervousness about opening night for Tate and the orchestra, but it felt like something more.

Something . . . unsettled.

She crossed to the darkened window and stared out for several moments, moonlight casting the world beyond in a silvery sheen. The clock on the mantel ticked ever faithfully, its face reading half past one.

Rebekah yawned and drained her cup. When she set it back on the tray, her gaze fell to the bundle of letters from her grandmother. She fingered the ribbon, then remembered something she had yet to do.

And the task, though small, heartened her.

She untied the ribbon and found the last two letters she'd read from the stack, then retrieved her Bible and crawled back beneath the covers. She turned the first letter over.

Genesis 31:49

She reread the prayer on the back, then looked up the passage her grandmother had noted . . . and smiled. "'The Lord watch between me and thee,'" she read aloud, "'when we are absent one from another.'"

Oh, Nana . . . "I love you so much," she whispered, able to picture her grandmother's sweet smile even now.

She reached for the second letter, reread the prayer, and turned in her Bible to the Scripture reference.

"And she said," she read silently, *"According unto your words, so be it. And she sent them away, and they departed: and she bound the scarlet line in the window."*

Rebekah frowned. Then read the verse again. What was that supposed to mean? She scanned the surrounding verses, somewhat familiar with the passage about Rahab, the prostitute, though it had been a long time since she'd read it.

She looked back again at the envelope to make sure she'd looked up the correct verse. *Joshua 2:21.* That was right.

She reread the prayer more carefully, her attention focusing on a specific sentence.

But what I find most difficult to reconcile, Lord, is how you force those you love to walk roads that we would never force our own loved ones to walk.

She thought of Tate, and how he was being made to walk a road that she herself would never have chosen for him. And yet God had. For some reason she couldn't begin to understand. Yet she was trying to trust.

She read the Scripture one last time but saw no correlation with what her grandmother had written. Maybe Nana had been off a verse or two.

Considering that likelihood, Rebekah scanned the next handful of chapters, but found nothing— other than being reminded that any army that had dared go up against the army of Israel hadn't fared well.

Feeling a yawn, she gave in to it and stretched her shoulders, sleep finally feeling within reach.

She put her Bible away, turned down the lamp, and pulled the covers up around her face.

But try as she might, she couldn't get that odd verse out of her mind. *Binding a scarlet line in the window . . .*

Her grandmother had been so careful in choosing all the other verses. Why would she have—

Rebekah sat up in bed.

Nana had used a red ribbon to tie the letters together. Rebekah flung back the covers, the skin on the back of her neck prickling. Whether from the chill or the possibility of a discovery, she didn't know. She turned up the lamp and crossed to the desk for the ribbon she'd laid aside. She moved back to the lamplight and held the ribbon up to examine it, bit by bit, but saw only hand-drawn flowers and fanciful curlicues. Nothing that would—

Words. There were words written amidst the drawing. Or more rightly, someone had written over it. She squinted and held the ribbon at an angle in order to see it better.

To whoever finds this, in the event of my passing, please see that my granddaughter, Rebekah Ellen Carrington, receives these letters. Revelation 21:3–4

Heart pounding, Rebekah read the words again. Then searched the rest of the ribbon, both sides, looking for anything else. But that was all. Her throat tightened. Her *grandmother* had put the letters in the hutch. But why?

One solitary reason stood out in her mind. And tears burned her eyes. She drew in a thready breath. Had her grandmother known she was going to die? Had Barton Ledbetter . . .

Rebekah squeezed the ribbon tight in her hand. *Oh, dear God.*

Barton had stolen her grandmother's money, and Delphia herself had said that he'd gotten rid of everything in Nana's room. Except for these letters. Nana had hidden those away beforehand.

The verse.

Rebekah grabbed her Bible and turned the pages, her hands trembling. She blinked to clear her vision. She read the Scriptures first to herself, her heart going to its knees as the vision of heaven came alive in her mind. Then she read the last verse aloud, needing to actually *speak* those words into the air around her.

" 'And God shall wipe away all tears from their eyes.' " She drew in a breath. " 'And there shall be no more death . . . neither sorrow . . . nor crying' "—she wiped her tears—" 'neither shall there be any more pain: for the former things are passed away.' "

Unexpected warmth moved through her. She closed her eyes and bowed her head. What was it Tate had shared with her only hours ago? Something Angus had said . . .

"We won't be leavin' this earth one minute before the good Lord wills it, nor one minute past."

For the longest time, Rebekah stood in the silence, eyes closed, clinging to that thought. Then she turned down the lamp, ribbon clutched in her hand, and crawled into bed, more convinced than ever that there was an afterlife, and that—however her grandmother had died—Nana was waiting for her there even now, along with her father, and Demetrius.

And with a peace she couldn't begin to understand, much less explain, she closed her eyes and slipped into sleep.

A thrum of anticipation filled the concert hall as patrons streamed in through the back and side doors, their attention captivated by the enormity and splendor of their surroundings. Rebekah peered through the curtain's divide, watching it all. But mainly, her gaze kept returning to the four empty seats in the front.

In Emil's letter to Tate earlier that week, Emil had written that he, Angus, and Cattabelle would arrive an hour before the start of the symphony. But it was already half past six. And the symphony started at seven.

"Any sign of them yet?"

Rebekah turned, surprised—yet also not—to see Tate standing in the wings. He should be back in his office, concentrating, reviewing the music one last time. This night was so important to him. She glanced back through the curtain, then shook her head.

Please, let them get here.

She'd offered to meet Emil and his parents at the train station, but Tate had assured her Emil knew the way. Now she wished she'd insisted. But at least she was sitting with them, so they wouldn't get lost in the sea of people afterward.

She joined Tate in the shadows along the side curtains, activity buzzing all around them, everyone intent on the preparations at hand. But for Tate—and even her, in a way—the months, and lifetimes, of preparation were done. Or at least, paused in the moment. Now only the culmination awaited. For him . . . in a matter of minutes when he conducted his symphony. For her . . . in a matter of weeks. *If* Maestro Leplin extended her an audition, the probability of which didn't bode well at present. Weeks had passed since she'd written to request an audition, including Tate's recommendation. She'd heard nothing back. But she decided not to dwell on that for now.

This night was about Tate. And Angus. And a son honoring a father.

She sneaked a glance at him beside her, saw the tense set of his jaw, the singular focus in his gaze, and knew he shared her nervousness. Yet his burden was much greater. She'd assisted him in writing the symphony, yes. But she wasn't the conductor, the composer.

He'd poured his heart onto the page, the contents now measured in beats and rests, melodies and harmonies, textures and tempos, sharps and flats. Not unlike one's life. But to have that life—all your work, creativity and inspiration, bits and pieces of your heart that you'd poured onto the page—about to be shared with the world and put on display for all to see, and to judge . . . A shiver spread through her.

She prayed the world would be gentle. No, not gentle. She looked again at the man beside her. She prayed the world would be *worthy*.

"I'll leave you to focus," she whispered.

"No." His hand closed around hers. "Stand here with me." His gaze turned appraising as he looked her up and down. "You look . . . stunning this evening, Rebekah. That's a lovely gown."

"Thank you. It was a gift from Mrs. Cheatham." She peered down at the gown made of iridescent silver taffeta and silk. It shimmered when it caught the light, making it appear almost white. "She knows I'm still in mourning, but she thinks with all the work that's gone into tonight, my grandmother would want me to *shine* a little."

The gently scooped neckline and sleeveless cut of the dress with its fitted waist suited her. As did the full skirt and low-heeled silver slippers. A far simpler ensemble than the glamorous off-the-shoulder affair many women in the audience were wearing, but she was thrilled to have it.

Tate's gaze held approval. "While I didn't have the pleasure of knowing your grandmother, God rest her, I wholeheartedly concur with Mrs. Cheatham's opinion."

Rebekah smiled in appreciation. She'd shared with him about finding the ribbon that bound the letters her grandmother had hidden. They'd discussed the possibilities of what it meant, and had come to the same conclusion—that they would likely never know for certain. As far as they knew, no one had seen Barton or heard from him. He'd simply disappeared that day after he'd tried to—

No. She refused to think about that. Not tonight.

She stared up at Tate, admiring him. And while she *did* appreciate his compliment, she also found his gentlemanly politeness irritating. Where was the Tate who had flirted with her? Sparred with her? Who'd swept her behind the ticket booth in Chicory Hollow and kissed her with a passion that made her lie awake at night and wonder at the mystery between a man and a woman.

She *knew* he loved her. She saw it in his eyes every day, in the way he watched her when she was talking, or playing the violin, or helping him compose. Or even how he'd briefly taken her hand a moment ago. But how to get him to admit his love for her?

Or more importantly, admit it to himself?

She made a show of looking at him the way he

had her. "You're quite a handsome man yourself, Nathaniel. Then again . . . I don't need to see you in black coat and tails to realize that."

He smiled, and the tension in his jaw lessened. His gaze moved over her face and settled on her mouth. An intensity lit his eyes, and a flush swept her from head to toe, leaving her slightly light-headed. She knew every one of his expressions—including when he read her lips as she was speaking. And this particular look, to her delight, had absolutely nothing to do with a lack of hearing.

Maybe that other Tate wasn't lost to her after all.

"Maestro Whitcomb?" Mr. Cox, the stage manager, quietly approached. "Twenty minutes, sir."

"Thank you, Mr. Cox."

Mr. Cox. Rebekah raised an eyebrow. "You remembered his name this time." She did her best to look impressed.

"I'm working harder to remember people, and their names. To notice them, compliment their work."

Her playfulness faded. "I think that's wonderful, Tate."

"I would think you might. It's a trait I learned from you."

More touched than she could say, she glimpsed the orchestra members filing in from the back of the stage, taking their seats and beginning to tune their instruments, and the weight of the moment set in.

Judging by the deep breath Tate took beside her, he felt the same.

"Would you look again, please?" he whispered.

She did, and her heart clinched tight. She returned to his side. "Not yet. But I'm *sure* they'll be here."

"Maybe something happened. Maybe the trip down the mountain was harder for him than they expected. Or maybe his health took a—"

"No, Tate." She could feel the turn of his thoughts. "Your father is fine."

"You know as well as I do, Rebekah, that if something had happened to him, they wouldn't send word until after tonight. They wouldn't want to do anything to—"

"Your father will be here—with your mother and Emil. You just wait. When you walk onto the stage, they'll be sitting right there. And I'll be sitting right beside them."

He briefly bowed his head and rubbed the back of his neck.

Oh no . . . "You're not feeling another one of your—"

"No, I'm fine," he whispered. "It's . . . the usual tension."

She breathed a little easier. She'd prayed for him and for this particular night for weeks now and was grateful when she'd learned Dr. Hamilton was praying as well. The man said as much in a note to Tate earlier that week. It felt good to know she wasn't alone in knowing—and caring—about what was happening to him.

A silent, unexpected awareness quickened her pulse, and Rebekah lowered her head, humbled, and reminded . . .

She'd *never* been alone. And neither was Tate.

"Ten minutes, Maestro," Mr. Cox said softly from behind.

Coming from the other side of the stage curtain, a hushed cacophony of voices, laughter, and twitters of conversation, all charged with excitement and anticipation, reached through to them and seemed to electrify the air.

"I need to take my seat," she whispered.

Eyes closed, he nodded.

Struggling with what else to say to him, how to encourage him, she gave his hand a brief squeeze, and was almost to the rear stage door when she turned around and walked back.

She took his hand and threaded her fingers through his. "Tate, I know you want your father here. You want him to hear what you've written for him. But whether or not he's in the audience this evening or whether he's"—her voice caught—"at home . . . somewhere else," she whispered, thinking of her own father and of Demetrius, "he knows you love him, he knows you're grateful for all he gave to you. So you walk out there and perform tonight as though he's here. Because he is." She placed a hand over his heart. "And always will be."

Saying nothing for a moment, Tate brought her hand to his lips and kissed it. "I wish . . . I had more to offer you."

Tears filled her eyes. "You have already given me more than I ever thought my heart could contain. Don't you see . . . It doesn't matter to me that in a few days, or weeks, or perhaps months you may not be able to hear me, or the world around you. That doesn't change my feelings for you."

"But what kind of future can I offer you, Rebekah? Think about it. Who wants to hire a deaf conductor?"

"You know as well as I that when Beethoven wrote his Ninth Symphony, he was almost completely deaf."

"I am no Beethoven, Rebekah."

"No," she whispered. "You're not. You're Nathaniel Tate Whitcomb, son of Angus and Cattabelle Whitcomb of Chicory Hollow, Tennessee, and you have been brought to this moment in your life to do this. And I am so grateful to have been allowed to be here to witness it."

He pressed her hand on the place over his heart. "You have done more than witness it. I could not be doing this tonight, or have even finished the symphony, without you."

"And don't you ever forget it . . . *Maestro Whitcomb*," she said softly.

A slow smile tipped one side of his mouth. "Do I hear an inflection of sincerity in that address, Miss Carrington?"

She laughed. "Yes, but don't let it go to your head."

He pressed a kiss to her forehead, then an even softer one to her lips. "No, my love. Only my heart."

38

Her heart full, Rebekah paused on her way to the stage door and looked back at Tate, grateful for the darkness and the opportunity to watch him unobserved. She so wanted this night to be perfect for him. And for his parents to see, for the first time in their lives—though, prayerfully, not the last—what a magnificent conductor their son had become, and how much he credited them with his success.

She could hear Edward Pennington, director of the symphony board, offering the introductory welcome to the audience, and was amazed at the clarity of the man's voice, even standing back here where she was. And they hadn't even raised the curtain yet. She recalled Marcus Geoffrey explaining the acoustics of the building to her. It would appear he'd done his job well.

But if she didn't get to her seat soon, she'd be forced to wait until after the first movement.

"Whoa, not too much there."

The deep whisper sounded as though it came from right beside her, yet Rebekah didn't see anyone nearby.

"It helps me when I play," someone whispered back.

A man laughed in a hushed tone.

"A *little* helps you when you play. A lot will . . ."

Rebekah strained to hear but couldn't make out the rest. One of the voices sounded familiar to her, yet she couldn't place it.

"So you're doing it, then?"

"Of course, I'm doing it. I do this, and I can write my own ticket anywhere."

"Well, you best stop drinkin' that or you won't be writin' anything. Much less playin'."

The shuffle of footsteps, and a side curtain moved, not six feet from her. Out stepped two men. A stage worker she'd seen on occasion. And . . . Darrow Fulton.

Standing in the wings, Tate couldn't see whether his parents were in their seats yet or not. While he knew that what Rebekah had said was true—about his father already knowing how grateful he was—he still wished them here.

Listening to Edward Pennington drone on and on, Tate wondered if the man might speak all night. But he finally finished, and Mr. Cox gave Darrow Fulton his cue. As first violinist and concertmaster, Fulton preceded Tate onto the stage.

Seeing Fulton, the audience applauded. Fulton paused and—as he always did—bowed with all the flourish of a European prince, then he turned and nodded for the oboist to sound the tuning note. The oboist played an A, pure and clear, and all the other instruments tuned to it.

Tate wished he could be more confident in

Fulton's ability to play the violin solo this evening. During the final two practices, Fulton had managed to play all of the notes correctly, but there had been little feeling in the piece. That was Fulton's problem—not connecting emotionally with the music he played. The man was brilliant, in one sense. And completely trammeled in another.

Which was particularly bothersome, because, as Tate had told him the other day, the interlude in the fourth movement was the heartbeat of this symphony. Tate had considered, numerous times, assigning the solo to another musician, but Fulton was the most experienced violinist in the orchestra. If *he* could scarcely manage it, then the second or third chair could hardly be expected to do better.

Darrow Fulton took his seat, and Mr. Cox gave Tate his cue. With a deep breath, Tate walked onto the stage.

Applause rose like a clap of thunder, filling the heights of the auditorium. Though every one of his mentors had insisted a conductor walk onto the stage with focus straight ahead, oblivious to his audience, Tate couldn't resist looking.

But three of the second-row seats were empty. Save for Rebekah's. His gaze briefly connected with hers, and it felt as though his entire world was tethered to the warmth of her smile.

He paused beside Fulton, who rose. Tate shook his hand, which was clammy to the touch. Tate gave him a look that said he trusted Fulton's nervousness would quickly shake out in the first movement.

Tate stepped up to the dais and waited for the applause to quiet behind him. As he picked up his baton, an image flashed in his mind. It happened in an instant. He was back in the cabin, in his parents' bedroom. His father was abed. Tate could feel the worn fiddle in his grip, and the prayer he'd prayed on his lips. *Please, Lord . . . for him. Let me do this for him.*

He looked down at the symphony score lying open on the stand before him and saw, instead of notes, all the ins and outs of his life that had led him to this moment. All the people with whom his life had intersected in order for his path to lead him here. How incredibly unlikely it was that all of that would have happened to a boy born in the hills of Chicory Hollow. As the magnitude of that orchestration set in, the prayer returned. *Please, Lord . . . for him. Let me do this for him.*

But even more, Lord Jesus—Tate briefly closed his eyes—*may I do this for you. Because of all you've done for me.*

He raised his baton and the instruments lifted in unison, every musician's gaze fastened on him, waiting, anticipating.

And though Tate couldn't remember ever having done this before, nor having even thought of doing it . . . he smiled at the men seated in a semicircle before him, and the light that had resided in their eyes seconds before paled in comparison to the eager excitement shining in them now. And with a flick of his wrist . . .

Music poured forth.

First the strings, then woodwinds, brass, and percussion. The music flowed through him, around him, and he could only imagine how it sounded as it swirled and soared behind him. Time seemed to stand still even as he was aware of the symphony's progression.

They were nearly to the middle of the first movement before he realized he hadn't bothered yet to look down at the score. Then he saw them. Tabs in his music.

The first one read: *1st movement, middle.* And he smiled to himself. *Rebekah.* The woman knew him almost better than he knew himself.

The first movement flowed into the second, then the third. And with the exception of some flatting by a musician in the first-violin section—he shot a glance at Darrow Fulton, whose face was bathed in sweat—the orchestra played flawlessly.

Tate could hear every instrument. Every pianissimo, every crescendo. And as the fourth movement approached, his heart pounding with exertion and excitement, he felt both a shudder of anticipation—and of uncertainty.

He saw movement in his peripheral vision and looked over. It was Darrow Fulton . . . wiping his face with a handkerchief? A face decidedly more pale than it had been moments earlier.

Tate caught Fulton's attention, his own gaze feeling daggerlike, and the man gave an almost imperceptible nod of his head. Which Tate found far from reassuring. But at least Fulton was still committed to playing the interlude.

The third movement built toward its finale, each section of the orchestra brilliant in clarity and tempo, until the movement's final note pierced the air and hung suspended. Tate scanned the musicians, the metronome inside him counting off the final four beats. Then he gave the cue, and . . .

Silence fell, save for the last, fading chord in C minor soaking deep into the fabric of the draperies and upholstered seats, the polished wooden floors, and the willing souls of those gathered.

Tate took a breath, raised his baton, and the majestic, triumphant strains of the violin and cello in C major rose to life, followed by the clarinets and oboes, trumpets and trombones.

He looked over at Darrow Fulton seated scarcely six feet away feet away and could see the man's fingers shaking as he gripped his bow. Still, Fulton played, as written in this section, in perfect unison with the other violins. A good sign. The man was simply nervous about the solo. Understandable. But he could do it. Tate cued the brass section, then percussion, and the strength of the instruments soared, circling round and round him. Truly, this must be what it was like to live within the music.

Filled with an uncommon joy and only measures

now from the interlude, Tate looked back to the violins to see Fulton give him an almost imperceptible shake of his head. Tate's heart all but stopped.

Fury ignited his veins, hot and explosive. Only measures away from the interlude, and Fulton does this?

Tate flipped to the next page of the score, reading ahead, his thoughts racing, colliding, twisting like a whirlwind inside him. He had no choice, he would simply have to proceed without the—

From somewhere backstage—the strains soft at first, then rising like the first blush of dawn— came the sound of home, of the hills and hollers, the mountains and the mist, the church in the meadow . . . and Vivaldi. Tate's throat closed tight.

He read confusion in the other musicians' faces and quickly regained control. The interlude gradually escalated in strength and volume, the clarity of the grueling arpeggios both astounding and soul stirring, their rapidly ascending and descending notes each living their own distinct, yet brilliant life.

And as he listened, he heard, as though for the first time in his life, the ethereal beauty of the violin. As if the curtain to eternity fluttered ever so slightly and notes, as yet unsung on earth, slipped through by the Hand of Grace. Judging by the faces of the musicians sitting before him, he gathered they shared a measure of his thoughts.

Nearing the final movement of the solo—the measures he and Rebekah had collaborated on most—Tate cued each instrument section until, one by one, their volume fell away to a whisper. And the ghostly beauty beyond the curtains rose once again with a power and fluidity that—true to Mr. Geoffrey's word—filled every corner of the auditorium . . .

Before finally yielding again to the soft strains of misty mornings and the hills and hollers of home. Tate's chest ached as he thought of his father, who he feared was listening from beyond the veil.

"Come, thou fount of every blessing, tune my heart to sing thy grace. Streams of mercy never ceasing, call for songs of loudest praise."

He couldn't be certain, but he wondered if he heard the faintest chorus of voices behind him. Or maybe . . . they came from within.

"Teach me some melodious sonnet, sung by flaming tongues above. Praise the mount, I'm fixed upon it, mount of thy redeeming love."

In his mind, he pictured a little girl, her auburn curls bouncing, as she wandered down to the slave cabins behind her house, drawn by a language that needed no words and that knew no boundaries. Not of rank or privilege. And certainly not of color.

He smiled as he caught snatches of the chords and distinct rhythms from "Barbara Allen," "Pretty Polly," and "The Cuckoo," and could all but hear Opal's sweet voice singing along. But it was the dissonance of themes from "Wayfaring Stranger" that wove a cord around his heart and pulled tight, helped along by the memory of Rebekah's voice as she sang that night in the cabin.

Becoming almost a part of the music rather than simply its conductor, he cued each section, and the music and volume built to a crescendo again, one last time. And he listened as closely as he could, struggling to memorize what he heard, knowing there would come a day—no, countless days—when he would close his eyes and reach deep within him, back to this moment, wanting to live in the midst of this music again.

How much he'd taken for granted in his life, and how much he would miss. But also, how much he had to be grateful for.

He turned the final page of the score and felt the turning of a page within him. As the last note faded, silence settled over the auditorium. Yet Tate was hesitant to lower his hands, to give permission for the moment—and this part of his life—to be over.

Finally, he relinquished . . .

And thunder broke for a second time as applause and cheers rained down. He turned and faced the audience. Their affirmation swelled and broke over him, again and again, in a bittersweet tide of gratitude and praise.

He bowed at the waist, his gaze returning to

the four empty seats in the second row. Then he straightened and, with a sweep of his arm, acknowledged the orchestra.

"Bravo!" someone cried from an upper balcony.

"Bravissimo!" another followed, which seemed to open a floodgate.

Tate raised his arm, trying to quiet the crowd, knowing there was one more thing he wanted—needed—to do. But that only encouraged their praise. He bowed again. Then after another moment, he tried a second time.

"Ladies and gentlemen," he called out as the cheers and applause subsided. "At this time, I would like to invite the master violinist who performed the solo in the fourth movement to join me on the stage, so that we might show our appreciation."

Without delay, a round of applause rose again.

Yet . . . no Rebekah.

Tate caught a glimpse of iridescent silver in the shadows offstage, then saw her peering at him from behind a side curtain. Hidden from view of the audience, she smiled sweetly but shook her head, then laid a hand over her heart and pointed back to him. He knew what she meant.

But this night was about so much more than him.

He held out his hand to her, determined that she be part of this evening. Uncertainty in her features and violin in hand, she walked onto the stage. And like gushing water forced through a sieve, the applause suddenly fell to a trickle, then to nothing as disapproving gasps and murmurs filled the void.

Until finally, only silence.

Where seconds earlier joy and celebration abounded, now tension stretched taut, and Tate felt responsible for every raised eyebrow and dark look. Yet in some expressions—women, mostly, but even a few of the men—he read intrigue and even . . . awe.

"Ladies and gentlemen, it is my extreme privilege to introduce this evening's master violinist . . . Miss Rebekah Ellen Carrington. Please join me in showing her our—"

"This is *beyond* the pale!" came from somewhere near the front.

"Disgraceful!"

"Unseemly conduct!"

The responses gained momentum and scattered *boo*s joined in to form an unseemly chorus. Edward Pennington began the exodus, his grip on his wife's elbow, then others from the symphony board followed as a hissing sound serpentined its way through the crowd. Groups of naysayers—a dozen here, a handful there—rose from their seats and filed toward the outer doors, from every section and every level of the balcony, parading their offended sensibilities like badges of honor.

Rebekah started to walk offstage, but Tate grabbed her arm and gently pulled her back. With a wounded look, she pleaded with him to let her go. But as much as it hurt him to see her being hurt, he shook his head. Angry with the patrons leaving, he was even more so with himself for insisting she come out here. He should have known better. But she *deserved* to be recognized for her talent and all that she'd—

Somewhere off to his left, someone began clapping.

One brave, daring soul.

And the auditorium fell silent.

He looked upward, searching for who it was. And the instant he spotted her—Mrs. Adelicia Acklen Cheatham—a second person joined in, followed by a third and a fourth, their approval unwavering, even if greatly outweighed. Then he saw who was standing next to Mrs. Cheatham, and an ache of surprise and gratitude filled his chest.

His father. With Adelaide Cheatham in her private box? Tate heard Rebekah's soft gasp beside him just as he spotted his mother and Emil seated in the box as well.

Tate lifted his hand to them, his father's face brimming with emotion, love, and pride—an image Tate knew he would carry with him forever.

As the applause continued and increased, he heard a noise behind them and turned to see all of the violinists tapping their stands with their bows, a time-honored tradition of showing appreciation and honor to the soloist. All of the violinists except Darrow Fulton, whose face was decidedly less pale, and instead was flushed with anger.

Rebekah smiled at the musicians, her eyes brimming.

"Encore!" someone called out from the auditorium, and a chorus of voices swiftly took up the cry. "Encore!" "Brava!"

Tate looked over at her to find her already looking at him.

"Miss Carrington, would you mind greatly if I were to conduct you in an encore performance?"

"I would be most honored . . . Maestro Whitcomb."

He gave instructions to the orchestra, then turned and gave them to Rebekah. When he looked back, Darrow Fulton was gone. Tate's gaze moved from the empty seat one over to Mr. Adams, the second-chair violinist. And Adams nodded, a measure of pride and gratitude in the act.

Tate lifted his baton, knowing this encore would be the truer test—not of Rebekah's skill. That had been established without question. But rather, whether the patrons would accept the vessel from whom the music they loved poured forth.

The orchestra began eight measures before the interlude, then Rebekah joined. The gracefulness and beauty with which she played—her arms, her neck, the curves of her shoulders, the expressions on her face—were as moving and mesmerizing as the music itself. And it occurred to him that the curves of a woman's body were much like those of a violin—both of extraordinary beauty.

Watching her, Tate knew again that she'd been

born to play this instrument. And based on a furtive glance behind him, the spellbound audience agreed.

Nearing the end of the fourth movement, he cued the violins, then woodwinds—then tossed a sharp look back at the violins. They'd anticipated the decrescendo far too early this time. A mistake they rarely made. He signaled the musicians, demanding more, but their expressions simultaneously registered confusion.

Then a *pop* sounded in his ears. And like a train moving farther and farther away, its whistle growing more distant by the second, the music faded until only a distant buzzing sounded in his ears.

The orchestra was still playing. The violins bowed together in perfect unison, moving as one. The cellists, the horns, the percussion did the same. But he heard none of it. And yet . . . he did. He could hear it in his heart, in the faces of the musicians, and he could see it in the tears slipping down Rebekah's face.

Was this what it was going to be like? Alone within himself while in a room surrounded with people. A world within a world. And not a world he welcomed.

He blinked—feeling outside of time—and realized that the orchestra had stopped. He couldn't remember when or how, but his hands now rested at his sides, baton still in his grip. He laid it on the podium, the simple act so strange without its corresponding sound.

Wondering why the audience wasn't applauding yet, he felt a touch on his arm, turned, and saw Rebekah, then realized his mistake. Love and understanding spilled down her cheeks, and she gestured toward the auditorium.

Tate turned to see every man and woman on their feet, clapping their hands, their faces jubilant, many tear-stained. He looked up toward Mrs. Cheatham's box and found her waving her silk handkerchief in the air, Dr. Cheatham clapping enthusiastically beside her. Tate watched his father laughing and applauding, his mother and Emil doing the same.

And all of this . . . from music. Which God had gifted to him. And he, in turn, had gifted back to God. How odd then, for his gift to be taken at the precise time he'd finally learned that knowing the Giver was far more important than honing the gift.

Another popping sound, this time painful, and Tate winced. But the pain subsided quickly, and he realized he wasn't dizzy. Not in the least. Dr. Hamilton had said there would be stages.

A sound like waves in the distance moved toward him, and he gradually recognized it as applause.

He heard a soft whisper beside him. "Take a bow."

He turned and took Rebekah's outstretched hand. "Only . . . if you take it with me."

39

As the curtain closed to thunderous applause, Rebekah turned to Tate, still holding his hand, not wanting—or willing—to let go. He drew her into his arms.

"Thank you," he whispered into her ear.

Head against his chest, she hugged him tighter. "Thank *you*. You were magnificent, Tate." She drew back slightly, a little breathless, the music and exhilaration still flowing through her. "Are you all right?"

He nodded, his expression full of emotion. And love.

"And your parents! And Emil!" She laughed. "Your father heard it, Tate! He heard what you wrote for him."

He exhaled, his eyes misting. So much said in a single sigh.

"Excuse me, Maestro . . ."

Mr. Cox, the stage manager, approached, and Tate leaned closer to the man. A telling sign.

"I'm sorry to interrupt you, sir," Cox continued. "But we need to get you to the foyer. And, if I might be so bold. . . ." The older man smiled. "I believe Miss Carrington should accompany you."

"By all means she should, Mr. Cox." Tate took her hand.

Mr. Cox led them to a door just offstage that

Rebekah had tried before when snooping around the new opera hall, but she'd always found the door locked. Using a key, he opened it and motioned for them to precede him.

Before them, a long narrow hallway with a barrel ceiling stretched for what seemed like forever, the golden glow of oil lamp sconces providing ample light and a warm invitation. But it was what covered the walls and ceiling as far as Rebekah could see that rendered her speechless. She felt as though she were standing at the portal of heaven.

"A secret tunnel." Tate's voice sounded overloud in the sudden stillness.

Mr. Cox laughed and locked the door behind them. "To get from the stage to the lobby in timely fashion. Mr. Geoffrey thought of everything."

"I'll say he did." Rebekah ran a hand over the murals, reminded of those she'd seen on the kitchen walls at Belmont. "Do you know who painted all of this?"

Mr. Cox beamed. "A lady by the name of Claire Monroe. She did quite a lot of the painting in this building, ma'am. A most talented artist, if I may say so."

"Yes," Rebekah whispered. "Yes, she is."

An expanse of azure blue sky, as pristine and realistic as she'd ever seen captured with paint, extended down the corridor. Rays of sunlight broke through wispy clouds so authentic looking she would've sworn she felt a breeze and saw them move. And mountains in the distance so green and lush they looked otherworldly.

Mr. Cox gestured. "Follow me, sir . . . ma'am. Lots of people are waiting to congratulate you both on the other end."

Tate squeezed her hand, and Rebekah followed, taking in the beauty surrounding them, and thinking of his parents and the pride she'd seen in their faces. Especially Angus.

As she walked, she spotted angels dressed in white robes peering from behind clouds and even standing on distant mountaintops. Some of the angels were tall, others short. Some were thick, others thin. Various shades of hair color too. And—her admiration for the artist suddenly deepened—some were light-skinned and others dark. And without exception they were all smiling, laughing, even clapping. Then she realized . . .

"They're not angels," she whispered. "They're people."

Nearing the end of the tunnel, Tate slowed, and Rebekah soon realized why. He began reading the words written in elegant script on the wall . . .

" 'Wherefore seeing we also are compassed about with so great a cloud of witnesses . . .' " His deep voice seemed more so in the hush of the tunnel. " 'Let us lay aside every weight, and the sin which doth so easily beset us, and let us run with patience the"—his voice caught—"the race that is set before us.' "

Threading her fingers through his, Rebekah read

on silently, the Scripture passage somewhat familiar to her, but not one she knew well.

"One afternoon," Tate said softly, "I saw Mrs. Monroe standing here in the tunnel. She'd asked Marcus Geoffrey if she could paint it. He said yes, of course. And she asked me if I had any ideas. These verses were on my mind at the time. They're some of Pa's favorites that he taught me when I was young. That's all I told her. And then she created all of this."

Rebekah reached out and brushed her fingers over the image of a black man standing on a distant hill, his expression bursting with joy, his arms raised heavenward. And she saw Demetrius clearly in her mind's eye, as though he were standing there with her. Same as moments earlier that night as she'd played.

Tate pulled her close and kissed her hair. "Demetrius heard you tonight, Rebekah. As did your father. I'm certain of it."

Tears in her eyes, she nodded.

"Maestro?" Mr. Cox asked softly.

Tate smiled. "Yes, we're coming."

Mr. Cox slipped the key into the lock, then paused. He glanced back, yet seemed hesitant to meet their gazes. "While I have the chance, may I say to you both that tonight was . . . Well, special doesn't begin to describe it. And to you, Miss Carrington, my mother, God rest her soul . . . was quite the fiddler when she was alive. She would have loved to've seen you up there, ma'am."

Rebekah gently touched his arm. "Thank you, Mr. Cox."

He dipped his head, then turned and opened the door.

The first person Rebekah saw was Mrs. Cheatham, standing with Tate's parents across the grand foyer, a sea of people between them. Rebekah's eyes locked with hers, and Adelicia smiled. But the smile held a message, it seemed, though Rebekah couldn't decipher it. And knowing Mrs. Cheatham, she wasn't sure she wanted to.

She followed Tate as he cut a path straight for them, both of them accepting congratulations as they worked their way across the crowded foyer and past the massive staircase where patrons continued to file down from the balconies. Only then did she think of the people who had stormed out of the opera hall earlier. That had hurt more than she'd thought possible.

But, in turn, the joy that had come with playing, with giving God her best, and with feeling the love, warmth, and appreciation from the people who'd remained . . . Then seeing Tate's parents and Emil there in the balcony!

That more than soothed the hurt away.

"Maestro Whitcomb!"

Halfway across the foyer, Rebekah turned to see a distinguished-looking older man approaching, his features keen with earnest. A woman of like age followed. Tate let go of

Rebekah's hand and embraced the man, clapping his shoulder as though they were old friends.

"Rebekah . . ." Tate leaned close, giving her a look. "I'd like you to meet Dr. and Mrs. Ronald Hamilton."

Realizing who the man was, Rebekah was overwhelmed with gratitude. "Thank you, Dr. Hamilton, for what you did for Angus. And for your care . . . of this man here." She looked at Tate, who was already looking at her.

"It is I and my wife, Christine"—Dr. Hamilton gestured beside him, his wife's expression full of kindness—"who are honored to have been here tonight. Truly, Maestro, if you'll allow me . . . Beethoven being dead, only Nathaniel Tate Whitcomb could make him alive again."

Tate shook his hand. "Thank you, sir," he said, voice husky.

"And, Miss Carrington . . ." Dr. Hamilton took her hand in his. "As you played tonight, my wife and I both whispered to one another . . . that we heard angels sing."

Rebekah hugged them both, and as they parted, Tate and the doctor vowed to keep in touch often.

Rebekah followed Tate through the crowd toward his waiting parents, and seeing Angus, even at this distance, she was struck by how much taller a man he seemed. Then she realized, she'd only seen him abed before.

Tate reached his family first and drew his father into a hug that Rebekah knew she'd remember the rest of her life. Just as she would remember every detail about this night. Angus whispered something to Tate she couldn't hear, and Tate hugged him again, struggling to maintain his composure.

But the closer she came, the more aware she grew of the weary set of Angus's broad shoulders and the shadows of fatigue and prolonged illness lining his face. Watching Cattabelle and Emil, and even Tate, she sensed they saw it too. And even as she thanked God that Tate's father was here tonight, she prayed for him—and for the days ahead.

Seeing Tate with his father made her miss her own father so much. She wished her mother were here. She'd invited her, several times, but her mother had declined, saying she wanted to be home "when Barton returned." There had still been no word from or news of the man. It was as though he'd vanished. Which, with everything in her, Rebekah hoped was true.

"We're so proud of you too, Rebekah," Cattabelle said, breaking into Rebekah's thoughts. "You looked so purty up there, darlin'. All shiny and sparklin' like the first star o' night. You started playin' and Angus and me just took to cryin'." Cattabelle drew her into an embrace that meant more to Rebekah than Tate's mother could know.

"Thank you, Cattabelle," she whispered, then noticed the woman's dress. A simple homespun, but so beautiful. And it looked new. She thought she recognized the fabric as the material Tate had brought his mother—a floral print with a coordinating fabric in cobalt blue. "You look lovely tonight, Cattabelle."

"Yes, you do, Mama," Tate whispered, lifting his mother off her feet when he hugged her. He looked over at Emil. "Thank you, little brother, for seeing our folks safely here."

Emil nodded, his expression filled with pride. "Sorry we got here a little late. We had some trouble at one of the mines."

Angus cleared his throat, and Rebekah caught the almost imperceptible shake of his head. She thought Tate saw it too.

"Then the train outta Knoxville was runnin' behind," Emil continued, "so we had to wait. Pa 'bout got off and started to walk his way here!"

Everyone laughed, including Adelicia, who stood quietly by, watching it all. Rebekah could only imagine what she was thinking. And how on earth had Tate's family ended up sitting with her and Dr. Cheatham in their private box!

"I take it you all have met one another," Tate said, broaching the subject before Rebekah could.

"Oh my gracious, yes." Cattabelle smiled. "This nice lady here done saw us askin' at the window for what tickets we's supposed to have. The man, bless him, couldn't seem to find 'em. We kept tellin' him we was here to see our son lead the music. That's when Mrs. Cheatham come over and swapped howdys with us. She was late gettin' here too. Which was good for us, 'cause she helped get it all ironed out."

"I'm so grateful, Mr. and Mrs. Whitcomb, that we happened upon each other when we did." Adelicia included Emil in her nod. "It was an honor for Dr. Cheatham and me to sit with you this evening."

"Oh no, ma'am." Angus shook his head. "The honor was ours altogether. I felt like a king sittin' up there lookin' down."

Adelicia smiled. "And rightly so, sir, on such an evening as this. We're all excessively proud of your son. As you are, I know."

Tate bowed in response to Mrs. Cheatham's praise.

"Miss Carrington?"

Rebekah turned to see Eleanor Geoffrey and her husband, Marcus, along with another couple Rebekah didn't recognize. Tate made quick introductions, deftly including Eleanor's relationship to her *aunt* Adelicia as well as crediting Marcus with designing and building the opera hall.

Rebekah looked more closely at Eleanor, detecting a subtle difference in her new friend that she couldn't quite place. Then Eleanor happened to catch her eye—and smiled. And Rebekah knew. She grinned, overjoyed for the couple.

"Next," Tate continued, "may I introduce Mr. and Mrs. Sutton Monroe. Mrs. Monroe is an artist and is responsible for many of the paintings and frescos all around us tonight."

As hellos and congratulations were exchanged, Rebekah took the opportunity to tell Claire Monroe how much she appreciated the mural in the tunnel.

"Thank you so much, Miss Carrington," Claire said, a trace of France in her voice. "And it was such a privilege to hear you play tonight. An experience I hope to repeat many times in the future." Claire glanced at her husband. "Now if you will excuse us, our son waits for us at home with my mother-in-law."

"And I'm betting he's waiting none too patiently," Sutton chimed in.

"Miss Carrington, a word, please," Adelicia said softly.

"Certainly, Mrs. Cheatham." Rebekah stepped off to the side, aware of Tate watching them.

Adelicia looked at her for a moment before pulling something from her beaded evening bag. "Imagine my surprise, Miss Carrington, when this arrived for you as my husband and I were leaving Belmont this evening."

Mrs. Cheatham held out a piece of paper that Rebekah soon realized was a telegram. She read it . . . and could scarcely breathe. She laughed, then looked at Tate, who again was already watching her.

His mouth gradually tipped in a smile.

"You knew?" she mouthed to him.

As his parents engaged Marcus Geoffrey in questions about the new opera house, Tate joined

Rebekah and Mrs. Cheatham. Rebekah handed him the telegram.

He looked up after reading it. "I told you Maestro Leplin would be a fool not to grant you an audition."

Rebekah hugged him. "It was your letter of recommendation that opened the door for me."

"Perhaps." Then he looked at Adelicia. "Or it could have been someone else's as well."

Rebekah turned. "Mrs. Cheatham?"

Adelicia merely shrugged. "I've known Crawford Leplin for a number of years now. And while he's very good, Miss Carrington, I'll warn you . . . he's no Maestro Whitcomb."

Tate laughed.

"But did you see the date he wants me to audition? It's only two weeks from now!"

Adelicia waved a hand. "Two weeks is plenty of time to get to New York. After all, Pauline's recital is this coming week, so you'll be done with your most important work here." Her expression all seriousness, the woman's tone hinted at jest.

Rebekah smiled. "Your daughter is doing splendidly, Mrs. Cheatham, and I'm certain—"

"Maestro Whitcomb!"

They turned to see Edward Pennington striding toward them, looking even more displeased now than he had when exiting the auditorium earlier, if that were possible.

Pennington walked to within inches of Tate, his face and neck a bright crimson. "As director of the symphony board, it is my responsibility to inform you that the board has decided that your . . . *talent* is no longer needed here in Nashville. You are hereby—"

"Mr. Pennington"—Mrs. Cheatham's tone held polite censure—"this is neither the time nor place for such a discussion. May I suggest that we—"

"And may I suggest, *madam,*" Pennington countered, "that you allow the men on the board to decide as they see fit!"

In the space of a heartbeat, Adelicia Cheatham's expression went from one of caution to outright warning, and Rebekah fought the instinct to take a backward step.

"Mr. Pennington"—Adelicia's voice was velvet and steel—"may I remind you that the Nashville Philharmonic exists solely because of the contributions of our patrons. Of which, if you will look around you . . ."

Rebekah did, and noticed that the conversations closest to them—far fewer in number than earlier—had grown very quiet.

". . . you will see that the majority of our contributors very much enjoyed tonight's performance. So may I suggest yet again"—she raised her voice a bit when the man opened his mouth to speak—"that we pursue this discussion with *all* of our major donors next week."

Rebekah heard the not-so-subtle reminder lingering beneath the statement, and apparently so did Pennington. Because he glared at Adelicia, then at Tate, the muscles in his jaw cording tight, and with a huff, stalked away.

Rebekah let out her breath and noticed that even Adelicia seemed to breathe a little easier.

"Maestro Whitcomb . . ." Adelicia extended her hand to him, and Tate kissed it. "Thank you, sir, for a *most* enchanted evening."

"Thank *you,* Mrs. Cheatham."

"It's a wonderful blessing to have your parents here, Maestro. They're fine people. And so very proud of you." Emotions flickered across Adelicia's expression, too many to count. "As you should be of them."

Tate held her gaze, then nodded. "I am, Mrs. Cheatham. Very much."

Adelicia blinked several times, then seemed to stand a little taller. "I'll bid you both good evening. Miss Carrington, don't be too late tonight. Pauline has a lesson in the morning, remember." And with a look that told Rebekah Mrs. Cheatham would speak with her at greater length some time later, Adelicia took her leave and joined Dr. Cheatham, who waited near the door.

Tate whistled low. "I would not want to be on that woman's bad side."

Rebekah smiled, watching Mrs. Cheatham walk outside into the beautiful spring evening, the patio full of lingering patrons still visiting with one another. "And I'm beginning to think that the woman doesn't have a bad side, Tate. Only one that's misunderstood . . . from time to time."

Tate moved to rejoin his family, but Rebekah caught his arm.

"Adelicia Cheatham is a formidable adversary, Tate. But tonight has likely cost you your job."

He covered her hand on his arm. "We each have our own race to run, Rebekah. And part of mine . . . includes yours now. Wherever that takes us."

She loved him more than she could say. "Still, I—"

He pressed a finger to her lips. "May I suggest we pursue this discussion later, Miss Carrington?"

Smiling despite her concern, she followed him back to his family, only to find them in deep whispers—that swiftly ended when Angus, Cattabelle, and Emil saw them.

Tate looked at his brother. "What's happened at the mine? Is it Rufus? Was he hurt?"

"It's none of the miners, son." Angus ran a hand through his hair, a gesture Rebekah recognized. "It's . . . one of the bosses. At least, they think that's who he was. Hard to tell now, they say."

"They found a body." Emil kept his voice low. "At the bottom of a deep ravine. Man was beaten real bad before his throat was—"

"No coarse talkin'," Cattabelle whispered, glancing around them. But the foyer was mostly empty.

"Before they made sure he was good and dead," Emil finished. "The body's been out there a while.

Nothin' found on him, they said, but a ticket stub from Nashville."

Rebekah met Tate's gaze and wondered if he was thinking the same thing she was. She was almost ashamed at even having the thought, much less hoping it was true.

"Was he one of the bosses from your mine, Emil?" Tate asked.

"Don't know yet. I'm supposed to go by there tomorrow, as soon as I get back. But I had nothing to do with it, Witty. Honest."

The look that passed between the two brothers told Rebekah that Emil was telling the truth—but also that he knew who had done it. And yet, if the highlanders had judged that man at the bottom of that ravine as deserving of death—which seemed to be the case—no one would ever know what really happened to him.

Tate was the first to speak up. "I think it's best we get on back to the house."

Rebekah nodded, loving the touch of highlander she heard in his voice from time to time. As they crossed the foyer, she glanced over at the framed portraits of the proud masters lining one of the walls—Mozart, Handel, Beethoven, Bach, and Haydn. She'd been there the afternoon the workers had moved the portraits from the old hall and had rehung them here. Her gaze traveled to Tate's portrait, a few feet away, the beginning of a new collection. A collection she feared would include another new conductor before the paint on Tate's portrait had scarcely dried. But Washington Cooper had captured his likeness so well. Especially the warmth and humility that defined the man she'd come to know and love so dearly.

They walked into the cool night air, and the breeze—laced with lilac and the hint of summer—seemed to wash away the ugly remnants of the conversation from moments earlier. A carriage was waiting.

Tate opened the door and leaned to whisper in her ear. "I need to get my father home. He needs a good rest before tomorrow's trip back home. I'll take you to Belmont afterward."

She nodded, then glimpsed a boy loitering at the edge of the crowd of lingering symphony patrons. He drew her attention, first of all, because children usually didn't attend symphonies. And secondly, because of his worn clothes, tattered britches and—

The instant Rebekah recognized him, he reached into a man's coat pocket. She grabbed Tate's arm. "It's him, Tate! It's *Billy!*"

Tate looked in the direction she pointed. "I don't see any . . ." Then he stilled. "Why, that little . . . He's the same kid who kicked me in the shin!"

"Tate!" She gripped his arm tighter. "He's taking that man's wallet!"

"Billy!" Tate called, and the boy froze.

Billy's head whipped around, and when he saw them, he smiled.

"Emil! You see that boy in the red cap?" Tate asked.

"You mean the one runnin'?"

"That's the one." Tate grinned. "You up for a chase?"

"Brother, when am I not?"

ONE WEEK LATER

Rebekah stood beside Tate on the ridge, remembering the first time she'd ever looked out over these mountains. It had been nighttime then, unlike this morning. But either way, the vista moved her as few things ever had. The Appalachians inspired an indescribable feeling of vastness and eternity as mountain upon mountain layered the horizon, wisps of clouds trailing off the highest peaks, strewn like torn tufts of cotton held aloft by the wind. And above it all, a mantle of azure blue extended as far as she could see.

"Perhaps we shouldn't wait for Emil," she whispered, so only he could hear. She glanced over at the preacher and Tate's family—all thirty-six of them, minus Emil—standing around visiting and waiting. She'd met his married brothers and their wives but still couldn't recall all their children's names, or keep straight who went with whom.

She'd asked Tate jokingly the other day if this was all of his family, and he'd admitted there were more. He had aunts, uncles, and cousins scattered all over the area, and he'd heard about some relations on his father's side in Georgia, although he'd never met them.

Tate tugged a curl at her temple. "Let's give him a while longer. He's supposed to give you away, after all. He told us his business for the mining company would have him back in time for the wedding. And sometimes the train from Knoxville runs late, as we well know."

His gaze lingered on hers, then lowered to the laced-up bodice of the white wedding dress some of the women in the holler had sewn for her that week. Rebekah read pleasure and anticipation in his gaze and smiled. The gown, a simple homespun, was so lovely, and just what she wanted for this place, this day. And this man.

She reached up and touched his face. "I wish your father could have been here."

Tate's focus trailed to the hill beyond, where they'd buried Angus only a couple days ago. "He *is* here, Rebekah. I know he is. Same as yours."

She smiled and slipped her hand through the crook of his arm.

Tate's family had left for Chicory Hollow the morning after the symphony—his father clearly weakening. She and Tate had attended Pauline's recital together on Monday morning—the girl gave an exemplary performance, and Rebekah had felt such pride in her student. Then Rebekah and Tate caught the last train for Chicory Hollow that afternoon, arriving only hours before Angus stepped into eternity, with all of his children gathered around his bed. Tate had handed her his father's fiddle, and she'd played Angus's favorite song as the family "sang him home," as Cattabelle phrased it.

Tate had read a poem at the graveside—one his father had written for *his* father—and he'd barely made it through. Despite the rugged demeanor of every highlander man who attended the funeral, there hadn't been a dry eye among them.

Tate pulled her closer and covered her hand on his arm. "I'm sorry you couldn't convince your mother to make the trip."

"So am I. But she took the news better than I thought she might." Rebekah focused on the farthest mountain peak she could see, still trying to come to grips with the news herself. It had only been three days since authorities from Chicory Hollow had confirmed the body as belonging to Barton Ledbetter. After getting Tate's opinion, she'd decided it best to make the trip back to Nashville to tell her mother, and Delphia, in person. And she'd insisted that Tate stay with Cattabelle. The woman had just lost her husband. She needed her eldest son. The trip had made for a long two days in an already exhausting week, but it had been the right decision.

"Mother's constitution has grown so much

stronger recently. I see more and more of the woman she used to be. Maybe Delphia's right. Maybe those *powders* that Barton claimed were from Mother's doctor weren't anything of the sort."

"Whatever he did or didn't do, he's gone now. For good. And don't you worry, between us, we'll win your mother over."

Rebekah nodded. There'd been so much heartache in recent days. Yet also so much joy. How could the two abide so closely to one another? And yet they did. Like dissonance and harmony. It took both to make the whole.

"William Angus Whitcomb!" Opal yelled, tiny hands on hips. "You give me back my doll right now!"

Billy froze, doll in hand, and smiled. "How 'bout you come and make me!"

The spark in Opal's eyes, backlit by a grin, told the truer story as the two children took off running across the ridge. Tate and Emil had caught Billy that night following the symphony. And by the time Angus, Cattabelle, and Emil were headed back to Chicory Hollow the next day, it had been decided. With no one else to ask but Billy, they'd sat down with him, and the boy—fighting tears he'd tried in vain to keep inside him—had agreed to go live with them in the mountains. Even considering Angus's passing, Billy would receive far more love and dedicated upbringing in these mountains than he would have if he'd stayed in Nashville.

Plus Cattabelle had another boy to love on. And Opal, the brother closer to her own age that she'd always wanted.

"I think I see Emil comin'!" Benjamin called out.

"See?" Tate gave Rebekah a quick kiss on the lips. "I told you he'd make it."

"No kissin' 'fore the vows is taken!" one of Tate's married brothers yelled out, which only encouraged even rowdier comments from the others.

Grinning, Rebekah felt her face go warm.

"You'll get used to it," Tate whispered. "We highlanders aren't nearly so proper as you level landers."

Laughing softly, she turned to watch for Emil, but Tate gently turned her gaze back to him.

"You know how much I love you," he whispered. "And how much I believe in you."

She nodded.

"We're going to New York next week, and if Maestro Leplin is as wise as I think he is, he'll offer you a position there in New York. But if that doesn't work out, we'll discuss what our next steps will—"

"Even if it *does* work out, Tate, and Maestro Leplin says yes, we have your position in Nashville to consider. Don't forget, Mrs. Cheatham leveraged her very considerable influence so you could keep your position." She squeezed his hand. "For as long as you—"

He gently drew her a few feet away from the others. "I resigned, Rebekah."

"You didn't!"

"I did."

"Tate . . ." She shook her head. "We said we were going to talk about it first."

"No, *you* said we were going to talk about it first. I never actually agreed." He gave her a look.

She sighed. "I wish you would have—"

"It's *your* time now, Rebekah. You helped me fulfill my dream, now I'm going to do everything I can, for as long as I can"—he cradled her face—"to help you reach yours."

Tears rose in her eyes. "I love you, Maestro Whitcomb."

"Finally, the woman gives me the respect I'm due."

She laughed and stood on tiptoe to kiss him, hoping at least one of his brothers would see. Hearing the whistles, she knew she'd succeeded.

"Emil!" Opal called out and started running for him. Billy followed, hot on her heels.

Rebekah turned to look, and went still inside. It was Emil. But he wasn't alone. A man and woman were with him. "Wait," she said softly. "That's Esther. From Belmont. What is she doing here?"

"Rebekah," Tate whispered. "There's something else you need to know, my love."

She turned to him, and the emotion in his eyes caused her own to water. She looked back at Esther walking arm in arm with the man beside her, his gait encumbered by a limp. And he walked with the aid of a . . .

Rebekah's heart buckled. She found it hard to breathe. Much less to comprehend that—

"Go to him," Tate whispered.

And she did. She ran as fast as she could, across the ridge, back through the years, and into his arms. "Oh, dear Jesus," she whispered, hugging Demetrius tight, his soft laughter like music to her.

"Hello, sweet child," he said in the voice her heart remembered.

After a moment, he loosened his hold, but she held on tight, which only made him laugh all the more.

Finally, she stepped back, wanting to take him in. And though she still recognized the Demetrius she loved, the person standing before her was a mere shadow of the robust man she'd said good-bye to only ten years ago. What Barton Ledbetter's cruelty had done . . .

Fresh tears welled up in her eyes.

"*Shhh* now, Miss Bekah." Demetrius stepped closer, leaning heavy on his cane. "Don't you go cryin' for me none. The Lawd's been good to me, child. And him lettin' me see you again is livin' proof of that."

Rebekah's breath came hard. "I've missed you so much."

His smile was a gift. "I been missin' you too, Miss Bekah."

Remembering, Rebekah pulled Buttons from her

dress pocket and held the wooden carving out to him. "I've carried it with me all these years."

"So I see." Demetrius took it from her. "That cute little pug never had him much of a nose to begin with. And what little he got now is all but gone."

Rebekah laughed along with him.

"Hello again, Miss Carrington," Esther said with a smile, not a hint of discomfort or evasion about her now. On the contrary, her warm brown eyes met Rebekah's without hesitation.

Feeling a presence behind her, Rebekah turned to see Tate. "Demetrius, Esther, may I introduce my husband-to-be, Tate Whitcomb."

"Demetrius." Tate offered his hand. "Good to meet you, sir." He nodded to Esther. "Ma'am."

"Good to meet you too, Mr. Whitcomb."

Tate slipped an around Rebekah. "The morning after you told your mother and Delphia about your stepfather, before you left to come back here, I got a telegram. From Delphia."

"Telling you he wasn't dead," Rebekah whispered, a few of the pieces already jarring into place.

"I'm sorry if what we done hurt you, Miss Bekah." Demetrius reached for her hand. "But your grandmama and Delphia, they done it to keep me alive. If Mr. Ledbetter had ever got wind that he didn't kill me, he would'a come back to finish the job for sure."

"My grandmother knew?"

"Yes, ma'am." Demetrius nodded. "Was her idea. She said he thought me dead, so why not go ahead and make it that way. She paid for my funeral. Then paid for my care when I's healin' too. Only a pocketful of people was wise to the truth."

"So you lost all of your friends because of me."

He shook his head. "Way I looked at it, I got to keep the ones I really liked. Then got rid of those I didn't."

Everyone laughed.

"But I gotta tell you, ma'am"—Esther's smile faded a bit—"you 'bout scared us to death that day you showed up at Belmont. I didn't know who you were at first, but I soon learned. And every time I saw you, all I could think about was Mr. Ledbetter and what he done to my man. And what he'd come back and do, if he found out."

Demetrius slipped his hand into Esther's, the love between them evident. "We thought about leavin' town, but it's hard enough to find a good place to live out your days. And the Cheathams are kind folks. Then when we found out you was only stayin' for a while . . ."

Though Rebekah still had a thousand questions, more of the puzzle pieces fell into place. And there'd be time—sweet, precious time—to ask them all.

Demetrius looked long and hard at Tate, then grinned. "I always figured that with Miss Bekah bein' 'cross an ocean all them years, she'd find

herself some man from a far-off place to marry."
He made a point of looking around. "And sure
enough, she did!"

Tate laughed along with everyone else.

"Come on, big brother." Emil grabbed him
around the neck. "Let's get this hitchin' done so
we can eat! Virgil and Banty sent some of their
best moonshine. But"—his voice lowered—"don't
tell Mama."

Minutes later, thanks to Cattabelle rounding
everyone up, the music started—Emil on the
banjo, Rufus playing the dulcimer, and Benjamin
the mandolin. Rebekah stood with her hand
tucked into the crook of Demetrius's arm, her
grandmother's red ribbon in her grasp.

"Thank you for giving me away, Demetrius."

"I'm proud to be doin' it, Miss Bekah, since
your own fine father can't be here."

They waited as Opal traipsed down the path
before them, dropping flower petals onto the field
grass.

"I got a message from Mrs. Cheatham for you
too, child." Demetrius's brow furrowed. "She said
somethin' 'bout you borrowin' her red case for
your trip to New York. Said you best come by
and get it before you go. That she knows you'll
take fine care of it."

Rebekah smiled. If auditioning on the Molitor
Stradivarius didn't get her into the New York
Philharmonic, nothing would.

As Demetrius walked her toward her future,

627

even as he anchored her to her past, Rebekah's gaze locked with Tate's. Never could she have orchestrated the events in her life in such a way that this would happen. Only God. The *true* Master Conductor.

"Who gives this woman to be married?"

"I do, sir," Demetrius said, fatherly pride in his voice. Then he kissed Rebekah on the cheek.

Tate drew her to his side, and as they said their vows, Rebekah noticed him watching her lips as she recited hers. When the preacher finally announced that it was time to kiss the bride, Tate smiled and kissed her full and long on the mouth, much to the delighted whoops and hollers of his brothers. Then he drew back slightly and whispered, "I'm not sure I heard that well enough, Mrs. Whitcomb. Would you mind repeating it?"

And so she did.

Author's Note

Dear Friend,

Thanks for taking yet another journey with me to Belmont Mansion in Nashville, Tennessee. When I first began brainstorming the three Belmont Mansion novels, the themes came easily, thanks to Mrs. Adelicia Hayes Franklin Acklen Cheatham, the mistress of Belmont, and her special affinity for three things—art (*A Lasting Impression*), nature (*A Beauty So Rare*), and music (*A Note Yet Unsung*).

So when I came across the history of women in orchestras in my research, I immediately knew the female protagonist in this novel would be a woman aspiring to be in an orchestra. Many of the situations depicted in this story are straight from history, and the struggles Rebekah Carrington endured were common for female musicians of that era. However, though a very few enormously brave, tenacious, and oh-so-talented women managed to gain acceptance into symphonies in the latter nineteenth and early twentieth centuries, it was generally well into the 1970s before orchestras worldwide finally began to welcome females into their ranks.

To find out more about the historical details included in this story, visit the book page for

A Note Yet Unsung on my website (www.Tamera Alexander.com) and click the "Truth or Fiction?" link. You'll also find links to music from this book on that page, in case you want to listen along!

As far as we know, Adelicia Cheatham did not own a violin, much less the real Molitor Stradivarius. However, considering her wealth, she could have owned such an instrument if she'd so desired. Until recently, the owner of said Molitor Stradivarius has been the famed violinist Anne Akiko Meyers. If you haven't heard Ms. Meyers play the Molitor, please treat yourself and indulge in that pure pleasure. I spent countless hours listening to classical music as I wrote this story—including the work of Anne Akiko Meyers—and my appreciation for classical music and its composers grew infinitely.

The opera house depicted on the front cover is the Odessa National Academic Theater of Opera and Ballet in Ukraine (circa 1880s). I took artistic license placing an opera house of this size and elaborate style in Nashville in the 1870s and modeled the opera hall in the story after this theater in Ukraine.

The physical ailment Tate suffered from is based on the disorder that some present-day physicians believe plagued Beethoven—the then undiagnosed disorder of otosclerosis (caused when one of the bones in the middle ear, the stapes, becomes stuck in place, hence preventing sound from traveling through the ear). The first successful operation for otosclerosis was performed in 1956.

Whatever became of Adelicia Acklen and the Belmont Mansion? Adelicia left Nashville—and Dr. Cheatham—in 1886 and moved to Washington, DC, with three of her adult children. The exact cause of her separation from Dr. Cheatham is not known. Adelicia died on May 4, 1887, while on a shopping trip to New York City. She is buried in Nashville's Mt. Olivet Cemetery in a family mausoleum with her first two husbands and nine of her ten children. March 15, 2017 will mark the 200th anniversary of Adelicia's birth.

Months before Adelicia's death in 1887, she sold her beloved Belmont. In 1890, it was opened as a women's academy and junior college. In 1913, the school merged with Ward's Seminary and was renamed Ward-Belmont. The Tennessee Baptist Convention purchased the school in 1951 and created a four-year coeducational college. Today the mansion is owned by Belmont University and is operated and preserved by the Belmont Mansion Association, which invites you to visit and walk through nineteenth-century Nashville history.

Finally, the poem included in the story entitled "The Last Load" was written by my father-in-law, Fred Alexander, for his own dear father upon his passing. When I came to that scene between Tate and his father, Angus, Fred's poem just naturally fit into place in my story. Fred passed away in January 2016, so he never knew I was using his poem in this book. But he'd always wanted the two of us to write together. So Fred . . . thank you for sharing the page with me, as well as your life—and your wonderful son.

Until next time, friend,

Discussion Questions

1. Rebekah is gifted in a way that isn't socially accepted in her day. Yet she still strives to achieve her dream. How do you relate to her stubbornness and tenacity? What decisions, if any, would you have made differently? And before reading this novel, were you aware that women weren't allowed to play the violin in public in that era?

2. What caused Rebekah's grandmother to accelerate the plan for Rebekah to be sent to study in Vienna? Do you think this decision was justified? Abuse issues (and potential abuse issues) are handled so differently today versus the nineteenth century (or even thirty years ago). Discuss the differences in how society then and now chooses to handle such occurrences and whether we have progressed in that regard.

3. As mentioned in the author's note, Tate's illness was otosclerosis, yet it went undiagnosed due to the level of medical knowledge at the time. Is anyone in your life deaf, or going deaf? What have you learned from them? What an incredibly frightening prospect for anyone, but especially for a composer. At one point, Tate contemplates how odd it is that finally, once he's learned to use his gift for

God, his hearing may be taken away completely. Discuss the spiritual aspects surrounding this possibility and whether you believe God not only allows bad things to happen to those who love Him, but that He sometimes specifically brings those challenges into their lives, and why.

4. Adelicia Acklen Cheatham, the real woman who built the Belmont Mansion in 1853, is a prominent secondary character throughout the Belmont Mansion novels, and *A Note Yet Unsung* is no exception. Discuss her character arc through this book and—if you've read *A Lasting Impression* and *A Beauty So Rare*—throughout the series. What do you like most about Adelicia? What do you like least? How are you able to relate to her?

5. In every one of Tamera's books, there are cameo appearances of a character or characters from other series (like old friends dropping in to say hello). Did you catch the cameo appearance in this novel? Who was it, and what novel was he/she originally in?

6. Based on Rebekah's past experience with musicians, she's certain Tate is struggling with an addiction. When faced with the possibility of losing her dream, she takes matters into her own hands, follows him, and confronts him. Review that confrontation (Ch. 19 and 20). What does she accuse him

of? If given her same circumstances, how would you have handled the situation? Have you or someone you loved ever struggled with an addiction? Were you aware that the substances mentioned in this novel were used by musicians in the nineteenth century to enhance creativity?

7. Tate is somewhat embarrassed about his family and about Rebekah meeting them. Could you relate to his feelings? Has there ever been a part of your life that you've been hesitant to let others see? Please share.

8. Tate struggles throughout the story to finish his symphony. Where is he finally able to complete it? And why do you think that is? What does this say about him? And even about us (if the same sentiment holds true for you as it does for Tate)?

9. Darrow Fulton was Rebekah's childhood nemesis, of sorts. Did you have a childhood nemesis? How did that person shape you in younger years? And if you've been so fortunate (or unfortunate, as the case may be) to cross paths with them again, what was your experience? Any lessons learned?

10. Rebekah's relationship with her mother was estranged, at best. And Barton Ledbetter being in the picture only complicated things. What issues do you believe were at the heart of the rift between Rebekah and her mother? Can you relate to those issues? If yes, how?

11. Toward the end of the novel, Rebekah and Tate are led down a long tunnel in the opera house. What does she see? And who does the depicted scene remind her of? Were you surprised by how that relationship in her life turned out? Or did you expect it?

12. Do you have a favorite scene in the novel? A favorite character? What is the takeaway message for you from *A Note Yet Unsung*?

13. "Come Thou Fount of Every Blessing" held special meaning for both Rebekah and Tate. Do you have a favorite old hymn that means a great deal to you?

Please take a picture of your group (holding up your books!) and share it with Tamera at TameraAlexander@gmail.com. Be sure to include first names of all those pictured. Tamera would love to share the picture on her Facebook Page.

For the complete discussion guide for this novel—including recipes from the story—visit the book page for *A Note Yet Unsung* at www.Tamera Alexander.com.

With Gratitude to . . .

My family . . . you're simply the best. Thank you for all the times you love me anyway.

Karen Schurrer, my editor at Bethany House Publishers. Where do I begin, dear friend . . . This is our ninth book together, and I've learned so much from you. Not only about writing but about life. And love. And courage. Bethany House will not be the same without you. But I know you're following the course God has marked out for you. And that your dear Jeff is part of that "great cloud of witnesses" cheering you on. All my love and gratitude for the past twelve years, and every best and sincerest wish in your future endeavor. Every life you touch will be blessed.

Raela Schoenherr, editor at Bethany House Publishers, for sharing your editing expertise on this story. And for your kind patience as it came together.

Helen Motter, for sharing not only your editing expertise, but your knowledge of classical music history—and your passion for playing the violin.

Natasha Kern, my literary agent, for sharing your depth and knowledge of storytelling with me. You inspire me.

Jeannie (Dickey) Phipps, for sharing your

experience of being deaf. You helped me get inside Tate's head in a way I never could have on my own. Bless you, sweet cousin.

Deb Raney, my writing critique partner, for carrying me all these years. I know, I know . . . I'm gettin' heavy.

Mark Brown, Jerry Trescott, and the staff at Belmont Mansion for letting me live in Adelicia's world—and for inviting me (and all my readers) so lovingly into her home. I couldn't have written these books without you.

My Bible Study Fellowship group for the BSF study of the book of Revelation last year. You inspired me, challenged me, and helped kindle within me a deeper longing for the Lord Jesus and our forever Home. #thebestisyettocome

You, my reader . . . One of the truest joys in writing comes when you connect with these characters and their stories, and then reach out to me. A thousand thank-yous for taking these journeys with me.

Jesus Christ, who orchestrates this earthly walk with perfect timing and who weaves the dissonant chords of this life—every hurt and every tear—into a Masterful symphony for His glory and for our eternal good. *If* we will but surrender to Him. Your will, your way, Lord—not my own.

TAMERA ALEXANDER is a *USA Today* best-selling novelist whose deeply drawn characters, thought-provoking plots, and poignant prose resonate with readers worldwide. She and her husband make their home in Nashville, not far from the Belmont Mansion.

Tamera invites you to visit her at:

Her website: www.tameraalexander.com
Twitter: www.twitter.com/tameraalexander
Facebook: www.facebook.com/tamera.alexander
Pinterest: www.pinterest.com/tameraauthor/
Group blog:
www.http://inspiredbylifeandfiction.com/blog/

Or if you prefer snail mail, please write her at:

Tamera Alexander
P.O. Box 871
Brentwood, TN 37024

Discussion questions for all of Tamera's novels
are available at www.tameraalexander.com,
as are details about Tamera joining
your book club for a virtual visit.

Center Point Large Print
600 Brooks Road / PO Box 1
Thorndike, ME 04986-0001 USA

(207) 568-3717

US & Canada:
1 800 929-9108
www.centerpointlargeprint.com